THE NIGHTJAR

Deborah lives in the UK, somewhere south of Glasgow and north of London. She's the proud owner of two brilliant boys and one very elderly dog. When she's not writing, she can be found watching her boys play football in a muddy field, or teaching in her classroom. Occasionally she cooks. Her family wishes she wouldn't. *The Nightjar* is her first book.

Follow her on Twitter: @TheVimes

THE NIGHTJAR

DEBORAH HEWITT

PAN BOOKS

First published 2019 by Pan Books
an imprint of Pan Macmillan
20 New Wharf Road, London N1 9RR
Associated companies throughout the world
www.panmacmillan.com

ISBN 978-1-5098-9646-2

Typeset in Janson by Jouve (UK), Milton Keynes
Printed and bound by CPI Group (UK) Ltd, Croydon, CRO 4YY

Visit **www.panmacmillan.com** to read more about all our books
and to buy them. You will also find features, author interviews and
news of any author events, and you can sign up for e-newsletters
so that you're always the first to hear about our new releases.

Seb and Archie – to infinity and beyond

THE NIGHTJAR

PROLOGUE

The pears in the orchard had ripened too early. Their swollen carcasses littered the grass, a rotting feast for the ants and fruit flies. He could smell the sticky juices from the terrace, mingling with the nauseating sweetness of the garden's wildflowers. It was too hot for September, and Helena's beloved hydrangeas were wilting. They lined the terrace like a guard of honour, heads bowed respectfully and yellow-brown petals shedding in the late-evening sun.

Tyres crunched over the gravel drive at the front of the house and he stiffened, a tumbler of whisky halfway to his mouth. The amber liquid caught the fading light, and its reflection danced like fire across his hand. He put it down without drinking and closed his eyes. The air was alive with moth wings and the rhythmic churring of birdsong. A soothing white noise. Calm. Peaceful. *A lie.*

'S . . . Sir? John?'

His eyes snapped open. The boy – *Vincent, the gardener's son* – was trembling. His thin face was tanned and streaked with dust and tears. The boy's hand was anchored to the patio door, as though he were preparing to flee through it and into the safety of the house. *Another lie. Nowhere is safe.*

'Sir, the police . . .'

John stared at him blankly before nodding. The boy slipped back inside, his trainers crunching through the patio window glass, strewn over the carpet.

John looked down at himself – at the polished shoes, the dinner jacket and crisp white shirt. His tie had worked itself loose and his left cuff was undone. *Police.* He ought to greet them. He smoothed down his rumpled shirt and straightened his jacket, wiping the blood from his hands on the lapels.

The music was still playing when he moved towards the house. A warped, tinny sound crackled from the antique gramophone and echoed through the hallways of Cranleigh Grange. Helena had gifted him the gramophone on their wedding day.

He couldn't breathe.

The music was still playing, but there was no one left to listen. All the diners were dead.

He clutched at his chest. *It was too tight; he couldn't breathe.* He staggered across the terrace, stomach convulsing with cramps, and gripped the iron railings for support. He retched into the hydrangeas, but nothing could disgorge the images of the dining room from his mind.

Broken shards from the mirror glittered over the lush carpet. Streaks of blood painted the upturned dining table, his mother's desperate fingerprints stippling the oak . . . His elderly father was splayed on the wing-back chair, spine bent backwards; his sister-in-law was slumped on the floor beside his brother's lumbering form . . . and there was Helena, cut down by the bay window, blood spreading out beneath her like a rose in bloom. If he had been home an hour earlier, he might have saved her . . .

He stumbled down the steps to the lawn. No. He would not greet the police. He would not follow them back into that room.

He would not show them the pale dove's feather in his pocket, stained pink at the edges: the calling card of the beasts who had slaughtered his family.

Vincent's nervous footsteps pattered onto the terrace behind him.

'Sir!'

The police officers were hammering at the front door with increased urgency now. Soon they would discover the gate that led to the back of the house.

'Sir, the baby is alive!'

He wheeled around, and Vincent held the child out to him. Soft tufts of dark hair and brown eyes . . . *Helena's* eyes. He recoiled – from the child, the boy, and the awful, awful scene in that house.

But there was something in the baby's hand . . . He frowned. It was a hydrangea. One of Helena's beloved hydrangeas. The wilted flower was clutched tight in a little fist. The pale stem was mottled brown, the faded petals withered and curled.

'What's . . . What's happening?' murmured Vincent in awe.

The baby's arm jerked and the flower began to straighten. The stem grew thicker, rich greens bleeding through the plant's cells, giving it a healthy vibrancy. The withered petals smoothed, the colour deepening, becoming a vivid mauve. Then the flower head quivered and the mauve faded into a soft purple . . . then cream . . . He stared at the baby, shaking the flower as the petals opened and closed, as if by command.

The child gurgled and his chest tightened again. *Helena's eyes . . . Helena's hydrangeas.* This was wrong. Wrong.

John shook his head. 'The child . . . should have perished with its mother,' he rasped.

'But sir—'

3

His arm snapped forward and he hurled the whisky tumbler across the garden like a missile. With a clinking thud, it struck the trembling boy clean in the face, slicing through his eyebrow and cheek.

The boy stared at John in shock, clapping a hand to his face as the blood poured through his fingers and onto the baby's vest. In the child's quivering fist, the flower rotted to dust.

John moved away, his eyes glassy and his legs leaden.

Behind him, the baby began to scream.

1

The trouble began on a bitter November morning, when Alice Wyndham left her flat and found a box on the front doorstep. It was entirely unremarkable: a plain brown cardboard cube about twelve inches wide. The only odd thing about it was that every inch was wrapped in clear adhesive tape.

For Alice Wyndham, the label said. *Do not open.*

She stared at it. Who on earth would send a parcel and give instructions not to open it? A glance at her watch made her wince. *Damn.* Her bus was due in ten minutes. She could *not* be late today. The mystery of the box would have to wait.

She quickly stowed the package in the hallway and hurried down the path. Head bent into the biting wind, she failed to spot the driver of a nondescript black car, watching her with mild disinterest. Robert Lattimer was slender, with skin the colour of weak porridge and a cultivated ability to hide in plain sight. He glanced up from his notepad and carefully inscribed *Alice Wyndham, box number 326* on a blank page. His pen hovered over his notepad, and after a moment's hesitation he added, *Aviarist?*

Half an hour later, Alice was mentally composing her own obituary. Of all the things she'd expected this morning, death by psychotic bus driver was not one of them. Still, it might be preferable to what was waiting for her at the office. A full contingent of the senior managers would be arriving soon, ready to listen to her presentation – her first since she'd joined the company over a year ago. Her best friend, Jen, had promised her a bottle of prosecco if she got through it. Privately, Alice thought she stood a better chance if she had the prosecco *before* the presentation.

She tried to recall the opening lines. *The survey of customers who complained about our concessionary stores revealed that . . . that they . . .* Shit. What *had* the survey revealed? Her handouts were in the office. Why had she left them there?

Without warning, the driver stamped the brakes, and Alice lurched forward, her knees hitting the chair in front. There was a flash of blurred movement outside and the doors burst open. A swirl of icy rain drenched the front-row seats.

She closed her eyes as a little old lady clambered on-board. *Concentrate. The survey revealed—*

Something brushed her shoulder. The old woman was looming over her, engulfing her in a waft of Yardley's English Lavender.

'Hello,' she croaked, staring at Alice with cataract-riddled eyes. She looked too old to exist, like something long dead that had been dug up and stuffed.

'Do you mind if I sit here?' she asked.

Alice smiled politely. There were plenty of other empty seats, but Alice was a magnet for lonely pensioners. It was something to do with her face – a wholesome, rosy-cheeked sort of face that spoke of chastity and virtue. Though if she was in any way chaste it wasn't through lack of trying. Old ladies loved her face. Men? Not so much.

'Of course,' she said. 'Let me move my bag.'

When the bus finally rolled off, it ploughed through a cluster of magpies and the birds scattered, pinwheeling into the dull skies above Larkhall Park.

The old woman watched them intently. 'Pretty little things, aren't they?' she said, waving a bony hand, her fingers fluttering like the birds' wings.

Alice's heart sank as she watched one lone magpie swoop back over the roof of a newsagent's. Great omen . . . *One for sorrow.*

'I know what you are,' the old woman continued.

Alice's brow furrowed.

'I know what you are,' she repeated.

There was a bewildered pause. This was all a bit existential for a Friday morning. 'I'm a customer complaints researcher for a shoe company,' said Alice, with a confused smile.

'No,' said the woman. 'That's what you *do*, not what you *are*. I know about the birds.'

Alice stiffened. Birds? Where was the polite but stilted conversation about traffic jams or bad weather? Hardly anyone knew about her fear of birds, and it was the last thing she wanted to be thinking about this morning.

'What do you mean?' Alice asked slowly. 'You can tell . . . I don't like birds? Is that it?'

The woman nodded but fixed her with a stern look, as though personally offended by Alice's ornithophobia.

'Birds are incredible creatures,' she said, her reedy voice stretched thin. 'Did you know the bald eagle mates for life? Faithful. Loyal. Now tell me this: are those not qualities you admire?'

Alice winced. Even the bald eagle had a more successful love life than she did.

'I . . . appreciate what you're saying . . .'

7

'Sylvie,' the old lady supplied.

'Sylvie,' said Alice. 'Well, birds are just . . . The thing about birds is . . .'

Her throat tightened, and she turned away. It was the thing she most disliked about London. She didn't mind the traffic, the noise or the unfavourable odds of being murdered. It was the birds she detested, and London was riddled with them. Ravens in the Tower, swans on the Thames, pigeons . . . everywhere. They'd blighted her entire childhood, and now, the only place she liked to see them was on her dinner plate.

They sat in silence for the rest of the journey, the rain slamming against the glass with malevolent intent. At Trafalgar Square, Alice hauled herself upright and edged past her neighbour.

'Just a moment, dear.'

Sylvie was teetering up behind her, swaying on her little matchstick legs.

'This is my stop too. Could you help me off?'

She held out her arm, and after a brief pause Alice took it and led her carefully into the full might of the thundering rain.

'Thank you,' said Sylvie as the bus rolled away. 'Would you mind seeing me across the road?'

Alice glanced helplessly at Trafalgar Square: one of her least favourite places in the city. She had no umbrella, and she'd hoped to sprint all the way to work.

'Please?' said Sylvie.

Alice felt a pang of guilt. She could hardly say no.

'Of course,' she said, flashing Sylvie a strained smile.

She squinted into the rain and wrapped one arm around the old woman. As soon as a gap opened up in the traffic, she propelled Sylvie across the road and plunged reluctantly through the square's mass of pigeons.

The rain had plastered her hair to her face. Perfect. Just the impression she wanted to make to her bosses.

'Okay then, well you have a nice day,' she said, preparing to dart away.

'Wait a moment,' said Sylvie, snatching at her wrist. She was staring at something. Alice glanced over her shoulder, but only saw Nelson's Column towering above.

'I haven't been quite truthful with you,' said Sylvie.

Alice smiled distractedly. 'Look, if this is about – oh, I don't know – the benefits of RSPB membership or—'

'It isn't. It's about the box.'

Alice's mouth fell open. 'Sorry, did you just say "the box"?'

Sylvie nodded.

'Which box?' asked Alice. 'Are you saying *you* sent the box I found on my doorstep?'

'I did.'

Alice let out an astonished laugh. 'But—'

'Listen to me, Alice,' Sylvie said quietly.

'How do you know my name?' asked Alice, growing uneasy. 'Who are you?'

'I don't have time to explain,' Sylvie wheezed. Her breath was coming in shallow bursts, and her skin had turned the exact colour and texture of parchment.

'I left the box for you just in case I didn't meet you today,' she said, forcing a smile. 'But I wanted to see you, to make sure I had the right person.'

'The right person for what?' asked Alice.

The smile fell from Sylvie's lips and she stumbled backwards, her heels scattering pigeons as she went. With a soft moan, the old woman's knees sagged, and Alice shot forward and threw an arm around her waist.

'Shit! Sylvie?'

Small and slight though Sylvie was, Alice could barely hold her up. She cast a panicked glance about her at the commuters hurrying past.

'Help!' she yelled. 'Call an ambulance!'

The old woman's eyelids flickered and she sighed a deep, rattling breath. Her fingers fumbled blindly at Alice's collar and tugged her closer.

'The birds,' she whispered. 'You mustn't spurn them . . .'

'*What?*' said Alice. 'No, Sylvie, that's not—'

'Crowley . . .' she murmured. 'Crowley is coming for you, Alice. You're not . . . safe. Once I go . . . you won't be safe.'

'Shh,' said Alice. 'It's okay. Don't try to speak.'

She caught a glimpse of movement. A security guard had peeled away from The National Gallery. He rushed down the steps towards her, followed closely by two luminous yellow blurs. Paramedics.

Raindrops glistened on Sylvie's face and pooled in the hollows of her collarbones.

'Someone's coming,' Alice said, her voice trembling. 'They're going to take you to the hospital. Okay? Just hang on.'

Sylvie's eyes flew open, alert and wild.

'*Alice,*' she hissed. '*Open the box!*'

With one last, futile gasp, the breath left her body and she fell limp in Alice's arms, her brow smoothing at the last.

Something seemed to change in the air. A stillness stole over the square and hushed the fluttering of wings and the pecking of the birds. The pigeons crowding Trafalgar seemed to freeze in a silent tableau of respect. It held for just a moment, like an intake of breath, and then it broke. Motion and noise snapped back into the city and every single bird rose, whirling into the sky above Nelson's Column – a teeming, churning mass of wings and feathers and claws.

'Did she hit her head?' a voice barked. 'Are you a relative? Is she on any medication?'

The paramedics had appeared and were shouting questions at her that she couldn't answer.

'What?' she mumbled in a daze.

With frustrated sighs, they snatched Sylvie from her arms and pushed her away. They lowered the old woman to the ground and began to count out loud as they compressed her creaking chest. But they were too late.

Alice stood in silence, the rain falling around her like white noise, like sand through an hourglass, as the strange old woman met her death in Trafalgar Square. The birds watched from the tops of the surrounding buildings, lining the slanted roofs and parapets like mourners at a state funeral.

2

Her hands were shaking so much that she dropped her swipe card twice before managing to open the electronic doors. The office was deserted – the desks empty, the phones silent – and she knew a brief moment of elation. Maybe there'd been a fire alarm and they'd evacuated the building. But then she heard cups chinking nearby and realized they were all crowded into the conference room. *Great.*

She quickly peeled off her sopping coat and scarf as she scanned her desk for her handouts.

They weren't there.

She surveyed the horror of her empty workstation. Maybe someone had taken them into the conference room for her? She nodded. Right. She took a breath and marched in, smiling manically at the expectant faces. A cry went up from one of her workmates, Ryan.

'Call off the search! She's arrived!'

There was a rumble of corporate-style laughter – like a herd of braying donkeys – and she cast a frantic eye over the room, searching for her documents.

An irritated voice rose, and the room fell silent. 'Shall we begin?'

Mr McGreevy, the most senior of the senior managers, peered at her over the top of his laptop and snapped the lid down sharply.

'Yes,' she croaked. 'Of course.' She cleared her throat, and her eyes alighted on Sandra, the office gasbag. She was watching Alice with a smirk, and suspicion as to the fate of her handouts curdled in Alice's stomach.

McGreevy sighed. 'Can you please just get on with it?'

'Okay,' she said, turning to face the front. 'Thank you all for coming. And I apologize for my punctuality.'

McGreevy grunted. '*Lack* of punctuality.'

She took a deep breath. 'Over the past year, surveys relating to our concessionary stores have revealed that the quality of our shoes is our customers' biggest concern. Twenty-four per cent of buyers returned their shoes within thirty days.'

'Which shoes?' said McGreevy.

'Sorry?'

He poured himself a drink from the water jug on the vast central table. 'Presumably, there's a manufacturing problem. Which shoes were returned?'

'That's a great question,' said Alice's line manager, Colin, nodding along like a deranged puppet. Grovelling creep.

'Well . . . I did have some handouts with the details, but . . .'

McGreevy stared at her, his lips puckered.

'I—Well, as a matter of fact,' she rallied, 'I can show you a pair from the line. Because I actually purchased some myself and . . . if you can just see, right here, where the stitching has started to fray—'

In horrible slow motion, her foot swung up and *somehow* caught the jug. McGreevy stared, immobile with shock, as the water chugged over his paperwork. There was a mass scramble to evacuate seats before the gushing water spilled onto clothing.

McGreevy glared at her, a nerve pulsing above his eye. She glanced down. There was a wet electronic crackle. Oh God. *His laptop . . .*

'Alice,' Colin murmured. 'I'd like a word in my office.'

Colin sat opposite her, arms folded across his massive chest and a pensive look on his face.

'So. Bit of a cock-up, wasn't it?'

She nodded mutely. Through the window, she could see Sandra, Colin's personal Rottweiler, fixing her blonde hair with a hand mirror. It was a perfectly coiffured 1980s-style disaster.

Colin grunted and sat back. 'Aside from turning up late *and* nearly electrocuting McGreevy, what I don't get is how the *fuck* anyone can give a presentation without handouts.'

This was it then. The moment she was handed her P45.

'Yes,' she said. 'Look, Colin—'

'The look on McGreevy's face when you shoved your foot under his nose was priceless though,' he interrupted. 'I think he thought you were going to give him a lap dance.' He winked, and her cheeks flamed.

Please. Kill me now.

'What are you doing tonight?' he said.

'Tonight?'

He grinned. 'I want to see you at The Piggery and Poke. Eight p.m. for my birthday session.'

Alice's face remained impassive, but her internal organs shrivelled at the mere thought.

'We're *all* going,' he said. 'If you don't come, it's going to look like you're turning down opportunities to bond with your colleagues. McGreevy wanted you gone, but I put in a good word for you – and here's your chance to prove yourself. What do you say?'

What she *wanted* to say would probably get her fired on the spot. She bit back a groan at the memory of last year's birthday drinking session. Colin standing up to raise a toast – to himself – his shirt half unbuttoned and beer spilled down his front. 'Alice!' he'd bellowed at her. 'I've got a nice big present to show you later. I'll take you back to mine so you can unwrap it!'

She pulled a strained smile. 'I – Colin, tonight I really just want to get an early night. I'm . . . really shaken up by something that happened on the way to work.'

'Great. See you there.'

He turned back to his computer, and Alice slunk back to her own desk. When she reached it, she froze. Her missing handouts were on her keyboard . . . next to a caricature she'd doodled – *and binned* – in the last staff meeting.

'You want to be careful where you leave your rubbish,' said Sandra – the subject of the unfortunate doodle. 'I found those last night.'

She gave a vengeful smile and sauntered off. Bloodyfucking office harridan. In Alice's brief absence, a Post-it had been left on her monitor, and she snatched it up.

> *Someone rang while you were in with Colin. Lee Crow?*
> *Leah Crow? Didn't get a number. Said it was important*
> *but* <u>*personal*</u>*.*

The *personal* had been underlined. Twice. To underscore the fact that such calls were banned at work.

She frowned. She didn't know anyone with that name. And to

get personal calls suggested you had a personal life. Which she didn't.

It was probably a mistake.

The next call came several hours later, at 4.45 p.m.

'Alice, hi, it's Dan from reception. There's a man down here asking for you, but he doesn't have a visitor's pass. Shall I send him up?'

Alice scrubbed at her forehead. She wasn't important enough to have visitors at work. She barely had her own chair.

'What's his name?'

There was a pause. 'Mr . . . Crowley, I think he said.'

Crowley. She blinked. Crowley. Crow-lee? Something niggled at her memory. Lee Crow? She scrambled for the Post-it note she'd binned earlier. The underlined *personal* leapt out at her.

A vision of a small, wizened figure rose in her memory. *Crowley is coming for you . . . You're not . . . safe.*

'Hello? You still there, love?'

She shook herself. 'Sorry, Dan, I was just . . . Can you ask him what he wants?'

She heard muffled voices, then, 'Er . . . He says he's got an important message for you about your destiny.'

'My destiny?' she said flatly. 'Who is he – God?'

'He says he wants to talk to you about a gift you've received.'

'What gi—' She cut herself short. The box?

'He looks a bit . . . agitated,' whispered Dan. 'I think you'd better come to reception.'

As the lift jerked its way down, Alice slumped back against the cool mirrored walls. Three identical brown-eyed Alices were reflected back at her, all with weary expressions and brown hair that rebelled against any notion of sleekness.

Clearly, a mistake had been made in giving her the box, and she would just explain that to this Mr Crowley. It was a misunderstanding – that was all.

Her confidence wavered when the lift doors opened and she spotted her visitor, arms folded with a grim look on his face. It wasn't a pretty face. Impossible, with that Roman nose. As in, a nose from an era that predated plastic surgery. He shook his hair – dark brown and overlong, reaching past his cheekbones – out of his eyes and looked at his watch.

She made to step out of the lift but paused. He was quite . . . striking, actually. Definitely not her type, but there was something arresting about the set of his jaw and the dark eyebrows.

He seemed completely out of place, given the tailored designer suits and carefully groomed hair of the other people milling around the waiting area. His long, dark coat, faded black trousers, scuffed boots and high-necked white shirt made him look like an undertaker. Maybe he'd been sent from whichever funeral parlour was dealing with Sylvie's body. But if so, what did he want with her and how had he found her?

The more she looked, the more convinced she was of his sinister intentions. She stabbed a thumb at the lift buttons to take her back up to floor thirteen. She missed. Her thumb crunched the alarm button instead. Typically, given her day so far, the lift wailed like a banshee.

'Damn,' she mumbled, jabbing urgently at the keypad.

Her visitor's head snapped up and their eyes met. He hurried towards her, shouting, 'Miss Wynd—' but the doors slammed mercifully shut and the lift swooped upwards. Alice slumped backwards and breathed a sigh of relief.

Colleagues were preparing for the end-of-day cut-and-run when she reached her desk again. She logged off her computer and yanked her coat on, thinking hard. Someone dressed like a furious undertaker had tracked her to her office, and wanted to rob her of a gift she hadn't asked for in the first place. What was Jen going to say? With Jen's track record of bad romantic choices, she'd probably ask for his number.

Alice had just reached the door when twenty telephones started shrieking behind her, and she paused. Hands snatched them up and heads turned to stare at her with narrowed and curious eyes. Voices simultaneously assailed her.

'Hey, wait, Alice, it's for you. It's—'

'Yes, she's here. Alice, it's—'

'I'll shout her. Alice! Wait, there's a guy asking for you, called—'

'Alice. It's Mr—'

'—*Crowley*.'

A hush descended on the office, and her colleagues looked at each other in confusion.

'Wait,' said Sandra. 'How can we *all* be talking to the same bloke at once?'

Alice wrenched the door open and fled.

Before it slammed shut behind her, she heard Sandra say to someone, 'She's on her way down.'

Bitch.

3

She really couldn't have choreographed it any better if she'd tried. Mr Crowley was glaring at the lift with a pinched expression on his face, evidently waiting for her to re-emerge. But when the metal doors sprang open, it was a cleaner who trudged out instead, dragging a massive industrial hoover. Mr Crowley spun away in irritation, and Alice, peeking from around a corner, took the chance to race down the last flight of stairs unseen and slip through the fire escape at the bottom.

She hurried into the alley at the rear and made her getaway along the quieter back streets. Jen was due to get out of work early, and they were meeting up for the journey home. They'd been living together since they'd left university four years ago, but their friendship long predated their London years.

She and Jen had lived in each other's pockets since they'd been old enough to climb the fence between their parents' gardens, in Henley-on-Thames. They'd learned to ride their bikes together; their families had both holidayed in Wales; they'd picked the same subjects at school, and helped each other get over their first broken hearts. When Alice had found out she was adopted, it was Jen who'd helped her come to terms with her new reality. They might have had different surnames, but they'd always considered themselves sisters – and there was no one Alice trusted more in the world.

A short walk to Charing Cross in the rain was offset by a long wait outside Jen's IT support office. Alice was drenched by the time Jen emerged, the wind whipping her red hair across her glasses.

'I've seriously had enough of this weather,' said Jen as they dived onto the number 87. 'I'm emigrating.'

Alice grinned as London blurred past them. They'd been plotting their escape since they were teenagers, while everyone else their age was busy drinking cider in the park.

'Where to?' asked Alice.

Jen sighed. 'I would literally move abroad tonight – if someone gave me a free plane ticket and accommodation.'

'Well, I have a tent and a weekly bus pass, but that's all I can offer,' said Alice. 'Now, if you hadn't dumped Giuseppe you could have had—'

'Chlamydia,' scoffed Jen. 'Thanks, but I'll pass.'

The rain was coming down harder now, exploding against the window and starbursting across the glass.

'So, how did your moment of fame go today?' Jen asked.

'I think it's fair to say my presentation went craply.'

'Craply?'

'If it isn't a word, it should be. And Sandra wasn't even the worst part.'

She told Jen about the box, Sylvie and the mysterious undertaker.

'Wow,' said Jen. 'That poor woman.'

There was a respectful pause, then Jen said, 'So . . . what do you think is in the box?'

'No idea.'

'What about money? She could have been a Miss Havisham-style benefactor.'

'Actually,' said Alice, 'Abel Magwitch was the benefactor in *Great Expectations*, not Miss Havisham.'

'Shh,' said Jen. 'Don't spoil this for me. It's our destiny to be rich.'

'Jen, get a grip. People don't leave money to complete strangers.'

'But why else would that Mr Crowley guy want it?'

The rain was bouncing off the pavements when they stepped off the bus, driving across the road in great horizontal gusts. Alice staggered into their hallway, battling to close the door while Jen pounced on the parcel.

'For Alice Wyndham,' Jen read aloud. 'Do not open.'

Alice shrugged and peeled off her wet coat.

'Do you want to do the honours then?' asked Jen, thrusting the box under her nose.

She stared at it. She couldn't explain why, exactly, but she was fighting the urge to hurl the parcel out into the street.

'No,' she said firmly. 'I don't.'

Alice collapsed on the living room sofa, keen to keep her distance from the box, but Jen followed. There was a long pause, and then Jen tentatively said, 'What if I get some scissors and have a quick look? If it's something great I'll tell you what it is. And if it's rubbish I'll bin it, okay?'

Alice nodded reluctantly, and Jen left to grab the scissors. Out in the hallway, the doorbell rang.

'Can I help you?' Jen's voice floated into the living room.

'I'm looking for a Miss Alice Wyndham.'

'What do you want? You're not a bailiff, are you?'

Alice poked her head into the hallway and sucked in a breath. A tall man with a nose that may well have been carved out of granite peered at her over Jen's shoulder. The man from her office.

Jen grinned and glanced at Alice, a question in her eyes. Alice shook her head. She knew exactly what Jen was thinking, but cold, taciturn men were not her thing – no matter how oddly striking she found them.

What was he doing here?

'Are you stalking me?' she asked, narrowing her eyes and fumbling for the first weapon she had to hand – an old netball trophy.

'Don't flatter yourself,' he said impatiently. 'I just want to talk to you about the gift you received. I know you have it.'

Alice pushed Jen out of the way and made to slam the front door, but he darted forward to fill the doorframe.

'Look, Mr Crowley,' she said, in a voice full of polite restraint, 'I didn't ask for that box and I don't want it. So you can have it. In fact, I insist.'

Jen drew a sharp breath and grabbed Alice's wrist. 'Hang *on* a minute,' she whispered.

'My name is Crowley,' he said, with an exasperated sigh. 'Not *Mister* Crowley. It's a forename. Rhymes with *jowly*.' He smiled blandly, but she swore his eyes tracked down her face and paused somewhere below her *jowl-free* chin.

Outrage dug deep into Alice's bones. Was he calling *her* jowly? What the actual fuck? She might have to put up with Sandra's catty remarks all day long, but this – she made to slam the door shut, until his pained intake of breath stopped her.

'Wait. Please. I . . . apologize. It has been a long and difficult day.'

'Oh, don't worry,' she said, her voice sweetly acidic. 'I'm a masochist. I love it when strangers turn up on my doorstep to insult me.'

'I didn't actually insult you,' he said. 'You inferred.'

'Because *you* insinuated.'

He winced apologetically. 'May we start this again? You received something from . . . an acquaintance of mine. Sylvie.'

'An acquaintance?' she said. '*Hardly* – she warned me you were dangerous. But you can have your box, all right? I never asked for it anyway. Here.'

She snatched it from Jen's hands and shoved it at him. But he made no move to take it.

Relief flitted across Crowley's face. 'Good,' he said. 'That's hers; I recognize the handwriting. Now open it. *Please.*'

This was not what she'd been expecting.

'You want *me* to open it?'

'Well, it does have *your* name on it,' he said offhandedly, earning a glare from Alice.

'But . . . she said you were coming for me. I thought it was because you wanted the box.'

He raised an eyebrow and turned to Jen.

'Well?' he said. 'Help her.'

Jen jumped to attention, apparently catalysed by the fact that he wasn't going to contest ownership of the box. With great enthusiasm, she hacked the lid off with the scissors.

Inside was an envelope with Alice's name on it. That was all. No money, no great mystery. Just an envelope.

'Maybe it's . . . a cheque?' said Jen.

Alice pulled it out, hesitantly. Crowley's shoulders relaxed just a fraction at the sight of it, and he stepped back, leaving him clear of the threshold.

'So it *is* you,' he murmured in wonder.

In a daze, Alice nudged the door with her hip, and it slammed closed. Evicted from the flat, Crowley rapped sharply on the wood.

'Open the door,' he shouted. 'Please – I haven't finished speaking to you.'

'Why did she say I was in danger?' Alice said to the locked door. 'If you don't want what's in the box, then what *do* you want?'

'You're not in danger from me,' he snapped. 'I've come for you precisely *because* you're in danger.'

She ignored him, but Jen shouted, 'If you don't get away from our property we're calling the police!'

Alice was vaguely aware of an explosion of muffled cursing beyond the door as she drifted into the living room with the envelope.

Jen stared at her expectantly.

Alice swallowed and then tore into the paper. Something light and soft fluttered gently to the floor.

It was a feather.

Talk about an anticlimax.

4

They both stared at it incredulously. A feather? Sylvie had given her . . . a feather?

Alice cleared her throat. 'Well . . . she was very old. She might have been going a bit senile.'

Jen plucked the feather from the carpet and examined it. 'Maybe it's rare? *Collectible* rare. Why would she leave it to you if it was worthless?' She straightened up, a look of dawning horror on her face. 'Hang on. Don't you think it's strange that she left you a feather? With your – you know – your *history* with birds?'

Alice shuddered. Growing up, Jen was the only one who'd believed her about the birds. She'd been there when everyone at school found out about her *anxieties* and the teasing hardened into bullying. She was the one who, after they'd studied World War Two in Year Nine, had declared that Alice was officially Poland, and that she'd do battle with anyone who dared make another move on her. Jen was the only reason Alice had survived secondary school.

She shook her head. 'It doesn't matter. It's either a joke, or . . .'

Jen peered inside the torn envelope. 'There's a note,' she said. 'Look.'

She passed the small, folded scrap of paper to Alice, who

opened it warily, squinting at the spidery scrawl. 'A gift. From my sielulintu to yours.' She turned the note over, but there was nothing else.

'What's that supposed to mean?' said Jen. '*Sielulintu*? It sounds exotic. Don't you think? Some sort of rare exotic bird?'

The feather was an unremarkable brown, streaked with beige flecks. Not very exotic at all.

Jen pulled her phone from her pocket. 'Maybe there's a market for rare feathers,' she said, clearly still hopeful about a windfall. 'Let's google it.'

Sylvie had mentioned birds on the bus. She *knew* about the birds. So was Alice being paranoid or was there more to it?

'How'd you spell it?' asked Jen, whipping the note out of Alice's hands. 'S-i-e-l-u-l-i-n-t-u. Ha! That's – well – okay, never mind.'

'What?' said Alice, curious now despite herself. 'What is it?'

Jen grimaced, but cleared her throat and read out loud: 'The sielulintu is a mythical soul-bird linked to Finnish paganism. Legend has it that the sielulintu bird delivers your soul to your body at birth and stays with you throughout your life. It protects your soul while you sleep – when you are most vulnerable – and at the moment of your body's death it flies away, carrying your soul with it. The sielulintu was believed to be the soul's courier and guardian.'

'Right,' said Alice, releasing a deep sigh. 'So – just to be clear – I've inherited a feather from a mythical bird?'

Jen blinked. 'Yes.' There was a pause in which they simply looked at each other. 'Maybe . . .'

'Please,' said Alice. 'It's someone's idea of a joke. I just want to put my pyjamas on and read a book.'

Jen stood up and dropped the feather onto the coffee table. 'Go on then. I'll put the kettle on.'

'I can't,' Alice said. 'I've got to go to The Piggery and Poke.'

'Why?'

'It's Colin's birthday. He didn't *exactly* say he'd fire me if I don't go for a drink and "bond" with my colleagues, but it was heavily implied.'

Jen frowned. 'That's blackmail. Tell him to bond with your fist.'

Alice's scalp was tingling as she pushed herself to her feet and realized she'd picked up the feather without thinking. She tried to shake off the feeling, but the slight movement caused her vision to flicker. Bright flashes popped in front of her eyes, and she tilted alarmingly. The living room carpet lurched underneath her and she slid sideways.

'Woah, are you okay?' asked Jen, grabbing her.

She'd *heard* something too. A fluttering noise, like a giant butterfly: soft wings wafting at the air. It was . . .

The blood drained instantly from her face and she had to bend over, hands on knees, to suck in a deep, calming breath.

'Alice?'

She opened her eyes and was relieved to find that the room had stopped moving.

'I'm okay. Just felt a bit . . . I must've stood up too quickly. Will you come with me tonight?'

'I suppose I'll have to,' said Jen. 'If you faint at Colin's feet, the pervert might bundle you into the boot of his car.'

Dried blood had clotted under one nostril, though the rain had washed some of it away. Vin leaned in close, his eyes raking her dismissively. She smelled. It wasn't the rank stench of death – he was used to that, and besides, the refrigeration was keeping her fresh – it was the musty old-woman scent that made him sick to his stomach.

'The death certificate was signed an hour ago,' said the mortuary attendant. 'I'll send the copies upstairs once I've—'

'No,' said Vin. 'I'll take them with me. All of them.'

There was a brief but uncomfortable pause.

'What about the body?'

Vin stood back to examine her. Her thin hair was too patchy to cover the liver-spotted scalp underneath. The strip-light on the wall backlit the fine white hairs so that she looked like she was wearing a halo. Funny, he thought, how appearances could be so deceiving. He absently raised a hand to his face and prodded the scars that laddered his cheek and eyebrow.

'Cremate her,' he said.

The attendant hesitated. 'Doesn't she have any family? We usually bury unknowns in case a relative comes forward after—'

'Just burn the bitch,' snapped Vin.

He was not in a forgiving mood. She'd dumped over three hundred of those boxes around London. For three years. She'd been trying to throw them off the scent – trying to overwhelm them with sheer numbers. She'd filled the boxes with sawdust and all kinds of worthless shit to confuse them.

He grinned down at her.

But it hadn't worked. Lattimer had tracked and logged every single box. And one of his administrators was checking the log right now. In the next hour or so he'd have the names and addresses of everyone who'd received one of her boxes this week. One of them would have received *the* box – she would have known her time was running out.

His pocket vibrated and he snatched his mobile phone out.

'Vin Kelligan.'

He listened in silence before licking his lips in anticipation. 'You've narrowed it down? How many?' There was a pause. 'Five? She sent five in one week? Jesus. You're sure about this, Lattimer?' There was a short pause. 'Fine. So what names have you got for me?'

Vin's face hardened into a frown, and the scar that sliced his cheek in two grew taut. 'Your signal's cutting out. Say that last one again . . . Alice what? Wyndham? Good, got it.'

5

'How do I look?' asked Alice as she hurried down Kentish Town Road towards her inevitable doom.

'Great. The dress is a man magnet. Trust me.'

'I don't *want* to look great!' she said, alarmed. 'I want to look horrendous. You said this dress was a man *repeller*!'

'It is,' said Jen. 'On me. I can't wear red with red hair. It suits you, though.'

Alice winced and wrestled the dress lower to cover her knees. 'I knew I should've worn the tartan trousers. Tartan sends a clear message: not interested.'

Jen raised an eyebrow.

As they reached a kerb, a group of dapper, bearded men surged up alongside them, and Alice was jostled over the road in their midst. She saw something flash out of the corner of her eye and frowned. Something soft fluttered above the group and wafted cold air onto her skin. She glanced up, but there was nothing there. Weird. For a second she'd almost thought there were wings—

No. She shook her head. It couldn't be. Not after all this time. It was just because of Sylvie – she'd locked all those thoughts about birds away in her mind. And that's all they were: thoughts.

She quickened her pace, propelling Jen inside The Piggery and Poke's doorway.

'What's the matter?' asked Jen.

'I . . . Nothing,' Alice puffed. 'I just thought – nothing.'

Jen pulled a face. 'You need a drink.'

There was a small side room inside called the Poke, which was used mainly by regulars older than Methuselah, but the biggest and most popular room was the Piggery. As the roars and chatter washed over her and she surveyed the crammed room – the sweating people squashed together, swilling beer and squealing with laughter – Alice couldn't help but think it appropriately named.

'Hey, hey, hey!' shouted Colin over Ryan's head. 'Here she is. Come with a special gift this year, I hope? About time you presented me with your birthday suit . . .'

He licked his lips suggestively, and revulsion rose in Alice's throat. She took in the room – the group in black suits drinking wine, the immaculately made-up girls knocking back shots . . . the middle-aged woman with 1980s hair. Sandra was grinning triumphantly as she wound a path through the crowd, followed by a dark-haired man.

Alice's eyes widened as she closed in.

'Look,' she hissed to Jen. 'I don't believe it. It *must* have been a fucking joke! The whole thing – the box, Sylvie, that stupid feather. Jesus. He's probably Sandra's boyfriend.'

'Who is?' said Jen, glancing over her shoulder as she paid for their drinks.

Alice stabbed a finger across the pub. At Crowley, who was standing by Sandra's elbow, affecting supreme boredom as his eyes drifted lazily around the room. Their eyes met and she froze. His gaze flickered to her pointing arm and he raised an amused eyebrow.

'I bet they're laughing about me over there,' she said, turning to face the bar. 'First the handouts for my presentation, now this feather thing. *Bastards*. But this is elaborate on a whole different level. I mean—'

'Alice, what the hell are you talking about? Are you seriously suggesting that pensioner put on a BAFTA-winning performance and pretended to die in your arms?' said Jen. 'You said there were paramedics there and everything.'

'Okay, well explain to me how Crowley and Sandra know each other.'

Jen shrugged. 'Maybe they don't. He followed you home. Maybe he followed you here too and they've just hooked up tonight. Maybe she's got a fetish for toy boy undertakers.'

A short cackle burst from Alice. 'All right. Well, that's my conspiracy theory obliterated, I suppose.'

When the bartender struck up a flirty conversation with Jen, Alice turned to watch Crowley, only to find he was staring straight at her. Her cheeks coloured and she glanced away. She wouldn't give them the satisfaction of knowing they'd rattled her.

A burst of laughter erupted from her colleagues, and she closed her eyes. When she opened them, she was staring directly into the mirror behind the bar, which reflected the whole room. The whole room, which was full of people and—

'Birds!' she gasped, but the sound was swallowed by the noise of the pub. Her stomach fluttered and she clutched the wooden bar-top.

She tipped her head back, eyes wild, watching the flock as they crowded the air above the drinkers' heads. *Birds. Indoors. Dozens of them*. There was no uniformity to their motion, no sense that they were a flock with a common purpose – and yet they seemed to be the same breed. They circled the pub's stone columns or else flitted from one end of the Piggery to the other. Wings were outstretched or pulled in close to their feathery bodies, beaks closed or chirping or slicing at the air—

'What did you say?' said Jen, breaking off from her banter with the bartender.

Alice stared at her, open-mouthed. Jen couldn't see them. Her friend, the bartender, the other pub customers . . . No one could see the birds but her. She was having bird hallucinations. *Again.* She couldn't speak, so she shook her head. Jen gave her a puzzled smile and resumed her conversation.

A bird swooped towards Alice, its outstretched wings perilously close to her face. The pointed beak clicked and darted towards her, so close it almost scraped along her cheek.

Alice turned on her heel and fled through the crowd. She burst through the pub's front door and sucked cool air into her lungs. She was gasping, trying to still the pounding in her chest.

Why now? She hadn't had these . . . these delusions for years. They'd started when she was seven and stopped at sixteen because she'd managed to repress them. She still remembered the morning she'd blurted it out to her mum over the breakfast table.

'I can—I can see birds,' she'd stammered. 'All the time.'

Her mum had given her a bright smile and plonked a bowl of cornflakes in front of her. 'Well of course you can, darling. There are lots of birds in this country.'

'Yes, but I can see birds in the house and at school,' she'd replied. 'There's one sitting on your shoulder right now.'

It wasn't exactly up there with 'I can see dead people', but her parents had been worried enough to send her to a doctor – ostensibly to make sure she wasn't suffering with bad eyesight, but really it was to check she wasn't a crackpot.

Seeing birds that no one else could see was clearly not normal.

And make no mistake about it: no one *could* see the birds; she'd checked with her classmates. Either they were real but invisible to everyone else, or she was genuinely delusional. Even at the age of seven, she'd realized that neither of these options was good.

Fearful that her parents might send her away, she'd told a flummoxed doctor – in one of her many appointments – that the birds had vanished. A pronouncement that was undermined by the invisible bird sitting on his desk, staring at her.

He'd promptly diagnosed her as suffering from nothing more than a wild imagination and sent her relieved parents on their way.

After that, she'd had her bird delusions fairly infrequently. And by the time she'd left secondary school, she'd managed to block them out completely.

So why now? Why here? Was it because Sylvie's incessant babbling about magpies and eagles had stoked her subconscious and sparked their return? Was she losing her mind again?

'Cigarette?'

She started. A man was leaning against the wall beside her, puffing on a stubby roll-up. She immediately searched out the air above him, and let out a sigh of relief to find it bird-free. She shook her head.

'No, I – I don't smoke,' she stammered.

'Sensible.'

She nodded. 'Sensible. The code word for boring.' Boring was good. She *wanted* to be boring.

He chuckled and stamped the cigarette out with the heel of his boot. 'Oh, I don't know. Sensible girls know what they want. And I like a girl who knows her own mind.'

She flushed and looked the other way, watching the cars zing past.

'Everything okay?' he asked.

She turned to find that he'd sidled closer. Close enough that she could see the ragged edges of a white scar slashed across his cheek and another bisecting his eyebrow. He was quite a bit older than her, but somehow the scars and his nearly shaved hair made it hard to guess how much.

'I'm fine,' she said, frowning at him.

'You don't look fine,' he said.

'Oh really? How do I look?'

He paused and examined her. 'Beautiful.'

She snorted. 'Well now I know you're lying,' she said. 'No one has ever accused me of being beautiful before. Wholesome, yes. Oh, and of course *jowly*.'

'I only say what I see.' He grinned, his eyes wandering over the dress.

Her cheeks burned uncomfortably. 'Yes, well . . . you're probably drunk.'

'I'm definitely *intoxicated*,' he said with a wink. 'Let me buy you a drink.'

'Thanks,' she said, stepping away from him, 'but my friend's already bought me one.'

A lazy smile played around his lips. 'I'll see you later then. I'll be waiting right out here.' He whistled softly. 'I'd wait all night for a woman like you.'

She resisted rolling her eyes and darted back inside the pub. But once in the narrow corridor, her courage deserted her. Would the birds still be in there? She steeled herself and swung open the door to the Piggery. A wall of black loomed over her, barring her way.

'What the—'

Crowley's strong hands grabbed her and urged her backwards, into the side room that was the Poke.

'Get your hands off me,' Alice hissed, shoving him away.

'I was watching you from the window.'

Her mouth fell open. 'So you *are* stalking me then? I don't think your girlfriend would be very pleased.'

His face registered confusion.

'Sandra?' she prompted.

'Don't be absurd – I only met her a few hours ago. When you raced from your office, after I simply wanted to talk, I had to find someone willing to give me your home address.'

'She handed my address to a total stranger? What a cow.'

'I can be quite persuasive when I want to be.' He shrugged. 'It was imperative that I spoke with you, but you rudely ejected me from your flat so—'

'Why are you here?' she demanded.

The look on his face soured. 'Stay away from that man.'

'I beg your pardon?'

He frowned at her. 'The man you were talking to outside. Stay away from him. He's dangerous. When Sylvie warned you that you weren't safe, it was because of *him*.'

'Is that so? Well, he hasn't been following me all day. He didn't try to force his way into my flat. He hasn't dragged me into a side room.' She suddenly became acutely aware that the room was empty. 'What do you even want?'

Crowley's eyebrows drew down into a glower.

'Forget it,' she said. 'I have enough to deal with without all this nonsense.' Alice shoved past him, and he dived to stop her from leaving, pushing the door closed. She could feel his chest heaving, pressed against her back, and she stiffened. 'Stay away from me or I'll scream blue murder,' she said quietly, before forcing the door open and slipping through it. She crossed the narrow corridor and entered the Piggery. Noise and warmth washed over her.

Sandra had broken away from their work colleagues and was hovering anxiously nearby as though waiting for someone. Crowley, obviously. As Alice took a step forward, she glimpsed the dreaded birds again, and her legs weakened. Just as before, they filled the air in a teeming, churning mass. But every blink swept them clean away. Birds. No birds. Birds. No birds. What was happening to her?

Light-headed, she briefly covered her eyes with her hands. Her skin was clammy and her legs weak. She needed to go home.

'Jen?' she croaked. A few heads nearby turned, but none were Jen's.

The room wouldn't stop spinning and blinking in and out of existence. Birds. No birds. Birds. No birds. A ruffle of wings swiped near her head and she jerked away. A hand made a grab for her, but she shook it off and staggered outside once more.

'Hey, slow down! Slow down!'

She tripped over the pub's threshold, and the scarred cigarette smoker caught and steadied her.

'I knew you weren't fine. Here,' he said. 'I'll get you into a taxi.'

She squinted at him through narrowed eyes, afraid of what she might see. No birds. She blinked. Still no birds. She exhaled and hugged her arms across her chest.

'I don't think I'm very well,' she mumbled.

'Come on,' he said. 'We'll share a taxi and I'll make sure you get home safely. You look like you're going to faint.'

'I—No, I'm okay,' she said, swallowing.

'Let me get you home,' said the smoker, tugging at her wrist.

'No. Honestly, I'm fine. My friend is still in . . .' She trailed away as she caught sight of a dark figure lurking behind the window, staring at her. Crowley. She turned to the man beside her and nodded shakily.

'That would be good, thanks,' she said. He grinned and urged her towards the kerb, threading his arm through hers. 'I – I don't even know your name.'

'Vincent Kelligan. Call me Vin.'

'I'm Alice.'

'Nice. I like it,' he said, as though she'd asked for an opinion on it.

She frowned and glanced behind her. Crowley had gone from the window. Relieved, she tried to extricate herself from Vin's arm, but he tightened his hold. He was tall and stocky: a good three or four stone heavier than her.

'We don't want you fainting in the middle of the road, do we?' he said as he steered her across it.

'No, but—'

'Alice!'

She whipped her head around. Jen was standing on the pavement.

'That's my friend,' said Alice, pulling back towards the pub.

Vin's fingers dug into the soft flesh of her arm, and she inhaled sharply at the pain. His mouth tightened and he yanked her forward with a violent tug, making her stumble. Manoeuvring his arm around her waist, Vin pulled her against him. She could feel his hot breath dampening her collarbone.

'Hey!' shouted Jen. 'What the hell are you doing?'

Alice searched Vin's face. She fought off the waves of panic. He wasn't smiling now. Eyes narrowed, he was pulling her relentlessly forward, not to a taxi but to a sleek black car.

'Get . . . off me,' she choked. Crowley's words echoed around her skull. *He's dangerous.*

There was movement in some bushes just ahead. She caught a glimpse of a face hidden among the tangle of greenery – another man, significantly older, watching her blankly. Her eyes pleaded with him for help. But he just gave an imperceptible nod and stood there like a voyeur.

With a desperate growl, she lunged sideways to dislodge Vin, but he lurched with her, grabbing at her dress to keep himself upright. She managed to twist her arm free and clawed her nails into his face. *Yes!* He hissed and lashed out with his foot, but she slammed her shoe into his shin. His grip loosened and she dived beyond his reach.

'Alice!'

She spun back to the road and let out a whimper of relief when she saw Jen hurrying through the traffic.

'I'm calling the police!' shouted Jen. 'That sick pervert! He was trying to force—'

A scream tore from Alice's throat, but it was lost in the shriek of brakes. A blur of white metal shot past her, the paintwork turned yellow by the tungsten streetlamps. It careered straight into Jen, sweeping her off her feet with a sickening thump. *No!* She crunched down onto the car's bonnet and ricocheted off the windscreen. Glass exploded across the tarmac, the shards embedding themselves in Jen's hair and skin as she smashed onto the road, broken.

'*Jen!*'

Alice stumbled over to the bloody figure lying twisted on the ground and hurled herself on top of the shattered glass, ignoring the sharp fragments slicing her legs.

'Jen, Jen, are you – Oh God. Oh *God*—'

Terror lit up her nerve endings and she could hardly breathe. *This can't have happened. This can't have happened.* Her shaking hands slid through blood, trying to stop it from pumping out – trying to force it back in.

People poured out of the pub and stood staring in shock. A siren filled Alice's ears, seeming to wail alternately closer and then too far away. She was aware of rain. Great, fat droplets pelted the wreckage and battered the exposed skin on her legs and the oozing, jagged cuts on her knees. She shivered under the stinging onslaught and let her eyes close.

Come on, Jen, she demanded silently. *Come on, come on, come on.* Her fingers blindly curved up to Jen's neck and pressed down, searching. There was a faint pulse ticking beneath the skin. *Hold on*, she begged. *Please* . . .

When the paramedics dragged Alice away and wrapped a blanket around her, the crowd started to disperse, shaking their heads and retreating to the warmth and safety of The Piggery and Poke. But Alice's eyes were fixed on the figure being lifted onto a gurney in the middle of the road. It was her fault. Jen was lying there because Alice had abandoned her in the pub. If she hadn't left with Vin Kelligan . . . If she hadn't been stupid enough to leave with that – that *criminal*, then Jen would never have had to chase after her – would never have been on the road in the first place.

She was too dazed to flinch when a voice dipped close to her ear and whispered, 'Don't go home. Whatever you do, you must not go home. He'll find you there,' before melting away.

6

Her hands were clean. She knew this to be fact because she had scrubbed them a dozen times in the past three hours. And yet they were not clean. She sat at the pillow end of her bed, cocooned in a flowery quilt, staring at her palms. She had been drenched in Jen's blood. Every time she closed her eyes it wasn't birds she saw now; it was blood, soaking into her red dress.

A light flicked on in the hallway, and she heard the creak of a foot on the stairs. She tensed, but the light went out and the footsteps retreated. Her parents were worried about her. She knew that. When she'd phoned from the hospital they'd come straightaway. Her mum had folded her into a crushing hug while her dad had gone to speak to the doctors. No, there was nothing wrong with her. No, the cuts on her legs didn't need stitches.

No, they couldn't all go and see Jen.

They'd whisked her back to Henley and insisted on telling Jen's parents too – even before the police had sent officers around to break the news.

'We've known the Parkers for thirty years,' her dad had said gruffly in the car on the way back. 'They're going to need us.' He'd braced himself and then gone next door to explain what had happened. He'd offered to take them to the hospital, and by the time he'd returned, hours later, he'd been grey-faced and shaken.

'She's stable,' he'd said. 'But she's in a coma.'

'My God,' she'd whispered. 'A *coma*?'

Her mum had packed her off to bed then. Her old childhood bed in her old childhood bedroom. The one she and Jen used to top and tail in when they'd begged for sleepovers, even though she only lived next door. The one still cluttered with her old bookshelves, sketchbooks and ancient posters. It suddenly seemed portentous. Had they kept it perfectly preserved because they'd known she'd do something stupid and would have to come back?

But she wasn't supposed to come back. Not yet, and certainly not alone. That was the deal; the friends had shaken on it before they left for uni. Once they'd graduated, she and Jen were moving to London to get brilliant creative jobs and make their names before setting off on a round-the-world adventure. First stop, France. They'd visit the artists' corner in Montmartre, where Jen would play guitar on the street while Alice sketched tourists for cash. They'd been naive enough to think there was romance in poverty, but it was more than that. It had been a promise: that no matter what happened, they'd always circle back to each other.

She scooted further down the mattress, and a wet nose snuffled into her ear. Bo, the podgy Westie terrier she'd had since she was twelve. Her scrawnier sister, Ruby, wouldn't be far behind. The worst thing about living in London was not having her dogs. Bo settled on the bed, and Alice listened to the sound of the little dog's breathing, feeling her own begin to relax.

When the doorbell rang and shattered the silence, Alice stiffened and the dog leapt up beside her. Through the sound of Ruby's excited barking downstairs, Alice caught snatches of her mum's voice as it drifted up the stairs. 'Terrible . . . Coma . . . Yes, officer . . . Cup of tea . . .'

When her bedroom door creaked open she tensed, but a familiar figure leaned into the doorway – five foot nothing, with bobbed, greying blonde hair.

'Mum?'

She bustled into the room, and Alice tried to focus on her mum's face in the dim light.

'There's a plainclothes policeman here, darling. He just wants to talk to you about the accident. Do you want me to stay?'

Alice shook her head, and her mum smiled so sympathetically it pained her.

'I'll bring a nice sweet cup of tea up then. Come on, Bo, give her some peace.'

She escorted the elderly dog from the room and disappeared. Another figure loomed into view. This one taller, darker, more menacing.

'*You?*' Alice gasped.

Crowley nodded.

She dived for the lamp on her bedside table, and the room was suddenly awash with yellow light. In the flick of the switch, Crowley had swept closer, standing over her bed like a big black crow. She scrambled upright and his coat caught the spray of light. The fabric was *not* black; it was the darkest shade of sea-weed green. Same as his eyes, which were lined with long, thick eyelashes, and were currently focused on her.

Him? He was a police officer?

'I'm not a police officer,' he said, as if he could read her thoughts.

'You're not—' Her voice caught.

Alice was suddenly very aware that she was alone with someone who had been following her all day, and who had now manipulated his way into her parents' home.

'Get out,' she croaked. 'If you don't, I swear I'll—'

She jumped up onto the bed and grabbed for the lamp again. She pulled it close to her chest and prepared to swing it. There was a twang, and the room was plunged into darkness. She'd pulled the plug out.

'Shit!'

She hurtled off the bed and yanked the curtains open so that a stripe of pale moonlight cut across the room.

'I know what you saw tonight,' he said. 'I know about the birds.'

She dropped the lamp. Whatever she'd been expecting him to say, it wasn't that. She slumped onto her mattress and tensed as he came closer, but he raised his hands to signal he meant no harm.

'Who are you?' she demanded. 'And how do *you* know what I saw?'

He gave her an assessing stare. 'Tell me, Alice. Do you believe in magic?'

Her eyes darted sideways to meet his, and hysteria shot through her. Magic? Oh God. He was just as insane as she was.

'We don't call it magic, of course. But the simplest explanation will suffice. The birds you have been seeing are –' he pulled a face – '*magic*.'

She narrowed her eyes. 'Someone *told* you, didn't they? Who've you been speaking to? The only people . . . Was it someone I went to school with?'

He sighed and lowered himself into the plastic desk chair in the corner of the room, crossing one elegant leg over the other.

'You are, it seems, more remarkable than you look,' he drawled, earning a sharp glare. 'You can see birds invisible to the naked eye. Magic, Alice. *You* . . . are an aviarist.'

There was a long, stunned pause, broken finally by Alice's laughter.

'Something is amusing?' he asked.

Her shoulders shook as the laughter threatened to give way to sobs. All this . . . Sylvie, Jen, the birds, the accident – nearly being dragged into a stranger's car. It was too much.

'Yes,' she said, taking a deep breath and wiping her eyes. 'My whole sorry life.'

He opened his mouth to respond, but she cut him off.

'Please. Would you just leave me alone?' She dragged her mum's spare slippers from under the bed, shoving her feet into them. 'I don't know who you are, I don't know what you want, and you know what? I don't even care any more. Just leave. I can't deal with this. In the last twenty-four hours, one person has died on me and my best friend might not survive the night.'

He moved away, and for a second Alice thought he really was going to leave. But he diverted to her wardrobe door and ran his fingers along the edges.

'The door's that way,' she said.

In silence, he stroked the handle of the wardrobe door and then yanked it open.

She leapt off the bed.

'We got off on the wrong foot,' he said. 'But I'm here to *help* you.'

'Help with what?' she asked, her voice rising, as she surged forward and shoved the wardrobe shut, hiding the rack of her old teenaged clothes.

'Vincent Kelligan,' he said abruptly.

Her eyes widened. 'The creep at the pub? What about him?'

'I was pleased you took notice of my warning and didn't return to your flat.'

'That was you who said that?' She shook her head. 'I didn't go back there because my mum insisted I come home with them. It wasn't anything to do with *you*.'

'At least one of you was thinking sensibly. Anyone would think common sense doesn't run in the family.'

'Yes, well, I'm adopted,' she shot back.

He ignored her comment. 'Sylvie knew you would be in danger once she gave you the feather, so I promised her I'd keep you safe. Vin Kelligan wants you, Alice. And he'll come looking for you again.'

'Well, who the hell is he and what does he want? There are easier ways of picking up women than kidnapping them, you know?'

Crowley looked at her steadily. 'Come with me – somewhere that Vin won't be able to reach you.'

'What?' she said, blinking in confusion.

'Staying here puts your parents in danger,' he said, his tone growing urgent. 'Vin Kelligan's organization will soon find you at this address.'

'Are you *raving*?'

'And your friend – the girl in the coma,' he pressed. 'I can help you to save her too.'

'Jen?' she asked, startled.

He nodded. 'Come with me, and I'll tell you the *only* way to save her life.'

'Come with you where?'

He pointed at the wardrobe.

She stared at him. 'My best friend is in a coma, and you want me to play *Narnia* with you? You need to get the hell—'

He jerked the door open again and her words fell away. The wardrobe, which only seconds ago had been spilling over with her old clothes, now contained nothing at all. Nothing but hollowed-out darkness.

'Will you come with me?' he said, gently this time. 'To save your friend?'

It could have been the empty wardrobe, or it could have been the crushing sense of grief, but her sanity felt like it had long since left the building – so she only nodded and moved forward. She barely heard the *snick* of the door closing behind them.

The darkness swallowed her whole, and her feet twitched and pedalled in mid-air. There was no floor – she was falling! In her panic, she hurled herself at Crowley, latching onto his coat.

She flailed her feet again, but there was no dislodging the bewildering truth. She was standing on nothing. But she *wasn't* falling. She was buffeted by gusts of icy wind that billowed upwards, from the place where the floor should have been. The wind swirled around and into her, cutting at her skin through her thin nightdress.

Her hair was blasted across her face, into her mouth, obscuring her eyes. She brushed it away as Crowley arched backwards, pulling her with him like a limpet fastened to his coat, and spun back to the door. He pushed on the handle and it flew open. Light blazed into her eyes and she fumbled her grip, losing her hold on him. She stumbled into the light and clattered to her knees. Floor. *Now* there was a floor.

Alice opened her eyes. Dirty yellow linoleum. She frowned. Her old bedroom carpet was a patterned dusky pink – all the rage a decade ago. But how did—

Her head jerked up. She was faced, incongruously, with tins of baked beans. Rows and rows of them. Spaghetti hoops, packet noodles, soup, tinned corned beef. Shelves of tinned foods towered over her, and she reared backwards.

'Where's my bedroom?' she asked, making no attempt to muffle the panic in her voice.

Grinning, Crowley dropped down beside her. 'Magic. I tried to tell you, but you wouldn't listen. We have indeed passed through a magical doorway in your wardrobe, Alice.' He stood up. 'Welcome to Narnia.'

She stared after him as he strode down the aisle. Overhead, a light flickered and buzzed, illuminating yet more shelves and dirty lino.

She rose to her feet in a daze and willed herself to follow. The aisle curved around to reveal a till, manned by a girl with a pinched face.

'You buying anything, or what?' she asked.

Alice shook her head, dumbfounded, and the girl huffed and turned away.

There were red signs hanging from the ceiling, yelling at her in obnoxious capital letters, *BUY ONE GET ONE FREE!!!* Alice gulped and hurried away, bumping into a wire basket full of mouldering fruit. It was marked *ALL BANANAS HALF PRICE!* She took a deep breath.

Narnia was a shithole.

7

He was waiting for her on the pavement outside the shop. The light from the pulsing fluorescent sign in the window (*24-HOUR NEWSAGENT'S*) was spasming on his back and shoulders, bathing him in reds and blues.

She shivered and he glanced at her. For a second she thought he was going to offer her his coat, but he just strode off down the street.

'Hey!' she yelled, startled by his sudden retreat. 'What the hell is going on?' She scuttled after him, cursing her mother for loaning her a pair of slippers instead of something more practical.

She hurried past shops with shutters rolled down and across roads that led to the types of narrow, dingy alleyways beloved of robbers and murderers. Cars flew past her, headlights blazing and engines roaring. She ignored the catcalls and laughter exploding from the doorway of a nearby pub, and the shouts of 'Are you lost, darlin'? Bedlam's that way!' She couldn't even blame them; what must she look like?

She reached a busy junction and stopped. She squinted at the buildings towering over her. Was this Edgware Road? And that was Oxford Street, wasn't it? But . . . how could she be here, when she'd just been in Henley, nearly two hours away?

What if she was losing her mind? What if she'd gone to the hospital after Jen's accident and they'd committed her? How did anyone actually *know* what was real and what wasn't?

A floating head appeared from around the corner and she flinched. Crowley. Her guide on the journey through her own insanity.

'What are you waiting for?' he hissed.

She was trembling on the pavement. 'Where am I? Am I ill? Are you a hallucination?'

His expression finally softened at the sight of her erratic shivering, and he tore off his coat. He threw it around her shoulders and she exhaled gently, letting the warmth – *his* warmth – envelope her.

'Walk with me,' he said. 'Let me show you something. If you don't like what I have to say, then I'll take you home. Okay?'

There was an expectant look in his eye, and the tightness in her chest abated. She gave him a reluctant nod and allowed him to steer her around the corner, where they were met by Marble Arch. It stood in a sparse flow of traffic that surrounded it like a moat, and it glinted, bone white, in the moonlight.

He coaxed her onwards as he spoke. 'There was a bird, once, known as the sielulintu: the soul-bird . . .'

Alice looked up at him sharply, and he hesitated.

'You've heard of it?' he asked, giving her a quizzical look.

'There was a note in Sylvie's envelope,' she said. 'Jen googled it. It's a Finnish myth. Basically, every soul has a magical bird acting as its bodyguard?'

He nodded thoughtfully, and she allowed him to lead her across the road.

'It's no myth,' he said. 'The soul-bird is as real as we are. It's a nightjar – a species of nocturnal bird from the Caprimulgidae family. Small feet, long, pointed wings, earth-coloured feathers patterned like tree bark. The birds you have been seeing are nightjars. Everyone has one – but they are invisible to all but aviarists.'

'That's . . . what you called me before.'

'Yes. You are one of maybe a dozen known aviarists in the world. I know of only one other in the United Kingdom.'

Alice shook her head. *Ridiculous.*

'The feather,' he said. 'In the box.'

'What about it?' she asked.

'That was your catalyst. It was a nightjar feather that Sylvie passed to you. She, too, was an aviarist. You touched it and it awoke something in you. Something that had been buried. It allowed you to *see.*'

'I was already able to see,' she said. 'That's the problem. I've seen those birds for half my life.'

'*Half* your life.'

'I forced myself to block them out.'

'Exactly,' he said. 'The feather tore down whatever barriers you had built for yourself. It brought the birds back.' He paused as though searching for the right words. 'Aviarists are born, not made, Alice. The ability to see nightjars is an innate skill, but it takes a dying aviarist passing on a feather from their *own* nightjar to fully awaken this ability.'

She shuddered and glanced away. Marble Arch was busy. It would be easy to shout for help if she really needed it – so why had he brought her *here*?

'What happens if aviarists don't receive a feather?' she asked.

Crowley shrugged. 'I suppose their early promise fades, like any talent not pursued.'

'Then I don't want it,' she said promptly. 'Sylvie's feather. I don't want it. The birds will leave me be and I can be norm—'

'Sighting nightjars is a rare gift.'

'A gift?' She grunted. 'Hardly a gift to spend all of your childhood in social isolation.'

'Spare me the angst,' he said. 'Others would kill for a single glimpse of a nightjar.'

'Bird-watching a popular hobby, is it?' she muttered.

'Aviarists do more than watch. The skilled ones study nightjars; they read them – understand them. They know that the nightjar is a mirror of the soul it guards. They can therefore perceive a person's emotions and memories, and determine when someone is lying. The human soul is an open book to a well-trained aviarist. Every thought, every feeling a person has can be determined by examining their nightjar. Rumour has it that some can manipulate the mind and coerce emotion, while others can even reunite dead souls with their nightjars. It is,' he repeated, 'a gift.'

Her face was flushed and the seeds of a stress headache were gathering at her temples.

'I need you to listen to me,' he said, 'because this is important.' He stopped and put a hand on her arm, his eyes burning with intensity. 'Your comatose friend is hovering between life and death, suspended in a state of eternal sleep – like a perverse Sleeping Beauty.'

Alice opened her mouth to protest, but what was there to say? It *was* perverse. And it was all her fault.

'She won't wake up,' he went on emphatically. '*Comas* . . .' He hesitated and let go of her arm. 'It's complicated. The trauma her body sustained in the accident tricked her nightjar into believing that death was imminent. Her nightjar – her soul-bird – has flown away, leaving her unprotected and weak. And now it's only a matter of time before her soul escapes and leaves the shell of her body behind.'

'Right,' she said flatly, her voice loaded with scepticism. 'You expect me to believe—'

'I don't expect you to do anything,' he said, but the impassioned look in his eye said otherwise. 'I'm simply relating to you the facts and offering you an opportunity. Your friend won't die without her soul. Not immediately, anyway; the hospital's machines will ensure her body keeps functioning. Perhaps she will prove resilient and live another forty or fifty years, fast asleep and withering to a husk in front of her loved ones.' Alice blanched. A flash of sympathy crossed Crowley's dark features, but he added, 'Without her soul, she can never wake up.'

'People wake from comas all the time,' she mumbled. Actually, she had no idea how often people woke up from comas. But she was absolutely certain that if anyone were to wake up, it would be Jen. She'd do it just to spite the odds against her.

'With her nightjar gone, this is no ordinary coma,' he said earnestly. 'Without her soul she's nothing but an inanimate lump of flesh and bone. All that's keeping her alive, Alice, is the almighty power of medicine – but that only sustains her body, not her mind. She needs her nightjar returned so it may guard her soul before it too leaves, and also keep it safely inside her. It's the only way she might stand even a moderate chance of recovering.'

Alice shook her head, fighting the panic.

'No,' she said. 'It's all – It's not real. It's because I've been hallucinating again. All this—'

He pulled her closer, his eyes searching hers. 'It *is* real,' he said firmly. 'You're an *aviarist*. You've seen the soul-birds with your own eyes. You, and only you, can find her nightjar and bring it back. And then, with her soul protected and safe once more, she'll wake up. *You* can save her.'

You can save her. The words ran in a loop through her mind. But she couldn't save Jen. She couldn't because what he'd told her wasn't true. It had taken her years to work out what was imaginary and what was not, and this – this was pure fantasy and nonsense, and she ought to go home. She jerked away from him and prepared to flee.

'I can prove it,' he insisted. 'Really, I can. So you weren't convinced by finding yourself in front of Marble Arch, in the middle of the night? You believe that to be another hallucination? Fine. Then let me prove it again.'

She stopped walking. Dear God, but she was tired. Would he take her home if she agreed? She nodded, motivated by sheer exhaustion.

They had reached a standstill in the curving shadow of the arch, and it was colder there. She drew Crowley's coat tighter around her. A gaggle of women tottered past. They were giggling and shoving each other good-naturedly, and she felt a pang of loneliness. *Jen.*

'Okay,' she said at last, her voice numbed. 'Supposing I'm not ill, and this is all real. According to you, everyone has a nightjar guarding their soul, stopping it from escaping?'

He nodded.

'Then why can't I see yours? Or anyone else's? The birds have gone. I don't know where . . .' Her eyes followed the women across the road. There were no soul-birds pursuing them at all.

'You see them inconsistently because not only have you repressed them, you are also inexperienced. You've not yet learned to see them on command. It's an innate skill, but it must be honed with practice.'

She exhaled softly and buried her chin into the coat collar. It smelled comforting – sandalwood and a hint of wood smoke.

'My wardrobe –'

'Was a shortcut. A doorway from your house to here.'

'And here is?'

Crowley laughed. 'Westminster, of course.'

She nodded, a strained expression on her face. 'Not Narnia.'

'No. Although through there,' he said, pointing at the centre of Marble Arch, 'is the Rookery. And it's through there that I can keep you safe from Vin.'

'But—'

'It's through there,' he repeated, 'that you will *find your friend's nightjar*.'

'Her name's Jen,' Alice said quietly. 'She has a name.' She turned to look at him. 'And what's the Rookery?'

'It's home,' he said, directing her gaze back to the Arch.

She frowned. There was nothing through it except litter bins, a department store and an office block. No rooks, no birds and definitely no magical nightjars.

'You know,' she said, 'maybe you're the one who's . . .'

She trailed away, her attention drawn to the centre of the Arch, where the air had begun to shimmer and ripple like a stone thrown into water.

'*Now*,' said Crowley. He moved past her, through the Arch, beckoning her to follow him. 'Do you see?'

Confused, she stepped forward, into the archway. The air felt soupy. It was like pushing her way through a barrier of spider webs that stretched and tore against her face. Crowley encouraged her onwards, until she appeared on the other side. What Alice saw next made her brain recoil and her breath catch in her throat.

Oh God, he was right. He was actually right. The busy streets with parking meters and telephone boxes were gone, and the flash car shops and grandiose buildings of Park Lane had vanished. Her eyes swept back and forth, taking in the dray horse pulling a wagon of beer barrels behind the oldest London bus she'd ever seen. The front end looked like a tractor and the back was a winding ribbon staircase to the open-topped deck. An advert for a tobacconist's was stretched across the side.

Wrought-iron street lamps stood sentry nearby, humming like foraging bees and casting a soft, flickering glow over the classic cars rolling past her. There were no road markings and the street signs were coated in a thin film of grime, making them unreadable in the dim light. If this was a fantasy, it was . . . the most elaborate hallucination she'd ever had.

A building loomed out of the darkness directly in front of her: a limestone behemoth with a domed roof, flanked by two jutting wings and surrounded by well-manicured gardens.

'This isn't Marble Arch,' she said. 'This is . . .' She spun round. The Arch itself was still behind her, solid and reassuring, but Edgware Road and Oxford Street were nowhere to be seen and, instead, open space stretched ahead of her. Greenery and grassland, and shimmering water. She recognized this place. It was the same, but . . . different. *Wilder.*

'That's St James's Park,' she managed. 'Jen made us camp out there once because she's a closet monarchist, but the police kicked us out. But if that's St James's . . .' She squinted into the park, and then stared back at the limestone building over her shoulder. 'Then *that* should be Buckingham Palace. Except . . . it's not.' A sudden rush of vertigo made the ground sway beneath her feet. If she could just stop, just for a second. 'I think I'm going to—'

Crowley grabbed her elbow. 'Steady now. Breathe.'

He stared into her eyes, forcing her to focus on him rather than the pounding in her skull. She gulped at the cool city air until her head cleared and the world shifted right-side up again.

'Better now?' he asked, more kindly this time.

She nodded, and he set her back on her feet and abruptly stepped away, leaving a respectable distance between them. Maybe he had girlfriend issues, she thought vaguely.

It was beginning to rain again, a soft pattering of drops sinking into her hair. She opened her mouth and the drizzle settled on her tongue.

'It smells different. It *tastes* different.'

'That's the exhaust fumes here,' explained Crowley. 'And horses.'

She shook her head. She didn't understand. 'What have you done with Buckingham Palace? Where's it gone?'

'It was never here to begin with,' he said, his voice laced with amusement. 'The Rookery is a republic. It has no monarch, so needs no home for one. That building over there is not *your* palace. It's known here as Goring University. Did you know that before Buckingham Palace was built, there was another building on the site, called Goring House? It burned down in 1674. Or so historians have been led to believe. What actually happened was that it was stolen . . . and brought here. The entire house – limestone walls, domed roof – and all of its contents.'

She stared at him.

'Alice,' he said. 'You are not in London. Marble Arch is a doorway into another city. A twin city.' Crowley grinned properly for the first time. 'Welcome to the Rookery.'

After several moments of thick silence, Crowley said, 'I presume you have questions.'

His comment seemed to kickstart her brain, and she became aware that the rain was falling harder now. 'Where did this place come from?'

He glanced at his watch. 'Choose a question that requires a shorter answer.'

'I don't *know* which questions have short answers!' she said, throwing her arms in the air.

He moved off again, and she was forced to hurry after him in a daze.

'That's Buckingham Gate,' she said, pointing at a long road in the distance. 'At least *that's* not changed.'

'Actually, it's Goring Gate.'

'*Goring* Gate?'

She stopped, turning back to the limestone building. So there was no Buckingham Palace. Instead, this Goring University was on the same site, housed in a building that didn't even exist in *her* London? Her brain rebelled at this rewritten history, but she focused on the many windows scattered across the pale facade – some still lit despite the late hour.

'I want to touch it,' she said, her voice hoarse. 'I want to make sure it's real.'

'Touch what?'

She pointed at the so-called university, and he scoffed, 'If it's not real, I wasted several years of my life in there for nothing.'

She gave him a stubborn look.

'It's midnight,' he said with a sigh. 'It's cold and wet, and you're wearing what can only be described as a net curtain and a gentleman's coat. We need to go before you die of hypothermia. Or worse – before *I* do.'

'A *gentleman's* coat? What exactly *is* your definition of a gen—'

'If you don't want the bloody coat, Wyndham, I'll have it back,' he said peevishly.

She pulled it tighter around herself and shook her head. 'Please, Crowley. Prove the building is real. Prove . . . everything is real, and I'll come quietly.'

The ghost of a smile twitched at his lips. 'Promises, promises.'

He stalked past, and didn't stop until they'd crunched over the broad gravel path and were standing at the foot of the entrance steps.

'The main door is just inside the cloisters,' he said. 'It closes at midnight and any students still inside the university must use the temporary sleeping accommodation on the upper floor. You can't go inside, but you may touch it, if you wish.'

Alice didn't need to touch the door. The steps would do. She knelt down and extended a trembling hand. The stone had been worn smooth by footsteps and time. It was . . . old. Old and therefore . . . permanent. But how?

Crowley raised an eyebrow. 'Done? Good.'

'Wait,' she said. 'If this is . . .' She shook her head, bewildered. 'Why is Marble Arch here? Why isn't it in Mayfair?'

'Because this is where it was first built, in the nineteenth century. In London, before it was moved to Mayfair, the Arch was originally an entrance to Buckingham Palace. Since the Rookery has no palace, it serves as an entrance to the university and as a door to our sister-city, London.'

He walked along a narrower path that circled the university, leading her past one of the wings and round the side. Through the darkened ground-floor windows Alice could see narrow corridors lined with books and wooden benches.

They soon reached what looked like a crooked stone shed, hidden behind a row of fir trees in the gardens. Crowley gave her a sharp nod and opened the door.

'Old janitor's outhouse,' he said. 'Just a store room now, but it has a door so it'll do for travelling. Shall I return you to London?'

She stared at him, fumbling for the right words. He'd been right about the building; maybe he was right about Jen too.

'Can you show me *more*?'

His eyes brightened, and he nodded. 'Let's start by satisfying a curiosity. Yours *and* mine.'

He urged her through the door and closed it smartly behind them. She was weightless. The floor was swept from under her. Again. Her legs gave an experimental kick in the nothingness as a fierce wind tugged at her hair.

'Where are we?' she murmured into the darkness, the chilly air making her eyes water.

'The void,' said Crowley. 'The barren space between worlds. You may think of it as a corridor, leading to infinite doorways. The trick is merely in knowing where you want to go.'

At that, another door swung open, and he steered her out onto a wide pavement. She glanced over her shoulder. A building made of white Portland stone towered over her. On the other side of the road, a similar building rose above the street: an imposing colossus with lined stonework and thick pillars supporting the first floor. It felt . . . familiar. The name, however, meant nothing to her. Above the entrance to the building was a stone plaque, inscribed with *House Pellervoinen*. They must still be in Crowley's London.

Soft drizzles of rain caught in the glow of the iron lamps and shimmered across her path; it seemed like the dark street was cloaked in mist. As they crossed the road, she spied the dome of St Paul's Cathedral rising above the rooftops in the distance and almost stopped in surprise.

She knew this place. There was supposed to be a statue here, commemorating Rowland Hill, the inventor of postage stamps. She peered up at House Pellervoinen, and her memory sharpened. In her London, this was the site of the old General Post Office HQ. And right next door was . . .

'That's Greyfriars,' she said.

'Yes,' said Crowley.

Alice jogged along the pavement towards it, him following for a change, her legs cold and her nightie trailing along the wet stone.

She'd had lunch once in the ruins of Christchurch Greyfriars. In their early days of London life, Jen had humoured her insistence on weekend trips to historical sites. They'd eaten corned beef sandwiches in the gardens, and Jen had pretended to listen while Alice explained the history of the church. Only the west tower and two walls had remained standing after it was pummelled by bombs in the Blitz. Instead of knocking it down, a wild garden had been allowed to spring up in the destroyed building's shell. And where the old stone pillars had once stood, there were now tall wooden frames built to support climbing roses and clematis. In her London, it was beautiful. Here, it was . . . breathtaking.

The west tower and its two rough stone walls were still standing, exactly as they did in London, but this Christchurch was much more than a broken shell. The roof and walls that had been destroyed by the Luftwaffe's bombs in one London still existed here. They were not, however, made of stone. Instead, they were built from enmeshed boughs and twigs of willow, horse chestnut and cherry blossom. The building was a living, breathing entity, the absent walls knitted from vines and branches: a perfect hybrid, half stone and half botanical.

As she watched, the colour of the branches' leaves began to change, shifting from greens to bright autumnal oranges and dull browns. The wind ruffled the leaves and they fell away from the building, scattering themselves across the pavement. The branches making up the walls were stark and bare for several long moments, before new buds and shoots burst along them like wildfire. *Springtime.* Blossoms and silvery catkins spilled out from the buds, and lush patches of leaves thickened in depth. She watched in amazement as the blossom drifted down in the breeze and caught in her hair.

'How is it doing that?' she asked. 'Christchurch is—'

'But this isn't Christchurch,' said Crowley. 'In the Rookery, this is House Mielikki. Can you hear the music?'

She strained to listen through the snapping and creaking branches and the rustle of wind through the leaves.

He gestured at the arched boughs that formed an entrance to the building. There was no door, just an open gap that led inside. There was no carpeting on the ground; instead, the dimly lit corridor had an indoor path, with a carpet of wild grasses and flowers rising from spongy earth. Fresh scents carried on the air, and Alice's ears picked out the strains of slow, rich folk music. Violins and tambourines and lilting penny whistles sang into the night, and there was something about the tune – haunting and wistful – that filled her chest and almost lifted her off her feet. Mesmerized, she stepped forward, through the gap and into House Mielikki. The wicker ceiling was strung with tiny lights that led her along the corridor, towards a doorway at the far end. She could hear laughing voices and the chink of glasses nearby. Was it a dance hall?

'Alice?'

She turned in a daze, just in time to see the vines creep across the gap, knitting together to close the entrance and imprison her inside. Crowley's face was striped by the criss-crossing branches. She couldn't reach him. Alarmed, she snatched at the vines, cracking them and tearing them apart. They crumbled in her hands like ash, leaving a space big enough to squeeze through. She darted outside, flying at Crowley. He caught her by the shoulders and glanced down at the ashy handprints she had left on his shirt.

'What is that place?' she asked.

'Think of it as . . . an exclusive, members-only club,' he said. 'Sylvie was a member, once. I wondered if you might be given the same courtesy.'

'I don't understand.'

'No,' he said. 'I don't expect you do.'

She shivered. The rain was falling harder now.

'You've seen enough of the city for one night,' Crowley said, directing her back the way they'd come, towards the neighbouring House Pellervoinen. There were warm lights in its windows as they approached the grand Edwardian building.

'Are they related to each other?' Alice asked. 'House Mielikki and House Pellervoinen?'

'In a manner of speaking,' he said, his eyes searching the dark streets, apparently set on returning them to the doorway by which they'd arrived.

A thunderous rumble from the entrance to House Pellervoinen echoed along the street, and Alice instinctively moved closer to Crowley. The granite door to the building slid heavily to one side, stone scraping against stone, and a man sauntered down the steps and past them, shoes clicking on the pavement. There was a strangled shout from the other side of the street, and a woman in a long dress raced past him. She hurtled up the steps, apparently determined to enter the building before the door shut.

As her foot slammed onto the top step, however, the door vanished. The grains of rock shifted in the surrounding stone brickwork and, like wind blowing the sand across a beach, brick dust poured along the building to fill the gaps around the door, until only a smooth, flat wall remained.

'I know you're in there!' the woman yelled, hammering on the stone. 'I know you're with her!'

Crowley quickened his pace and led Alice across the road, towards the door that had brought them here. As he opened it, she saw House Pellervoinen's ornate architecture change again. The grains in the walls' surface began to churn, and poured across the facade like a wave, smoothing out the patterned stonework. A curved band emerged from the middle of the building, followed by geometric shapes around the windows. It was morphing into the art deco style.

'My God,' she whispered. She wanted to draw it.

Crowley spun her away and into the void, slamming the door shut behind them. In the confined space she could smell wood smoke and spices again.

He opened the door abruptly and ushered her back through it.

They were standing very close together, and Alice was shocked when he moved suddenly away, as though she'd contaminated him. Her cheeks burned with embarrassment. *More* girlfriend issues on his part? But still, sniffing strange men in closets? Nice work, Alice. Wait till Jen—The thought instantly shrivelled and died, and a wave of pain washed over her.

They had emerged onto a tree-lined street full of old houses – and it seemed she still wasn't 'home' in her London. She glanced back at the door she'd exited, which had wooden boards hammered across it. A sign nailed to the front read, *Unsafe. Condemned.* Above that, a fly-poster was pinned to the rotten wood, showing an image of a white feather stamped with the words *He is Coming*.

'Did we just come out of a locked, derelict—'

'Yes.'

Alice hesitated, her eyes drawn back to the poster and its declaration. 'Who's coming?' she murmured.

'Elvis,' Crowley said.

Her eyes widened. 'What? Really?'

'What do you think?' he asked, gently mocking now.

She flushed. 'I *think* I'm having the weirdest night of my life. So forgive me if Elvis seems entirely plausible.'

He was already walking across the road, but Alice hesitated. A couple, arms linked, were strolling towards her. They could have been her grandparents, back in their prime; they looked like they'd just stepped out of a black-and-white picture, complete with cloche hat, greatcoat and trilby.

The woman's laughter spilled along the street and she clutched the man tighter, using him as a shield from the worsening rain. He murmured something to her and swept his arm up in a circle. There was a sudden silence. The air seemed to quiver and glitter in front of Alice, and she squinted into the night. The rain: it had stopped – not because the clouds were empty, but because it had stopped *falling*. All along the street, droplets hung motionless, suspended in the air. A bead of rainwater floated just above Alice's nose, shining like a jewel in the moonlight. She flicked it gently with her finger and it pinballed into the darkness.

The man in the trilby jerked his hand and the rain shot upwards, defying gravity as the drops were thrust back up into the dark sky. Alice gasped out loud as the water soaking Crowley's coat and her nightdress wrenched itself free of the fabric and the drops lifted into the air, leaving her almost dry. Across the road, the woman reached up and kissed the man's cheek in apparent thanks.

'Okay,' Alice croaked, hurrying down the steps. 'That's . . . strange.'

Crowley was skulking by a spiked metal railing; beyond it stood a Georgian townhouse that looked a little more neglected than its neighbours. The panelled sash windows were flaking and the white stucco on the lower half of the building had faded to a dull grey. There was a plaque screwed into the brickwork by the front door: *Coram House*.

It was, in spite of the air of benign neglect, a very grand house. She'd seen houses just like it in glossy society magazines: all varnished wooden floorboards, luxurious furniture, sheepskin rugs and huge gilded mirrors. Crowley swung open the front door and attempted to usher her inside.

'Oh no,' she said, batting his hands away. 'I'm not falling for that again. You can save your vanishing-floor act for someone else.'

'This is a perfectly ordinary doorway,' he said, stepping through himself. 'See?'

She followed dubiously. 'Whose house is this?'

He flicked a switch and light burst from a brass candelabra on the ceiling. It was not precisely what she had been expecting.

'Jesus,' she breathed.

'We've already been through this,' he said, a faint smile tugging at his lips. 'My name is *Crowley*. Though I won't deny I have certain messianic qualities.'

Alice ignored him as she edged deeper into the hallway. It was . . . hideous. The patterned walls clashed horribly with the tartan-style avocado-coloured carpet. *Tartan*. There was a rimless mirror above her that reflected the migraine-inducing nightmare tenfold, and near the stairs a mahogany console table was being suffocated by an army of lace doilies. Resting on top was an ancient Bakelite telephone. It was as if the entire decade of the 1930s had vomited all over the hallway. And not in a good way.

She tore her eyes from the decor and spotted a sign on one of the inner doors. It said *1a*.

'You will stay here,' said Crowley.

'Don't *tell* me what to do,' she said testily. 'That isn't what I asked you, anyway. Who lives here?'

'You do. Or at least . . . I strongly advise that you do.'

Alice's mouth thinned, and apparently sensing an explosion in the offing, Crowley added, 'The house comprises four apartments and an attic. 1a belongs to Jude. The floor above, 2a, is home to Sasha, and yours is on the third floor, though you will find it is numbered as 2b. Naturally, you will be expected to earn your keep during your stay.'

'Hang on,' she said as he moved deeper into the hallway. 'I'm only here because you said you had a way of helping Jen. I'm not staying here. I'm not – I'm not going to *live* here. This is temporary. A one-night deal.'

Crowley stopped at the bottom of the staircase, and his eyes deliberately targeted the slippers and the windswept nightdress sticking out of his coat.

'A one-night deal?' he said softly, the faint hint of suggestion colouring his voice.

She sucked in a breath, blushing. 'That's *not* what—'

His sudden amusement transformed his face, surprising her despite her irritation, but then he turned abruptly and continued up the stairs.

'Look,' she said desperately, trailing after him, 'you said my parents were in danger. I can't just abandon them if—'

'If you go back to London, *you* will put them in danger. Vin and his men can't use your parents against you if they can't find you.' He was staring at her intently.

'Why do you care, anyway?' she asked. 'Why are you helping me?'

'Sylvie,' he said roughly. 'I made her a promise. I owe it to her to keep you safe. The Rookery *is* safe.'

Alice frowned. None of this made any sense. She had barely known the old woman, and why would she herself be in any further danger from Vin?

'Stay here and you can help your friend,' Crowley murmured.

She hesitated. It was an irresistible incentive.

'*How?*'

He seemed to take this as a sign of acceptance and sighed with apparent relief. 'Rescue her nightjar.'

She nodded, but there was a long pause while she wrestled with the absurdity of it. Rescue the mythical bird that was supposed to be guarding her friend's soul? The one that had taken early retirement and deserted as soon as she'd fallen into a coma?

'Rescue Jen's nightjar,' she said slowly. 'Just like that?'

He gave her a brief smile. 'I didn't say it would be easy. But it can be done; I'm certain of it.'

'And you'll help me? With Jen – if I agree to stay?'

He nodded. 'First, you will be required to train – to practise *seeing* nightjars, understanding them. I'll find you a tutor.'

'At the university? That Goring place?'

'No,' he called over his shoulder. 'Call it ... an apprenticeship.'

She grabbed his sleeve. 'Why can't *you* train me?'

He twisted to face her, from the step above. She hadn't realized they were standing so close, and braced herself for his usual abrupt movement away, but he remained still. A thick silence fell between them, and a warm flush rose up the back of her neck.

'I ... can't,' he said at last. 'I'm not an aviarist.'

Alice sensed he wanted to say something else – there was a piercing gleam in his eyes that she couldn't read – but, without another word, he turned and continued up the stairs.

9

She slept like the dead, and when she first awoke, the horrors of the previous day seemed utterly fantastical. It was only after a few moments, curled beneath the polyester blankets, that icy-cold awareness began to drift down and settle on her like snow. Jen. The accident. The return of the invisible birds.

Alice's eyes flew open and she found herself dazzled by the beams of light striping her pillow. She hadn't shut the hideous floral curtains before climbing into bed the night before; she'd merely traipsed inside after Crowley, who had pointed at the bed and said, 'Yours. Get in.'

There had been an awkward moment when she'd just looked at him in horrified silence, thinking he meant to climb in beside her. He'd read the panic on her face and had given a short laugh before striding out of the room.

She inspected it now. An apartment, he'd called it, but really it was just a room. Even calling it a bedsit was probably an offence under the Trade Descriptions Act. There was a small fireplace against the far wall, but it didn't look as though it had been lit this century – hence the chill in the stale air.

It wasn't the worst place she'd ever slept in (that honour would have to go to her ex-boyfriend's shed). After the horrors of the hallway, she was at least thankful for the tasteful cream wallpaper with leafy patterns and the minimalist wooden floor and plain rug.

There was very little furniture: just an iron bedstead, a hard wooden chair, a writing desk and, instead of a wardrobe, a wooden coat rack with a shelf. There was no toilet, just a chipped sink and a dusty mirror. The kitchen facilities consisted of a travel kettle and a cup, both of which sat on the chair in lieu of a countertop. There didn't appear to be any teabags, sugar or milk. *So.* A cup of hot water for breakfast then. *Marvellous.*

A knock at the door caused her to snatch the blankets up to her chin.

'Hello? You in there?' came a disembodied female voice.

Alice held her breath and stared at the door in a panic, willing the woman on the other side to go away.

'There's breakfast downstairs if you're hungry. We share a kitchen on the ground floor. And a bathroom on the first. I don't know if Crowley mentioned it. He didn't tell me he was bringing in a new tenant till this morning, so . . .' The voice trailed away. 'Right. Well, just come down if you want some food. Or not. No pressure.'

There was another pause, and then the sound of footsteps retreating. Alice let out a gusty breath and flopped backwards onto the pillows. Her stomach roared. It had been a long time since she'd eaten. Excellent, she thought – she had to introduce herself to a total stranger while wearing her mum's nightie and a pair of furry slippers. Crowley had, of course, taken back his coat.

When she stepped into the kitchen, Alice was hit by a welcome blast of heat from a massive tiled fireplace. Pine wood crackled and burned inside it, spilling its mellow scent into the house. Crowley's scent, she realized.

A young woman with dark skin and dandelion hair was sitting at a table in the middle of the room, spooning a small mountain of yoghurt into her mouth. At the sight of Alice in her nightwear, she nearly choked.

'Morning,' she croaked. 'Alice, right?'

Alice nodded.

The stranger wiped her eyes and waved her spoon at her chest. 'I'm Sasha. I'm in 2a. Floor below yours. Mind yourself on that fire; it'll melt that polyester right onto your skin.'

Cheeks flaming, Alice gathered up her ugly nightie and edged away from the fireplace, plonking herself into one of the mismatched chairs by the table. Sasha stared at her with something like anticipation, but Alice wasn't sure what she was waiting for.

The painful silence stretched thin, then Sasha slumped back in her seat, exasperated.

'Okay, you need to do something more interesting than this.'

'I do?' said Alice, bemused. 'Like what?'

'Like . . . look into the depths of my soul and tell me what you see. Crowley said you're an *aviarist* – do what aviarists do! Tell me what my nightjar looks like,' Sasha urged. 'What's it doing?'

'I can't see it,' said Alice. 'Sorry.'

'So . . . what?' said Sasha, narrowing her eyes. 'You're saying I'm soulless?'

'No, I can't see *any* of them . . . except sometimes by accident.'

Sasha considered Alice for a second or two before shaking her head. 'You're not an aviarist then. Crowley's having me on.'

'You're probably right.'

'Have you *ever* seen a nightjar?'

'I've seen . . .' Alice paused, then nodded. 'I think so. Maybe.'

Sasha stood up and tossed her spoon into the sink. 'I'd better finish getting ready for work. You really can't see anything?'

Alice shook her head, and Sasha sighed.

'You're the Mona Lisa of aviarists.'

Alice didn't bother masking her confusion.

'Have you ever seen that thing in real life? It's tiny. You hear all about it, you think it's going to blow your mind, and then when you're standing in front of it, it's like . . .' Sasha's nose wrinkled. 'Size of a postage stamp.' She shrugged. 'Sorry. No offence, but you're the first proper aviarist I've ever met, and . . .'

'I'm a postage stamp?' Alice supplied.

'Pretty much. But hey, it's early days.' Sasha swung her coat over her shoulders and smoothed the lapels. It was a woollen oxblood greatcoat and she'd teamed it with an old-fashioned plaid blouse, dark trousers and battered military-style boots. She looked like she shopped in two different decades, in whichever department she felt like.

'Crowley left that for you, by the way,' she said, nodding at the table. 'He found it in his coat pocket. Said it was yours.'

Alice glanced at it. It was Sylvie's feather. She wasn't inclined to pick it up.

'Help yourself to whatever food you can find in the cupboards,' said Sasha. 'We've not done the weekly shop yet, but Nella – she lives next door with her husband, Gideon – she donates a box of this weird Finnish bread she makes every Saturday. Korvaputty . . . Korvapuusti?' She shrugged. 'Anyway, there's still some left in the breadbin if you fancy it.'

'Thanks.'

'Jude's already gone to bed – he does a lot of night shifts at the Royal Mint – but—'

'Are my ears burning?'

A tousled head appeared around the door jamb, and Alice shrank into her nightie. Why did she have to be dressed like the ghost of someone's grandmother? *Why?*

'This is a bit late for you, isn't it?' Sasha asked the newcomer. 'I've been creeping around the kitchen all morning so I didn't wake you.'

'I didn't get out of the Mint until half an hour after my shift ended,' he said, navigating his wheelchair into the room. 'There was a problem with one of the dies.' He turned to Alice. 'I'm Jude. Are you . . . ?'

'This is 2b,' said Sasha. 'She's moving in.'

'Nice to meet you, "to be . . . "' He paused. Sasha was staring at him expectantly. 'I'm supposed to make the classic pun here, aren't I? But I refuse.'

'Killjoy,' said Sasha.

He grinned. 'Is the kettle on?'

'No. Do you want me to boil one?'

Jude shook his head. 'This will do.' He reached into the storage bag on the arm of his wheelchair and pulled out a newspaper and a travel flask. He tossed the newspaper – *The Rookery Herald* – onto the table and held up the flask.

'Can I interest you?' he said to Alice.

She nodded. 'Thanks.'

He fished out a pair of plastic mugs, unscrewed the flask and poured two cups of tea.

'What's your name, 2b? I'm sure your mother didn't name you after a type of pencil.'

'It's Alice,' she said. She blew a curl of steam from the mug and stared into its murky depths.

'Everyone's usually gone to work by the time I get home,'

he said, stifling a yawn. 'Are you a permanent addition to the household?'

'I don't think so.'

'Guess what she is,' said Sasha, grinning broadly and gesturing at Alice's head. 'No, you'll never guess – let me tell you. She's . . .' She paused for dramatic effect. 'A *postage stamp*.' She turned to Alice. 'No offence.'

'None taken.'

'A postage stamp?' said Jude. 'Has someone spiked my tea?'

'Fine,' said Sasha. 'For clarity, she's an aviarist. I'd go for the dramatic pause again, except she can't actually see any nightjars so I'm not sure she warrants one. No offence.'

Alice sipped her tea, beginning to feel mildly offended.

'Crowley's found an aviarist?' asked Jude, surprised. 'Where did he find you?' He was staring at her with quiet interest.

'In London – the other one.'

His eyes lit up and he wheeled closer. 'I have a photograph collection,' he said. 'London in the post-war years. Could I show it to you sometime? I'd love to know how much it's changed since the photographs were taken.'

'You've never been?' she asked.

He shook his head.

'Only you,' Sasha told him, 'could find a Londoner more interesting than an aviarist.'

Jude yawned again – this time reluctantly. He was clutching his mug between both hands, hunched down in the wheelchair, his pale blue eyes regarding her calmly. His tanned face was narrow and angular, his jaw showing the first signs of stubble. A lock of unkempt dark hair bounced down over his forehead, and he swept it back with his fingers.

Well, crap. Her new housemate was actually James Dean, circa

1950 – he even had the plain white T-shirt. There was probably a leather flight jacket in his wardrobe too.

'Aviarists are a bit of a fascination around here, because of their rarity,' he explained. 'People want to know what aviarists see.'

He smiled, and Alice found herself blushing and wishing she'd brushed her hair.

He held her eye for a moment longer, before another yawn broke across his face and he gave up trying to stifle it. 'I'm sorry, I can't keep my eyes open,' he said. 'I've got to call it a night.'

'It's morning,' said Sasha.

'Not to me it isn't,' he said, rolling backwards. His chair clanked against something metallic, and he paused. There was a bucket of water on the floor behind him, collecting a steady stream of drips from the ceiling.

'Leaky pipe needs fixing?' said Jude.

'It can wait,' insisted Sasha. 'Have your sleep first.'

Alice looked up at the ceiling. There was a small damp patch blossoming over the plasterwork among several other dried-out yellow stains, as though flooding was a regular occurrence.

'Alice, it was lovely to meet you,' said Jude. She gave him a wave, and he spun round and headed for the door to 1a.

Sasha stared down at Alice with pity in her eyes. 'I've seen that nightdress before,' she said. 'On the old lady in *Titanic*. Do you have any clothes with you?'

'No.'

'If you're quick, I'll drop you off at my favourite shop on my way to work. You'll have to wear something of mine on the way there.'

'I don't have any money.'

Sasha shrugged. 'Crowley will be back soon. Maybe he'll sort you out with—' A sprinkle of water splattered onto the floor and Sasha froze.

Alice glanced up at the ceiling.

'Where did—'

She fell silent as a gush of water fountained up from the gaps between the kitchen floorboards. Was . . . the *floor* leaking? Another mighty spray dashed the legs of the table and splashed the walls before receding and pooling around its entry point. Alice watched, bewildered, as water chugged out across the floor. It gathered pace as it flowed, and she had to whip her feet up onto the chair to save her slippers.

'Rubbish pipes,' Sasha said quickly, backing away. '*Jude!*'

Another spurt of water erupted from beneath the floorboards and whipped across the kitchen like an erratic hosepipe. Alice was too late to duck. The splash hit her right in the chest, leaving her drenched and shivering.

'When you said I looked like the old lady on the *Titanic*,' she gasped, 'I didn't think you meant *literally*.'

There was a rumbling in the hallway, and then Jude appeared, looking perfectly calm amidst the sodden chaos.

'You'll need to lift the boards,' he said.

He cast out an arm and flicked his fingers upwards. There was a buzzing noise, followed by a series of soft pops. The nails hammered into the floorboards around the leak worked themselves free and . . . *sprang* into the air. Jude's fingers twitched again, and dozens of rusted and bent nails shot across the room and landed in his open palm.

'The boards,' he repeated.

Sasha shook her head, wild-eyed. Her fingers groped for a pendant hung around her neck, and she clutched it tightly. Jude turned to Alice instead, who was staring at him in shock.

The nails – they'd flown across the kitchen as though he'd *summoned* them. Magnets, she quickly decided. He must have used industrial-strength magnets . . .

'Alice, can *you* lift the boards?' he said, disrupting her thoughts.

Two inches of water had quickly eaten up the floor, so she left her slippers on the chair. Icy liquid splashed up her ankles, but she scrambled forward to lift the now-loose boards, making a gaping hole in the kitchen floor. Inside, a thick metal pipe was spewing water from a fist-sized hole.

She glanced over at Sasha, who was rooted to the spot while the water rose. Three inches now. What was the matter with her? Some sort of phobia?

Another splatter of water hit Sasha in the face and she flinched in fear.

'Okay, let's get out of here,' said Alice. She forded across the room and grabbed Sasha's arm, tugging her towards the doorway while Jude inspected the pipe.

Another spray of water shot out and drenched the tabletop, and Alice hesitated. Sylvie's feather. *Her* feather . . . With a frustrated sigh, she doubled back and snatched it to safety before ploughing over to Sasha and bundling her out of the room.

They decamped to the pavement outside. Alice was cold and wet, standing on a city street in her nightdress – again; it was fast becoming her signature look. Through the open front door, she could see the water seeping from the kitchen and advancing towards the hallway.

'It would be a real shame if the tartan carpet had to be replaced . . .' she said.

There was no response from Sasha, so she shuffled closer to the kitchen window to watch Jude through the glass. He glanced down at the floorboards' nails in his hand: misshapen and serrated. Then he slammed his other hand down on them and crushed them between his palms. Alice winced, but Jude appeared unfazed. He *kneaded* the nails into a lump of metal as malleable as plasticine, flattened it to form a disc and hurled it at the damaged pipe. It steamed through the spray and slammed onto the ragged hole, and its molten edges merged with the metal of the pipe, closing the gap.

The water stopped, and Alice's mouth fell open in disbelief. Who *were* these people? She darted a look at Sasha and inhaled sharply. The birds – the birds were back. Her first instinct was to scarper, but she swallowed it down and forced herself to remain still. No – no more running. She took a shaky breath and lifted her gaze . . .

Sasha's bird – her *nightjar* – watched her through shining black eyes. It sat on Sasha's shoulder, its pincer claws alternately squeezing and releasing her arm. She clearly couldn't feel it – she was leaning against the wall, her hands shoved into her coat pockets, an occasional shudder running through her body.

The nightjar's feathers were soft and downy, the earthy colours forming a simple pattern. Half the feathers lay flat, but the other half were ruffled, as though they were growing in the wrong direction. It seemed . . . agitated, flicking its tail feathers and jerking its head.

There was a thin, silvery ribbon of light tethering the bird's leg to Sasha's left wrist. It was ethereal and translucent, so fragile that it seemed to be a trick of the light. She'd never seen it before in her previous bird 'visions'. What *was* it?

In a flurry of rustling, the bird's head spun in her direction. Before she had time to talk herself out of it, she reached out a trembling hand and stroked the bird's soft head. *Face your fears*, she thought grimly.

The nightjar flinched and peered down at her, its eyes two inky black pools like the glassy surface of a lake. The light from its luminous cord pulsed vividly, haloing the nightjar's head, and Alice was entranced. Her eyes locked with the bird's and the street suddenly blinked out of existence around her . . . *inky black . . . surface of a lake . . .* She felt herself mentally pitch forward, into the bird's gaze . . . and broke through the surface.

She sank into the bird's mind like a stone. Cold terror trickled through her body, and the sound of rushing water roared in her ears. Not a lake: an ocean. A child's voice rose above the noise of the crashing waves in her head, screaming and spluttering. Weighed down by sodden clothes, dragging her under. And under. *Zara!* Guilt and anguish abraded every cell of her body. *I've killed her!* Her heart exploded in her chest and her head split open like a walnut.

Alice staggered sideways with a gasp, her hand falling away from the nightjar and her head pounding. What *was* that? A vision of the future? A memory?

Sasha was staring straight ahead, an apprehensive expression on her face and her fingers still clutching her necklace for comfort – the pendant contained an iridescent gemstone Alice had never seen before.

'The water's stopped,' Sasha croaked.

Despite the short, confused pause, she seemed oblivious to whatever Alice had just done.

Alice pressed the heels of her palms into her eyes. She took a steady breath and willed the pain in her head to recede. What was happening to her?

'I've fixed the pipe,' said Jude from the hallway.

Alice's hands fell away, but it still seemed too bright outside. She squinted over at Sasha, and suddenly realized she was gripping Sylvie's feather. Her fingers snapped open and it fluttered to the ground. Sasha's nightjar instantly vanished, and relief unwound in Alice's chest.

'It's all clear,' Jude called again. His drenched hair was slicked back and his T-shirt was soaked. Everything seemed hazy now – she'd been so sure she'd seen him crush nails with his bare hands and fix the pipe using metal he'd melted without any tools, but that was patently absurd. It must have been a trick of the light, or tiredness . . .

'Jude,' she murmured. 'What exactly do you *do* at the Royal Mint?'

He smiled. 'I have a licence to print money.' He rolled his wheelchair to the front door. 'But I really want to get into metal engineering and weaponry. I rent a small forge in Spitalfields.'

She nodded absently and stared down at the feather; it lay on the ground like a corpse, and she couldn't bring herself to pick it up again.

'What in *God's name* is going on?'

Crowley was standing on the other side of the road, staring at them all in disbelief.

10

The kitchen door swung open and Crowley frowned down at them. Frowning seemed to be his default expression.

'Come back in,' he said.

After insisting they continue to wait on the pavement, he'd somehow managed to dry the room in minutes. The fire was roaring in the grate and there wasn't so much as a teaspoon of water on the floor.

'How did you get rid of the flood?' Alice asked, her eyes flitting up to his face.

'Evaporation.'

His gaze moved past her to study Sasha, who had remained in the hallway. The numbness that had gripped her seemed to be wearing off.

'Everything okay?' he asked.

Sasha hesitated, then shrugged. 'Fine.'

His lips pursed and he continued to watch her, apparently unconvinced.

She rolled her eyes at him. 'I'm fine. Same can't be said for you, though. You look like shit this morning, Crowley. You need a decent night's sleep.'

He raised a sardonic eyebrow and shook his head. 'Sasha. A delight, as ever.'

She grinned and sauntered away.

He turned back to Alice and gestured at the table. She sank into a chair and watched patiently as Crowley dumped his undertaker's coat on the back of a seat and vanished into the hallway. He returned a few seconds later clutching three black bin bags.

'Your things,' he said, dumping them at her feet and lowering himself wearily into a chair.

'My things?'

'You needed clothes, didn't you?'

She punched a hole in the nearest bag and peered through it. 'You've been to my *flat*?' She glimpsed underwear through the gap and winced.

He nodded, and the realization hit her: this really wasn't going to be a short stay.

'My parents –'

'I told you,' he said. 'If you go home—'

She waved his words away. 'I need to let them know I'm okay. You dragged me out of the house in the middle of the night. They'll think I've been kidnapped. Or arrested, since you told them you were a bloody policeman.'

'I've taken care of it. As far as they're concerned, you left to help the police with their enquiries and returned to London for some normalcy.'

'My mum would never believe I'd go without saying goodbye,' she said. 'Let me phone them.' There was an old-fashioned Bakelite in the hallway; she'd seen it last night.

'Our telephone systems are internal. Write them a letter and I'll deliver it, if you must, but you can't call London from here.'

'But where *is* here?' she asked.

'As I said last night, this is the Rookery.'

She gave him a dark look. She'd had an inglorious start to her day and was in no mood for riddles. 'And what is the Rookery, exactly? You said it was a twin city. A twin of London.'

'It is.'

'Well, where did it come from? Why can't everyone else see it? And what you said about the birds . . .'

He rubbed his palms across his face and sighed.

'Oh, I'm sorry,' she said hotly. 'Am I boring you? It's probably the sort of thing you do every day, isn't it? Stalking people, kidnapping them from their childhood bedrooms, telling them that magic is real and then locking them up in an old house. Bit tiresome after a while, I expect.'

She grabbed the jug of orange juice on the table and poured herself a shaky glass before taking a slug and slamming it back down.

He raised an eyebrow. 'Finished?' he asked blandly.

She gave him a grudging nod.

'What do you know about religion?'

Alice paused, surprised. 'I have a degree in history,' she said. 'We took a module that covered religious texts, but that was years ago, back in—'

'How widely read were you? Did you cover just the Abrahamic religions, or paganism too?'

She stared, at a loss for a response.

'I'll skip ahead and put you out of your misery, shall I?' he said. 'The reason I can travel through doorways and you can see magical birds is because we are special – you, me, all of us here in the Rookery.'

'Special?'

He nodded.

'Are you . . . ?' She hesitated. Could she seriously be considering saying this out loud? She took a deep breath. 'Are you a wizard?'

He smirked and shook his head. 'No. *We*, Alice, are not wizards; *we* are a species.'

She scrubbed a hand through her hair. Sometimes, in the mornings, Jen pointed out that she had her skirt on back to front, or had toothpaste sprayed over her blouse. This was the first time she'd woken up to be told she was an entirely different species.

Finally, she said, 'Why did you ask me about religion?'

'Because several hundred years ago, the Christians went on a conversion spree, targeting pagans all over the world.'

'The crusades?'

He nodded. 'Campaigns were waged all over the globe, suppressing paganism, eradicating heresy and fighting over symbolic lands. Holy wars and forced baptism on a grand scale.'

She frowned. 'What's this got to do with—'

'Before the conversions, the Finnish pagans believed in the existence of the Väki, a magical race of elf-like creatures. When I said that we are a species . . .' There was a heavy pause.

'I am not a fucking elf,' she said flatly.

'No.' He laughed. '"Magical creatures", however, is an adequate description. With Europe executing witches and Christianity being imposed across the world, often at the end of a sword, our ancestors decided to make a break for safety. Most headed for the heart of England and built the Rookery as a safe place for their families to live.'

'You're telling me I'm a . . . Väki?' Alice said weakly. 'What does that even mean?'

'Väki means both "supernatural power" and "folk". We are "folk" with unusual powers.'

She stared at him. Jude had summoned those metal nails . . .

'The four Masterbuilders who built the Rookery were called Ahti, Pellervoinen, Ilmarinen and Mielikki,' he went on. 'They shared their names with the old Finnish heroes and gods.' He paused, then added, 'Perhaps the founders of the Rookery truly *were* Finnish gods, or perhaps they were simply the most powerful Väki of their time – their history is somewhat murky and we may never know for sure. But it is thanks to their ingenuity—'

'House Mielikki and House Pellervoinen,' Alice interrupted, seizing on the strange yet now familiar words. 'Those buildings from last night . . . Did they build those too?'

'They built the *foundations*.'

'You said they were exclusive, members-only clubs.'

'Indeed they are.'

'What about the other two builders? Do they have clubs – I mean, houses – too?'

He nodded. 'House Ahti can be found at Baynard's Castle, on the riverfront. It no longer exists in your London; I believe its ruins are buried beneath a dual carriageway now. House Ilmarinen is on the north side of Thames Street, in the old London Coal Exchange – another building demolished in London. Here in the Rookery, we appreciate good architecture.' He hesitated. 'Should I continue?'

She nodded.

'Most of the powers we've been given are descended from the four Masterbuilders and the other, less powerful Väki who followed them here.'

Her gut churned as she tried to assimilate this information. It just *couldn't* be true. Yes, she'd seen plenty of strange things recently – the couple in the rain last night, Jude, Sasha's nightjar – but . . .

'No.' She shook her head. It just wasn't *logical*. 'There has to be a simpler explanation. Magic bloody powers?'

'We don't call them magic powers. We call them legacies – because they're our genetic inheritance.'

Alice pursed her lips. Her biological parents, whoever they were, were dead. All she'd inherited from them were her brown eyes and wide hips. If all this was true, why had she been adopted in London instead of the Rookery?

'Look at this,' Crowley said. He pressed his palm against the tabletop. The table juddered and faint curls of steam – no, not steam, *smoke* – seeped out from beneath his hand. A bright spark leapt out from the gap between his fingers and snagged on the wood. Alice lurched backwards in shock when a whip of glowing orange fire lashed across the table, crackled briefly and vanished.

'A trick,' she said desperately. 'A small one. Quite basic, really, considering what David Copperfield can do. In Las Vegas the magicians can pull helicopters out of their sleeves. They'd probably—'

Crowley rolled his eyes and flicked his index finger in her direction.

Her hair burst into flames.

'What the *hell*?' She threw her chair back and hurtled towards the sink, flames dancing across her head like Medusa's snakes. With a panicked cry, she spun the taps, and icy water splattered into the basin. She was seconds from thrusting her head under the tap when the flames dissipated. She reached up to pull at the singed clumps of hair . . . but her hair was fine. Her usual bird's nest, yes, but otherwise . . . fine.

She whirled around to face Crowley.

'That,' she breathed, 'was low.'

He sat back in his chair, folding his arms across his chest, looking amused. 'We all have our little talents.'

'You're a – a human flamethrower! How did you *do* that?'

He shrugged. 'DNA. My point, Alice, is that the things you and I can do—'

'I can't do that. I can't – That fire – I can't do—'

'No,' he said. 'The magical genetic lottery doesn't bestow the same legacies on us all. Members of House Ilmarinen are practisers of fire magic.'

'And that's . . . what you are?'

'I am many things. We are, all of us, a product of hundreds of years of interbreeding. When it comes to legacies, most of us are a jack of all trades, but with certain dominant specialities. One of my specialities happens to be with fire.'

'Then . . . what else is there?' she demanded.

'The traditional legacies are those drawn from the physical environment and its elements. For example, those descended from Ilmarinen are typically skilled with fire and metals, whereas Ahti's children are skilled with water. Pellervoinen's with stone, rock and the doorways.'

Alice cleared her throat, the hypnotic music she'd heard last night still ringing in her ears. 'What about . . . ?'

'Members of House Mielikki are skilled with wood, forestry and wildlife.'

Her pulse picked up its tempo. 'Wildlife as in . . . birds?'

'That was certainly the case for Sylvie,' Crowley said in a musing tone.

'Are all aviarists descended from Mielikki then?'

'Not necessarily, no,' he said. 'I believe the link to forestry and animals was purely coincidental in Sylvie's case. The traditional legacies – water, metals, forestry and so on – are passed on through the generations. However, there are other skills – evolutionary quirks, if you will – such as the ability to sight nightjars, necromancy, hemomancy—'

'Necromancy is death magic?' she asked. 'And . . . what's the other one?'

'*Hemo* relates to blood,' he said. 'These skills are . . . anomalies, and they're rare because they're not inherited through successive generations; they're random aberrations. Hemomancers and necromancers are very unusual, but not extraordinary. I can name a few dozen in the Rookery alone. But there is nothing so rare as an aviarist.'

He plucked Sylvie's bedraggled feather from his pocket and laid it flat on the table. She'd left him to pick it up from the pavement. She didn't want to touch it again.

'Well,' she said at last, 'that was a really great story.'

'It's not a story.'

'Of course not.' She sighed wearily. 'Congratulations on your fantastic DNA. Ilmari-something?'

'Ilmarinen,' he said. 'I've proven myself sufficiently skilled with fire to have been granted membership of House Ilmarinen. However, among other things, Pellervoinen created the doorways, and I also have a prodigious talent for travelling.'

'So you're a member of House Pellervoinen too?'

'I don't have sufficient aptitude with stonework,' he said, but his tone was hesitant. 'If I have Pellervoinen's blood in my veins, then I inherited only the ability to open any door I choose.'

'What about the others?' Alice asked. 'Sasha and Jude? Are they—'

'Jude also belongs to House Ilmarinen. He has an immunity to fire, but his real skill lies in metalwork. He's a very talented blacksmith. He works two jobs – one at an armoury, and another at the Royal Mint.' He smirked. 'Yes, I know. A Royal Mint despite an absence of royals.'

Alice was only half listening to him. She balked at the very idea of it, but . . . she had seen some incredible things in the past twenty-four hours.

'I can't do any of those traditional legacy things,' she said. 'Fire, water, stone . . . none of it. What makes you think I'm a Väki?'

'You're an aviarist.' He glanced pointedly at the feather and then leaned back in his chair. 'You may have inherited only very weak legacies from your ancestors: recessive Väki traits and, instead, dominant human traits. Our bloodlines have become mixed,' he explained, then sighed quietly. 'Anyway. We can do things that others can only dream of, Alice. And therein lies the danger.'

He paused, as though expecting some sort of response to this, but when nothing was forthcoming, he added, 'We're unnatural. There are people on the other side of Marble Arch who think we're monsters. Devils. An affront to all that is good and pure and should therefore be wiped out.' He pushed his hair back from his face and continued more calmly. 'Your run-in with Vin Kelligan . . .'

She sat up, suddenly more alert.

'He belongs to a group of people – they call themselves the Judicium, the Judgement. *We* call them the Beaks – *beak* being old English slang for *judge*, you understand . . .' He paused, lost in thought for a moment. 'The crusades ended several hundred years ago. But some of those crusaders squatting in Finland, they discovered us; they knew we had escaped them and they never forgot. They followed us here and handed down their own stories about the devils living on the other side of the wall.' He looked up, his eyes meeting hers. 'All these long years, their intention has remained the same: break down the wall and wipe out the Rookery and the Väki.'

Crowley lapsed into silence. His eyes glazed over, staring blindly at a spot over her shoulder. After a moment, he added, 'Vin Kelligan belongs to the Beaks, which means that you're already on their radar, Alice. They've been waiting for Sylvie to die in order to find and capture her replacement. They want you – quite badly – and they're powerful.'

Alice's lip curled at the memory of Vin's pinching fingers digging into her flesh. 'Not that powerful,' she bluffed. 'Vin wasn't even strong enough to bundle me into his car.'

'I'm not talking about brute strength,' he said. 'The Beaks have *authority* in London. Originally, they were just a renegade outfit, but a few hundred years ago they were enfolded into the government. Now, they're an official but clandestine branch of the Ministry of Defence, headed by Sir John Boleyn. You're unlikely to have heard of him, but he has a blinding hatred of the Väki and extensive resources at his disposal. The Beaks are now actively seeking out Väki living in the mainland – the outside world: London and beyond. And they're destroying them.'

'But that would make it state-sanctioned murder . . .'

'Your point? Magic, or whatever you want to call it, is a threat to national security. I could walk into your beloved Buckingham Palace tomorrow and burn it to the ground, and not a soul could stop me. The Beaks prey on that fear, and now they can do whatever the hell they like in London, just as long as they do it quietly.' He cleared his throat. 'Anyway, it doesn't matter. You'll be safe here. They can't venture into the Rookery without damaging themselves.'

'But why me?' she asked desperately as he made to leave the table. 'I don't understand what Vin and those others want with me.'

He paused. 'Your skill with nightjars could be dangerous in the wrong hands,' he said. 'The Beaks want to *use* you against the rest of us, and I cannot allow that. Sylvie was too frail and too blind to be useful to them – but you are not.'

'Use me how?'

He sighed and scooped up the feather. 'I think that's quite enough talk for one morning, don't you?'

'No, I bloody well do not! What do the Beaks want me for?'

He shook his head. 'Later. I have several other things to attend to while you get ready.'

'For what?'

'For work. You won't be staying here rent-free.'

'Work? You're taking me back to London?'

He frowned. 'No. You *must* stay in the Rookery.' Her mouth tightened in response, and he continued in a softer tone. 'Alice, I know that all of this is new, and strange, but it is necessary. You're not safe in London.'

He gave her a searching look that went on just a beat too long, before he straightened up and his reserve snapped back into place. 'Besides,' he said smoothly, 'I've already found you a new job and a tutor.'

'But I've—'

'You will be working for the Bow Street Runners – the Rookery's equivalent of the Metropolitan police force.'

'Are you kidding me? A job in the police? Don't you have to be . . . trained to be a police officer? Properly trained?'

'Yes,' he said. 'But fortunately you already possess the necessary skills outlined in the job description.'

'Really?' she said suspiciously.

'Of course.' He grinned. 'You *can* operate a teapot, can't you?'

11

Bow Street Station was a grand old building made from pale, serrated stone, its pitted surface resembling a giant cheese grater. The entrance sat at a blunted corner of the building, by a pavement busy with harried police officers in dark uniforms (Runners, Crowley called them) hurrying in and out. Crowley, with Sasha in tow, had escorted Alice from the derelict building opposite Coram House – Coram itself being locked to outside travel. They had exited through a purpose-built doorway set into the wall of the Royal Opera House, opposite the station.

'You'll be working for Proctor Sinclair in the archivist's department,' he said, steering her around a pothole in the road while Sasha trudged behind them in silence. 'He's also agreed to tutor you.' He paused. 'For money.'

Her eyes widened; she was penniless.

'*My* money,' he clarified. 'You can reimburse me later. But for God's sake, learn quickly. The old merc's charging by the hour.'

'Is he an aviarist then?' she asked.

'Yes.'

'He's the only other one in the UK?'

'Yes. He is, however, useless. He's half-blind these days; he can't see his own reflection, never mind nightjars.'

As they neared the entrance, a woman leaning against the wall eyed her with curiosity. The woman was selling newspapers from a rack on the floor, but she shuffled closer to peer at Alice, who felt like an exhibit in a zoo.

'It's your clothes,' said Sasha. 'If you're going to wear main-lander's clothes, you need a coat to hide them under so you blend in.'

She paused. Sasha was right. Everyone she'd seen in the Rookery so far looked like they shopped in the 1930s, give or take a decade.

'My favourite shop is just over there on Floral Street,' Sasha said, pointing at an army and navy store about twenty metres away. 'They sell coats.'

'No,' said Crowley, his mouth pinching.

'You just said she's got to reimburse you for her training. What's a coat compared to that? She'll get a wage soon, and they're second-hand anyway.'

'We'll be late.'

'Skinflint,' said Sasha. 'Come on, I'll get you one and we'll put it on your tab.'

'No, honestly,' said Alice, rapidly growing mortified. 'It's fine. I'll—'

Sasha took no notice of her feeble protests as she propelled her over the road, leaving a stationary Crowley to glare after them.

Alice had never been to Floral Street in London, though she'd shopped at nearby Seven Dials and Neal's Yard. The narrow cob-bled street that Sasha dragged her down was chaotic with small terraced shops, draped with canvas awnings, crammed almost on top of each other. The signs out front advertised everything from English tea and confectionery to barbershop haircuts, priced at ten crowns each.

She recognized none of the brands on display in the windows.

The confectioner's was a hodgepodge of unknown toffees, liquorice, striped rock, Motoring Chocolate, Oxo Chocolate and aniseed balls, all stored in glass jars, cardboard packets and metal tins.

'Don't you have any supermarkets?' she asked.

'No,' said Sasha. 'Most of the things you eat in London are a luxury here. Even the chocolate.'

No Dairy Milk? Alice was horrified.

The shop next to Gribbon's Military Garments was a monolithic building advertising swathes of fine cottons, expensive wools and *Buttons only two shillings a pair!*

Sasha managed to stride into Gribbon's, grab a coat, take it to the counter and pay for it before Alice had even reached the first rack.

'See,' she said, shoving the coat into Alice's arms. 'No-nonsense shopping. Try it on.'

'Try it on *after* you've already bought it?'

Sasha shrugged.

The coat was a well-worn, funereal black, and it had clearly been made for a very short man with broad shoulders.

'Thanks,' she said. 'I really appreciate it.'

Sasha gave her an appraising nod. 'Nice. You look less like a mainlander now and more like the rest of us. You owe me twelve sovereigns, by the way.'

'By mainlanders, you mean Londoners?' said Alice.

'Not just Londoners – everyone on the other side of the Arch.'

'Is the Arch the only way to pass from London to the Rookery?'

'No,' said Sasha. 'There are a few others, but the Arch is the easiest, if you're not an experienced traveller. It's basically an open door.'

'Then why don't Londoners come through by accident? Why doesn't anyone know about this place?'

'It only opens to us,' said Sasha. 'Mainlanders *can* come through, but only if a Väki brings them in. And it's not good for them.'

Alice turned to look out of the shop window. There was some sort of herbal medicine shop directly opposite, called Forrester's. A sign in the window declared, *A tincture, tonic and liniment for your every need! Willow, hawthorn, oak, beech, alder, pine, ash and many more*. There were shelves of tiny glass bottles in the window, and huge signs boasting, *The Rookery's best birch sap tonic – antibacterial, anti-tumour, anti-poor health!*, *Beat flu with our quality cedar bark tea* and *Eradicate sore muscles with our poplar anti-inflammatory salve!*

There were herbalist shops in London, but she couldn't recall any with tree extracts as their unique selling point. It seemed sort of quaint and parochial.

'It's not exactly Harley Street, is it?' said Sasha, recapturing her attention.

Alice shook her head, caught off-guard.

'I don't understand,' she said, trying to straighten things out. 'How did all this *get* here? A whole city. And it's not a perfect mirror of London, is it? Because there are places here that don't exist any more in London?' She shook her head and sighed.

'I'm starting to really enjoy your company,' said Sasha, with a grin. 'Being around you makes me feel like a bloody genius.'

Sasha stepped outside, pivoted Alice around and headed back towards Bow Street and Crowley.

'When the Rookery was made, they couldn't build the whole place from scratch; they were fleeing persecution and on a deadline. So they used London as a . . . template. And then, over the years, the Rookery Council – our government – has built it up to cope with the fact that more people live here now. They used Pellervoinen's lot – they work with stone – to add more buildings. They stole some of them from London – places that were being knocked down anyway; places that wouldn't be missed. They just dragged them through here instead, like—'

'Goring House,' said Alice.

'Exactly.'

'You can steal a building?'

She nodded. 'Some are stolen. The rest they just copied. Or borrowed. It's complicated. We share some of the same streets and buildings, but the space inside them is different.'

'But the Rookery doesn't look like modern-day London. If they were copying it, it should be identical.'

Sasha shook her head. 'They stopped modelling it on London in about 1930. Why do you think the place looks like a time warp?' She sighed irritably. 'They haven't even upgraded the electricity systems since the thirties, which is why we have blackouts every few months; it's impossible to get new technology to work without short-circuiting the whole street. I don't know why I even bother paying my taxes. I sometimes wonder about going to one of the other Väki cities.'

'Cities?'

'Like ours,' said Sasha. 'Why? Did you think London was the only twinned city?'

'I . . . Well . . .'

Sasha laughed. 'Of course it's not. But if you go to one of the others, they won't call themselves Väki. The Finnish settled the Rookery first, so they've always been the dominant culture and language here. But in New York, for instance, they go by "the aes sidhe". That's because the Celtic magical folk – Irish, mainly – established themselves in the United States during the crusades. I guess they didn't fancy London. Right choice, given the bloody taxes.'

Alice was speechless. 'Do most of the Väki live here or on the other side – the mainland?' she asked eventually.

Sasha grew serious. 'Some hide their legacies and take their chances with the Beaks. But it can be difficult – legacies can be involuntary, like a reflex action, triggered by fear or stress. Plus, the Väki generally show small signs of different legacies when they're babies – all spontaneous and difficult to keep under wraps. But there are some . . .' She paused. 'Some Väki have legacies so weak they get to live out their whole lives in the mainland, never realizing they're not completely human. Flying under the radar. Living ordinary lives.'

There was a wistful tone in her voice, and it was on the tip of Alice's tongue to ask Sasha what her legacy was – given her reaction to the flooding, it couldn't be water – but the sound of running footsteps and a furious shout wiped her mind blank.

'Stop!'

A tall young man in a threadbare jumper hurtled towards her. Following far behind were two heavy-set police officers – Runners – faces red with the effort of giving chase. The buttons of their navy uniforms glinted in the cold daylight.

'Get him!'

One old man made a shambling grab, but missed. The others milling around seemed to become inordinately fascinated by the shop windows. The man had put some distance between him and the Runners and was nearly upon her now. He was so close she could see the whites of his eyes. There was something bundled under his arm – stolen goods?

He stared her in the face as he approached, arms and legs pumping, and grinned. Then he had the audacity to *slow down*, as though dismissing her as a threat, and her pulse raced. The bloody nerve of him . . . If nobody else was going to stop him . . .

She shot out a foot and clipped his ankles. He tumbled side-ways in a clatter of long legs and landed on his back with an *oomph*. The bundle under his arm – paper – rolled away; he grabbed it and tried to pull himself upright.

'Oh no you don't!' shouted the smaller of the Runners. He yanked something from his pocket – bizarrely, it was an acorn. He tapped it with his finger and the seed shell cracked open. A green shoot burst from the acorn, changing colour as it rapidly length-ened and thickened, until it resembled a fully grown tree branch. The Runner threw it and it whipped across the cobbles, wrapping itself tightly around the thief's legs, locking him in place.

'He just grew . . . from a seed,' Alice mumbled.

Sasha shrugged, and Alice swallowed thickly.

The larger Runner nodded at her. 'Thanks,' he panted, before approaching the man tangled on the floor.

'What did he steal?' asked Alice.

'Nothing,' said the Runner. 'He's been putting up posters illegally.'

Fly-posting? She'd helped the police catch a fly-poster? But that was nothing! She glanced down at him, shackled on the cob-bles, and her cheeks flushed with regret. No wonder everyone else had let him pass; he was hardly a hardened criminal.

'Come on, Captain Marvel,' said Sasha, nudging her up the street and trying not to laugh.

Alice looked back over her shoulder, but the Runners had closed in around the man and she couldn't see him. Probably for the best.

Crowley's voice broke through her thoughts.

'At last,' he said. He was leaning against the station wall where they'd left him, his hands in his pockets and a peevish expression on his face. 'The prodigal daughters have returned.'

Sasha rolled her eyes. 'I'll catch you later,' she said to Alice. 'Maybe for lunch; I work on the second floor.' She paused. 'And hey, nice coat.'

Sasha took the stairs two at a time and vanished from sight. Alice hovered outside, feeling oddly guilty about the coat as well as the fly-poster now.

'Shall we?' said Crowley, gesturing for her to enter.

It was cool and dark inside the station, the walls lined with wood panelling and the type of vintage tiling she remembered from tube stations in London. The ceiling was grand. Buckingham-Palace-Sistine-Chapel grand. Standing beneath it made her feel a strange sense of awe.

There was a wrought-iron barrier fencing off half the entrance hall, manned by a uniformed Runner behind a desk. Like the others, he wore a navy tunic with silver buttons, pulled tight over his paunch.

The Runner had the flushed cheeks and purpled, bulbous nose of a hardened drinker. He grunted at Crowley and took a slug of coffee, thumping it down on the tabletop, where it sloshed over a pile of papers.

'Heavy night, Chalmers?'

'Heavy morning,' said the desk clerk. 'Wife wants a divorce.'

Crowley's eyes widened briefly. 'I'm sorry to hear that.'

'Don't be,' said Chalmers. 'Been celebrating in The Rook's Nest since midnight.' He grinned. 'Now then. Who's your friend?'

'Alice Wyndham,' said Crowley. 'First day in the archives. I'm escorting her down there.'

Chalmers nodded and ducked his head down behind the desk. He reappeared after a moment or two.

'Here she is,' he said, slapping a small rectangle of card down on the counter. 'She's been signed off, but we don't have her membership on record.' He turned to Alice. 'Do you belong to a House?'

'Coram House,' she offered.

An awkward pause followed, until Crowley sighed. 'She has no House affiliations.'

'Not even associate membership?' asked Chalmers.

Crowley shook his head, and Chalmers gave her a kindly, if patronizing, smile. 'Maybe you're just a late bloomer.'

She could sense Crowley smirking beside her. She refused to look at him.

'Just need a sample then,' said Chalmers. 'Left hand, please, love.'

'Pardon?' she asked.

'I need your ring finger,' said Chalmers.

She stared at him blankly.

'Don't worry, I'm not proposing.' He winked. 'Maybe when the divorce comes through though, eh?'

He took her hand with a grin and tugged it gently across the desk, palm upwards. A shot of pain spiked through her little finger, and she gasped and snatched it back. A bead of blood had welled up on the tip.

'Finger on the card, please,' said Chalmers.

'You just stabbed me,' she said, incredulous.

'Steady on, love. We're not talking samurai swords and vital organs here,' he said with a rasp of laughter. 'Come on. Stamp your finger on the card.' He caught her hesitation and added, 'No stamp, no security clearance.'

She pressed her finger to the card.

The iron barrier clanged open and Chalmers waved them through. She gave him a cheerless goodbye and trudged into the expansive hall-cum-waiting-room. There was a quiet hum of activity in the air. Heads were bent over desks stacked with paperwork, and there was an insistent scratching of pens. Lockers lined one wall, while rows of alternating metal and wooden chairs lined another.

A Runner escorted a slouching older woman to one of the metal chairs. He pushed her down into it, and Alice sucked in a breath as the arms of the chair writhed and clanked then suddenly sprang across her. They wrapped around her chest, trapping her firmly in the seat. She didn't even flinch; maybe she was used to being arrested and restrained in magical iron chairs.

A muffled shout rang out, and Alice jerked around. A pale young man in rumpled clothes was being restrained by two burly Runners. It was the fly-poster she'd tripped. With his scruffy, straw-like hair and rangy build, he looked more like an environmental protester than a dangerous fugitive.

He was clenching a wad of papers in his fist.

'Watch my arm – not so tight!' he shouted. 'God, your priorities are a real shit-show, you know that? Here!'

He tossed his papers into the air and they floated across the hall. One slid to the floor by Alice's feet, and she bent to examine it. There was a drawing of a white feather on the page, under a line of text proclaiming:

He is coming.
The Fellowship of the Pale Feather.

The Runners hauled him to the other side of the room. He caught Alice staring and locked eyes with her. Her face was hot with remorse – but his mouth twitched at the corners and, very slowly, eyes bright with merriment . . . he winked.

The Runners bundled him into a lift in the far wall. They

yanked the gold grille across and he sank out of view. The little floor show now over, Crowley hustled Alice in the same direction, punching the button to summon another lift. She hovered by the one that had just departed, but he shook his head.

'That one only takes you to the cells,' he said. 'Unless you have a criminal history that I don't know about, we're taking the ordinary lift.'

She glanced at the poster in her hand while they waited.

'This is what he was fly-posting? I've seen this before,' she said. 'When you first brought me here.'

'They're all over the place. You can't avoid the damn things.'

'He is coming,' she read. 'What's this advertising? A *Game of Thrones* fan club?'

He stared at her blankly.

'"Winter is coming"?' she prompted.

This earned no response.

'Never mind,' she mumbled. 'So what is this Fellowship of the Pale Feather then, if it's not a fan club?'

'They're death cultists,' said Crowley.

'A death cult,' she repeated with a frown. 'What's that supposed to be?'

He raised an eyebrow. 'The clue's in the name.'

She paused. Right. 'So . . . *who's* coming?' she asked. 'Is it supposed to be a warning or something?'

'Just the usual: that the Fellowship have predicted the apocalypse again. It happens every year. You'd think they'd get embarrassed when the world keeps stubbornly failing to end, but no. I suppose they think the laws of probability mean they've got to get it right eventually.'

She nodded towards the other lift. 'I got him arrested,' she said morosely.

'Don't worry,' he said, glancing down at her. 'They'll shove him in a cell for a few hours until he's bailed by his comrades, and then he'll go straight out and continue his fly-posting. Rinse and repeat.'

She stared at the floor with a thoughtful look on her face, and he sighed as their own lift swooped into view. 'Come on – if you stop to humour the nonsense of every cult and lunatic in the Rookery, you'll never get anything done.'

'Well, I'm humouring you, aren't I?' she replied tartly.

He rumbled with laughter – a pleasant, deep baritone – and steered her into the open lift, one hand on her arm.

Her arm tingled with pleasure.

Odd.

Proctor Sinclair, resident archivist and her new tutor, was a tall, skeletal old man with spidery hands and permanently red eyes. He was also a complete arsehole, a fact she'd realized about three seconds after meeting him. She'd stuck out her hand for him to shake and he'd merely stared at it before turning his back on her and wandering off with Crowley.

When they reached Proctor's dusty basement office, he sniffed and looked her up and down critically. 'You'll be archiving old cases,' he said. 'That's how you'll get paid. That clear?'

She nodded.

'As for the other stuff . . .' He shifted uneasily. 'I'm not promising anything. I'll give you some basics. Some tips, but . . .' He shrugged. 'Take it or leave it.'

'We'll take it,' said Crowley.

Proctor grunted. 'So why the urgency?' he asked Alice. 'Crowley says you're on a deadline.'

She shoved her hair out of her eyes. 'I am. My best friend's nightjar has flown away and I need to get it back.'

'Flown away? It's—'

'Precisely,' said Crowley. 'Now if you don't mind, Proctor, I'm paying you by the hour, so could we begin?'

Proctor's lips turned down and he rubbed his nose. 'If she wants to learn about nightjars she'll have to put in a full day's work first.'

Crowley's eyes darkened. 'You listen to me, Sinclair—'

Proctor showed a mouthful of stained teeth – the grin of a man who knows he's holding all the aces. 'The quicker she works, the more time there'll be at the end of the day.'

He shuffled over to a huge desk in the corner while Crowley glared at him in mutinous silence.

'You can start by filing away everything related to the old Adderstone Forgery case,' said Proctor, returning to dump an armful of folders into her startled arms. 'The files stay closed. They're confidential – you can read the case name on the front but no more, or you're out of here.'

'Okay,' she said slowly, fixing a polite – if flustered – smile on her face.

'I'll return shortly after four o'clock then,' said Crowley, striding for the door. 'I trust you'll find that a more convenient time to take my money, Proctor.'

Alice watched him go in a sudden panic. 'Wait! You can't just leave me here on my own,' she said.

'Work shy,' mumbled Proctor.

She ignored him. 'You can't just drag me to this bizarre place, thrust me into a new house and job and expect me to be okay with it. Forty-eight hours ago I had a different life.' She dumped the folders on the floor by her feet.

'Funny,' Crowley said quietly. 'Forty-eight hours ago, your comatose friend had a different life too.'

A muscle in her jaw twitched as she stared at him. 'You really think I can help her if I stay?'

'It's the *only* way you can help her.'

She gave him a sharp nod, and he turned on his heel and vanished through the doorway, abandoning her to the mercies of Proctor and his towering stacks of paperwork.

'Are you going to file those or not?' he growled.

'Yes,' she said with a sigh.

Alice carried the pile of papers over to the cabinets and methodically began putting them away. The entire basement was a repository of information about an array of topics so wide-ranging it was a wonder it all fitted into one room. It was like a library, and she'd always felt at home in libraries. She could do this.

After a while, she sensed that Proctor was watching her from behind his desk, but she gave no outward sign that she'd noticed. He was probably checking she wasn't snooping in the files. She worked diligently for another hour or so before accidentally meeting his gaze.

He was staring at her, his bloodshot eyes fixed hard on her face, but it was a wonder he could see anything at all. His eyelids were a mass of burned scar tissue, and she wondered what had happened, whether he'd been caught in a fire. Not that she'd ever dare ask.

'Are there any more folders?'

His stubby pink tongue darted out to wet his lips. 'On the drawers in the corner.'

She paused, resting her back against a filing cabinet by the wall. Above, a tiny, high window was the basement's only source of natural light. There was an enormous ugly vase on the cabinet, and the leaves of the begonia inside tickled her neck.

'Can I ask you something? Are you a member of a House? Mielikki or Ilmarinen or—'

'Never bothered applying for membership anywhere,' he said. 'I'm an aviarist. What do I care about the traditional legacies?'

'But,' she battled on, 'do you think I could possibly—'

'The Houses don't let just anyone join,' he said gruffly. 'There are tests – *trials* – to pass. You've got to prove your legacy is strong enough. If you don't know what kind of Väki you are by now, yours definitely isn't. But you're an aviarist. So it doesn't matter if you haven't got a House. If you learn properly, you'll be better than all of them.'

Alice glanced over at his vexed expression. She strongly suspected he was talking to himself as much as her. Still, she couldn't help but be a little deflated.

'My turn to ask you a question now,' said Proctor. 'Your friend . . .' He hesitated. 'How'd she lose her nightjar?'

'Car accident.'

He sat back in his chair.

'She's in a coma,' she continued. 'Crowley said the coma tricked her nightjar into flying away. The bird thought she was dead. So now . . . I have to get it back before her soul abandons her.'

Proctor snorted. 'You're going to waltz in and rescue her nightjar? Just like that?'

She paused. 'Yes.'

He stared at her, but she held his eye without looking away. After a moment, he nodded. 'How? How are you going to get it back?'

'I'm . . .' She sucked her teeth while she thought about the answer. She had a goal; what she didn't have was a plan. How *was* she going to get it back?' 'I'm going to find out where it is,' she said slowly. 'And then I'm . . . going to go and pick it up.'

Simple. Exactly like going to collect a takeaway.

'Find out where it is?' he asked. 'You don't *know* where it is?'

Something about his tone made her feel like a complete halfwit.

'Well, do you?' she shot back.

'Course I do,' he said, a crooked grin on his face. 'It's where they all go. All the freed nightjars, they go to the Sulka Moors. Everyone knows it.'

Sulka Moors. She mouthed it under her breath, trying it out on her tongue to see if she recognized it, but it felt foreign and strange. Yorkshire and the North West had lots of moors, but she'd never heard of the Sulka Moors before.

'How do I get there?' she asked, her breathing quickening. 'Can you help me to—'

'You can only go to the Sulka Moors once,' he said.

'Once? Why only once?'

He shook his head in open amusement. 'Because it's where you go when you die. Crowley didn't tell you? Sulka Moors is the home of Death. It's the land *of* Death.'

She frowned. 'So by Death you mean . . . ? Sorry, can you help me out here, because—'

'The Grim Reaper!' he barked, making her jump. 'Tuoni. The Pale Rider. Lintuvahti. The Lord of Death.'

'But—'

'Death,' he said, 'is the ultimate aviarist. What did you think happened to nightjars when people die?'

'I – Well, I don't—'

'They're set free,' Proctor said. 'There's a cord tying them to us, and it gets cut so they can fly off to him. He takes the nightjar and he cages it in his aviary, The Black Menagerie. So if you want to get your friend's nightjar back, you're going to have to sneak into the moors and steal it from his aviary. What do you reckon he'd do if he caught you red-handed, eh?'

Alice swallowed convulsively. Her thoughts swirled around her, a merry-go-round of the strange and macabre. She had to travel to Death's home? And steal from him? And – Death was real? An actual person? Or Väki, or whatever the fuck? And she had to sneak into his Black Menagerie and – oh God. OhGodohGodohGod.

'But . . . I can't,' she murmured. 'I can't get to his aviary because you said – you said you can only go to the Sulka Moors once: when you die.'

'That's right,' he said in a smug tone. 'Bit of a conundrum, isn't it? Still, you sounded pretty sure of yourself, so I'm sure you'll figure something out.'

He grinned at her and busied himself with his desk. She watched in silence while she grappled with his revelations and tried to organize her scattered thoughts. Jen's nightjar thought she'd died in the car accident so it had flown away, to a cage in Death's aviary: The Black Menagerie. Right. Maybe she should phone one of those no-win-no-fee accident claim firms off the TV. *Have you been injured in an accident that wasn't your fault? Suffered hearing loss or muscle pains? Lost your nightjar and can't afford to replace it? We can help.* A burst of hysterical laughter welled up in her chest and she fought to tamp it down. *Focus, Alice. Embrace the New Normal.*

She shoved her hands into her pockets and slumped miserably into a chair. A cascade of paperwork fell from the seat, but she ignored it. Her fingers had brushed something smooth and pliable in her pocket. She pulled it out and stared at it in silence.

It was the Fellowship of the Pale Feather's leaflet. The *Death* cult – capital *D*.

Her fingers curled around the paper and she stood up abruptly, her head buzzing. It wasn't a plan. But if she was going to rescue Jen's nightjar from Death, then the first place she could start was with his worshippers.

She looked around the dingy basement, at the alphabetized cabinets looming over her like mini skyscrapers . . . the dingy basement, which was a *repository of information*.

She glanced over at Proctor, her throat dry. He was busy rifling through his desk drawer. How long would he be preoccupied? Long *enough*? She held her breath and padded quietly in the opposite direction, scanning the labels at speed. There it was: The *F* cabinet.

> *FELLOWSHIP OF THE PALE FEATHER*
> *Historically known as The Valkovane. Leader: Marianne*
> *Northam (see separate file), successor to Michael Greaves.*
> *The group is notoriously private, but Runner agents have*
> *previously infiltrated the Fellowship, posing as would-be*
> *members. Current address unknown; the group remains*
> *mobile so as to avoid detection.*
>
> <u>*Background information*</u>
> *The group calling themselves the Fellowship of the Pale*
> *Feather are worshippers of Tuoni, the Lord of Death, who*
> *is commonly referred to by his title, the Lintuvahti.*

She paused, the Fellowship folder open on her lap. Lintuvahti? If his name was . . . She rescanned the words. If his name was Tuoni, why did they also call him Lintuvahti? It sounded like another Finnish word, like Ilmarinen. Was he another Väki – a Masterbuilder of the Land of Death – or . . . was he *actually* Death?

She glanced over her shoulder, nerves buzzing with tension, wary of Proctor pouncing on her – but he was still busy; he hadn't noticed she'd stopped filing. She dropped her eyes back to the page and hurriedly continued.

> *Members believe that, since all who are born eventually die, all life in the Rookery exists only in order to serve Death. They believe that the act of dying is a sacrificial gift to honour the Lintuvahti. Past leaders of the Fellowship preached that the group was duty-bound to slaughter both Rookery and mainland citizens en masse, in order to provide the Lintuvahti with a surfeit of sacrifices. This viewpoint fell out of favour following the Cranleigh Grange dinner party massacre (see separate file). There are indications that the group now believes that the Lintuvahti himself will select an agent to become his conduit for murder. Informants have revealed that the Fellowship believes only a child of the Lintuvahti's bloodline is 'genetically pure' enough to act as Death's proxy. Evidence suggests they are awaiting this proxy, who will be capable of massacring all life on earth in a final 'cleansing' or 'purge', with the Fellowship taking their rightful place by the Lintuvahti's side, rewarded in the Sulka Moors for their faithful service.*

So – the apocalypse, then? Crowley was right? Alice sighed. Well, this was a cheerful bit of light reading, wasn't it? She gently closed the bulging folder – there were six altogether – and reached for the next one, labelled *evidence file*.

Flipping it open, she saw a handful of glossy pages on top. She snatched one up and recoiled. It was a photograph of a dead young woman, her pale skin marred by purple bruises. Her dress was torn and her bare legs were painfully thin. She lay on a damp pavement in a twisted heap, her neck bent unnaturally. She'd clearly fallen from a great height. There were others, depicting similar scenes: bodies of men and women lying prostrate, limbs snapped and contorted, faces mottled with livor mortis.

She grimaced. Were the Fellowship murdering people? She thought back to the page she'd read: *The act of dying is a sacrificial gift to honour the Lintuvahti* . . . Had these all been sacrifices to the so-called Lord of Death?

'I knew you couldn't be trusted,' grunted Proctor. He was staring down at her, his nostrils flaring with anger.

Alice's eyes widened and she lurched to her feet, mortified.

'I'm sorry, I was just—'

'Put. Them. Back,' he growled. 'The photographs, put them back.'

She dropped to her knees and hurriedly stuffed them back into the folder, but then paused.

'Did the Fellowship kill these people?' she asked, figuring she now had nothing to lose.

'What do *you* think?' he jeered.

Her jaw set, she eyed him silently.

'Marianne Northam is a con artist,' he said, eyes narrowing at her lack of contrition. 'She convinces them they'll be rewarded by her so-called Lord of Death – when he comes to sweep away all life in the Rookery.' He shook his head disdainfully. 'They sacrifice themselves, thinking they'll be rewarded for being among the first to voluntarily go to the moors. Pathetic.'

Alice glanced at the grisly file – a folder full of corpses – and shuddered.

Shit. *Death. Sacrifice.*

The Sulka Moors was the Land of Death; the place you went to only when you died; the place where Jen's nightjar was caged.

'Will I have to *die* to get into the moors?' she murmured.

12

'Busy?' drawled Crowley.

Alice startled, reflexively squeezing the pages between her fingers. *Yes*, she replied mentally. *Busy plotting the best way to euthanize myself.* She stood up and slapped the photograph folder down on a cabinet.

Proctor glanced at his watch, and Crowley rolled his eyes.

'I can assure you I'm as punctual as ever,' said Crowley. 'And you'll be glad to know I've brought a little friend to help out.'

He whipped an arm out of view and herded a grinning Sasha into the basement.

Proctor frowned at her. 'You sure you want her poking around your nightjar, Hamilton?' he asked. 'Invading your privacy? Spying?' He glanced at the folder. 'She's already got a taste for snooping.'

Sasha glanced sideways at Crowley, who was stony-faced. 'She's not going to invade my privacy,' she said, but the grin was fading fast. 'Wait. *Are* you?'

'I don't think so,' said Alice.

'Good,' said Sasha.

'More fool you,' muttered Proctor. 'Well, go on then. Do it.'

Both Alice's eyebrows shot up. 'Do what?'

He gave an irritated sigh. 'Look at her nightjar. Examine it.'

She hesitated. What sort of training was this supposed to be? If she could already 'do it' then she wouldn't need a tutor, would she?

Proctor gestured at Sasha, but Alice frowned. She'd seen Sasha's nightjar once, but it hadn't exactly been a roaring success.

'I've never been able to see them on command,' she said. 'They just . . . appear when they want to. I don't have any control over it.'

'Yes, you do,' Proctor said, then nodded to Sasha. 'Sit down, Hamilton. And wipe that expression off your face – don't give her anything to work with or we'll end up with a false positive.'

Sasha's face was carefully blank as she lowered herself into the chair behind Proctor's desk and crossed her arms over her chest.

'Here,' said Crowley. He pressed a feather – Sylvie's – into Alice's hand. 'The feather was your catalyst. Until you're fully trained you should be able to—'

A bird fluttered into her vision.

'*I can see it*,' she whispered.

'You're sure?' Crowley murmured, coming closer. He was watching her with anticipation, a nervous but ardent gleam in his eye that she could make no sense of.

She nodded. The bird was standing by a heavy book on one of the shelves behind Sasha. Its feathers were tawny-coloured, half smooth and half rumpled, with a simple flecked pattern. A pair of dark, shining eyes regarded Alice warily, submitting to her inspection with an air of defiance. Did it remember their last encounter?

A luminous ribbon of light bound the bird's leg to Sasha's wrist. It was so ethereal Alice wondered if it was really there at all. It glimmered in the dusty basement, the thread suffused with a warm glow. She started forward, her hand outstretched to stroke the translucent cord, to see if it was tangible, but Proctor grabbed at her sleeve and pulled her back.

'Manners,' he hissed, shoving her arm back down. 'You don't touch it. Ever. Might as well slice open someone's chest and shove your hands in.'

Any questions she'd had about touching Sasha's nightjar in the street instantly shrivelled up. Had she already broken some terrible unwritten rule?

'What *is* that?' she asked.

'It's the cord that ties the nightjar to the body. The cord that gets cut when you die – that's how your nightjar escapes. Usually it takes your soul with it when it goes. But, like with your friend, sometimes the nightjar leaves before its time, and it leaves the soul behind, unprotected.'

She looked over her shoulder, to catch a glimpse of her own nightjar. Where was it?

'Do I have a nightjar?' she asked.

'Yes. But an aviarist can't see their own. Not until they're about to die.'

'Oh,' she said, deflated. 'But maybe you could describe—'

'My eyes don't work right any more,' he snapped.

She cleared her throat awkwardly and nodded. Maybe she could settle for a glance of Proctor's nightjar instead. As a fellow aviarist, wasn't it likely that their nightjars would share similarities?

Her eyes drifted back to Proctor. His nightjar was perched on his shoulder, hunched over, its beak up close to his neck. It was a scrawny thing, half bald, with scrappy feathers. Its gaze was fixed on Proctor's Adam's apple, like a vulture about to pounce on a piece of carrion.

She shuddered at the sight of it. Okay, well . . . hopefully there were no similarities with her own.

Sasha sat forward in the chair. 'What's my nightjar doing?' she demanded.

Alice's eyes darted up to refocus on Sasha's bird. 'It's—'

'Don't tell her yet,' said Proctor. 'You've got an advantage. You tell her what you can see and you lose that advantage. She could change her nightjar's behaviour to influence your reading – it's difficult but not impossible.'

Sasha sat back, her mouth a thin line of pent-up frustration.

'Don't give me that look,' growled Proctor. 'We're not here for your entertainment. You'll be told what you want to know at the end.'

Sasha nodded mulishly, and Alice used the brief impasse to search for Crowley's nightjar too. It was hiding behind his back – not just leisurely sitting or flying there, but quite literally hiding. From over his shoulder she could just about sneak a few glimpses of its jutting beak.

'Does the nightjar correspond to your first impressions of *Sasha*?' asked Crowley, with a pointed glare at Alice.

With a guilty start, she tore her eyes from the spot just over his shoulder and refocused on Sasha's nightjar.

'I . . . don't know.'

Proctor slammed his hand down on the desk, and both Alice and Sasha jumped. 'Who's doing the teaching here, Crowley?' he snapped. 'You or me? Reading nightjars is an *art*. It takes dedication and it can't be rushed. But if you don't need me I can just—'

'My apologies,' said Crowley, though he didn't look in the least bit apologetic. 'Continue.'

Proctor's eyes narrowed and he trudged closer, long, bony arms loose at his side. Alice fought the instinct to rear backwards as he thrust his finger at her face.

'You don't deserve this gift you've been given,' he rasped. 'If this is the best you can do, forget about saving that nightjar.'

A hard knot of anger flared in her abdomen and cramped her stomach. He didn't even know her – how fucking dare he! There was a rustling, slithering sound somewhere nearby, but she was too focused on Proctor's face to register it. She glared at him, her fists clenched.

'Your little friend might as well *die*,' he said, 'because you're too—'

Alice exhaled forcefully and there was a sharp crack behind her. She spun round. The ugly vase on the cabinet had fractured. The roots of the begonia plant seemed to have swollen in size and burst the vase open – but how? Water glugged out, pouring over the Fellowship file.

'The photographs,' she gasped, snatching them to safety and shoving them back into the cabinet.

Proctor was red-faced. He took a step backwards, his flustered gaze swinging between Alice and the broken vase. The plant's unravelled tendrils had snaked across the cabinet's surface as though reaching out for him.

Crowley stood watching her with a curious, approving smile on his face.

'Proctor,' he drawled, 'I'm paying for your expertise, not your opinion. Don't bother putting limits on her expectations – she will exceed them; I'll make sure of it.'

A warmth stole over her, but she didn't dare look at him. Proctor's mouth opened to bark a retort at Crowley, but he seemed to think better of it. His face soured, but he turned back to Alice.

'Fine,' he grunted. 'I'll tell you what you need to know about nightjars, and I suppose you might surprise me.' He paused. 'The nightjar reflects the soul it protects. You want to know what's in someone's soul, you watch their nightjar. Aviarists – we can see the things people want to hide. All their fears, their secrets, their lies, their private humiliations – *right there* in front of us for the taking.'

He took a step backwards and turned away from them, wringing his hands in what was clearly an attempt to calm his trembling excitement. When he faced them again, his gaze was coolly detached.

He missed this, Alice realized. His failing eyes had robbed him of the chance to worm his way into people's most secret, innermost thoughts. What exactly had he used his gift *for*?

'Ask her some questions,' Proctor told Alice roughly. 'Some she'll answer with a lie, some the truth. Your job's to tell the difference. Look for changes in her nightjar's behaviour. Ready?'

Confused, she nodded and fixed her gaze on Sasha's bird. Questions? She wanted to ask about the drowning girl she'd seen when she'd stroked Sasha's nightjar, but it didn't seem appropriate now.

Crowley cleared his throat. 'Perhaps you might start with her name,' he suggested, earning a scowl from Proctor.

'Right. Okay . . . What's your name?' she asked, feeling faintly ridiculous.

The question seemed to put Sasha at ease, however, because her shoulders relaxed and the muscles in her face grew less taut.

'Sasha Marie-Antoinette Hamilton.'

Alice raised an eyebrow. 'Marie-Antoinette? Like—'

'"Let them eat cake",' said Sasha. 'Yeah. Her.'

Alice refocused on the bird. It hadn't changed at all. She wasn't sure what sort of changes she was supposed to be looking for, exactly.

'You ever played poker?' asked Proctor.

She shook her head.

'Then you'd better start. You need to look for tells. Clues. In a game of poker, people hide their weaknesses and their strengths, but there's always a tell. It might be a cough or shaky hands, or talking too quickly. Could be anything. But with nightjars, the tells are easier to spot. People can put on a mask in real life, but it's harder to mask what you can't see.'

She nodded and turned back to Sasha.

'Is your name . . . Simon?'

Sasha's forehead creased with amusement. 'Really?' she said, sweeping her hand down her not-unimpressive chest.

The bird looked the same as ever. No tells, no giveaways – nothing.

'Is your name Simon?' she asked again.

Sasha paused. 'Yes,' she said, plucking her necklace's pendant out from her collar and displaying it with a smile. 'My name is Simon and I hate pretty necklaces.'

Alice watched the bird more closely. It was subtle. So subtle she almost missed it. Its head ducked slightly and it pulled its wings closer to its body. Just for a second it had closed in on itself, like a flower in reverse bloom.

'I think it worked,' she said, shaking her head in disbelief. 'I'm a *lie detector*.'

'Ask her something else,' said Proctor.

Possibilities raced through her mind – something general, like whether the aes sidhe Sasha had mentioned had a different, Celtic version of the Sulka Moors, or whether it was the same place with a different name . . . But instead, she asked the question she hadn't had the chance to ask earlier.

'What's your legacy?'

Sasha stiffened. 'I don't have one,' she said flatly, shoving the necklace out of sight.

The nightjar ducked again, but afterwards, it flapped its wings in agitation.

'I think . . .' Alice pointed at the irritable nightjar, half a smile on her face. They were trying to catch her out, right? 'Is this another one you've answered untruthfully?'

Sasha leaned forward, the spark of confrontation in her eyes. 'You're calling me a liar?'

'What? No,' said Alice, alarmed at the abrupt change of mood in the room. 'It's just for the . . . training, isn't it? Do you really not have a legacy?'

Sasha tilted her chin defiantly. 'I'm non-practising.'

Alice forced a smile to break through her confusion. 'What does that—'

'Ask her something else,' Crowley intoned quietly.

Alice looked down at her lap, embarrassed by whatever mis-step she appeared to have made. So much for showing appreci-ation for the coat.

She decided to keep things simple. 'You said you work on the second floor. Are you a Runner?'

Sasha chuffed out a bitter laugh. 'No. I'm a civ, like you. A civilian worker in the publications department. Technically, I *am* the publications department.'

'So you're a journalist?'

'No, I'm a—' Her smile faltered. '*Dogsbody*,' she said, flash-ing a grin that was about as fake as Jen's Chanel handbag. 'Next question?'

The bird was staring at Alice with a preternatural calm. It was quite unnerving. 'I don't think . . . the police in London have their own newspaper,' she mumbled lamely.

'The Runners don't either,' said Sasha. 'It's a pamphlet, not a newspaper. All it does is list wanted criminals and stolen items, with the odd reward thrown in for a bit of excitement.' She nodded at Crowley. 'Where do you think he gets most of his work from?'

Alice frowned.

'He's a thief-taker,' Sasha explained. 'Aren't you, Crowley? Like a freelance Runner, only the trouble is that sometimes he ends up doing work for the wrong side.' He glared at her, and she grinned. 'What? Was it a secret?'

'That's enough,' he said.

There was a hacking cough from the corner of the room, and Proctor wiped his mouth on his sleeve. Alice had almost forgotten he was there. With his hunched posture and emaciated frame, he seemed more suited to skulking in the shadows than filling a room with his presence.

'I didn't realize you were paying me for timewasting, Crowley,' he muttered.

Proctor shuffled into the centre of the basement, staring at Alice with an odd look on his face.

'What's next then?' she asked, taking a step towards him.

He started at her question, and his heel clipped the leg of the desk, sending him crashing into a nearby cabinet.

'Are you all right?' she asked as he rubbed his shoulder.

He threw up a hand to ensure she kept her distance. 'I'm fine,' he growled. 'You—You leave me alone.'

'O-kay,' she muttered, bending to scoop up the broken porcelain.

'Would you prefer to do this session somewhere quieter?' asked Crowley, with concern. 'Perhaps if you came to Coram House for a session in the evenings, you could sit comfortably while—'

'No,' snapped Proctor, his voice tremulous. 'You know what?

Forget it. All of it. You can keep your bloody coin, Crowley. I'm not a teacher, and I never wanted to be one.'

He grabbed his trench coat from the back of his chair and trudged through the basement, pointedly avoiding Alice. The door slammed shut and an awkward silence smothered the room.

'Well,' said Crowley, 'you're popular, aren't you?'

Alice huffed her embarrassment and gave a sidelong glance at the door.

'It's difficult for him,' said Crowley. 'You're a reminder of what he's lost.'

'What time is it?' she asked.

He frowned. 'What?'

She ignored him, caught up in her thoughts. One thought in particular. It had come to her quite suddenly: a solid goal; a plan. She knew what she had to do next.

'He might still be here,' she murmured.

'Who? Proctor?'

She didn't respond. She dived for her coat, bundled it under one arm and hurtled out of the basement, with Crowley's cries of 'Alice!' chasing her down the corridor.

13

The entrance hall was quiet when she crept from the lift and furtively summoned the one next to it. It was only when she had slipped inside – and felt her stomach lurch as it plummeted – that she allowed herself to actually breathe.

The lift landed with a soft bump, and Alice took a moment to gather her thoughts – which were screaming about ill-conceived ideas – then yanked the grille aside and stepped out. She was in the alcove of a grim, stone-walled corridor. There were green porcelain tiles on the floor, as though an interior designer had attempted to give the place a makeover but had admitted failure before he reached the walls and ceiling. A row of cubicles stretched out along one side of the corridor, cordoned off by bars. She was in the bowels of the building – in the cells.

It was eerily silent. No doubt the layers of thick stone acted as soundproofing. *Soundproofed cells.* She shuddered and forced herself to stride forward, ears primed for footsteps or the sounds of torture.

But there was nothing. No one. Just an expanse of narrow corridor and uniform iron and wooden bars. Presumably, they doubled up on the bars to prevent escapes; iron bars alone were unlikely to hold a metal Väki, like Jude.

She picked up the pace, her heart beating furiously. Empty cells blurred past her as she increased her speed, her casual jog turning into an all-out sprint. Where was everyone?

A door materialized, set into the stone some fifteen metres away. It swung open and a man in a long, dark coat swept out into the corridor.

Crowley.

'Looking for someone?' he enquired.

Alice bent over, her hands on her knees and a stitch tearing at her stomach. 'Just . . . out for a stroll.'

He inspected the corridor and nodded, a wry smile on his face. 'Scenic.'

'Yep.'

He watched her in silence while she regained her breath.

'Why are you down here, Alice?'

'I thought I'd try to break someone out,' she said flippantly. 'Then I realized the only person in the cells was me. It's a Kafkaesque nightmare.' He gave her a withering stare, and she sighed. 'I was trying to find that man from the Fellowship. The one they arrested for fly-posting. I thought he'd be down here. He got into that lift,' she said, waving a hand at the alcove at the other end of the corridor . . . which now appeared to have vanished completely. 'What the hell? Where's it gone? What is this place?'

'Holding cells.'

'So why is it empty down here?'

'It's not really,' Crowley said. 'But you have no authorization to be here. Unauthorized personnel find the cells like *this*. Denied access to both detainees and the Runner guards, trapped in an expanse of endless corridor. The *actual* cells are . . . nearby – but you can't get to them.'

'Oh,' she said. She knew it had been too easy. 'Well, why didn't you tell me that before?'

He rolled his eyes. 'It's lucky Chalmers saw you sneaking into the lift. Otherwise, you'd have been stuck here until their 1 a.m. patrol. Ready to leave?'

Alice frowned and folded her arms. 'No.'

'It was a rhetorical question.'

'I need to speak to that Fellowship fly-poster,' she said, 'and I'm not going anywhere until I do.'

Crowley's lips pinched, and he leaned back against the stone wall.

She let her arms drop. 'Please, Crowley? If there's a way you can get me access to him . . .'

'Every door in this station is locked,' he said. 'You can't travel from one doorway in this building to another.'

'But . . . you just came through a doorway.'

'I told you. I have a unique talent for doorway navigation. Few doorways in the Rookery can keep me out – and virtually none inside Bow Street. Why do you think the Runners employ me as a freelancer? Better I occasionally work with them than against them.'

'So you can get me into the *real* cells?' she pushed.

He studied her face. 'For what?'

She considered her response. 'I want to speak to the leader of the Fellowship – Marianne Northam – and I think the fly-poster guy could help me.'

His eyebrows flew up. '*Northam?*'

'Proctor said Jen's nightjar is in the Sulka Moors. Home of Death. Just a minor titbit you forgot to mention. And, Crowley, if I've got to go there, I need to speak to "Death's" worshippers. They could tell me all sorts of things.' She stared up at him, eyes pleading.

He put his hand on the small of her back and guided her firmly into the open doorway.

'I'll do your laundry for a month,' she said, pressed against him in the darkness. 'I'll—I'll—'

He bent to her ear, his breath hot on her neck despite the cold black void between the doorways.

'If you're going to barter, you'll have to do better than *that*,' he said suggestively.

Her cheeks burned. 'What do you think I am?' she spluttered. 'I'm not going to—'

'Tea,' he said. 'On demand. Any time I ask for it. You will be my personal tea slave. How does that sound?'

She swallowed. 'Well, I'm against slavery in any form. But . . . okay. Tea's good.'

A slice of light cut through the darkness, and Crowley shooed her out of another doorway, into . . . the station's grand entrance hall. Very definitely *not* the cells.

'You were supposed to be taking me to the—' she began, her voice loud with indignation.

'And *you* were supposed to be playing by *my* rules,' he said, plucking the feather from her sleeve cuff. 'I think this thing's addled your brain. I won't be taking you anywhere near that madwoman. We're going home.'

'But—'

'I take my tea black,' he said, unable to stop a growing smile. 'No sugar. I didn't agree to your terms, but you did agree to mine.' He threw her a disarming wink and strode off towards the barrier blocking the exit.

A small congregation of Runners and backroom staff were waiting to clock off.

'Hurry up, Chalmers! Some of us have homes to go to!' shouted a balding Runner waiting in line.

The officer manning the barrier scowled at him. Each person, in turn, was swiping their arm over a small metal plate inlaid into the desk beside the barrier; then once they'd been successfully 'scanned', Chalmers let them past. Alice gave a quick smile and held her hand over the metal. Chalmers saw it first. His mouth fell open in surprise as the metal rectangle curled at the edges and snapped shut around her wrist, binding her to the desk. She tried to tug her hand away, but she was fixed fast.

A handcuff, she thought in shock.

'What's—'

'You're bloody well kidding me,' said Chalmers. 'You? It was your first day. What've you done?'

Alice sat with her hands clamped between her knees, staring at the room's wood-panelled walls in silence. She didn't know how long she'd been waiting.

She took a deep, shuddering breath and scrunched her eyes shut. She'd been in the Rookery for less than twenty-four hours. Apparently plenty long enough to get herself marched to a Runner interview room, under caution. Under caution for what, exactly, wasn't clear.

There was a click as the door opened, and her head snapped up. A tall, lean man, maybe in his early fifties, stepped into the room and shut the door. She shot out of her seat, fuelled by her outraged sense of injustice. But the regal way he held himself and something about his clothing – a burgundy waistcoat with a shabby blue greatcoat – put her on guard. He didn't look like your average Runner. He looked like a down-at-heel military general.

His hair was a thick, silvery tangle, and fierce, slanting eyebrows framed slate-grey eyes – focused entirely on her.

'Miss Wyndham,' he said softly. 'Please, take a seat.'

'You have the wrong person,' she said as she lowered herself.

He sat down opposite, carefully positioning a brown folder on the table in front of him.

'You are *not* Alice Wyndham?' he asked.

'No. Yes. I mean, I'm her, but whatever it is you think I've done, you're wrong.'

He said nothing, flicking slowly through the file.

'You are new to the Rookery,' he said, scribbling something down on a fresh page.

She nodded. Under the table, her knees bounced with nerves.

'And yet you managed to acquire a job in this highly regarded institution in just a short space of time.'

'Yes.'

'Your references must be remarkable . . . and I would like to say it's a pleasure to meet you, but I fear that may be premature under the circumstances.' He paused. 'I'm Reuben Risdon, commanding officer of the Runners and your new employer.'

She opened her mouth but couldn't think of anything to say, especially about the references, so closed it again.

He sighed, took a small tin from an inner coat pocket and flipped the lid. 'Yes. Quite.' He took a pinch of finely ground tobacco – snuff – from the tin and rolled it between his fingers before giving it a sharp sniff. 'Who are you?' he asked suddenly.

She blinked. 'Pardon?' He already knew her name. Did he think she'd given him a fake identity?

'A young woman in a dead-end job in London, living a life so ordinary your own neighbours don't remember your name. You turn up here with Crowley, in a city of magical opportunities, the possibilities endless. And yet he ensconces you in a house and provides you with . . . another dead-end job. Why?'

She was so taken aback by his line of questioning she couldn't think of a response.

'I've been making inquiries,' he said. 'Your references, Miss Wyndham, were *not* remarkable. In fact, they were non-existent.' He paused. 'Why did Proctor Sinclair help Crowley secure you a job in the archives? The pair are known to despise each other. The bad blood between them goes back years; the accusations Proctor levelled at Crowley left a stain he's never quite managed to cleanse.'

Alice tensed. What sort of accusations?

'Coupled with that,' he went on, 'Sinclair is known for his reclusiveness. Why, then, would he agree to endure your company in the basement?'

She had no answers for him. The job was Crowley's doing, not hers. 'Maybe the workload was getting on top of him,' she suggested.

Risdon sat back. 'Maybe, indeed.'

He said nothing for a whole minute, and her tension grew. He studied her face, his grey eyes bright with suspicion, searching for something – a weakness in her story, maybe. Finally, he seemed to make some sort of decision and shook his head.

'Explain to me why you attempted to gain access to a secured area on your very first day,' he said.

Her eyebrows shot up. *The cells.* This was about her unauthorized trip to the cells. She almost sagged with relief. Trespass was nothing. They couldn't throw her in prison for wandering into the wrong room. 'I got lost,' she lied. 'I was looking for the bathroom and took the wrong lift. Luckily, Crowley rescued me.'

Risdon stared at her shrewdly, and the silence yawned out between them.

'Trespass is a very serious offence,' he said. 'Particularly when it happens in a heavily restricted area, as an apparent attempt to gain access to our criminal suspects.'

She sat up straighter, her body suddenly rigid. He was right; it didn't look good. Did they think she had a masterplan to infiltrate the station and swipe one of the criminals out from under their noses?

'No, wait. None of this was supposed to—' she started, then stopped. 'Are you arresting me?' she asked quietly.

He slid his tobacco tin off the table and pocketed it. 'No. I'm suspending you from your employment without pay, pending further security checks.' He paused. 'Consider yourself fortunate. Any further transgressions *will* result in your detainment.'

She sighed. Never let it be said she didn't know how to make her parents proud. There was a pang of loss in her chest. Crowley had said he'd deliver a message to them; she'd have to write something convincingly banal so that they wouldn't worry – or go to London looking for her.

Risdon pushed back his chair and rose.

'Proctor Sinclair has never had the protection of a House,' he said mildly. 'It has made him bitter and intolerant – yet he had, apparently, been prepared to tolerate you. I find that very interesting.'

She kept her face carefully blank. She wanted, suddenly, to reveal that she was an aviarist, and explain that Proctor and Crowley were helping her muddle through this new discovery. But, faced with the hard look in Risdon's eyes, the words just wouldn't come.

'You've found yourself plunged into a confusing new world,

and Crowley seems to be your anchor in the storm,' he said softly. 'Allow me to advise. An anchor stops a ship from coming adrift, but it also weighs it down, rendering it sinkable. Crowley may not be the lifeline you need.'

14

Alice shuddered and tugged the blanket tighter around herself. Her eyes were gritty with exhaustion; she'd spent at least eight hours staring at the ceiling, replaying Risdon's words. Why had he warned her against Crowley? And what was Proctor's old accusation against him? Her confusion was threaded with anger at her own stupidity. She'd charged off to the cells without any real thought to the consequences. Okay, she couldn't necessarily have predicted it would result in a suspension on her *very first day*. But it was a stark reminder that she was operating blind in this world. She was tired of feeling so hopelessly ignorant.

She prided herself on her ability to carry out research. At university, the hours of work she'd put into her dissertation, not the exam, had sealed her passing grade. It was the story of her life. She'd dug up vast amounts of reliable information at her godawful job – statistics, market research – and then blown her presentation. She was top-class backroom staff but a dreadful fieldworker.

Now Jen was the exam she couldn't afford to fluff, and yet ... she already had. Her suspension meant she couldn't search Proctor's basement for any more information. She'd blown her chance of squeezing information from one of Northam's followers, and her first session with Proctor had resulted in him storming out. If she didn't make progress soon, Jen might . . . She exhaled shakily. She didn't like the direction of her thoughts. She needed to get out of bed before she drove herself mad.

She checked to make sure the coast was clear, then shot across the corridor to the toilet in the winceyette nightdress (Crowley hadn't packed her beloved pyjamas). She was just returning when she heard Crowley sneak up behind her.

'Are you going to waste the day sleeping?' he asked.

'I can't sleep. That's the bloody problem.'

He frowned. 'It's almost midday and you're still wearing your mother's nightdress. What does that say about your state of mind? We have things to do.'

'If I'd known there was a dress code, I'd have taken a leaf out of your book and worn my best mourning clothes.'

His eyes flashed, and she paused. That had got under his skin, but why?

He followed her as she flopped back onto her bed, and loomed into the doorway. His dark hair fell messily over his collar.

'Oh, please. Stop with all the looming,' she said. 'What are you? Jane Austen's Mr Darcy reject?'

'I beg your pardon?' He raised an eyebrow, but she hadn't provoked a reaction this time.

'And talking of books – *I need books*,' she said earnestly.

He narrowed his eyes.

'I need to know more about the Rookery, about aviarists, the Fellowship – about *everything*.'

'I can tell you,' he said stiffly, 'if you'd only listen.'

She shook her head, thinking again of Risdon's warning. 'But you didn't tell me *anything* about Marianne Northam and her followers . . .'

He stared at her. 'All this nonsense about wanting to speak to the death cultists – I didn't realize it'd be necessary to explain why ingratiating yourself with the leader of a death cult is an appalling idea.'

She shook her head. 'It's a good plan. I need to get into the Sulka Moors – home of Death. And surely they know most about him. Maybe I can meet Marianne and . . . infiltrate the Fellowship for information.'

'You are ridiculously naive. Marianne Northam is *dangerous*.'

'Then I'd better make sure she doesn't find out.'

'And how are you going to *find* Marianne? The Fellowship are notoriously secretive, and constantly on the move – no one even knows where they are.'

'Fine,' she muttered. 'Then what's your grand plan anyway? Do you even *have* one?'

He glared at her, but she stood her ground, for Jen's sake – and Jen's time might be running out.

'Just give me some time,' he said at last. 'I'll get you to the moors safely. You don't need Marianne.' His expression relaxed, and he shook his head with a sigh. 'It would be a dereliction of my duty to Sylvie if I saved you from Vin and the Beaks only for you to die at the hands of Marianne's deranged group.'

Alice thought of the corpse photographs and paused. Maybe he had a point.

'Why do you owe Sylvie, anyway? Who was she to you?'

Crowley's eyes grew shuttered, and she had the sense that the question had stung him.

'A friend,' he said quietly. There was a short pause. 'Will you trust me about the moors? I'll sort something out.'

She hesitated, before nodding. What choice did she have?

'I'll also get you your books. And I'll smooth things over with Proctor, so we can continue your tuition here. You're going to need it.'

He turned to leave, and she nearly thanked him. But she felt too troubled. *Crowley may not be the lifeline you think he is*, she remembered.

She studied Sasha's nightjar for a moment. Then she began to sketch out long, flowing lines that curved up around the head and sharpened at the beak. Her pencil scratched and glided across the page, her strokes softening for the feathers and hatching out the shading beneath the wings. It had been Sasha's idea to sketch the nightjar, in case it helped tune her fledgling 'magic' – though Alice suspected it was really so that Sasha could finally see her own soul-bird.

All through school, art had been Alice's release. When she'd been fighting to ignore the birds and the daily battleground of school life, she'd lose herself in drawings. Her old bedroom was littered with her sketchbooks, filled with drawings of her dogs. The visions of birds had eventually faded, and the need for cathartic release had lessened. So she'd gone for the sensible, academic option instead: a history degree and the promise of a more secure career path – which had taken her to shoe research. Look how well that had worked out.

Across the kitchen table, Sasha gasped, and Alice's focus slipped. 'Is that really what it looks like?' asked Sasha, skirting around the table to examine it greedily. 'Oh, mother of pearl, it is, isn't it?'

'It's not finished,' Alice protested.

Sasha's strong, dusky nightjar was calm, but its tail feathers kept fanning out, and Alice realized she'd got them wrong. She'd textured them with straight lines, but, on closer inspection, tiny whorls branched out from their edges.

'Let me just fix . . .'

She tugged the paper from Sasha's hands and snatched up her pencil, scratching into the feathers while the nightjar sat placidly on Sasha's shoulder. Alice finished with a satisfied sigh.

'I need to check the book,' she said, pulling a thick volume across the table towards her. *Magellan's Nightjar Compendium* – nearly as rare as aviarists themselves. According to Crowley, he'd had to sell his soul to get hold of this copy. There had only ever been one edition published, and it had been out of print for a century. He'd thrust it at her over a week ago, evading all questions about how he'd acquired it, so she'd pretended not to notice the graze on his top lip or the bruise blooming under his eye. The book was a godsend. She'd spent every waking hour poring over it, studying drawings and diagrams of nightjars and memorizing descriptions of behaviour and appearance long into the night.

She flipped through the pages and settled on the double spread of a nightjar that bore a passing resemblance to Sasha's. Magellan had captioned it: *Stevie Mohan, member of House Ahti. Note the distinctive arcs spiralling from the lined patterns.*

She glanced up at Sasha. Her nightjar had this same pattern. *House Ahti.* The patterns, Alice had discovered, often hinted at the legacy. Jude's nightjar, like those of other members of House Ilmarinen, had a series of short, intersecting lines on the breast feathers. And Sasha, despite her aquaphobia, *must* have the water legacy – so why did she hide it? Was it because of Zara – the girl Alice was now convinced she'd seen in Sasha's *memories*? Curiously, though there were many warnings about misuse of aviarist skills in the book, there was no mention at all of the ability to actually touch a nightjar. She'd been tempted to touch Jude's, to test her theory about the memories, but she didn't want to betray a new friendship by stealing a look at his private recollections.

'Can I keep the sketch?' asked Sasha, awestruck.

Alice smiled. 'I accept payment for sketches in the form of a trip to London.'

Sasha's brow wrinkled. 'What?'

Alice leaned across the table, her expression serious. 'Could you take me to London? Through a doorway? I want to see Jen and my parents, just to check they're okay—'

Sasha grimaced. 'Crowley's already warned me and Jude against it. The Beaks want you, so you're better off here.'

'Then . . .' She racked her brains for a new angle. 'Tell me how you learned to travel using the magic doors, or whatever they're called.'

'Doorway navigation takes years to learn,' said Sasha, tracing a finger over Alice's sketch. 'And the only shortcut is dangerous and expensive.'

'What's the shortcut?'

'You buy a skeleton key.'

The door flew open and Crowley appeared in the gap, a handful of books under one arm. His face was stony, but this wasn't particularly revealing; stony disapproval was his expression of choice.

'You will *not* be purchasing a skeleton key,' he said, dumping his books on the table. She glanced at the titles: a worn book with a broken spine, called *Uncommon Ornithology*, and a battered copy of *Trinity of the Mind, Body and Soul*.

'Excuse me,' said Alice, bristling, 'don't tell me what I can and can't buy.'

He gave her an exasperated look. 'Wyndham, you arrived here in a nightdress without a shilling to your name. You can't buy *anything*, and my charity does not extend to premature travelling escapades. Not yet, at least . . .'

Sasha muffled a laugh and vacated the room.

'Take me to London and I can get to a bank to repay your charity,' Alice countered, her cheeks pink.

'We've been through this,' he said patiently. 'London is off-limits. Write your parents and friend a letter, if you wish, but you can't visit.'

Alice's frustration boiled over. She was beginning to resent being told she had to stay here; the Rookery was a sprawling city, and yet she felt trapped. No Bow Street, no London; she might as well chain herself to Coram House.

'You said that Vin and the Beaks might be watching my parents' address?' she said. 'Fine. I'll write to them. But there's nothing stopping me from visiting *Jen* at St Pancras Hospital – why should the Beaks link Jen to me?'

He pinched the bridge of his nose. 'Of course they will link you. By now, they'll know *everything* about you.'

'Then what if none of my loved ones are safe?' she asked. There was a heavy weight pressing on her chest. 'What if the Beaks get bored of waiting for me and attack them anyway as punishment? Crowley, I can't stay here, knowing they might be in danger!'

'I've taken precautions. Trust me. I won't allow them to be harmed.'

'How?'

He frowned irritably. 'Jen will no longer be *in* St Pancras Hospital. I'm arranging for her to be moved so that Vin Kelligan stands less chance of finding her – and using her against you.

And as for your parents, I have their house under surveillance. All right?'

She hesitated. Was he telling the truth?

'You keep saying the Beaks want to use me against the people in the Rookery,' she said after a moment. 'How?'

'Not just those in the Rookery,' he said. 'You're a danger to every Väki living in the mainland. The Beaks can't distinguish us from non-Väki; aviarists, however, can spot magic users by their nightjars. The Beaks want you to find *us* . . . They want you to *find* people for them to murder.'

'But—'

'Alice, please. Focus on developing your nightjar sight; leave the rest to me.' He glanced at *Magellan's Nightjar Compendium*. 'You've been researching again?'

She sighed. 'Yes.'

He nodded, half a smile on his mouth, and she had the impression he was quietly impressed.

'Good for you,' he murmured, warmth in his tone.

She stole a glance at him, appraising him with an artist's eye. The Roman nose seemed to perfectly balance his features now – had she really once thought it too imposing? His overlong dark hair rested against his cheekbones, framing the hint of five o'clock shadow – and the graze he'd acquired when he'd secured Magellan's book for her still marked his top lip.

Their eyes met. His gaze seemed to hold such intensity that all the breath rushed out of her, and she turned back to her book, utterly thrown. She stabbed at the page with an unsteady hand.

'It's no use seeing nightjars if I can't find out how to get into the Sulka Moors without killing myself,' she said, injecting her voice with some force to make up for the confusing tension between them. 'If that's where Jen's nightjar is, *that's* what I should be focusing on. The Fellowship, not just the nightjars. I need to know how to get to the moors, and the Fellowship might be able to help. Why can't you *see* that?'

The heat in his eyes instantly chilled, his face swiftly transitioning into a blank mask. He stared at her, expressionless, then left the room. She listened in frustrated silence to his footsteps. Her eyes dropped to the books, but she was too discomfited to concentrate. *Trust me*, he kept insisting. It would be so much easier to do that if she could only see his nightjar.

'How many?' said Proctor.

Alice leaned further out of the open sash window. Surprisingly, given the way their last session had ended and his apparent distaste for both her and Crowley, he'd agreed to resume their lessons. They were now using unsuspecting passers-by for practice.

'It's harder when they're further away.'

'How many?' he repeated.

'Two,' she said, her eyes on the street below her. 'Two nightjars. One big, one small. The big one belongs to a businessman with a cane, but his nightjar is the scruffiest. The small one belongs to a woman walking a white dog. She's trembling, and her nightjar is stroking her face. She can't feel it, can she?' She paused and squinted into the distance. The sight of the dog-walker made her chest ache. Her elderly Westies would be so comforting right now.

Alice reluctantly withdrew from the window. 'I need a breather,' she said. She'd been holding the feather so long it was sweaty in her grasp. She flexed her fingers and it dropped to the floor.

'You need to practise *without* the feather,' said Proctor. He was sitting in the chair in the corner of the room.

'If I don't use the feather, I can't see any nightjars at all.' She pushed her hair back from her flustered face. 'Even with it, I don't always understand what I'm seeing unless I take to my books.'

'Forget the books. Follow your instincts.'

'The only time I've really been able to understand them was when—' She caught herself just in time. She couldn't tell him about touching Sasha's nightjar and catching a glimpse of her memories. Not after his warnings about the cord.

She bent to retrieve the feather, and her fingers found a knot in the wooden floorboards. She hesitated. There was a peculiar stubby nodule in the dark knot that she was certain hadn't been there before.

She frowned. 'Proctor, the cord – have you *ever* touched one?'

He eyed her warily. The burned scar tissue near his eyelids looked particularly raw today.

'It's dangerous.'

'Why?'

He hesitated. 'You mess with the link between a person's body and soul, and you'll rob them of strength and leave them in agony. And when their defence mechanisms kick in, they'll throw all their dwindling strength into an attack.'

He glanced at her, making sure she was listening. 'Touching a cord hurts the person it's attached to, but pain can flow the other way as well. Mental pain. All the worst emotions they've been feeling, all their turmoil and despair – sometimes even flashes of their worst memories. All hurled along the cord and into your mind.'

Sasha – so they really were her memories. But she hadn't touched Sasha's cord.

'The ability to touch a cord . . . is a weapon. But you risk your sanity if you touch one,' said Proctor. 'Bad enough to carry your own mental anguish, never mind drowning in someone else's.' He cleared his throat. 'That's what I've heard, anyway. Never touched one myself.'

She glanced at his nightjar. He was lying – she might be new at this, but Magellan and her own instincts told her that much at least.

'Only an aviarist can touch a cord,' said Proctor. 'But just because we can, doesn't mean we should.' His eyes flicked away from hers.

'What if you touch a nightjar itself?' she asked.

He frowned. 'You can't.'

'But what if you did?' she pressed.

'You *can't*,' he repeated. 'It's not possible. They're guardians. Protectors of the most precious thing in the world. They'd *never* let anyone touch them – they'd never risk endangering the soul. Nightjars can touch each other, so maybe your nightjar could touch mine – maybe, if they trusted each other – but *you* can't. There are some things even aviarists can't do.'

Alice pressed her lips together tightly. But she *had* done it. She'd stroked Sasha's nightjar. And it hadn't hurt Sasha at all. In fact, she had been oblivious. Was it possible she'd unlocked some aviarist skill that Proctor never had?

'Can I show you something?' she asked, moving towards Crowley's pile of books on her bed. 'This book mentions cloaking,' she said, trying to keep the tremble of excitement from her voice. 'It's only a few pages, but it says that the interconnection between mind, body and soul means aviarists can render themselves *invisible*.'

Proctor paused and looked away from her. 'Not invisible.'

Her shoulders sagged. She should have known it was rubbish.

'Just . . . unseen,' he continued.

She held her breath.

'Nightjars are connected to the body and guard the soul. If the nightjar knows you're not a threat, then maybe it'd dismiss you and turn its back on you. Maybe. I've heard of one or two aviarists who could force people's nightjars to look away from them – and because of the trinity, the soul *and* mind looked away . . . the eyes too, since the mind can affect your biology.'

'It's like a . . . perception filter,' said Alice.

'Yeah. Something like that. It's not easy to stop a nightjar from looking at you – they're constantly on guard – but if you can turn their eyes away, then their owner will be blind to you.' He shrugged. 'From the few examples I've heard, it's a waste of time, because it only lasts about a minute; no nightjar would relax its defences for long.'

'And . . . how do you do it?' she asked.

He scratched his chin. 'Hard to say. Maybe the best way is to have them think you're harmless, so they'll be at ease.'

'How?'

He sighed. 'Keep calm around them. Try meditating. I've got to go.'

She frowned. 'Will you come back?'

'Maybe.'

There was a knock at the door, and he limped over and yanked it open.

'Skulking around, Crowley?' he said.

Crowley's face was impassive. 'I came to see if there'd been any progress.'

'We're done for the day.'

Crowley peered at Alice over Proctor's shoulder. 'I've delivered your letter to your parents.'

She smiled her thanks. She hoped it had stopped them worrying.

Proctor grinned at Crowley. 'I'm off. She needs more practice. Are you going to volunteer?'

Crowley's lips thinned. Proctor barked a laugh, muttering, 'Thought not,' and roughly pushed past him. They listened to the sound of his unsteady footsteps thumping down the stairs before Crowley turned to her, his face unreadable.

'Forget about the Fellowship,' he said. 'I've found a better solution, but we'll need to act fast.'

'What sort of solution?'

'I know how to get you into the moors.'

'You do?' she asked, surprised.

His eyes darkened, and for a second she thought he wasn't going to respond. 'A necromancer,' he said. 'Only a necromancer can open the door to Death's homeland.'

15

'Here?' she panted, digging her fingers under her ribs to ease the stitch in her side. Crowley had insisted they walk part of the way to Clerkenwell, arguing that all the doorways near their destination would likely be guarded. The streets were steeped in shadows and they'd talked little on the journey.

'Pull your hat down to hide your face,' said Crowley as they neared an imposing Victorian building engraved with *Lead & Glass Merchants*. 'There will be very few women here, and the less attention we draw, the better.'

Crowley slipped his arm through Alice's and directed her into the building's shadow. 'There are . . . some things I haven't yet told you,' he said, leaning closer to whisper.

Her skin prickled.

'The Runners employ their own necromancer, but the art of necromancy is illegal,' he said.

She frowned. 'Isn't that a bit hypocritical?'

Crowley snorted. 'You think any organization headed by Reuben Risdon adheres to a consistent moral code?'

She said nothing. Crowley and Risdon clearly had the same low opinion of each other.

'The Runners' necromancer is Eris Mawkin,' he said. 'They

keep her on a tight leash. She's only allowed to practise her art if she practises it in their name. She's the one who gave me the tip-off about one of her kind being here tonight.'

'But . . . if you're already friendly with a necromancer, can't she just open a door to the moors for me?'

'Unfortunately not,' he said. 'The legacies don't always present in the same manner. She has an impressive set of skills, but she's never been able to open a door to the moors. However, she's been keeping her ear to the ground, and the man we're here to find tonight is Ronan Bishop.'

She paused to process this. 'Okay. So necromancy is illegal – but we're not necromancers. There's no risk to us, is there?'

'You misunderstand,' he said quietly. 'Most practising necro-mancers go underground, off-grid, to avoid the Runners. That's not an easy life. Everything is temporary: homes, jobs, families. To make money, they often end up dabbling in crime. This man – Ronan Bishop – is a stranger to me. He has no reason to trust me, and he isn't expecting me. He won't be hospitable.'

'Maybe if we offer to pay him—'

'He'll do nothing for us until he's certain we're not undercover Runners. He will be particularly alert to the possibility of a covert Runner operation tonight.'

'Why tonight?'

'Because he's holding an illicit dogfight for a shady gambling ring. And that is why this is not going to be pleasant.'

Thanks to the unsociable trading hours, the nearby Smithfield Market was blessedly silent as they continued down the street. The rank odour of animal meat was masked by a smell of tobacco smoke and stale beer.

Dogfight? Her stomach lurched.

'Keep your head *down*,' murmured Crowley. He led her to a

derelict building with a crooked sign marking it out as a warehouse. Every upper-storey window was smashed, and the woodwork was rotted. But they were headed for the yard round the back.

The gated passage leading to it was guarded by two hulking figures. Warm light poured out from behind them, and the rain-soaked pavement glistened in the darkness. Murmurs and a low rumbling of furtive conversation drifted towards them. Crowley nodded at the pair and slipped them some money. The men relaxed their stances, and Crowley and Alice moved towards the yard.

What struck her first was the heat. The stagnant air was oppressive, and flavoured with sweat, beer and filth. The space was hemmed in by brick walls from the buildings on either side and enclosed by a flat wooden roof. It was much larger than she'd expected. There was a table set up at one end, lined with a row of what appeared to be gin, rum and whisky bottles and a stack of shot glasses. A barrel underneath the table supplied beer on tap.

Men – they were all men – huddled around in groups, knocking back shots or swilling cloudy beer in pint glasses. Behind Alice, more were pouring into the yard, crushing her against the people in front. Feet were stepped on and elbows were jostled, but despite the undercurrent of electric anticipation, there were no angry complaints and no sharp looks. No one wanted to be the spark that lit the fuse tonight.

Alice felt a hand brush against hers and stiffened, until it squeezed gently and tugged her sideways through the crowd. Crowley. He led her over to a small pocket of space in the corner, where she could breathe more easily and take stock of her surroundings.

The yard was filling up – all except for a circular arena in the centre and one strip of land which made up about a quarter of the space. The latter seemed cordoned off, but there were no barriers; the crowd seemed to know instinctively to keep their distance. She glanced sideways and her muscles tensed – she grabbed at Crowley, eyes wide with alarm.

'Shh,' he mouthed. 'Shh, I know.'

His eyes bored into hers, trying to communicate wordlessly. He squeezed her hand in reassurance, and then let go.

They were standing near the holding area. The area everyone else was carefully avoiding. A few feet away were twenty or thirty of the most vicious dogs she'd ever seen. They were broadchested, scarred and muscular, with docked tails and ears cropped so short they looked like devils' horns. Their fur was patchy with grease and missing chunks of hair. All had jaws like bear traps. Short metal chains around their necks shackled each to a wooden barrel, weighted to hold them in place.

Along the back wall, there were half a dozen cages, but she couldn't see what they contained. The lantern lights placed their occupants in deep shadow. The central arena was covered in a thick layer of sawdust, and a wooden barrier, splattered with dried blood, divided it from the packed crowd.

She didn't want to be here. The dogs, the stench, the baking heat, the crush of bodies, the wooden roof trapping them inside . . . the thought of her two Westies, Bo and Ruby, being cornered in a place like this . . . She had to get out. She pushed off from the wall, lurching towards the exit in a haze of panic. Her breathing was shallow. She made it a few steps before Crowley grabbed a fistful of her coat and pushed her back against the wall, a warning in his eyes.

'Think of Jen,' he hissed.

'But this is—'

There was a screech of grinding metal, and all conversation abruptly died. The two hulking doormen had closed the gate, locking them in. Silence fell, and the atmosphere became more charged. People were looking around now, grinning and nodding, eager to begin.

Two men – one huge and lumbering, the other tall but skinny – dragged a pair of dogs to the enclosure. The skinnier of the men was pulling a brindle-coloured dog with hunched back legs and a cowering neck. Even from a distance, Alice could see the whites of its eyes. The man spat at it and yanked its chain. It yelped loudly, and there was a chorus of guttural laughter from the crowd.

'I'll take the piebald!' someone roared, pointing at the other dog – a snarling black-and-white-furred beast with teeth like daggers.

'Twenty-five to one on the brindle!'

Three men darted about the tightly packed crowd, wafting betting slips and taking money at speed.

'Final bets!'

There was a further burst of activity and movement, and Alice was shunted backwards. The crowd closed in around her, their sneering faces morphing together into something monstrous and predatory. The grasping bookies; the stench of testosterone; the animals' fear choking the back of her throat . . . Her senses were overwhelmed.

It seemed that every dog in the yard had opened its jaws and begun to bark – snarling, baying howls and deep, husky-throated growls. The floor seemed to judder with the cacophony of noise.

She closed her eyes briefly, her ears ringing . . . and when she opened them again, her stomach dropped as the yard erupted into a flurry of wings and claws: nightjars in every conceivable inch of space, smothering the air. She grabbed Crowley's arm, crushing it in her trembling fingers. It was an explosion of night-jars unlike any she'd ever seen – the flawed soul-birds of every savage in this arena. These were spiteful, sharp-beaked creatures, beady-eyed and menacing. They swooped at each other, pin-sharp claws extended to rake at feathered breasts, the fighting on the ground mirrored in the air. Alice buried her head against Crowley's shoulder, all of her childhood nightmares made flesh; she felt the dregs of her self-control slip away.

'Face your dogs!'

The handlers hauled the stocky animals to either end of the arena. They jerked the chains up, exposing the dogs' throats and keeping their teeth just out of reach, and forced them to sit facing each other. The men goaded them with shouts and commands and prodding fingers. Then the chains were removed and the handlers scrambled to safety.

The piebald black-and-white was the first to move. Its back legs bent and it sprang forward, mouth frothing and eyes glitter-ing with menace. The brindle twisted sideways to escape, but it was a beat too slow and the other dog slammed into it, knocking it off its feet. Splayed out on its back, the piebald sank its teeth into the other dog's neck, drawing blood, and shook it violently. The brindle didn't utter a sound – not a yelp or a howl. It scrabbled in the dirt, kicking up sawdust, and managed to squirm loose. It leapt to its feet, shaking in terror and dripping blood.

The piebald lunged again, lips pulled back and teeth snapping at the air. The brindle scuttled backwards into the wooden bar-rier, its eyes wide with fear.

'Crowley,' Alice wheezed, her gorge rising in her throat. 'It's barbaric. I can't . . .'

The brindle's handler leaned over the enclosure. For one foolish moment, she thought he was going to pull it out, lift it to safety, but he had a stick in his hand like a baseball bat. He jammed it between the dog and the barrier and used it to propel the dog back into the centre of the arena.

The brindle keened in fear, and Alice snapped. The crowd was reduced to background noise. Her vision tunnelled until it was a pinprick. The only thing she could see was him. The handler. He leaned over the barrier, resting on his elbows. His shirt sleeves were rolled up and he wore braces, with a cigar pinned to the elastic. Short, oily hair was half hidden under a baker-boy cap pulled low over his rat-like face. His nightjar was sitting on his shoulder: a rangy, greasy-looking thing with plain feathers and a razor beak. She was going to strangle his cord with her bare hands. Right here, in front of all these people. Proctor had said touching cords was a weapon that would cause agonizing pain. Well, she was going to have him on his knees, begging for mercy, and when he couldn't bear it any longer, she was going to throw him to the dogs.

She thrust herself into the crowd, shoving people aside, her every thought focused on reaching him. She could see the stubble on his jaw, smell the sweat stains under his arms . . .

'Alice, *no*.'

Crowley caught her elbow from behind and tried to pull her backwards. The brindle yelped in agony and she shrugged Crowley off with renewed force. The handler. She had to get to the handler.

'Don't lose your head,' he hissed.

He put both arms around her, bear-hugging her from behind. They were in the middle of the throng, but the fight hadn't finished and everyone was too engrossed to pay them much attention. Frustration expanded in her chest. Anger and helplessness – about the terrified dog, about Jen – surged through her. And the more Crowley tightened his hold, the more she felt she might explode with it. She tried to peel his hand from her chest and, quite by accident, her hand closed around the luminescent cord that bound him to his nightjar instead.

A shot of adrenaline and euphoria electrified her, robbing her of breath and leaving her light-headed. The cord was like warm liquid velvet in her hands. It was gloriously alive: a living thing pulsing in her grasp, pounding against the rhythm of her blood.

She smiled beatifically. There was a sudden burst of fluttering wings in the air behind Crowley. His nightjar! Giddy elation shot through her and she forgot everything else. The dog handlers, the bookies and their malevolent nightjars vanished. Crowley couldn't hide it from her now! She tugged at the cord, pulling his nightjar closer. But it grew thinner and fainter in her hands, and Crowley staggered sideways. She was confused. Where was the nightjar?

There was a buzzing sound in her ears and something rolled down the cord. It juddered in her hand, and she staggered as a wave of emotion swept over her. *Guilt*. Heart-sickening guilt throbbed up her arm and coursed through every vein, leaving her panting and dazed. *Crowley's guilt*. It was raw and wild; it sank into her mind, burrowed into her nerve endings. The taste of Crowley's guilt was like ashes in her mouth. What had he done to feel such awful shame?

With a pained groan, Crowley slammed to his knees in the dirt, clutching his chest and gasping for breath. His hair fell over his face, but she caught a flash of rapidly paling skin beneath his collar as he slumped onto the floor like a corpse. Startled, she released the cord, and it instantly glowed brighter.

'Oh God. Crowley, are you okay? Are you—'

'What's up with him?' someone shouted in her ear. 'Can't hold his beer?'

There were jeers of laughter, and Alice's panic rose several notches higher. What had she done? Here, of all places. Crowley let out a hiss of pain and pushed himself onto one knee.

'What . . . did you do to me?' he breathed, his voice ragged.

One look at his ashen face and she quailed. This was bad. She sobered instantly, regaining control of her sensibilities. 'I . . . I don't know,' she said.

Crowley took a great, heaving breath as he struggled to his feet. The crowd pressed in around him and he stumbled. She had to get him out of the throng. She hauled him towards the edge of the holding area. But they didn't quite manage it; his right leg buckled and they staggered sideways and crashed into the wall.

They'd fallen together, her arm trapped under him – and his body was crushed against her, pressing his warmth into her muscles. God, it felt like it had been so long since she'd been touched by another human, so long since she'd even been held . . .

'The brindle,' he murmured, freeing her arm and arching ever so slightly – and pointedly – away from her, 'is dead.'

Alice's eyes flew open as she stumbled away from him, her whole body flushed with embarrassment. What on earth was she doing? She spun around, grateful to hide her face.

The fight was still going on. The piebald had collapsed in the middle of the arena, bleeding out on the sawdust while the crowd shouted at it to get back on its feet, to attack. A deafening chorus of dogs and men urged the piebald on while the other dog staggered drunkenly around the arena, clearly exhausted. Crowley was wrong; the brindle wasn't dead – it was *winning*.

She felt absolutely nothing. Empty. Even when the dogs won, they lost. This was a fight won by men. Men who rustled betting slips and rattled coins in their pockets, who clinked shot glasses and laughed as the blood sprayed the sawdust like rubies.

'That dog is one of Ronan's – the necromancer's,' said Crowley. 'His brother is the handler. Look.'

She squinted across the yard. The rat-faced handler was talking with another man, this one shorter but with the same features: narrow face, long nose, thin lips. Ronan Bishop was the shorter of the brothers.

'Watch the brindle.'

She did. It had stopped now and was staring into space, eyes glazed. Oozing cuts pitted its shoulders and criss-crossed its back. Its nose was heavily scarred, and its fur was matted with blood.

Her stomach churned and her eyes watered with frustration, magnified by her humiliation with Crowley. She hated them. She hated every last one of them. Everyone who had watched this happen.

'Both dogs are dead, Alice,' whispered Crowley. 'But the winner is the last dog standing.'

She frowned, trying to piece together what he was telling her. She focused on the dog, the frightened brindle that had been forced into the arena. It still hadn't moved. It didn't blink. It wasn't even—

Alice's head jerked around to Crowley's and he nodded grimly. No one else had noticed. They were already making bets on the next fight.

The brindle wasn't breathing.

Her hand flew to her mouth, but she didn't make a sound. She stood watching the dog in shock; it should have been panting, but its chest was absolutely still. The brindle hadn't survived the brutal fight. Both dogs had died in the arena – but the brindle had won because no one else had realized. After all, it was standing on four legs. Its eyes were open.

She watched as the dog followed Ronan to one of the cages in the holding area and shuffled inside. They were rigging the fights. She understood it now. The cages along the back row were filled with dead dogs, all victors in their fights. It didn't matter if they offered up a weaker-looking dog. All they had to do was make the gamblers think their contender was still alive until the fight ended. The survivor won, and the Bishop brothers were pocketing the winnings every time.

Necromancers practised death magic. They raised people – and animals – from the dead. In a fight to the death, no dog owned by a necromancer would ever really die.

16

'There has to be another exit,' said Crowley. 'The brothers co-ordinated this event, and they won't risk getting trapped here if the Runners burst through the gate. Keep your eye on the brother. I'm going to find Ronan.'

He pushed off from the wall, still pale and clammy, and veered to the left. He kept to the edge of the yard, but his gait was sluggish and unsteady. Crowley wasn't Crowley without the arrogant stride. He looked debilitated, and it was her fault.

Alice turned to watch the dog handler. He was busy dragging another terrified animal towards the enclosure to wait its turn. There was a high-pitched yowl within the arena and a thump as something smashed violently against the thin barrier. As one, the crowd fell back, and a heavy man in a dirty overcoat staggered into her, forcing her back against the wall. A roar of laughter went up as the danger passed and the crowd surged forward again like a wave.

She stood on her tiptoes. The handler hadn't moved, and frustration nagged at her. What use was she out here? Even if she saw something, how was she supposed to alert Crowley? He'd gone off alone, stumbling and depleted, to meet a necromancer who might attack first and ask questions later. She hesitated for just a fraction of a second before making sure her hat – one of Jude's – was shading her face, and darted after him.

'—Runners are no friends of mine.'

The low murmur of Crowley's voice carried through the gloom, and Alice froze. They weren't far ahead. She held her breath and carefully picked her way closer. It was more squalid here. The roof hung lower, giving the space a more claustrophobic quality, and the floor was littered with heaps of sawdust, broken wood, rotten barrels and fragments of glass. She had thought the dogs' holding area was a dead end, taking up one side of the yard. But another, much smaller courtyard branched off from it, tapering off to another doorway between the buildings on either side. Crowley was right; they had a second exit.

Alice flattened herself against the wall, battling with the noise to focus on the words passing between Crowley and Ronan.

'I thought we might do business together,' Crowley drawled. 'That's why I'm here. I have no interest at all in disrupting your little sideline out there.'

'Who gave you my name?' said Ronan.

'One of your compatriots. Eris Mawkin.'

Ronan laughed roughly. 'Compatriot only when she wants something. Tell that hypocritical bitch to send no more of her *friends* to me.' He paused, then abruptly said, 'You can be on your way now, fella.'

Crowley sighed. 'No. I don't think so.'

Alice craned her neck to see what was happening. Ronan was a head shorter than Crowley, but they were standing an inch apart. Ronan's chest was pushed out and his face twisted into a snarl.

'Would you rather be chased out by my boys?'

Alice tensed, unsure whether he meant the doormen or the caged dogs. Crowley didn't seem in the slightest bit concerned, but there was a tightness in his jaw she'd never seen before and his fist was pressed into his chest as though to stem a sharp pain. He was trying to face down a necromancer, and she'd weakened him. She couldn't have chosen a worse time.

She took a moment to prepare herself. This was for Jen. This dogfighting necromancer could help her get into the moors. He might be the most hideous excuse for a human being she'd ever seen, but if he could help her save Jen then she had to get this right.

Something crackled. Her hearing sharpened. A wave of simmering heat rolled across the small courtyard, and fresh shadows were illuminated by a sudden glow. She sucked in a breath. The floor was on fire. Columns of twisting flame now danced between the two men, and Ronan had been forced backwards by the blinding heat. Fire dripped from Crowley's fingertips, and the air crackled with sparks.

Crowley's face was eerie, his expression made malicious by the play of light falling across his features. He flicked his wrist, and the roaring flames by his feet shot across the dirt to cut off Ronan's retreat. Ronan spun, his face twisted with shocked rage, and stabbed a finger in Crowley's direction.

'Don't you dare play this fucking game with me,' he hissed. 'You know what I am!'

Crowley stared at him coolly as the fire whipped across the ground, fencing Ronan in. Alice smiled inwardly. *Let's see how that bastard likes being enclosed himself!*

'Let's make this simple,' said Crowley, stepping closer, the flames licking at his boots. 'I'll tell you what I want, and what I'm prepared to pay, and you can agree to give it to me. Deal?'

Alice glanced over her shoulder. She'd thought . . . footsteps, maybe . . . but no one was coming. Either people were too wrapped up in the fighting to have noticed the sudden light, or they were too wary of the chained dogs to skirt past them. There was also, she realized, no smoke at all to alert anyone to the fire. She slid from her hiding place, keeping to the patches of darkness against the walls.

Palms open, Crowley snapped his fingers upwards, and the flames – head-height now – drew closer to Ronan.

Ronan's face was scarlet. His hair and face were soaked with sweat. He threw up an arm to protect his face, and the raging fire at his back leapt to consume his shirt. Alice's imagination was playing tricks on her; she had a vision of charred and blistered skin. And, despite the inferno, her blood suddenly chilled at the thought, and she staggered forward.

'Crowley, wait,' she said. 'This is too much, even for—'

He glanced in her direction, and his eyes widened in surprise. The fire stuttered.

'*Alice?*'

Ronan staggered from the flaming circle and dropped to his knees. His hands were bunched into fists, his face awash with hatred.

'You were supposed to wait in the—'

Ronan smashed his fists into the dirt, and an explosive peal of clanging metal rang out like gunshots. There were distant gasps of horror from the crowd and shouts for calm. Alice heard a series of thuds, and a heavy skittering sound scratched its way towards the small courtyard.

Crowley turned to her, his jaw set and a look in his eye that brooked no argument. 'The second exit,' he said, jerking his head in the direction of the other door. 'Go.'

'What? No! I'm not . . .'

He grabbed her by the arm and roughly shoved her behind him. She stumbled on the detritus cluttering the floor and tore open her knee on a sliver of broken glass. She hissed and pulled herself upright, just in time to see the first shadow detach itself from the roiling patch of darkness rushing around the corner.

Ronan's malevolent grin leered at her from a few feet away. Behind him, teeth and claws emerged from the gloom. Scarred faces, swollen eyes and bloody fur, exposed flesh and wounds that had cut right to the bone . . . The victors of the Bishop brothers' previous fights massed behind him: a savage army of the dead.

The glassy-eyed brindle swaggered to the front. A rasping growl resonated from its mangled throat. One by one, the other dogs took up the call, their hackles rising.

'Crowley,' she whispered, stepping up next to him.

He swiped his arm to keep her back.

'The other door,' he said through gritted teeth.

'Face your dogs,' commanded Ronan with a grin, raising both hands before snapping his elbows straight ahead. At his signal, the dogs galloped forward. A blur of blood and bone, flashing teeth and sightless eyes converged on them. Crowley swept his hand in a steady arc, and a whip of flame lashed the ground. He teased it higher, putting a wall of fire between them and the approaching horde.

It worked. The unnatural animals didn't dare close the gap, and Ronan merely watched them. Alice allowed herself a moment to track the brindle through the wavering flames. The heat distorted its appearance monstrously, but it was just . . . a dog. Only, instead of a wagging tail and lolling tongue, it was a congealing mass of scar tissue and abuse, and looking at it made her chest ache.

'We want you to open a door to the Sulka Moors,' she said,

finally finding her voice. She stepped out from Crowley's shadow, arms by her sides, deliberately presenting no threat. 'There's no need for all this,' she said, avoiding the brindle at the corner of her eye.

Ronan stared at her through the wall of dancing flames. He didn't smile, didn't flinch – nothing. He stepped back, and she thought she'd done it – that she'd cooled the situation before it escalated. But the second he spun away, the dogs staggered forward, into the fire.

Alice sucked in a horrified breath, but the dogs soldiered on. Their fur kindled with flame, slowly at first, then it raced across their chests and spines until it engulfed them. And then their skin began to char.

Crowley swore loudly and doused the fire with a swipe of his hand, but it made no difference and the dogs continued to march onwards.

He glanced over at her, his face gripped with indecision.

'They're dead,' he said.

She knew what he meant. They were already dead; it shouldn't matter that they were burning. But it did.

Ahead, a figure hurtled around the corner and stopped. It was Ronan's brother, the dog handler. He appraised them for a second or two before squaring his shoulders and driving forward at speed.

Pulse thundering, Alice scrambled past the pack of dogs and Crowley, only faintly registering that the dogs made no move to attack her. Apparently, they'd been set on Crowley's scent alone. The dog handler was hers. She might not have Crowley's skill with fire, and she might not be able to read nightjars properly without a book, but there was something she *could* do. She could see his cord from here, a rope of glowing incandescence looped idly round his waist.

She picked up the pace, racing straight for him, but he didn't even spare her a glance. He waved his hand as a ball of flame engulfed it. Had Crowley done that? The dog handler's face was tight with concentration, but he didn't seem to be in any pain. He thrust his hand into the air and the flame shot from his palm and hit the floor by Crowley's feet.

She drew up short, skidding on debris. No. The dog handler's legacy matched Crowley's own. Ilmarinen. He aimed a jet of fire at Crowley, who was backing further away from the growling dogs. It was only a matter of time before they launched their attack too, wasn't it?

'Alice!' Crowley shouted. 'Go after Ronan!'

She hesitated, torn between hurling herself at the dog handler and doubling back to support Crowley.

'Do *not* let him leave!'

Crowley's eyes flashed with anger, and a long sweep of his hand divided the yard in two, a line of blazing fire cutting her off from him and pushing her back towards the yard. She grimaced and spun on her heel, setting off after Ronan.

The yard was in chaos. The two dogs in the enclosure had given up fighting and were racing around the arena, trying desperately to jump the barrier. The crowd had erupted into a melee of flying elbows and fists. A pint glass soared across the yard and shattered above her head, showering her with glittering shards. She ducked away to avoid a pair of drunken gamblers.

The floor was strewn with discarded betting slips, and the table of whisky and gin bottles had been upended, leaving a sharp tang in the air. She could see no sign of Ronan in the disarray.

Fired up on losses and alcohol as they were, the crowd were

still not stupid enough to stray into the holding area. There were still two dozen dogs chained to beer barrels, and the crowd's agitation was infectious. The dogs – these yet living – howled and scratched at the ground, trying to shed their chains.

Ronan was crouching by the metal cages. He'd eased himself into the shadows, waiting silently while the commotion raged around him. Alice made use of the noise to creep into the holding area undetected. Ronan's face was blank, but his eyes scanned left and right. She kept to the edges as she slipped closer.

A dog missing one ear startled at her approach and let rip with a great, booming bark. She tried to shush it, but Ronan had already shot to his feet.

'I just want to talk,' she said quickly.

His mouth screwed up and he tipped his head, eyes fixed on hers, to launch a glob of spit on the dirt.

'Can we—'

His head whipped sideways, and the motion seemed to pull a rattling cage with it. The empty metal crate rocketed towards her like a missile. She dived to the floor among the terrified dogs, and it nicked her ear as it shot past. It crashed into a barrel and obliterated the latch, freeing a skinny dog fastened within. The dog seized its chance and hurtled towards the throng of men, who let out a great roar of shock and panic. Alice scrambled to her feet and tore across the yard as a bombardment of cages launched at her retreating back. *Metal.* Ronan Bishop wasn't just a necromancer; his other legacy was the same as Jude's.

The men had had enough of tonight's entertainment. Someone tried to kick at the liberated dog as it approached; another tossed a glass of beer at it. It was terrified; it was trying to escape, not attack. Didn't they realize? An idea began to form in Alice's mind. *Free the dogs.* Fear and adrenaline chased through her veins, and she swerved into the centre of the holding area, her heart hammering an erratic beat in her chest.

She lunged towards a barrel and tried to wrench off the metal latch that secured the nearest dog's chain. The restrained animal pulled at its bindings but made no move to attack. Maybe it knew she was trying to help.

'Shit!' she hissed as the latch held. She tried again, her palm bleeding, twisting the chain to weaken it.

Another of Ronan's metal cages shot towards her, and she gasped and threw herself to the left. It missed and smashed into a brown pit bull, flinging the animal backwards. It slammed into the brick wall with a muffled yelp of agony before falling silent, and Alice dragged herself upright, her head almost splitting with pent-up fury. She grabbed at the nearest chain, and in one swift movement, as though it were no stronger than paper, she tore the metal from the barrel.

Several metres away, Ronan paused. He looked down at his feet as a deep rumbling noise jarred Alice's senses. The floor juddered. The barrels vibrated, and Alice stormed towards him, her teeth clenched and a terrible wrath in her eyes. He took a wary step backwards, then another.

Alice's breathing was heavy, her heart pounding and her blood rising. She exhaled an explosion of breath and a deafening crack erupted through the yard. The barrels burst open simultaneously, the wood splitting and curling back on itself. The cowering dogs barked and whined and yanked at their restraints . . . and this time, the chains pulled free from the broken latches.

A scream went up, and the crowd surged towards the exit as every dog bolted for freedom. A gate had been opened and the gamblers jostled through the gap, escaping into the Rookery's streets. The dogs followed in a frenzied bid to escape.

Alice's anger evaporated, and she looked about in astonishment. Busted metal locks hung from the ruptured barrels. Why had *Ronan* unshackled the dogs?

A thunderous bang echoed around the yard, and her head darted up. The fleeing men had closed the wooden gate behind them, trapping her – and the remaining dogs – inside. They pawed frantically at the gate, their claws gouging furrows in the wood. Whimpering barks reverberated around the yard.

'We haven't fed them for days,' said Ronan, his tone conversational.

She narrowed her eyes at the implication.

'It gives them a vicious edge in the ring.' He smiled. 'When they're desperate, they'll eat anything.'

The metal cages he'd fired at her lay scattered around the holding area. He glanced down at one and toed it away from the wall.

'Up you get,' he said.

There was a pause, and then a chocolate-brown pit bull with a smashed nose and a broken spine lurched onto all fours and teetered out from behind the cage. Half its muzzle had been obliterated by the blow from the cage – the blow that had killed it. Ronan shrugged.

'This one's too defective to pass in the ring. But it'll do for now.'

The pit bull's head swung in her direction, its eyes vacant. A guttural growl emerged from its mouth, and she shuddered. It was *wrong*. Sick.

'Let it go,' she said quietly. 'Let it—'

'What? Rest in peace?' He laughed. 'Its soul *is* resting in peace. This thing – this body it left behind – is a puppet. A toy. I never did grow out of them.'

There was a shout from the far corner, and a blast of fire

spurted from the small courtyard. They both turned to watch it, briefly. It receded, and a chorus of snarling and muffled roars carried out into the yard.

'My brother, Elliot, is like my dogs,' said Ronan, unconcerned. 'He never loses a fight.'

He crouched down to the cage and pressed his hands against it. The metal began to warp and bubble, losing its shape at his touch.

'We came for your help,' said Alice, shaking her head in disbelief. How could it have gone so wrong? 'We didn't come here to fight, or—'

'But you did,' he said. 'Your friend in there tried to burn me alive.'

'No, he only meant to—'

'And look what happened to my yard.' He waved a hand at the upturned tables, broken glasses and smashed cages. 'The Runners will be sniffing all over the place by morning. I'll never be able to use this place again. You think you can use my secret against me? You think you can ruin my livelihood?'

'You torture animals,' she snapped. 'That should be a prison sentence, not a career choice!'

He nodded and focused on the liquefying metal in his hands. 'I'm going to pour this into molten steel down your throat,' he said calmly. 'And then I'm going to make a puppet out of what's left of you.'

Alice took a step backwards, one eye on the dog at Ronan's feet and one on him. Crowley would come to her rescue. The dog handler – Elliot – would be no match for him. Any minute, he'd come storming around the corner and firebomb this sick bastard, and this time she wouldn't protest.

She snatched Sylvie's feather from her sleeve cuff and clutched it in her fist. Her hand quivered. She only had to hold him off long enough for Crowley to get here. Ronan rose to his feet, working the shiny metal between his palms, and her stomach lurched. She took another step backwards, her breathing shallow.

His nightjar circled the air above his head, the cord pulling taut as it dipped its wings. It was small but lithe, with a stubby beak and manic, staring eyes that were fixed on her face.

Her courage wilted alongside her fury. She was alone, and she wasn't a fighter; she wasn't anything. She couldn't reach his cord *and* defend herself. And if she *missed* . . .

There was a blur at her feet as the sightless dog shambled closer, its dislocated spine poking through the skin. She gripped the feather tighter and focused on Ronan's cord. She'd have to make sure she didn't miss. Her fingers flexed in anticipation.

Its limbs jerky as a mechanical spider, the dog roared and suddenly pounced. She leapt backwards and landed among a pile of broken bottles with a crunch. Whisky and gin soaked through her trousers. She scrambled to her feet, but she was a beat too slow and the snarling beast clamped its teeth around her ankle. Sharp incisors lacerated her jeans, tearing the skin. She shrieked and kicked out with her other foot. The dog thumped to the ground, stunned, then hovered by his master – snarling.

Ronan was strangely expressionless as he trudged closer, scalding metal flowing through his fingers like liquid. *My God, he really is going to kill me.* Cold dread rolled through Alice's body and she pedalled backwards, limping and wincing in pain, but there was no escape. Her back hit the wall. *His cord*, she told herself. *Focus on his cord.*

A bellow sounded from the other courtyard, and a helpless moan escaped her mouth. Was that Crowley? A deep, resonant scream tumbled out into the yard, followed by a chorus of snarling, tearing sounds. Had Crowley been overcome by Ronan's puppets? She'd weakened him. It was her fault. Anguish squeezed her chest tight as she sank down, clasping her wounded ankle. Her fingers came away bloody.

'I told you,' said Ronan. 'I'd always bet on Elliot.'

He suddenly lunged for her. With a shriek of agony, she surged to her feet, the feather bloody in her hand. His glowing cord swung through the air, tantalizingly close, and she threw out her arms. Her fingers brushed the cord – just barely – and the compact ball of panic and terror coiled in her stomach unravelled and swept through her body, pulsing through her arms as she spread her fingers wide to grab the cord, to snatch it into her grasp . . . and missed.

17

Her lungs deflated in horror as her hand arced through the empty air and smashed against a low-hanging roof beam. Her palm smarted and her fingertips tingled with pain.

Something cracked – her wrist? No – the wood. A great tearing, splitting sound rang out, and a powdering of sawdust pattered onto Alice's hair. Her head darted up, just as the beam above her somehow, inexplicably, snapped in half. She dragged in a gasp of air, her eyes wild. *It was twelve inches thick. How –* Her thoughts skittered away from her as an ominous, deafening creak boomed through the yard.

Ronan saw it first. He looked skywards, his face ashen. 'What've you done?'

'Me?' she whispered.

The roof tilted sharply as the snapped beam released its burden. The remaining beams bowed under the extra load. The pressure built as the roof sagged further. Ronan's face fell and he turned tail and ran, just as the strained wood fractured and burst apart, triggering a succession of explosions that ran around the yard. Metal screws pinged from the brickwork like bullets as every supporting beam disintegrated.

Alice's feet slipped on the broken bottles and she threw herself back against the wall, crouching to make herself as small as possible. A wide plank of wood crashed to the dirt like a javelin. Ceiling joists and beams crunched down alongside it as the entire roof structure collapsed and shed its canopy. Red-brick grit and splinters rained down over the yard, and thick clouds of dust bloomed up from the debris.

Alice curled her arms around her head. Her ears had popped, and a distant ringing gnawed at her eardrum. She buried her face in her coat, her nostrils and mouth covered to stop the invading dust. She couldn't breathe, couldn't see, couldn't hear.

When at last the floor stopped vibrating, she opened her eyes, blinking rapidly. The air was thick with powdered grit; it filled the yard like fog. Vague, angular shapes rose out of the murk. She pulled herself to her feet, tripping on the loose rubble, and squinted about her.

The floor was heaped with the wreckage of fallen timber beams, lintels and joists. Slants of criss-crossed wood reached shoulder-height in places. The roof was gone, and with it the oppressive warmth. A chilly breeze gusted through the roof's carcass, overturning plastic sheeting and slivers of timber. Shafts of cool moonlight poured into the yard, casting eerie, misshapen shadows, some of which were moving. Alice tensed, but the shadows steered clear of her. The dogs cowered against the gate, too shell-shocked to bark. She had no idea how many had survived the falling timber.

A dry, rattling cough from the rubble caught her attention. She hesitated for a moment before venturing a hoarse, 'Hello?'

There was an answering moan.

Alice clambered across the fallen joists, her feet slipping in the crumbled sawdust. Blood from her savaged ankle had dripped into her sock, but she felt no pain now. She suspected she was in shock. She heaved herself across the pile of wood, swinging her legs over the hurdles in her path.

She found Ronan pinned beneath a ceiling joist, a length of timber crushing his chest. His hair was thick with dust. He blinked up at her.

'Help me,' he croaked.

She bent to heave the joist away, but paused. Her breath stilled and her legs trembled. She shook her head.

'Open a door to the moors for me,' she said.

'I . . . can't.'

She thrust her hand into her pocket and pulled out the blood-stained feather. His nightjar appeared, sitting on a beam, hunched with its eyes closed as though in pain.

Her face grimly determined, Alice put her heel on the joist and applied a gentle pressure. 'Open a door to the moors for me,' she repeated.

His shoulders shook, and he coughed loudly. 'I can't,' he hissed. 'Mawkin told your friend I could. But she's wrong. I can try, but it won't work. I've . . . I've never been able to do it. I'm . . .' He drew in a ragged breath. 'I'm not the necromancer you need.'

She stared at him in horror. His nightjar was rock-steady.

'No. No, you have to. All this . . . It had to be for something!'

But the nightjar showed the unpalatable truth. He couldn't help her. He couldn't help Jen. She turned on her heel and stumbled away, tripping and slipping on the timber, her brain buzzing with shock.

'Don't . . . Don't leave me here!' he rasped. 'I know someone who can help you!'

She wheeled around.

'Marianne Northam.'

'She's not a necromancer.'

'She's . . . She's found one. She wants a door opening as well. She came sniffing around me, once, but I was no good to her.'

She studied his nightjar. He was still telling the truth. Of course the Fellowship – the death cult – would have their own necromancer. She swallowed convulsively; her mouth was painfully dry. A frisson of nervous anticipation ran down her spine.

'Give me a name,' she said. 'And an address for Marianne.'

'Not . . . Not until you get me out.'

She moved towards him. The pile gave way beneath her, timbers sliding under her feet, and he hissed.

'Tell me how to find her,' she said. '*Then* I'll let you out.'

'Porto – Portobello Road,' he groaned, his face scrunched up in pain. 'Notting Hill. Number twenty-nine. Get me – *Get me out.*'

She shivered with nerves. This was it. This was how she was going to save Jen. She was getting closer . . .

'Alice!'

She froze. Was that . . . ?

'Alice, if you're behind there, stay back!'

Her head spun round and relief tightened her chest, making it difficult to breathe.

'Crowley?'

The entrance to the smaller courtyard was blocked by a heap of thick beams. She scrambled in the direction of Crowley's voice.

'Are you—'

Fire – a white-hot stream – blasted through the blockade and seared the beams that obstructed the way through. The timber exploded in a mushroom cloud of ash and charred wood shavings. The fire abruptly died out, and Crowley appeared in the gap, shoving the remnants of the roof aside and ploughing across the ruins. His hair was damp with sweat and his singed coat was smeared with dark, glistening patches of what could only be blood.

She slammed her hand over her mouth to stifle a whimper at the sight of him. She was on the verge of throwing her arms around him on impulse when he grabbed her by the shoulders and peered into her eyes, his expression dark.

'Are you okay?' he asked roughly. 'I *thought* you'd –' A haunted look crossed his face and he pressed his lips together.

She managed to nod. 'I'm okay.'

His eyes roamed over every inch of her, determinedly checking for mortal injuries. Finding none, he shuddered with relief and his shoulders sagged.

'Thank God,' he breathed. 'Time to go.'

He released her and hurried back the way he had come, his coat flying about behind him.

'Wait!' she said. 'Ronan is going to . . .'

She glanced over and trailed off. He'd gone. The joist had been rolled aside and Ronan had gone! But he still hadn't given her the name of Marianne's necromancer.

Something crackled, and she jerked around just as Crowley swore loudly. Ronan Bishop was leaning heavily on his brother's shoulder, his chest heaving and his face badly bruised. The dog handler had dragged him out. Elliot Bishop looked like he'd been through a mangle; his skin was a mass of cuts and burns. There was a tiny flame dancing along a mound of wood behind him, crackling and smoking gently. Elliot grinned. He sucked in a breath and exhaled forcefully, bending the flame in their direction. The flames leapt higher and ate into the timbers stacked all around. He waved at them venomously – and then was gone.

Fire now raced along the planks, consuming everything it

touched. Given the collapsed roof – the wood, the beams and joists – it was a death trap.

'We have to get out of here,' shouted Crowley. 'I can't put this out!'

'But . . . the dogs,' Alice said. 'They'll burn alive!'

She tried to tug him towards the main gate, where she could hear them whining, but he shook his head.

'Please,' he groaned. 'Just this once – *don't* be brave. Or *you'll* burn alive as well,' he yelled over the sudden roar of the fire. He was right. The fallen roof had blocked the main exit, and Elliot's flames were hurtling towards it, making it impassable. Choking black smoke curled away from the fire and funnelled up towards the open sky. The flames blazed through the rubble, sizzling and hissing and growing taller and more impenetrable with every second. They had to find a different way out – the second exit – *now*.

Crowley dragged her by the arm, slipping and sliding on the rubble. She turned her face away from the unbearable heat, but her neck nearly burned in the sweltering temperature. The air was too thin to capture a lungful. Her skin felt like it was going to melt right off her bones.

They skidded through the corridor and into the smaller court-yard. It was cooler here, but even by the time she'd turned around, the flames were catching up.

The door that led to the streets was unlocked; the Bishop brothers must have left through it only minutes prior. Crowley thrust her out through the exit, and she collapsed in a heap on the gloriously wet, cold pavement.

'Wait here,' he said.

'What?' she gasped. 'Where are you going?'

'The *dogs*,' he growled, striding back into the inferno without another word.

Alice staggered to her feet and raced back to the door, but fire blasted through it like a bonfire and pushed her back. She stared at it in shock. He hadn't been able to put out Elliot's fire. Could it burn him? Did his own legacy offer any defence at all?

She stepped away from the fiery exit and shivered into her coat. She couldn't seem to stop shaking. Her body was racked with shudders, her teeth chattering violently. Faltering, she stepped back, into the road. The warehouse's smashed windows were illuminated with flickering flames, quivering in the wind.

Dimly, she was aware of noise and footsteps, and distant sirens echoing through the city streets. The Runners would be here soon. She felt no concern. Prison, Jen, necromancers . . . She felt completely detached from everything. Untethered. The noise of the roaring fire drowned out every other thought.

Then the main gate burst off its hinges, exploding outwards with a thunderous boom. Alice reeled backwards, clutching at her throat as Crowley appeared in the gap like an avenging angel, his face streaked with charcoal and ash in his hair. He looked . . . *magnificent*.

A dozen cowed – but living – dogs poured out of the doorway behind him, fur blackened and singed, and Alice staggered forward to let him lean against her.

'This,' he said heavily, 'is why I prefer cats.'

18

There was something odd about her floorboards. Just under the edge of her bed, there was a dark knot surrounded by misshapen rings that spread outwards, like ripples in a pond. During Proctor's training session, she'd noticed a peculiar nodule in the centre of the knot. Now, a short twig appeared to be growing out of it.

She bent down on all fours and shuffled closer. The twig was an inch tall, with crusted skin. She poked it, and a chunk of it crumbled away. It had the consistency of a bad meringue.

'Polishing the floors?' asked Crowley. 'I suppose I could employ you as a housekeeper, now Risdon's thrown you out on your ear.'

Alice twisted to find him standing in the doorway.

'There's a branch growing out of my floorboards,' she said.

He raised an eyebrow. 'Between the exploding pipes and leaking ceilings, this house has always been susceptible to wet rot. That's likely just another fungus. I'll have it removed.'

She hesitated, unconvinced. 'I think it could be my fault the roof fell down at the dog fight – Ronan seemed to think so, even though I only hit the beam with my hand.'

Crowley frowned.

'And I thought he'd done it at the time, but what if *I* was the one who freed the dogs from those wooden barrels, not Ronan? And . . . that first day in the archives, when the begonia roots smashed the vase . . .'

'You think this is your handiwork as well?' he asked, flourishing a hand at the floorboards.

'I . . . Maybe.' She paused. 'Proctor said there are tests – trials – for House membership, so –'

'Forgive me,' said Crowley, 'but destroying a roof, some decrepit barrels, and a rotten floorboard strike me as typical of the Wyndham trail of carnage that follows you around – rather than a spectacular show of legacy strength.'

Well, what had she expected him to say? That the litany of wood-related disasters were proof she should be admitted to House Mielikki, and he'd take her there immediately? The memory of the folk music came back to her, swelling in her chest . . .

'What do you mean, typical Wyndham carnage?' she retorted, narrowing her eyes. 'I didn't ask for any of this. Everything that's gone wrong can be traced right back to that bloody box on my doorstep.'

'No,' he said, pinching the bridge of his nose as though the conversation was proving vexatious to his sinuses. 'Take responsibility. You powered off recklessly to the Bow Street Station cells, which led to your suspension for trespass. Somehow you managed to offend Proctor on your first day; you left me *weakened* so that I couldn't protect you from Bishop –'

She flushed. 'I said I was sorry about th—'

'Even your friend Jen wasn't safe from you,' he said carelessly. 'Your chaos saw her mown down by a car.'

All the breath rushed out from her lungs. He might as well have punched her in the stomach.

Crowley's face blanched; he'd realized he'd overstepped the mark. 'Alice, I didn't—'

'You can go now.'

She busied herself with her books, making a tidy pile with *Magellan's Nightjar Compendium*, *Trinity of the Mind, Body and Soul* and her drawing papers – she'd sketched Proctor's nightjar after their last session; her memory wasn't photographic, but it had never failed her when she put pencil to paper.

Crowley hadn't moved. He remained by the door, contrition in his eyes.

'Why did you come up here?' she said in a clipped voice. 'What did you want?'

'To talk about your training.'

Her icy gaze drifted over him. His nightjar was nowhere in sight. Why was he so determined to hide it from her? Proctor had said altering your nightjar's behaviour was difficult – but not impossible. Crowley had obviously mastered it, because she hadn't seen so much as a single feather. If she hadn't been able to hear it – the occasional flap of its wings and click of its beak – she might have doubted its existence.

'Maybe you're right,' he said reluctantly. 'Maybe you *are* a late bloomer and Mielikki's legacy is awakening – you're absolutely entitled to investigate that. But I would urge you to put it aside for now. Prioritize. You have a limited amount of time, and you should be devoting it to your aviarist learning and not becoming swept up in ideas about Mielikki. Mielikki's legacy will not help your friend.'

'Time,' she said. 'But exactly how much time *do* I have, Crowley? Maybe her soul has already left her body, so even if I bring her nightjar back from the moors, there's nothing left for it to guard.' It was a fear that had danced at the back of her mind for days.

His expression softened. 'There are avenues available to us, even if that is the case,' he said. 'A necromancer can summon the soul back from the moors. But they cannot persuade it to stay, caged in her body, without the nightjar there to prevent it escaping again. The nightjar,' he added, 'is *vital*.'

She sighed. 'Frankly, Crowley, your last plan didn't exactly go as we'd hoped. I don't want to rely on a last-ditch "avenue". It's time for me to put my own plan into action.'

'What . . . plan?'

She took a deep breath. 'I have to find Marianne and persuade her necromancer to help me. Thanks to Ronan Bishop, I have her address now.'

He flinched and then looked her square in the eye, enunciating slowly, 'No.'

She wanted to throttle him. 'Ronan said Marianne wants a door opened to the moors too. Maybe if she sees I want the same thing, we could work together. And maybe I don't need your help, or your permission for this. I'm an aviarist; maybe I could offer her something in exchange for—'

He snatched the feather out of her sleeve cuff.

'Do you see this?' he hissed. 'You think it makes you untouchable? One of only two known aviarists in the British Isles. You might be rare, but did you never stop to wonder *why* there are so few of you?'

'I . . .'

'Aviarists are revered by many, yes,' he said roughly. 'Because you can glimpse the most sacred part of us: the soul. But you can also reveal what should be private and untouchable. You can tell secrets. You can pry – and there are just as many who fear you for it. You're a danger. A threat to be eliminated.' He hesitated and returned the feather. 'Ask Proctor what happened to his eyes.'

'Someone . . . ?'

He nodded sharply, and dread coiled inside her stomach.

'If you storm into Marianne's vipers' nest and announce what you are, do not expect a warm reception. And with you dead, your friend Jen dies as well.'

Her momentary flare of excitement stuttered.

'Well, maybe it would be easier to just . . . let myself die,' she said challengingly. 'That's my fastest route to the Sulka Moors, after all.'

'That's a complete dead end.' He looked furious. 'Interesting that Marianne isn't volunteering to die in order to enter the moors, isn't it? She'd rather hide behind her so-called sacrifices.'

Alice hesitated, her eyes narrowed. 'So-called? You don't think they're really sacrifices?'

'I think Marianne dresses up murder as sacrifice and, as always, has her own motives.'

She nodded, uncertain of his meaning but growing tired of arguing.

'Trust me,' he said more gently. He dragged a hand through his hair. 'I'll find a way that doesn't involve the Fellowship.'

'I did trust you,' she said. 'But your plan failed. And Ronan can't open a door to the moors, but Marianne's necromancer can. I won't tell her what I am, if that makes you happy—'

'No.' His face was pale and taut with agitation. 'You don't understand what she's . . . what they're . . .'

Alarmed by his uncharacteristic discomposure, she put a reassuring hand on his arm. His shirt sleeves were rolled to the elbows, and his forearm was warm and strong beneath her palm. Crowley froze and glanced down at her hand. His eyes drifted up to meet hers and he gave her a searching look. Alice's throat dried out, and a thrill of nervous anticipation quivered in her stomach.

Then he stepped away and swallowed. 'You're right,' he said grudgingly. 'Of course. Marianne. It . . . must be done.'

They stared at each other for several moments before he nodded sharply. 'I will make the arrangements.'

He left abruptly, and Alice found herself following him out to the corridor, but he'd already swept down the stairs.

She closed her eyes, the blood pounding in her head, and leaned her forehead against the corridor wall.

What the hell was she doing? Why did he unsettle her so much? He could make her so cross at times, and at others she was just so *aware* of him.

'You okay?'

She spun around, startled, to see Sasha watching her. She was wearing a plastic anorak and had a towel slung over her arm.

'What?' Alice murmured, stepping aside.

'Just nod and say yes.'

She nodded. 'Er . . . Yes.'

Sasha grinned. 'Great. Glad we touched base.' She pulled open the bathroom door and slipped inside. 'Catch you later.'

'Wake up.'

Alice blinked sleep out of her eyes and stretched under the covers like a cat. This bed was so soft that—

'Wyndham, there's an oak tree growing from your floorboards. It's a Mielikki miracle.'

Her eyes flew open. A face was hovering over her, and she automatically yanked the covers up to her chin. Crowley. She squinted through the gloom, and he huffed and whipped the curtains open. There was a twig in leaf by her bed, but a distinct lack of actual tree. Early morning light blazed through the window, dazzling her, and she tugged the blanket right over her head.

'There's no bloody tree,' she said, her voice muffled. 'What do you want?'

The blankets were suddenly wrenched away and tossed onto the floor. Alice sat up with a gasp of indignation. She could have been naked under there!

'If you're determined to push ahead with your plan, we need to cover all bases. Rather than relying on someone else for transport, you're going to develop the ability to travel the doorways yourself.'

Her breathing quickened.

'I'm taking you to purchase a skeleton key,' he said, drawing himself up to his full height. 'You'll need one in the long run anyway. If you succeed in rescuing Jen's nightjar you'll need to be able to *return* with it, and to do that you must be able to travel home through a door. Doorway navigation is a vital skill.' He paused, and continued in a quieter tone. 'It will also give you a potential escape route, if things go wrong with Marianne. Get dressed. I'll meet you at the front door in ten minutes.' He paused to quirk an amused eyebrow at her. 'If you're even three seconds late, don't expect me to wait.'

He strode from the room, and she rolled her eyes. Well . . . *someone* wasn't much of a morning person, were they? Or an afternoon or evening person either, come to think of it.

'I'm ready,' she said, trudging down the stairs and pulling her ill-fitting new coat on over her jeans and jumper.

Crowley gave her the once-over as he stepped outside. 'If you say so,' he said, stifling a grin.

Instead of heading for the black door of the derelict building opposite, he started off down the street.

'Why aren't we using the doorways?' she asked.

He glanced over at her. 'Travelling can increase the heart rate. We want your body in its calmest state for this.'

What the hell was that supposed to mean?

'You will not say a word,' he said.

'Pardon?'

'That's a word,' he said in exasperation. 'Come on. Walk, and listen to my instructions.'

Play nice and he'll help you, she told herself as she trekked after him.

'You must resist the impulse to make small talk with the locksmith,' he said over his shoulder as he strode briskly along the pavement. 'Please do *not* make any mention of nightjars, Marianne, your suspension, the Lintuvahti or the Sulka Moors.'

'Why not?'

What was he going to do? Make her sign the Official Secrets Act, in case she blabbed about the colour of his nightjar, or how he liked his tea?

'Because I'm a private man, Alice. If he asks – as I'm sure he will – I'll tell him that you are an old friend visiting from London.' He gave her a contemplative glance. 'An old friend with . . .' He shrugged. 'I don't know. Leprosy. Or bird flu. He might not bother trying to chat if he thinks you're carrying a deadly infectious disease.'

'Yeah? Well, why don't you tell him you've got *swine* flu while you're at it?' she said. 'I'm sure he'll find that easy enough to believe.'

He chuffed out a laugh. 'Temper, temper.'

With a grin, he nudged her off the kerb and into the empty

road; her arms pinwheeled with shock as she was thrown off balance. He grabbed her waist to steady her and she clung to him reflexively. There it was again, the scent of pine smoke and cloves. She took a deep breath, inhaling him . . . Damn it! She reared backwards and hurried across the cobbles, away from him. What was wrong with her traitorous nose?

They walked in silence, and he led her down a crooked side street. It was unfamiliar, and she had no idea if it existed in her London. She noted Fortnum Family Investments as they passed: a shabby building with signs on the dark windows, advertising *Money-lending. Apply within*. It was in direct contrast to its brightly lit neighbour, Moores & Robinson Chandler's, which had the front door thrown open and the windows gently ablaze with the glow from hundreds of flickering display candles.

'Sod off!'

A man barrelled out of the chandler's doorway, chased out by a woman wearing a long leather apron and a fierce expression.

'We survived Edison and his lightbulbs,' she yelled. 'You can shove your bloody long-life candles!'

On the last angry syllable, every candle in her shop exploded. Alice stumbled backwards in shock. Roaring flames leapt from floor to ceiling as the tallow and wax bubbled. Golden light danced across the pavement and the air sizzled with suffocating heat. The whole shop was ablaze.

'Saints preserve us,' the woman growled. She hurried back to her shop, leaned into the flames and sucked in an impossibly deep breath. The fire died instantly, and the shop sank into darkness. She slammed the door shut.

'Did she suck out the oxygen?' Alice asked quietly.

Crowley didn't seem to hear. He led her past Derbyshire's Garden Perennials. Their display featured plants too young to sell, all sturdy green stems and shoots with buds that hadn't opened. But as Alice and Crowley passed, flowers burst out from the buds, blossoming so suddenly that a wave of unfurling rainbow petals accompanied them along the street, casting their musky scents into the air.

'It's like . . .' she breathed.

'Nature,' said Crowley.

Magic.

Alice glanced back at the sea of flowers, brightly coloured heads dancing in the breeze, and shook her head in astonishment – and longing. She could almost hear House Mielikki's mellow violin notes in her mind . . . Not looking where she was going, she smashed into a sandwich board directly in her path.

'Shit!'

She staggered sideways.

'You are the epitome of feminine elegance,' drawled Crowley. 'And thinking of your softer skills – don't engage Marianne in direct conversation either.'

'Excuse me?'

'Whatever you say to her, she'll use it against you. She's a liar and a cheat. Don't speak to her or listen to what she has to say. You're going for one thing only: to find her necromancer – and the other members might be able to give you that information anyway.'

She peered at him dubiously. 'It's going to be hard to ingratiate myself with them if I have to act mute around their leader . . .'

'Better mute than dead.'

'Your cheery optimism is so encouraging.'

'If you succeed, we'll toast a glass to your brilliance in every public house the Rookery has to offer. Satisfied?'

Alice pulled a face. Crowley would never admit to her brilliance in anything – which meant he thought she was doomed to fail.

The next street was the busiest yet. It was thronged with people, smartly dressed in their old-fashioned clothing. Almost all were wearing hats, and many were swinging umbrellas or canes. Newspapers were tucked under arms, and there seemed to be an unusually high number of moustache-wearers in the vicinity.

'She'll have a magical lock on the doors,' said Crowley. 'You won't be able to travel into the Fellowship's hideout directly.'

'Well, it would be bad manners if I did,' said Alice. 'If I suddenly materialized in her bedroom, she'd probably kill me before I got a word out, and who could blame her?' She glanced over at him. 'So how, exactly, do I get inside then? Disguise myself as—'

'You knock on the front door.'

She paused. 'I just . . . knock on the front door?'

He nodded. 'They will either invite you inside or refuse to answer.'

'That seems . . . surprisingly easy for a secretive death cult that regularly changes address to avoid the Runners.'

He shook his head dismissively. 'The problem is being allowed to *leave*. And no one reneges on their membership.'

She paused to look up at him. 'But I'm not joining, I'm only *visiting*.'

Crowley frowned, plainly unconvinced by her argument. 'My Pellervoinen blood gives me an advantage with the doors. And it's my hope that your skeleton key will also help with Marianne's door lock.'

'How?' she said. 'There's nothing special about *my* blood.'

He pursed his lips. 'Not yet, there isn't.'

She shook her head. 'But if I *can't* bypass Marianne's lock, and I *can't* leave—'

'You're as good as dead,' he said baldly. 'She'll add you to her list of sacrifices, valiantly throwing away their lives in honour of the Lord of Death and her secret machinations.'

'Well,' she said, shoving her panic aside, 'looking on the bright side, I *will* get some information to help Jen. Better than that, I'll find a necromancer who can open a door to the moors.' She looked at him for a reaction.

His expression was pained. 'I find your occasional optimism alarming. I much prefer your belligerent cynicism; it increases your chances of survival by at least ninety per cent.'

'This is the place?' Alice asked ten minutes later, staring up at the creaking sign. *Josef Skala: Surgeon & Master Marrower*. 'I thought we were going to a locksmith's. This looks more like ...'

She peered through the squared glass in the bowed shop window. There were two iron bedsteads covered in sharply ironed white sheets in the centre of the room, surrounded by shelves of medicine bottles, syringes, racks of knives, hacksaws and, between the two beds, an enormous brass contraption with wires and tubes spilling out of the top of it. It looked, in short, like some sort of medieval torture chamber.

'Josef Skala is an excellent surgeon,' said Crowley.

Her mouth fell open. 'But ... we're supposed to be going to a locksmith. To get a key.'

He raised an eyebrow and reached for the door handle. 'And so we are. A skeleton key. How else to make a skeleton key but to insert it into your bones?'

Alice remained outside as he entered the shop, rooted to the spot in horror.

'Well?' he called back to her. 'Do you want to travel or not?'

'Crowley!' cried a small, hunchbacked old man with a nest of wild grey hair. He had a surgical apron on and was wiping a blood splatter off his neck with a towel. 'How the devil are you?'

Crowley smiled with a trace of real warmth, and it was so genuine that Alice had to do a double take.

'I'm very well, Josef, thank you. And how are yourself and Mrs Skala faring?'

Josef tossed the towel onto a shelf and trotted over, to clutch Crowley in a blink-and-you'll-miss-it embrace. 'Not so bad,' he said.

'And Mrs Skala – she is recovered?'

'Oh yes,' he said. 'It was just a chest infection.'

'I thought she'd injured her hand,' said Crowley, frowning. 'The last time I was here, she was bandaged to her elbow.'

Josef smiled, for just a moment too long. 'It was nothing, really.' He turned to Alice and gave Crowley a broad smile. 'And who might your friend be?'

'I'm Alice,' she said. 'Nice to . . .' She spotted a bloody hand-print halfway down his apron and swallowed. 'Nice to meet you.'

He winked at Crowley. 'She's exquisite. I'm very pleased to see you with a—'

'We're just friends,' they both blurted out at once, and then glanced at each other suspiciously. Friends? Hardly. Whatever they were, it certainly wasn't that.

'Alice would like a skeleton key,' said Crowley. 'And I wouldn't trust anyone else with the procedure.'

'You flatter me,' said the old man, ushering her over to one of the iron bedsteads and unravelling a brass stethoscope. He gestured to her coat and she gingerly slipped it off. 'I had a fresh batch of donations in only last week,' he said. The cool metal of the stethoscope on Alice's back made her jump, and he patted her shoulder apologetically.

'Actually,' Crowley murmured, '*I* intend to be her donor.'

Josef dropped the stethoscope. It clattered to the floor and bounced off one of the bed's metal legs.

'You're offering to donate?'

Crowley gave a sharp nod. 'Only to her. You needn't think you can siphon off a few extra pints to fill one of those jars in your back office, old man.'

'As if I would!' He laughed loudly. 'But Crowley, this is remark-able!' He turned to Alice, his eyes bright. 'I don't know what you've done to him, my dear, but I couldn't be happier for you both. We must celebrate. I think I have a bottle of—'

'*Josef,*' Crowley warned. 'There's nothing improper between us, so please do not insinuate.'

'And why should it be improper?' he said, grinning broadly.

Crowley sighed and massaged his temples. 'How long will this take?'

'Four hours, or thereabouts,' said Josef. 'I suggest you make yourself comfortable.'

Crowley nodded and carefully positioned himself on the other bed. Josef hurried over and wrapped a tourniquet around his arm. Alice watched in mute horror as the little old man reached for a cannula with a long needle attached.

'Woah,' she said. 'You know, I'm not so sure I'm ready after all. You said I needed to feel calm, and actually—' She jumped to her feet.

Crowley's eyes snapped to hers, and she exhaled shakily.

Josef looked from one to the other. 'You're unfamiliar with the procedure?'

'The doorways respond to blood,' Crowley said patiently.

'Oh my God, this isn't helping!'

'You *can* be trained to navigate the doorways, but it takes many years of practice. And there are those – myself included – who were simply born with the ability.'

'Good thing too,' said Josef. 'Crowley here has been flee-ing to the Rookery since he was a frightened boy. I dread to think how miserable he'd have been if he couldn't use the doorways.'

Alice's eyes darted to Crowley, who was glaring at Josef with a furious expression on his face.

'Yes, *thank you*, Josef,' he said to the oblivious shopkeeper, his voice dripping with acid. 'As I was saying, some are born with the talent to travel. It's in the very marrow of our bones. We are our own skeleton key.'

She didn't like where this was going.

'I can pass on this skill to another by making a peripheral stem cell donation. Blood will be taken from me and transplanted to you, where it will eventually find its way to your bone marrow. The doorways should respond to the donated blood in your body. You'll need some recovery time, but you'll skip years of training, and you could be navigating within a fortnight.'

'Don't worry,' said Josef. 'I perform bone marrow transplants every day of the week.'

Bone marrow transplants?

'In just a moment, I'll put a central line into the big vein that leads into your heart,' Josef said kindly. 'You couldn't pass me that needle, could you, dear?' He waved at a solitary syringe, which looked more like a javelin. A sword. And the smiley-faced bastard was going to stab her with it.

Alice didn't remember leaving Josef's surgery. Or Crowley carrying her home, her head lolling against his chest with every footstep. She definitely didn't remember who had undressed her and put her to bed – though perhaps it was better to remain ignorant.

She rolled over, one eye flickering open in the darkened bedroom. What time was it? She fumbled for her bedside lamp, but her ribs ached and her arms were like limp spaghetti. She felt like she'd been kicked in the chest by a horse. The procedure had left her utterly zapped.

If she concentrated, she could almost hear the steady thump of her own heartbeat . . . her heart, which was pumping Crowley's blood around her body, seeping and spreading into the very marrow of her bones. She flushed in the darkness at the strange intimacy of it.

The sight of him lying casually on the bed flashed into her mind: his shirt unbuttoned at the neck and his sleeves pulled up to reveal the soft skin on the underside of his elbow. She'd watched him, his eyes closed, his throat exposed; vulnerable; the lines of his face utterly relaxed – despite the fact that his lifeblood was being drawn out of him and pressed into her.

There was a knock at the door. She opened her mouth to call out 'Come in', but her tongue felt so swollen that she only managed a grunt.

The door cracked open and Sasha strode in with a porcelain cup. She leaned over the bed, wearing a frown.

'Are you alive?' she asked suspiciously.

Alice managed a weak nod.

'Our next-door neighbour, Nella, made you this. It's willow bark tea – good for pain relief.'

Alice tried to push herself up, but her arms went from under her and she collapsed against the pillows.

Sasha sighed. 'I can't be your nursemaid. Sick people make me nervous.'

Alice croaked an unintelligible response. She tried to flap an arm to dismiss Sasha from the room, but the movement only made her wince in agony.

'Oh, fine,' Sasha said sourly. 'Here.' She slid a hand under Alice's head and pressed the cup to her lips, tilting the hot liquid into her mouth.

Alice grimaced at the bitter taste. She managed to spill half the tea on the bed covers but was too exhausted to care. Crowley hadn't even hinted that recovery would be *this* bad.

'Tastes vile, but thanks,' she murmured, flopping back onto the pillow. 'What time is it?'

'Late. Jude left for his night shift a couple of hours ago.'

Sasha's tightly curled hair spilled out from around a knotted headband, framing her face like a halo. She was wearing a pair of khaki dungarees with a blouse and her trademark military boots. She looked like a land girl, courtesy, no doubt, of Gribbon's Military Garments.

'So how are you feeling?' asked Sasha.

'Grim,' said Alice, her voice raw and cracked. 'How do I look?'

'Grim.'

There was a short pause. 'It's not catching, you know,' said Alice.

'I don't care about germs – I'm just wondering what to wear to your funeral.'

'Nice. I think you owe me a favour for that. To take my mind off the sickness?'

Sasha shrugged and plonked herself down on the bed, taking up more room than was strictly necessary. The necklace she always wore bounced out from her collar, and Alice squinted at it. The pendant was a shimmering gemstone set into a metal clasp.

'That's pretty,' she said. 'What's the gemstone?'

Sasha glanced down at it. 'Spectrolite. I never take it off; it's my talisman.'

'Talisman against what?'

Sasha's breathing stilled. 'Bad luck.'

'I could do with one of those right now,' mumbled Alice.

Sasha shook her head. 'Talismans should be personal to you. You need to take a reminder of your worst luck and turn it into something positive.' She clinked the pendant with her fingernail. 'I found this stone by a beach.'

Alice swallowed thickly, her mind immediately jumping to Sasha's memory of the drowning girl – Zara – and trying to piece this information together.

'Anyway,' said Sasha, slipping the necklace under her clothing, 'what's the favour?'

Alice glanced over at her copy of *Trinity of the Mind, Body and Soul* on the bedside table. 'Will you ... sit there while I meditate?' she asked, locating her feather and waving it at her visitor.

Sasha sighed loudly. 'God, you're weird. Fine.'

Alice focused on Sasha's nightjar, its busy eyes darting left and right as pin-sharp claws perched on the lampshade.

She shifted her gaze and closed her eyes. She'd tried meditation and relaxation techniques in her teens, when her nightmares had been filled with birds. This was very familiar ground. Gradually, her body fell limp. She was calm. Peaceful. *Harmless.*

The indistinct shape of Sasha's nightjar flickered through her eyelids as she opened her eyes. Harmless. She breathed steadily, imagining each exhalation releasing her benignity into the atmosphere and surrounding the bird.

Look away.

The nightjar continued to watch her. She tried to send her thoughts directly into its mind, persuading it, cajoling it. She'd already made a connection when she'd touched it.

Look away from me, little bird.

Its eyes never left her face.

'Look away,' she whispered aloud, driving the command through the glassy surface of its eyes, the windows to the soul.

It blinked. Once. Twice. Then it slowly turned its back on her. Alice gasped and her concentration slipped. The bird shot back round to stare at her, and Sasha grabbed her arm.

'What did you *do*?' demanded Sasha. 'Did you put me in a trance?'

Alice trembled with shock and excitement.

'It worked?' she gabbled. 'Did I –' Her words fled, and she succumbed to nervous laughter, which caused spasms of pain to rack her chest. But she'd done it – if only for a few seconds! She'd managed to cloak herself – to render herself unseen! The book was right!

'Did you do something to my eyes?' Sasha asked suspiciously.

Alice shook her head. 'No,' she murmured. 'Just . . . Doesn't matter,' she breathed into the pain. 'A trick, that's all. Have you ever been tempted to buy a skeleton key?' she asked, trying to distract herself.

'Don't need to,' Sasha replied. 'I've been practising for two years, and I'm pretty decent. Completely exhausts me, but—'

'Travelling?'

'Of course. Everything has a price, doesn't it? Travel too much, and it saps your energy so much that you can get stuck between the doorways. Permanently.' There was a warning in her voice. 'But you'll have no trouble, will you? Crowley's a brilliant traveller – best there is – which means you will be too.'

'Couldn't Crowley have donated for you too?' Alice asked weakly. 'Then you wouldn't have had to practise so much.'

'No chance,' said Sasha. 'I don't think Crowley has ever donated before. And anyway, sharing blood – with someone you know *really* well – isn't popular any more because . . .' She trailed away.

'What?' asked Alice, her voice laden with apprehension.

'It's nothing bad.'

'You've given me a disclaimer – of *course* it's bad.'

'It's not, it's just . . .' Sasha winced. 'When you've shared blood to make a skeleton key like *that*, well, the blood will always find itself.' She paused, frowning. 'Yeah, that's not very clear, is it? The doorways – they're sensitive to blood, so you and Crowley are sort of linked through the doors now. You'll be able to find each other. Even if you don't know where the other one is, you'll be able to press your hand to a door, your blood will sense Crowley's blood and it will take you to the last doorway he used. It's like Hansel and Gretel. Only, leaving a trail of blood behind instead of breadcrumbs.'

Alice's brow furrowed. 'But why is that a problem?'

'It's not,' said Sasha. 'It's nothing to worry about. Not. At. All.'

'*Sasha?*'

'Oh, fine. It's not usually a huge issue if your donor is truly anonymous. But if you know your donor . . .' She hesitated. 'Skeleton keys went out of fashion because people were misusing them. Checking up on each other, trying to catch each other having affairs.' She stood up quite suddenly. 'But that's not an issue with you and Crowley. I mean, you're not . . . married, or *together* or anything. He'd have no reason to want to check up on you, would he?'

A sense of uneasiness swirled in the pit of Alice's stomach. Always one step forward, two steps back. Why hadn't Crowley said that they'd be linked before she'd accepted his blood? He'd deliberately withheld all the facts. Now the blood that pumped through her bordered on something sinister. *Crowley may not be the lifeline you think he is.* Her thoughts kept circling to one thing: what was he – and his secretive nightjar – hiding from her?

19

Alice was awake and leafing through *Magellan's Nightjar Compendium* when Jude returned from his night shift. He was still dressed in his grubby work clothes when he opened her door. There was a smudge of oil on his tanned forehead, partially hidden by the messy hair.

'I've brought you some pain relief,' he said, pulling a travel flask from the storage bag of his wheelchair and pouring two cups of hot tea.

'Thanks,' she said, struggling upright against the pillows.

Jude's nightjar was perched leisurely on his shoulder, surveying her with quiet consideration. It shared the colouring of a sparrow – soft, muted browns – and it gave the impression of gentleness, if you avoided its sharp, intelligent eyes. She wanted to draw it for her collection.

'So Crowley tells me you want to join the Fellowship's human fodder programme,' said Jude.

She winced and shook her head. 'Don't believe everything he tells you.' She paused. 'Jude, why is it called Fellowship of the *Pale* Feather? They might expect me to know.'

He shot her a look, as though checking she was being serious. 'Death's nightjar is albino. White feathers, not brown like the rest. It's common knowledge around here. It's why the white feather is the Fellowship's emblem. It's also why the Fellowship have been desperate for an aviarist for years.'

She stared at him.

'The Fellowship . . . have been desperate for an aviarist?' she repeated slowly.

'Proctor didn't tell you?' He seemed genuinely surprised. 'The Fellowship have a *wild* theory that they can kickstart an apocalypse. They call it the Puhdistus – Finnish for the purge. They're desperate for it – they'd do anything to trigger that many sacrifices to the Lord of Death. But they believe it has to be initiated by Death's bloodline – his child . . . a child only an aviarist can identify.'

It was both ridiculous and familiar; she'd read as much in Proctor's files.

'Marianne's been searching for some sign of the Lintuvahti's offspring for years. Once upon a time, she was forcing Proctor to examine nightjars across the city, searching for the right one. You can see the attraction; the Fellowship worship the Lord of Death, who they've never set eyes on. But Proctor was supposed to be able to tell them, definitively, whether or not the Lintuvahti had a child. Their very own flesh-and-blood messiah, with an albino nightjar like his. And what's more, this child could bring on their Puhdistus – their apocalypse. Unfortunately for Marianne, someone dragged Proctor down an alleyway one night and poured scalding-hot oil into his eyes. That was the end of that.'

She shuddered involuntarily. 'You think that's why he was burned? Not because people are worried about aviarists revealing their secrets?' Crowley had said it was the latter; that's why he'd warned her not to tell Marianne she was an aviarist. And yet, all along, Marianne had *wanted* an aviarist. Why would he lie about that?

He took a sip of his tea. 'Hard to say. I think Proctor is perfectly capable of making enemies – without his aviarist skills even coming into the equation.'

'Proctor once made some accusations about Crowley,' Alice said. She tried to keep her tone light, but there was a stiff edge to her voice and her heartbeat suddenly seemed too loud.

'Proctor's paranoia got the better of him years ago,' said Jude.

'Maybe about the same time he lost most of his sight?' she pressed. Jude frowned. Alice studied him closely. 'How long have you known Crowley?'

'Too long,' he said. Then he smiled ruefully. 'Not long enough.'

'And do you trust him?'

'With my life. And if you trust him with yours, you'll stay far away from the Fellowship.'

'I can't,' she murmured, lapsing into silence.

'So what's your plan?'

'Oh, there's no part of my life that I've ever planned, which is why I keep making a royal hash of things.'

Alice slumped back against the headboard. 'However . . . I'm going to track down Marianne's necromancer,' she announced. 'And then I'll force him to do my bidding. That's my plan.'

'I'm not sure that's a plan,' said Jude. 'That's just an idea.'

She tipped her head back. 'Damn, I'm bad at this.'

'A plan would involve details. Such as, how are you going to get to the Fellowship? How efficient are you at using the doorways? Marianne bonds her cult members to her when they join – she controls them, all of them, like marionettes – so how will you persuade her to let you have the necromancer? There's got to be something in it for her.'

She sighed. 'I don't know . . .'

'This is where a plan would come in handy.'

She nodded, thinking. *Marianne wanted an aviarist.*

'Marianne is one of the most powerful hemomancers in the Rookery,' said Jude. 'She's dangerous.'

'Has Crowley persuaded you to talk me out of this?'

He smiled. 'No. Not exactly. And he used his own blood for the skeleton key, didn't he? He's trying to increase your chances of success.'

She stared up at the ceiling. Crowley had said Marianne would have a lock on the door to prevent people travelling directly into her base, which would also stop them leaving at will. That was . . . not at all sinister. She rubbed her eyes. On the plus side, Crowley's Pellervoinen blood would hopefully help her there . . . assuming she could actually use the doorways.

She turned back to Jude. 'Is there some sort of instruction manual for travelling?'

'I can do better than that – I can get you a teacher.'

Oh God, not Proctor again.

'Do it quickly,' said Sasha, three days later, when Alice was able to stand upright without excruciating agony. 'Once you've stepped through it you don't want to be in the void for too long. If you stay too long, you'll probably get stuck.'

Alice's hand loosened on the door handle. 'Wait. I can get stuck?'

'You won't get stuck. You just have to keep your concentration, that's all.' Sasha sighed irritably. It was becoming clear that she was a proponent of Proctor's teaching style: all stick, no carrot. 'Stop focusing on the negatives. Be bold. You know – boldly, go.'

'*Star Trek*?' Alice asked, amused.

'What of it? I grew up in Hackney, not the Rookery.'

Alice's eyes widened in surprise, but she decided now was not the time. 'Hang on. What if I go to open a door, it's locked, and *then* I get stuck in the void?'

'Stop dithering,' said Sasha. 'You're making me want to hurt you. And we're friends now, so that would be –' she grinned and made air quotes with her fingers – '"socially unacceptable".'

When Alice hesitated, Sasha sighed wearily. 'Some doors are always locked, okay? And some only open to specific people. Look, you don't need to know all the rules to travel less than ten metres. All you need to remember is: don't panic.'

'Right,' said Alice, swallowing thickly. She was so going to get stuck. 'Well . . . I suppose I'll . . . meet you there.'

Sasha's door. She concentrated on the shape of it in her mind's eye; on the colour of the paintwork; the shape of the hinges; the brass *2a* sign on the front. She opened her own door and stepped through.

It worked! Her stomach leapt with excitement. She was in the void. The in-between. Thank God for Crowley's genius blood! Now she just had to find the doorway to . . . Where was it she was going again? Sasha's . . . apartment door! 2a . . . *Sasha's door* . . .

She groped at the dark, empty space around her. Her fingers found nothing but fistfuls of air. Her pulse started to quicken, and she stumbled in a circle, her arms swinging desperately, searching for . . . something. Panic seized her chest and her breath hitched. She was going to suffocate in here.

Her hand brushed something spherical. A doorknob. She launched herself at it, clutching it desperately. *Please let it be Sasha's door* . . . A door materialized, growing out of the darkness. She twisted the doorknob, pushed forward . . . and dived through.

'Congratulations,' Sasha said, catching her on the other side. 'You did it.'

A smile spread across Alice's face. 'I did, didn't I?'

'Ready to go try again?'

She nodded.

'Kitchen,' said Sasha. 'I'll meet you there.'

She ended up in the bathroom.

'Bollocks.'

'Damnit!' Alice growled with frustration and slammed the door shut. Again. Eleven times she'd prepared to step into the void, and eleven times she'd just revealed the bathroom with its sink, anorexic bar of soap and ancient toilet.

'Perhaps . . . you're having second thoughts about meeting Marianne,' said Crowley, who was leaning against the corridor wall, a concerned look in his eye.

'I'm not.'

This was the moment. Finally. Days of travelling practice within Coram House and dozens of attempts to blind Sasha and Jude to her presence had led to this. Crowley had removed the block on outside travel from the house, to make it easier for her novice skills. Today, she was going to the Fellowship. She felt one step closer to Jen's nightjar.

'You're not ready,' he said. 'If you rush in before you can protect yourself, then—'

'I don't understand,' she interrupted. 'It was working.'

'*Within the house*,' he said, his expression growing tense. 'Outward travel is always erratic to begin with. Perhaps it would be best to do more practice.'

'Or perhaps your special Pellervoinen blood isn't all it's cracked up to be,' she retorted. 'And . . . why didn't you tell me about the *side effects*?' she continued, her voice thick with accusation. She'd been in too much pain to confront him for days, and she'd needed to pour her energies into practice. She'd unwittingly started to trust him, too. But now, a simmering anger burned at the edges of her mind.

His brow creased. 'What side effects?'

'That your donation for my skeleton key means we're linked,' she said in a brittle voice. 'That we'll always be able to find each other.'

The mood changed. Any hint of softness or concern gone, he gave her a flat, dead stare.

'You wanted a key, and I arranged one for you.'

'You lied.'

He blanched. 'I . . . did not.'

'You didn't tell me the full truth. It's the same thing.' She paused. 'Are you going to use the link to spy on me?'

His eyebrows drew down. 'I assure you, the day-to-day inanities of Alice Wyndham hold no interest for me whatsoever.'

'But the key *is* going to make it easier for you to keep track of me, isn't it?'

'Yes,' he said. 'Of course it is – that's the whole point! And the link is reciprocal, which means you'll be able to keep track of me. If you're so suspicious, maybe you should use the link to spy on *me*.'

'I just don't understand why you didn't mention it,' she said. 'If you had nothing to hide.'

He shook his head impatiently. 'I didn't say I had nothing to hide. We all have something to hide. The reason I insisted on using my blood was to help you.' His eyes burned with injustice. 'A drop of my blood will give you a fighting chance of escaping

Marianne's with the necromancer. And if it's not enough, I'll come for you and break the door down myself.' He shook his head bitterly. 'Besides which, since you're practically an endangered species, I thought that if you were ever hurt or attacked – anywhere – then I could use the blood link to find you and keep you safe. *For Sylvie's sake.* Satisfied?'

Her cheeks pinked, but she powered on. 'If it's that easy for you to open a door to the Fellowship, why don't you just come *with* me? We'll stand a better chance together.'

His face paled. 'I didn't say it was *easy* for me. There are things . . . You don't . . .' His lips pressed together tightly and he spun away from her. Eyes wide, she watched mutely as he wrenched open the bathroom door. This time, it did open to blackness.

'There,' he said. 'You're welcome.'

Silence swallowed them whole, and she closed her eyes.

'I'm . . . sorry,' she said. 'I didn't want it to happen like this – leaving for the Fellowship with angry words. I'm just . . .' She shook her head. She wasn't ready. Not for any of this. But maybe that was for the best: no thinking, just doing. She fumbled in her jeans pocket for Sylvie's feather and discreetly transferred it to her sleeve.

'Why was Sylvie so keen to keep me safe?' she asked quietly.

'Because she knew you were destined for her feather. Destined to be her successor. Destined to be on the radar of Vin Kelligan and the Beaks. It was a burden to her that she would be putting you in danger.'

'And now I'm your burden, am I?'

She looked up at Crowley. He was staring at a spot over her shoulder.

'No,' he murmured. 'Your safety isn't a burden.'

He lowered his gaze to hers, and there was a look of such powerful longing in his eyes that her cheeks burned and her mouth grew dry. A sudden and violent flood of nerves made her breathing shallow and her heart race.

'If I can't leave the Fellowship's building, you'll come?' she whispered.

'I will.'

'What if—'

'Trust me.'

His words hung in the air. *Trust me.*

And just like that, the moment passed. His expression changed and he withdrew, pulling himself behind the shuttered mask of indifference he so often wore. He cleared his throat and stepped through the doorway, into the void.

'Well?' he said, gesturing for her to enter. 'This is what you wanted, isn't it?'

Alice couldn't fight the warm buzz of excitement in her stomach as she stepped through, placing them inches apart. *Butterflies.* How could this abrasive man, with all his secrets, possibly be giving her butterflies? So what if . . . if the occasional glimpses of fire in his eyes hitched her breath? It was ridiculous. *She* was ridiculous. What would Jen say when she told her? Her stomach lurched. Probably, *What the hell are you doing, developing inappropriate crushes? Especially when I'm wasting away in a hospital bed and you're about to meet a death cult?* The butterflies evaporated.

'Will you check on Jen for me?' she asked suddenly. 'Just . . . make sure she's still . . .'

He sighed. 'If it will reassure you, yes.'

'And my parents,' she added.

Crowley allowed the door to close, and they stood silently in the dark for several long moments before she spoke.

'You know which door?' she asked.

'Yes.'

With the Fellowship constantly on the move to conceal their location, it would have been almost impossible to find them without the address Bishop had given her. But since they had it, Crowley had been out on a reconnaissance mission to select a nearby doorway.

'Remember, get only as close to Marianne as necessary. Believe nothing she says, and tell *no one* you are an aviarist.'

'Okay,' she said quietly. Crowley wasn't an aviarist; he had no way of knowing she was lying to him.

He looked down at her, a frown on his face. He opened his mouth to speak, and she steeled herself for his good-luck message, or useful parting advice, but his jaw snapped shut again and he stepped away.

'Aren't you—' Alice began, but he flung open the door and a shaft of blinding white light poured into the void. She stepped out, blinking furiously, onto a pavement. There was a row of familiar white houses opposite. She'd been to the markets near here in her London and had walked the streets – crammed with envy-inducing millionaires' houses – but . . . dilapidated was one way to describe *these* houses. Unholy mother of dumps was another.

The white paint was peeling off the walls of number twenty-nine, opposite. And the frontage was a jungle of trash and broken paving stones, furred with moss.

'So I just . . . knock on the door?' she said faintly, looking back at Crowley.

'Yes. It will either admit you or remain closed.'

'If there's some kind of password, you might have said earlier.'

'You may need to offer something to Marianne,' he replied stonily. 'A small reassurance.'

'Like what?' she asked, though she thought she could make an educated guess.

'Just knock,' he said, 'and we shall see.'

With one last glance in his direction, Alice took a deep breath and crossed the road. She crept up the stairs to the front door and paused. There was a stain on the woodwork. The door was black, so it was difficult to make out what it was, exactly. She dabbed her index finger into the liquid and pulled it back to examine it. Her fingertip was covered in congealing, rust-coloured blood.

Horrified, Alice hastily wiped her finger on her sleeve. She took a moment to gather her nerve, then grabbed the cast-iron door knocker. But as she knocked, raised notches oscillated and pierced her skin, leaving bloodied grooves in her palm. She hissed in surprise and snatched back her hand. So *this* was Marianne's small reassurance; to enter the home of a hemomancer, you had to gift her with some of your blood.

There was a click and the door shuddered open. A man's face appeared, shrouded in gloom from the hallway, his plain, dark nightjar visible over his shoulder. Alice acted instinctively, summoning the mental serenity she'd become familiar with in her sessions with Jude and Sasha. She smothered her panic. Her breathing evened out as she centred herself, and she stared calmly at his nightjar. *Look away*, she compelled. The bird slowly turned its back on her, and the man blinked in confusion as her cloak hid her from sight. She stepped to one side as he swiped a hand at the space in front of him; to all intents and purposes, she'd just vanished.

He paused for a moment, before shrugging and shuffling away – apparently deciding he'd imagined her. Alice gently caught the door before it closed behind him, and waited until he'd disappeared into the depths of the house.

She paused on the front step and glanced back at Crowley. He was watching her from the doorway across the road, his face impassive. She stepped into the hallway and glanced back once more, almost daring Crowley to stop her. But instead, he gave her a short nod, turned and departed through his doorway. Left to her fate – whatever that might be – she strode purposefully into the house.

20

It was like a Tardis. Dozens of rooms seemed to unravel before her, all of them sparsely furnished and lacking in comfort. Men and women were scattered throughout the building – some lying slumped on the floor, catatonic, and others sitting at tables, engaged in frantic debates. She edged cautiously along the hallway and poked her head into the living room. The air was thick with suffocating herbal smoke. She slipped back out into the blessedly cool hallway and sucked in a deep breath.

'I'm Bridget.'

Alice started. A small blonde woman with scraped-back hair and freckles was standing at her elbow; her nightjar was staring into space, glassy-eyed like a stuffed toy. Alice was just debating whether it would cause too much alarm to cloak herself again when Bridget spoke.

'Marianne knows you're here,' she said. 'Go to her.'

Alice's brain buzzed with nervous energy. But she hadn't even managed to get her bearings yet – and besides, it was the necromancer she wanted, not Marianne. Bridget gestured at a narrow, near-vertical staircase. Alice swallowed thickly – what choice did she have? – and took the stairs two at a time. She paused at the top, her eyes sweeping the cluster of doors along the landing. Silence. Which room was Marianne's?

Sylvie's feather was tucked into the inner cuff of her shirt sleeve, so it was touching her skin. She took a deep breath and tried to clear her mind. The rise and fall of her chest slowed, and the hairs on her arm stood on end as she listened . . .

There! Was that a flutter of wings? Her breathing sped up, and she hurried over to the door opposite. There was *someone* inside. She was sure of it. She exhaled softly, steeled herself and rapped on the door. She pushed it open without waiting for an answer and strode inside.

It was empty.

No Marianne, no furniture, no windows . . . *No windows?* She inhaled sharply and spun around to the door . . . but the door was gone. She was in a room with no entry or exit. A concrete box. She was trapped. Dread trickled down her spine. Was this a test? Or a punishment for trespassing, like in the Bow Street cells?

Alice pressed her lips together and lifted her chin. It didn't matter what it was; she was inside the heart of the Fellowship now, and she was going to make the most of it, for Jen's sake.

She began to explore the walls: cracked and crumbling, but bearing painted romanticism-style depictions of the most extraordinary scenes. Floor to ceiling, the paint was smeared directly onto the walls; outside an art gallery, she'd never seen anything like it.

A dark landscape, blotted with shadows, was stretched across one wall, dramatic clouds framing the image of a desolate desert city. Smudged trees towered over small white-washed houses. Weeping men and women were slumped on the steps outside, clasping each other, while sightless children lay sprawled in the dirt. A colossal shadow, shaped like a claw, reached across the scene, dark fingers creeping through the city streets and doorways. Above the trees, a white nightjar watched the deadly shadow, wearing a look of triumph. Alice's eyes roamed greedily across the wall. She'd always loved the work of J. M. W. Turner, and whoever had painted this artwork had tried to replicate his style: bold colour strokes, wild landscapes and an ethereal play of light.

The adjacent brickwork featured a huge depiction of a dark-haired woman lying on a clifftop. The wind raged below, scattering broken ships and sailors across the ferocious waves. One half of the woman's face was a skull. She rested on her elbows, a baby spilling out from between her legs as she gave birth in the storm; beside her, seven newborn babies lay discarded on the rocks, while another suckled at her breast, leaving her torso withered and rotting. It was beautiful and terrible all at once. Alice reached out a hand to trace the crooked horizon line, which split the waves and sky in two.

'Magnificent, isn't it?'

She spun round. A woman stood a few feet away, watching her carefully. Marianne. It had to be. She was a tall, lithe brunette with a streak of greying hair at her temple; her face was bird-like and her body so devoid of fat that if you touched her you'd probably cut yourself on her bones. Dozens of bracelets hung loosely from her wrists, and a brightly coloured ring adorned every finger. *She looks like a magpie*, thought Alice.

'The tenth plague,' said Marianne, her voice deep and velvety. She raised a casual hand to the first wall painting. 'The Angel of Death slips into the homes of the Egyptians and steals the life from all of the firstborn.' She stepped closer to the painting, smiling at the dreadful scene.

Alice knew the story. It was from Exodus in the Old Testament and the defining story behind the Jewish Passover. The Egyptians were keeping the Israelites as slaves, so God sent nine plagues to Egypt to free them. Nothing worked until the tenth plague, when the Angel of Death was sent to kill all the Egyptians' first-born children. The Israelites put blood on their doors so that Death would know to *pass over* them and spare their children. Alice frowned and looked down at her fingertip; there had been congealed blood on the Fellowship's door.

'But the nightjar doesn't appear in the biblical story,' said Alice, gesturing at the image of a pale bird sitting in the trees.

Marianne ignored her. She turned abruptly, and Alice's attention shifted to track her as she stroked her hand across the other wall, her fingers caressing the face and skull of the woman giving birth.

'And this is Loviatar,' she said softly. 'According to the Finnish myths, she's the blind daughter of Tuoni, of Death. Made pregnant by the wind, she became the mother of diseases: Pleurisy, Fever, Cancer, Colic . . . nine, in all. The one she's breastfeeding, sapping the life out of her, is Consumption. She offers herself up as nourishment for her children, and in doing so she happily wastes away. An allegory of perfect motherhood, don't you think?'

Marianne suddenly moved closer to Alice. Surprised, Alice stepped backwards, her heart thumping. She hit the wall as Marianne towered over her, a faded aristocratic beauty with a smile like a serrated knife. Alice had the sensation of a spider examining the fly trapped in its web.

She was not a young woman. Mid-forties, though the too-pale make-up powder and heavy mascara made her look a decade older. If she was chasing her youth, she was failing terribly. Her eyes were shark-like. Small and icy cold. Alice's skin prickled with dislike.

'But this,' she said, 'is the best of all.' Her fingers went to Alice's chin and tilted her head back. A third painting bore down on her from the ceiling. Marianne spun Alice around, her sinuous hands gripping her shoulders from behind and forcing her to examine the picture.

'A little glimpse of the future,' she said, her soft voice seeping into Alice's ears like a noxious gas.

The painting showed a devastated version of the Rookery: the city a dark, ravaged wasteland, buildings empty, swollen clouds choking the sunlight and the streets littered with corpses. Haphazard brushstrokes showed a dark figure standing over them, the wind whipping at his cloak.

'The coming purge,' said Marianne.

'Purge,' Alice repeated, staring up at the painting. 'The . . . Puhdistus? This is what you think Death is going to do? Kill everyone, like . . . an apocalypse? The tenth plague – but on a bigger scale?'

Marianne swatted the question away with a bony hand.

'The Lintuvahti may once have been an executioner. But not any more.' She glanced at the Exodus plague painting and re-focused on Alice. 'He's preoccupied by his own kingdom – a kingdom we're all destined to inhabit eventually.'

'Exactly!' said Alice, seizing on this gap in Marianne's insane logic. She wanted information from Marianne – solid information – but this was all starting to sound like the most ridiculous fantasy. *Apocalypses?* The *Lord* of Death? 'If everyone dies and goes to the moors eventually,' said Alice, 'what's the point in a purge? All it does is speed things up.'

Marianne's face darkened. 'Dying is compulsory. It requires no effort at all. For death to have meaning, it must be a sacrifice – something of value, wrenched away. There's always been honour in sacrifice.' She exhaled smoothly. 'The Lintuvahti doesn't *need* to waste his time ending our petty human lives. It's beneath him. And there are others who'd gladly perform such pleasures on his behalf.'

'Others?'

'Certainly. Only the purest can carry out the purge in his name.' Marianne gave her a pitying smile. 'Only his blood – his children – can act as his proxy. With my help, he'll send his children among us and they'll cleanse all life from the world, on his behalf. It will be our ultimate gift to him.'

Crowley was right. She was a madwoman . . .

The manic zeal on Marianne's face dissolved, and she straightened herself, suddenly businesslike.

'Now then. Given the efforts it must have taken to track us down,' Marianne said lightly, 'I'll assume you're here for something of great importance to you.'

Alice hesitated before croaking, 'Yes. I'm looking for some help.' Crowley was going to kill her for this – assuming Marianne didn't beat him to it.

'Then let us retire somewhere more comfortable,' said Marianne, withdrawing from Alice's personal space.

She strode towards the wall bearing Loviatar's image, and – Alice blinked rapidly – the brickwork slid aside, stones pivoting outwards and mortar dust blooming from the gaps as a hole opened up in the wall. Without pausing to break stride, Marianne marched effortlessly right through it. The bricks began to reassemble themselves, returning to their original positions, and Alice hurried after Marianne before the hole closed up.

The room she found herself in was so warm it was disorientating. It was busy with rugs, silk cushions and swathes of luxurious blankets on padded Queen Anne chairs. There were trinkets covering every surface: gold candlestick holders, hand-carved ornaments and gilded boxes. Two shelves were cluttered with boxes of sweetmeats, floury breads, cheeses and wines.

Alice stood at the edge of the room, breathing lungfuls of tepid, heavily scented air and trying very hard to keep her wits about her. Marianne surveyed her with a sly look on her face.

'Well?' she said. 'What's it to be? News from a loved one? Instructions about how to find your inheritance? Or perhaps you want to send a message?' Marianne smiled – a thin, reptilian smile. 'Yes. You're one of those, aren't you? Who died?'

Alice's mouth opened and closed. She shook her head. 'No one.'

Marianne appraised her for another long, uncomfortable moment, then folded herself elegantly onto a Queen Anne, her hands draped lightly over the armrests. The chair sat in the corner of the room like a throne.

'My time is precious,' said Marianne, 'so tell me what you *want*.'

Was this how the leader of the Fellowship earned her living? She sold her services as some sort of psychic who could speak to the dead? But . . . she was a hemomancer, not a necromancer.

Alice stepped further into the room. Marianne Northam's nightjar, which she could now see clearly, was a muscular thing with beady, unblinking eyes and wide, flattened feathers. It held itself in a proud, superior pose, perched on the back of the chair. The nightjar didn't endear Alice to its owner.

'I need to know how to travel to the Sulka Moors,' said Alice. 'I want . . . I'd like to speak to your necromancer. Please.'

The nightjar flapped anxiously before quickly regaining its composure. Marianne, meanwhile, stared at Alice with a bored expression on her face.

She sighed gently. 'Poor girl. You're confused. I can contact whoever it is you're mourning, but you can't *visit* them. The Sulka Moors are not a cemetery.'

She smiled again, and Alice shivered.

'Let me help you make peace with your loss,' said Marianne, her voice soothing. 'Sit. Make yourself comfortable.' She gestured at a pile of embroidered silk cushions on the floor, but Alice remained standing. Marianne rose from her chair and swept over to a narrow set of drawers. She retrieved a small velvet box and withdrew a brass-tipped scalpel from it.

Alice eyed the implement warily.

'It's a lancet,' said Marianne, rapping it with her fingernail. 'The message from your loved one must pass through me to you. I'm merely the channel, but you and I must be connected by blood for the message to travel between us.'

Her nightjar betrayed her. It was a lie, a ruse to get her hands on the blood.

Marianne smiled gently. 'I promise – it won't hurt at all.'

'No,' said Alice, standing straighter. 'I don't need a seance. I don't need to speak to anyone in the moors. I need to find a way to travel there without dying. *That's* the help I need.' Her heart slammed against her ribs in anticipation. 'You have a necromancer who can open a door for me. Ronan Bishop told me. I need to meet them.'

Marianne's face tensed, and she stood as still as stone. 'You made a mistake,' she said, 'coming here alone. Making demands, offering nothing in return.'

'I *can* offer you something.'

Marianne's eyes searched Alice's face. 'What could you possibly have that I want?' she murmured.

Alice swallowed thickly, her one ace card on the tip of her tongue.

'I'm . . .' *Time to blow Crowley's advice out of the water*, she thought. 'I'm an aviarist.'

There was a stunned silence, and Marianne's nightjar fluttered its wings in agitation.

Alice calmly watched Marianne's face for a reaction, expecting . . . She wasn't sure. Excitement, maybe? But instead, she only looked horrified. Wasn't she supposed to be pleased? Finally, an aviarist she thought she could use?

'I don't have time for your lies,' Marianne said quietly.

'I'm not lying. I can see your nightjar right now. It's—It's quite stocky – strong. It's standing on—'

'Shut up!' Marianne snapped.

'I can prove it.'

'I don't care.' A mottled blush crept up Marianne's neck, exposing her discomposure. 'I no longer *need* an aviarist.'

Frowning, Alice pulled back to study Marianne's nightjar. She seemed to be telling the truth. Had Jude got this *wrong*? Her pulse quickened; she'd gambled her safety on this.

'I thought . . .' She trailed away.

'What?' Marianne challenged. 'What did you think?'

'I thought that you would . . .' Her mouth was suddenly too dry.

Marianne grinned scornfully. 'You thought I'd find you useful? Well, I hate to disabuse you of that notion, but I don't.'

'But the Lintuvahti's bloodline. Don't you need help to identify the right person . . .' said Alice, backing away. 'For your purge . . .'

'Which is no concern of yours,' said Marianne. She gripped the lancet more tightly. 'My circumstances have changed. I'm looking to the future now.' She exhaled slowly, steadying her composure,

and looked at Alice with a placid expression. 'It may comfort you
to know that your sacrifice will be gratefully received.'

Sacrifice?

Every muscle in Alice's body tensed. Her hearing sharpened
and her vision narrowed to the woman calmly approaching her,
her skeletal fingers clutching the lancet. The blade caught the
light and glinted menacingly.

Alice prepared to launch herself at Marianne's cord. The only
weapon she had. It looped down between them as she approached.
It was incandescent and so very close. She glanced up at the
muscular bird. Its imperious stance was completely at odds with
Marianne's sickly smile.

She began to understand. Marianne controlled her followers,
bound them to her . . . It was the lancet. Marianne was going
to use it to worm her way into Alice's blood. She was planning
to use hemomancy to brainwash her . . . to persuade her to sacrifice herself. She could almost imagine how it would happen.
A soothing voice. A gentle nudge . . . Marianne held sway over
her followers because, once her blood was in their system, they
could be persuaded to believe anything, with just a few soft
prods.

The musky incense in the room made it hard to concentrate.
Alice's thoughts were like smoke, drifting away from her. *Defend
yourself!* She tried desperately to gather her convictions close, so
she could act, but action seemed impossible. Sluggish and heavy,
her body was drowning in quicksand while her untethered mind
floated away.

Alice didn't protest as Marianne swept closer. She shook herself in a bid to stay alert in the suffocating, scented heat, but the
incense burned her eyes and pressed on her lids like a weight.

'Don't bother fighting it,' said Marianne. 'You bequeathed

your blood to me when you entered the building. Just a drop. Just enough to . . . hold you still.'

She stroked Alice's cheek with the most exquisite gentleness. Alice's vision blurred and she moaned incoherently. *Awake . . . Stay awake!*

'If you give me a little more, you'll feel such wonderful peace.' Marianne brought up the lancet and traced the sharp tip over Alice's throat, along the trachea . . . sweeping around the curves of her collarbones . . . past the temples . . . sliding up towards her hairline . . . The sharp point pinched the skin, sending her nerve sensors into a frenzy.

Move! Now!

Panic stirred in Alice's chest. Adrenaline rolled through her body like a wave, smashing through her inertia. Her eyelids flew open and she gasped, turning her body, preparing to twist sideways.

But Marianne was quick. She lunged forward and her nightjar soared around their heads. Alice glanced up at it, momentarily distracted, as the lancet carved through the air . . . and sliced open the back of her neck.

She gasped and stumbled into the wall, face-first. She bit her tongue with a whimper. In a daze, she swept her hand to her neck and flinched as a searing bolt of pain hit home. Blood pumped from the gash and seeped into her collar. She pressed down hard as glossy ribbons of blood poured through her fingers and splattered onto the stone floor.

'You . . . You . . .' she babbled.

The stabbing pains in her neck were pulsing harder, sending thunderclaps of agony through her body. The back of her shirt was wet, and the hair at the nape of her neck was matted with blood.

Through her confused stupor, Alice registered that Marianne was watching her silently. She had made no move to advance her attack and was staring at her, not in triumph but horror.

'His blood,' Marianne rasped.

The room juddered. Alice couldn't tell if she was trembling, or Marianne, or both.

'You have . . . his blood.'

Alice opened her mouth to speak, but the room swam precariously and she pitched over at the waist. The stone floor rose to meet her and she turned her face away, bracing for impact.

With a strangled hiss, Marianne darted closer, and Alice flinched in expectation of a fresh assault. But strangely – inexplicably – Marianne reached out and . . . caught her. Alice's vision flickered. Her breathing deepened. The world shrank to a black dot and swallowed her whole.

21

Cold. That was her first sensation as she woke, her cheek pressed against a layer of cool silk, on a chaise longue. The air was sharp now, its frigid barbs driving into her bones, peeling the warmth from her skin. She pushed herself upright and wrapped her arms around her chest to quash the violent shivers rolling through her body. Fear had numbed the pain in her neck.

She appeared to be in a living room. It was immaculately laid out. Decadent wine-red curtains draped to the carpet; a round table and cushioned chairs sat to one side, and a staggering marble fireplace dominated the room. The room was, in fact, so immaculate she doubted it was ever used. The firebox was barren and there was no ash in the grate. The sash windows, which had been thrown open like gaping mouths, rattled with a fierce wind, leaving the room so cold as to be utterly inhospitable.

'He sent you in here for me.' Marianne swept out from the corner of the room, where she'd been waiting in the shadows. 'I barred the door to stop him getting inside, so he's sent you in, like a Trojan Horse.' Her clipped voice was glacial, and the temperature in the room dropped even further.

Alice frowned through her confusion and cautiously reached

for the wound on the back of her neck. She prodded the skin and hissed at the awful tenderness.

'Leave it,' Marianne said tersely. 'I stopped the blood loss. Don't aggravate it.'

The wound was closed. Only a ragged scab hinted that she'd ever been slashed with a scalpel.

'Why?' murmured Alice. 'Why did you . . . fix it?'

'Why are you here?' asked Marianne, dismissing the question.

'I told you,' she said. 'I need your necromancer.'

Marianne's mouth pressed into a hard line, and the deep red lipstick crinkled and smudged at the corners.

'Why?'

Alice hesitated before answering. Crowley had warned her against revealing too much – but Crowley wasn't here now, and Jen couldn't afford for her to waste time. 'My friend is in a coma,' she said carefully. 'Her nightjar is in Death's menagerie, and it has to be rescued. I need to go to the moors to find it.'

Marianne frowned. 'It sounds like your friend is cheating my Lord. All of our deaths belong to him.'

'Oh really?' Alice countered. 'Yours too, I suppose?'

Marianne stared at Alice, her eyes searching. 'Yes. Eventually,' she said after a moment. 'When the timing is appropriate, it would be an honour to go to him. We're his chosen few.'

A fresh draught exploded through the open windows and blasted across the room, leaving Alice racked with tremors. She felt as though she were caught in a slipstream. The chilled air burned her throat, and she ducked her head, seeking warmer air in the depths of her upturned collar.

'Whose Trojan Horse do you think I am?' she asked, her voice muffled. 'Crowley's?'

'You have his blood,' said Marianne. 'Diluted, but it's there just the same. Oily. It slides away when I try to grasp it.'

'He donated for my skeleton key,' said Alice. 'Why have you barred the door against him? What are you worried—'

'He doesn't *worry* me,' she said, her back stiffening. 'I tolerate his existence in the Rookery perfectly well. But if he's sent you in here to get me, then he's changing the rules we play by. If you—'

'I came to you for help,' said Alice. 'No other reason.'

Marianne stared at her, her roaming eyes subjecting her to a full scrutiny.

What was the history between Marianne and Crowley? Was this why Crowley had been so opposed to her seeking out Marianne? *Crowley may not be the lifeline you think he is.*

'Very well,' said Marianne. 'I'll help you.'

Alice's chest expanded. She *was* going to help, despite Jen 'cheating the Lintuvahti out of a death'? She tensed, waiting for the other shoe to drop.

'But there will be conditions.' *Of course.* 'My necromancer, August Rhone, is not here at present,' said Marianne. 'You will retrieve him and bring him here to me.'

'I . . . What?' said Alice, deeply confused by this unexpected turn of events. The necromancer wasn't even here? 'Where is he?'

Marianne smiled coldly. 'The Bow Street Station cells.'

Alice's mouth fell open.

'I can't open locked doors within the station,' said Marianne. 'But Crowley can. And his donation for your skeleton key means that you'll have that same access – at least, for a time.'

'But—'

'August was arrested on a minor charge some time ago. He ought to have been released within twenty-four hours, but, instead, he appears to be facing remand at Newgate Prison. I can't allow him to be sent there. You'll bring him here, and he will open a door to the Sulka Moors.'

She wanted her to break a criminal out of the cells, right under the Runners' noses? Alice's brain worked at lightspeed, processing the frankly preposterous idea and checking for holes – of which there were plenty. But . . . just supposing it was in any way possible – why couldn't she retrieve this necromancer and just steal him away? Why would she even consider returning him to Marianne?

'Once you've secured him,' said Marianne, who seemed to have sensed Alice's thoughts, 'I'll tell you what I know of the menagerie, the moors and its security measures.'

Alice's schemes slammed into a brick wall. 'Security measures?'

'Of course,' said Marianne. 'You didn't think you could simply wander into the moors as you pleased, did you? They have a failsafe to prevent unwanted visitors. It's far better protected than Bow Street Station.' She paused and offered Alice a tight smile. 'I have my own people in the station – Bridget among them. They'll provide some assistance.'

It was past midnight, and the drizzling rain hung in the air, a fine mist kissing Alice's face as she flattened herself against the wall. Bow Street was quiet – no pedestrians, few cars, little noise – but her luck only went so far. The moon was unusually radiant, bouncing light across the city and robbing her of shadowy hiding places.

As she approached the entrance to the station, her hand crept into her sleeve, seeking reassurance. She exhaled with quiet satisfaction. The feather was wedged in tightly; there was no likelihood of her losing it. She withdrew her hand from her woollen sleeve. Her fingertips brushed the feather's quill and tingled uncomfortably, the skin throbbing and pulsing; she didn't dare dwell on why. That had been part of Marianne's plan, and there was nothing to do but get on with it, no matter how repulsive she found it.

The entrance door was open, as expected. A quick scan through the gap showed less than a handful of Runners inside. One was sitting behind the barrier, reading a newspaper, and there were a couple of others at the booking-in desks, sifting through paperwork and yawning or swigging coffee. These were nearing the end of a late, eight-hour shift, and Alice hoped their tiredness would work in her favour.

She trekked silently up the steps and into the station hall, her heartbeat so loud in her ears it nearly deafened her. *Don't scuttle*, Marianne had warned. *Enter every room as though you own it, and no one will dare question your right to be there.* She was reluctant to take advice from a woman who thought the apocalypse was a perfectly sensible idea, but she couldn't deny that Marianne had a point.

She took a deep breath and strode across the hall, attempting to project an air of confidence. Her footsteps echoed sharply on the tiles, and a Runner glanced up from her paperwork – a slender, dark-haired woman. Alice nodded politely and marched on towards the barrier. She added the Runner's nightjar to the filing cabinet in her brain: a thin bird, about twelve inches tall, with glossy brown feathers and a grey throat.

The barrier was manned by a stocky, fair-haired man with a wispy moustache. His nightjar was small and round, with an abundance of beige feathers and dark stripes on its wings. There was no sign of Chalmers, the Runner who'd signed her in on her first morning. Marianne's enquiries had suggested he stuck to the day shift, as would anyone else she'd met there, or the whole plan would have been dust.

'Name?'

'Bridget Hogan,' she announced. She'd rehearsed for this – *Bridget Hogan, junior evidence archivist. I've been dragged out of bed to find a missing transcript, for a case that was urgently reopened late this evening.* But the fair-haired Runner didn't probe further, and she was cautious of offering too much information; the best lies were short and to the point.

He dropped a small white card onto the desk and gestured for her to put out her hand. Her stomach fluttered. The skeletal staffing on the night shift meant that they reverted to blood checks for unfamiliar faces requiring entry.

The Runner whipped out a small needle and jabbed it through Alice's index finger. A bead of ruby blood welled up from the pinprick, and her breathing calmed. After all, the blood wasn't her own. The real Bridget Hogan was a fully indoctrinated member of the Fellowship, and she'd generously donated a teaspoon of her blood. Marianne had inserted this just below the skin of Alice's fingertips with the aid of her magic. They'd prepared for this moment.

Without even glancing at her, the Runner rapped the white card. Alice pressed her finger to it, and he swiped it across the small square of inlaid metal on the desktop. Apparently satisfied that she was Bridget Hogan and had the necessary security clearance, the blond Runner pulled a lever under his desk.

'The lift is out of bounds after midnight,' he said. 'You'll have to take the stairs. Ground and first floors are open; the rest are locked up for the night.'

She'd expected this. Bridget had explained that in the early hours, the building was on partial lockdown to compensate for the smaller number of Runners on duty. The lift was restricted to transporting people to and from the cells; access to other floors within the building was limited to daylight hours.

'That's fine,' she said. 'I only need to grab a file. My office is on the first floor.'

The barrier slowly clanked open, and he waved her through into the hall. Her breath hitched. That was the easy bit done.

The huge hall doubled up as a waiting room and booking-in area for suspects. At this late hour, the place was almost deserted. The few Runners there were quietly getting on with their work. The sole suspect in the waiting room was an older man in a wooden chair, the armrests pinning him into the seat – but he was snoring gently.

The stairs were to Alice's left, but she needed access to the central lifts for the cells. There was no possible way to reach them unseen. So she had to make sure she *wasn't* seen.

She took a deep breath to prepare herself. The snoring man was of no concern. That just left the three Runners: the one at the barrier, the woman with the glossy nightjar and a lanky, bearded Runner behind a desk. Irritatingly, he was watching her progress as she cut across the hall. His nightjar was dark, with stiff feathers and hard edges, and a vigilant look in its eye.

An iron clock with hands like spears dominated the wall behind him. The steady ticking resonated through the space, and Alice knew, suddenly, that she could use it. She focused all of her attention on the hypnotic sound. *Tick* . . . Her breathing deepened and her erratic pulse found a stable rhythm . . . *Tick* . . . Her heartbeat slowed to match the clock's pace . . . *Tick* . . . A sense of calm resolve poured into her . . . *Tick* . . . A knot of tranquillity built in her chest and she exhaled, pushing it out, letting it flow into the atmosphere . . .

The watchful nightjar eyed her cautiously. She imagined reaching out to stroke it, her fingers gentle and innocuous. *I'm not a threat, little bird.* Her gaze shifted, her scope widening to include the glossy brown and the small beige nightjars. *Harmless. I'm harmless.*

'Look away,' she commanded, her voice barely a whisper.

The stiff-feathered nightjar blinked in confusion. Then, slowly, it shuffled sideways and turned its back on her. The Runner's eyes glazed over as though he were lost in thought, and then he shuddered and glanced down at his paperwork. The other nightjars followed suit, losing interest in her and turning away.

Gratification roared in her chest, but she quashed it instantly. No time for that. She could cloak herself from a single nightjar for around two minutes; for multiple nightjars – Jude's and Sasha's combined – she'd never managed more than sixty seconds. She hurried to the lift.

The clock measured out her invisibility in seconds. *Tick . . .* How much longer before the nightjars resumed their interest in her? Her eyes flew to the numbers clicking above the lift shaft. *Second floor . . .* She glanced over her shoulder. What was the lift doing on the second floor? It was supposed to be locked at night. *First floor . . .* The lights above the lift flickered as its descent continued. *Ground floor . . .* With a soft hiss, it came to a stop. At the desk behind her, the bearded Runner cleared his throat. *Get inside.* She had to get inside. Now!

With quivering hands, she pulled at the gold grille, preparing to dash inside. But instead, she fell back in dismay. The lift was already occupied. A bulky figure was hunched in the corner of the cramped space, his shadow spilling out across the tiles at her feet. It was a Runner. He was distracted by his watch, his fingers nimbly turning the knobs on the outer edge while he squinted at the tiny face.

Alice's eyes raced to find his nightjar, to blind the Runner to her presence, but her head was spinning. Where could she go? There was nowhere to hide! The figure finally looked up. A momentary spark of recognition lit up his eyes, and she quailed. It was Chalmers.

22

Chalmers.

She stood watching him in stunned horror. He knew she was suspended. He knew she'd been caught trespassing – trying to access the cells last time. What was he doing here?

He stared directly at her, his mouth puckered in bewilderment. Panic lodged itself in her airways and her throat closed up. Overhead, the hands on the clock seemed to judder and pause . . . and then, just as quickly as he'd appeared, he trudged past her, his eyes focused straight ahead and his expression blank. Was she cloaked? She hadn't even compelled his nightjar; why couldn't he see her? She watched him go, her mind feverishly searching for comprehension, before hurtling into the lift. She hit the button and sagged back against the walls when it sank, taking her away from the hall and down to the potential safety of the holding cells.

The stone-walled corridor was deathly quiet. There was no sign of movement in the barred cubicles stretched along one side of the corridor. This was, after all, not the home of the real cells. This was merely the failsafe – the trap for unauthorized trespassers.

She couldn't open a door directly to August's cell because she'd never seen the real thing. To travel, you had to be able to visualize your destination. She needed to see August's cell in person, and that meant only one thing . . .

She moved out from the alcove that housed the lift. When the gold grille and the doors disappeared moments later, she was unsurprised. But her stomach was heavy with dread, and she eyed the now-blank wall with trepidation. It was too late to back out of this plan; the course was set. She squeezed her eyes shut to snuff out the terrible visions she'd had of being caught in the wrong place. Chalmers. He wasn't even supposed to be on duty – Marianne had said so. He'd had the opportunity to expose her, and yet he hadn't taken it. Was he, like Bridget, one of Marianne's 'people'? The Runners had once infiltrated the Fellowship; now it seemed Marianne and her comrades were infiltrating them in return.

Alice shivered and propelled herself onwards, until she found what she was looking for: a door made of granite, midway along the corridor. It was the door Crowley had used to rescue her from this empty corridor. When she found it, she sat on the floor . . . and prepared to wait.

The abrasive rasp of stone scraping against stone startled her. Every muscle tensed. Then the granite door cranked open and a pair of leather boots stepped out into the corridor. *Finally. The 1 a.m. patrol.*

An astonished Runner stared down at her. It was evident that he'd never found anyone trapped here – until now.

'What the hell are you doing down here?' spluttered the Runner. He was a dark-haired man, probably in his late fifties, with watery blue eyes and a build like a rugby prop forward.

'I'm . . . a bit stuck,' said Alice.

'You're trespassing,' he said. 'Who are you?'

She scrambled to her feet and took a generous breath to steady her nerves. 'I'm Alice Wyndham.'

This clearly meant nothing to him. A frown darkened his face, and he seemed to regain his mental footing.

'Let's check you out then, shall we?' he said as he grabbed her arm and bundled her through the still-open doorway.

They hadn't known quite what to do with her. They'd performed a blood check, piercing the skin on her fingertip – she'd been careful not to give them the hand carrying Bridget's blood. And they'd confirmed she was indeed Alice Wyndham: one of their own employees, but suspended for a previous incident of trespass. They were loath to summon their commanding officer, Reuben Risdon, for advice in the middle of the night. So they'd opted for throwing her into an empty cell. Someone else could deal with her at a more godly hour. It couldn't have gone more smoothly.

Her cell was cramped and a heavy smell of damp hung in the chilly air. She tiptoed to the bars and peered out, into a corridor similar in layout but not design to the one she'd just left behind. Here, the tiles on the floor and walls were carved into unusual patterns, and the cell doors were made of intricately woven iron and oak. As an added precaution against travelling into the cells, the doors and patterned stonework changed frequently, so as to prevent easy visualization of the doorways – the work of House Pellervoinen, according to Marianne. Fortunately for Alice, their precautions were futile against Crowley's unique blood; he could open any lock, including those on the cell doors.

There were two blue-uniformed Runners playing poker at one end of the corridor. The dark-haired prop forward was smiling broadly at his cards, but a quick glance at his nightjar showed he was masking a poor hand.

'I win this hand, Rhone, and you can eat the lettuce-and-tomato sandwich my wife made for me.'

'Fuck that,' said another voice – Rhone, she assumed. 'I'm not ending my hunger strike for a salad. I want a greasy steak or nothing. Vegetarianism is an insult to my beliefs.'

She'd assumed Rhone was the other Runner, but the voice had come from a cell opposite. And that was when she realized. *August Rhone: the necromancer.*

'Your beliefs?' snorted the Runner.

'Absolutely. You can't worship Death and then refuse to eat dead animals. That's the ultimate insult.'

The lettuce-eater winced and tossed a coin onto the pile.

The other Runner – balding with a thatch of red hair behind his ears – clapped his colleague on the arm sympathetically. 'Don't talk about steak,' he said. 'He's living on those rabbit-food sandwiches.'

'I'll do you a favour, Whelan,' said August. 'I'll eat that pitiful sandwich, if you hate lettuce so much, if you give me that pack of cigarettes on the table.'

The dark-haired prop – Whelan – shook his head with a grin. 'Cigarettes are bad for you, Rhone, and I take my duty of care seriously.'

Whelan sat back in his chair and lit one of the cigarettes. Alice watched as the smoke drifted past her cell, her mind racing. They were relaxed and in good spirits. That could work to her advantage.

The guards' nightjars were reclining on the card table. By her calculations, the necromancer's cell was the last one on the row, right next to the guard table.

She stepped back, her stomach cramping with tension. Nearly there. She was so close now. The necromancer was within breathing distance, and once she had her hands on him, she would have instant access to the moors – and to Jen's nightjar. She exhaled slowly, quietened her mind and numbed her thoughts. It was time to extinguish any anxieties that might be a barrier to achieving a state of calmness.

Then she strode to the cell bars.

'Help!' she called out, her voice strong. 'Please help!'

There was a disgruntled moan and the sounds of chairs being shoved aside. Then, heavy footsteps, coming closer. She pressed herself into the corner of the room, to give herself the best view of the approaching Runners – and, more importantly, their nightjars.

The prop forward was the first to barrel towards her cell. She locked eyes with his dark nightjar. Then the balding redhead's bird, his nightjar squat, with soft, gingery feathers.

'Look away,' she murmured.

The nightjars averted their eyes and the cloak settled over her, just as the door opened and the two Runners burst inside with shouts of surprise.

'My God, where is she?'

She was ready. While they frantically examined every inch of the cell, with growing tones of disbelief, she crept silently past them, through the open door and into the corridor. She took care to tread lightly as she ramped up her speed and sprinted to the cell nearest the guards' table.

'Nice trick.'

She stumbled at the whispered voice in her ear. Of course – her cloaking had only worked on the Runners' nightjars. A man on the other side of the bars was frowning at her, a flaming match in one hand and a packet of cigarettes in the other. He slid one out, lit the end of it and inhaled. His eyes fluttered closed with pleasure, and he blew dragon-like plumes of smoke from his nose.

'Thanks for the distraction,' he said, pocketing the cigarettes. His eyes drifted open and locked onto Alice's face. His grin widened and he stood straighter, waving the smoke away.

'Am I about to get my first conjugal visit, or are you Whelan's angry wife?'

She recognized him. He was the fly-poster she'd seen on her first day; it was her fault he'd been caught, and she'd been suspended because she'd tried to reach him! *He* was the necromancer?

He reminded her, very strongly, of a handsome scarecrow. Tall and gangling, with dishevelled, straw-like hair and eyes a touch too big for his pale face. He was about her age, maybe a few years older, and he wore dark trousers and a too-big woollen jumper with holes in the cuffs. He stepped closer, and the shifting shadows threw his collar bones into sharp relief. He looked half-starved.

His nightjar was a large bird, resplendent, with its wings spread wide. Its body was a palette of rusty browns, chestnut, cream and copper tones, all streaked and spattered across its feathers. Ego personified, she thought. It was perched on his shoulder, preening itself.

Alice ignored him. She was intent on imprinting the vision of his cell door in her mind. It was firmly closed. But she had Crowley's blood, and nothing was closed to Crowley. Marianne had said so. She wrapped her hand around the iron ring on the door – the lock. She closed her eyes . . . and pushed. It opened – not to the cell, but to the void. *Shit.* Maybe this was the only way; it was the void's doorways that Crowley had mastered, not mere doors from one room to the next. She glanced over her shoulder, but the Runners had still not emerged from her cell. With a sharp breath, she leapt into the darkness. Icy wind gusted over her skin, enveloping her in a frozen caress. Teeth chattering violently, she closed the door behind her and refocused. *August's cell door* . . . *August's cell* . . . She groped at the chilly air. Her fingers found the iron ring . . . and pushed . . .

She stumbled into August's cell this time. Light blinded her and bright spots burst in front of her eyes. Startled, he caught her by the elbow and held her steady.

'Bloody hell, you're eager,' he whispered. 'I should warn you: I've hardly eaten in weeks, so my stamina's not the best, but I'll give it a bloody good effort.'

'Be serious, for God's sake,' she hissed. She flinched, hoping she hadn't been loud enough to attract attention, but the Runners hadn't yet reappeared. He gave her an amused smile.

'Marianne sent me,' she said. 'I've come to get you out of here.'

The smile vanished. His mouth slackened and he stepped away from her.

'Come on,' she said. 'We can use the same doorway.'

A thin crease appeared between his eyebrows, and he shook his head rapidly. 'No.'

'What? Come on! The guards will be back any second!'

He shrank back against the wall, his expression grimly determined. 'No. I'm not going back to Marianne.'

'But—'

'They tried to release me weeks ago, but I went on hunger strike. I'm not leaving this cell.'

She gaped at him stupidly. Of all the obstacles she'd considered, it had never once occurred to her that this prisoner might not want to be rescued.

'But *I* need you,' she whispered.

He opened his mouth, and she knew, suddenly, what he intended.

'No, wait,' she breathed. She started forward and threw out her arm in desperation. Her flailing hand latched onto the incandescent cord that linked him to his nightjar, and she tugged him closer.

She gasped. Warm and soft, it was like scooping up sand and letting it run through her fingers. It throbbed in her grasp, its vitality sending shivers of blissful pleasure through her arm. She smiled serenely, her gaze drifting from the cord to August's face. He was puce. His teeth were gritted and the tension in his jaw was causing a vein in his temple to twitch erratically.

'Please?' she murmured, tightening her grip on the cord.

His eyes bulged, and he didn't seem able to speak. The cord palpitated. A ripple surged through its length, and Alice faltered as a wave of emotion swept over her. Fear. Panic. Emotions that were not her own. They coursed through the glowing twine in her hands and shot up her fingertips. Memories followed. But not her memories: August's. Bodies – corpses – lay scattered on the floor. A woman stood over them, a scalpel in her hands. Marianne. Fear and panic magnified . . .

Alice's head seemed to crack open, and August's terror poured into the hole. Her grasp weakened and the cord fell away from her. August released a choked gasp and collapsed to his knees.

'I'm sorry,' she whispered. No wonder he didn't want to go back to Marianne. 'I . . . I'm . . .'

August dragged his head up and glared at her through red-rimmed eyes. 'What . . . did you do to me?' He licked his lips nervously.

'I'm sorry,' she babbled. 'I . . . I didn't realize . . . Please . . .'

There was a thunderous clatter of footsteps on the corridor tiles, and her anxiety swelled. The guards were coming.

'I swear,' she said. 'I swear on my life. I won't take you to Marianne. But if they find me in here, I'll . . . You have to come now,' she begged.

She moved towards him, and he flinched away. The dark circles under his eyes had grown darker and more pronounced. She could almost taste his fear.

She squinted out into the corridor as two running figures barrelled to a stop outside the cell.

'Get the key, Whelan!' the balding Runner shouted.

Alice glanced over at August. Panic knotted in her stomach.

'I'm sorry,' she said.

She dived at him. Her hand closed around his wrist and threw him off balance. In his weakened state, it was enough to tip things in her favour. She dug her heels in and swung backwards, hauling him with her. They tumbled headfirst into the still-open void, just as an ear-splitting alarm exploded into the darkness behind them.

23

The front door flew open and Crowley's face morphed from irritation to thunderstruck horror within seconds of the situation becoming clear.

'They'll have a warrant out for your arrest,' he said, ushering Alice and a very pale, unsteady August away from Coram House. 'This is the first place they'll look.'

He rushed up the steps of the derelict building opposite and threw open the door.

'Quickly,' he said. 'I'll take you to Jude's forge. No one will think to look for you there.'

He propelled August through the doorway first, then held out his arm to bar Alice from following him.

'Are you okay?' he murmured.

She glanced up at him. He was so tall. Had he always towered over her like this? Her pulse was racing from the night's events and her brain so fogged she couldn't muster a response. She nodded, but he seemed far from convinced. He leaned back to examine her fully, his eyes searching her face with such concern she suddenly found it hard to breathe.

'Marianne didn't hurt you?' he asked gently.

She faltered at the memory of the lancet ripping open her

neck, and he caught her hesitation. His eyes darkened, and she felt his body tense in the shadows.

She shook her head. 'No,' she croaked. 'She didn't.' It was only a partial untruth. Marianne had, after all, fixed her wound afterwards. She couldn't afford for Crowley to get distracted – not now, when she was so close.

'Did you check on Jen and my parents?'

'I . . .' He swallowed and pressed his lips together. He nodded sharply. 'They're fine,' he said, his voice hoarse.

He straightened, and his usual inscrutability slid over his face, his eyes becoming distant as he stepped away from her, into the void, and gestured for her to join him.

The wind was sharp and bitter. It lashed them with chilly gusts that drove into their bones. August was trembling violently. He drew closer to Alice, seeking warmth in the darkness.

'Where—Where are we going?' August managed.

Crowley looked from one to the other, his mouth tightening. 'Spitalfields,' he said curtly. 'You'll have to wait there while I attempt to resolve this latest Wyndham debacle.'

Alice was too numb with cold to react. She didn't care – not about Marianne or the Runners, or a warrant for her arrest. She had the necromancer. She had a route to the moors and to Jen's nightjar, at last.

'Can you reach my cigarettes?' August's voice was a dry whisper in the gloom.

She blinked rapidly and sat bolt upright. She'd been dozing fitfully, her head cushioned by Jude's blackened apron. Her eyes felt like they were filled with grit and ash. Maybe they were. Feeble beams of light filtered in around the doorframe and illuminated motes of dust in the air. Gradually, her sight adjusted to the dimly lit stone forge, and her eyes tracked over the array of anvils, leather bellows and metal pokers hanging from wall racks. There was a pack of cigarettes lying nearby in the dirt.

'Thanks,' said August when she awkwardly handed them over. He scratched at his straw-like hair and cleared his throat. 'You kept your promise, then,' he said after a few seconds of guarded silence. 'No Marianne.'

'I . . .' Alice's cheeks flushed. In the cold light of day, she was . . . ashamed. This wasn't self-defence, as with Ronan Bishop, his dogfighting brother or Vin Kelligan. This time, *she'd* attacked. And her only justification was that she'd needed him to do as he was told. She'd never believed in deliberately hurting anyone without good cause before – but last night she had.

'I'm so sorry I hurt you,' she said quietly. 'It's no excuse, but I panicked and—'

'Forget it,' he said, his eyes fixed on the drifting dust motes. 'Whatever it was you did to me, I can guarantee I've done worse.'

'That's . . . very forgiving of you.'

He shrugged, lost in thought. Then he sighed and turned to face her. 'We weren't introduced properly. I'm August Rhone. People call me Augie.'

'I'm Alice Wyndham,' she said. 'People call me . . . Alice Wyndham.'

He straightened his legs, wincing as he stretched. 'So . . . how did you end up in the cells? Was the whole thing one of Marianne's schemes to break me out?'

'Trespass,' she said. 'And . . . yes, kind of.'

His mouth snapped shut. 'I knew she was desperate to get me back, but I didn't think she'd go that far.' He forced a smile. 'One of the hazards of being irresistible, I suppose.'

Alice shook her head, and there was another long pause before she said, 'You're a necromancer.'

He said nothing. His fingers crept to his pocket, and he pulled out his small box of matches. He set one alight, held it against his cigarette and took a drag.

August's nightjar, with its extravagant palette of browns and beiges, was perched on his knee, watching her intently.

'I'm a practiser of the banned arts,' he said at last, tipping his head back to expel the smoke. 'I can't help what I am, but it's illegal to practise.'

'But . . . you were arrested for fly-posting, not necromancy.'

'Yeah,' he said. 'Thanks to you.'

She had the good grace to look embarrassed.

'Don't worry, you did me a favour. Why do you think I slowed down?' He grinned. 'In the past, I've been locked up for breaching the peace, public intoxication, motoring offences . . . If there was a crime syndicate specifically for petty offences like littering and inconsiderate driving, I'd be the kingpin of that gang.'

'Can't you stay out of trouble?' she asked.

He laughed. 'I *was* staying out of trouble; I wanted to get caught. If I'm locked in a cell for fly-posting, I can't be stuck in Notting Hill with Marianne, trying to open a door to the Sulka Moors for her so she can kickstart her apocalypse.' He tapped his forehead. 'See. Logic. Whelan thinks I'm the most brainless criminal in the city, because I always get caught, but I'm actually a fucking genius. I've tried telling them what she's trying to do. But the Runners have all the survival instincts of the dodo, and no one will listen, not even Reuben Risdon, the top man himself.'

'You really believe *Marianne* could start this so-called apocalypse?' she asked sceptically. 'I thought it was Death's child who was destined to somehow massacre everyone.'

'You don't seriously believe that bloodthirsty bitch would want someone else to take the credit, do you?' he said. 'She's got a whole plan all worked out.'

They lapsed into silence while she pored over what he had said. One thing stood out. She glanced over at him, her mouth dry. 'So Marianne's . . . been using you to try to open a door to the Sulka Moors?'

He nodded, and Alice exhaled shakily. Her heart was thumping with anticipation. Everything had led up to this one moment, this one thing she needed, to save Jen.

She took a deep breath. 'I need you to open a door to the moors for *me*.'

He dropped his cigarette, startled.

'I went to Marianne because I was desperate, and she told me how to find you. I tried Ronan Bishop, but he couldn't do it. You're my last hope.'

He snorted. 'You know Bishop, do you? Can't stand that bastard. I've always been a dog lover.'

'But will you help me?' she asked. 'Please. Whatever it takes to—'

'Tell me your story,' he said. 'Why do you want the door open?'

Alice bit her lip. Then she took a moment to gather her thoughts, and explained, falteringly, all that had happened to Jen and her nightjar. When she was finally finished, he cleared his throat.

'She must be something special, if you're prepared to go this far for her.'

'She is.'

August nodded, but there was a cagey look in his eyes. 'How do you know she's lost her nightjar? The only way you would know it was missing would be if you could see it – if you could see that it wasn't there, I mean. Which would mean you'd have to be—'

'An aviarist,' she said. 'If that's your question, then yes, I'm an aviarist.'

He whistled in surprise. 'Wow. My God, you must be the only—'

'Yes,' she said. 'A bit of a rarity, apparently. Although . . .' Her brow furrowed. 'I didn't actually see that Jen's nightjar was missing. Crowley told me.'

'But how did he know?'

'I . . .' She hesitated. 'I don't know.'

August shot her a sideways glance. 'Jesus. This feels like the start of a joke. An aviarist and a necromancer walk into a bar . . .' He laughed and shook his head.

Alice reached out and put her hand on his arm. He froze under her touch. 'August,' she said. 'Will you please help me?'

He looked away. 'Sorry. But I don't want to work for you any more than I want to work for Marianne.'

She snatched her hand back. Her stomach clenched with sudden anger. No. He couldn't do this.

'Why?' she asked, forcing herself to sound calm. 'If that's your legacy, what's the problem with using it for something useful?'

'Useful?' he said sharply. 'You think my legacy is useful? You think that opening a door to the moors is just a small, inane favour?'

He shook his head bitterly and took a drag of his cigarette to disguise the obvious trembling in his hands.

'You don't know anything about necromancy,' he said. 'You probably think we can raise the dead.'

'Can't you?' she asked, thinking back to Ronan and his dogs.

'Nope. Not possible.' He smiled wryly. 'I did once manage to reanimate a dead cockroach though. Regretted it instantly.'

Of course. Reanimation. Puppetry, not genuine resurrection.

'Not every necromancer is skilled enough to reanimate insects, you know.' He grinned. 'You want to talk about useful – can you imagine a more useful gift in life than being able to make your very own puppet army of undead cockroaches?'

'You could terrorize restaurants with them,' said Alice, trying to ease the tension. 'Blackmail them into paying you off.'

'Like the Pied Piper?'

'Exactly.'

He gave her an admiring glance. 'I've always found a cunning mind to be the most attractive quality in a woman. Which is probably why I'm flat broke.'

Alice pulled a tight smile. 'So what sorts of things *can* necromancers do?'

'Well,' he said, 'I know of this one guy who can touch something a corpse has worn and tell you exactly what killed them.' He shrugged. 'I can't do that. I know of another necromancer – a woman – who can eat meat and hear the cries of the animal as it was slaughtered. Nightmare. Can you imagine eating a hot dog while the pig squeals in your ear?' He sighed. 'Lots of different kinds of necromancers out there.'

'And you're the cockroach kind?' she said. 'Or the . . . door-to-the-moors kind?'

'I'm the kind who wants to live,' he said quietly. 'I'm not Marianne's first necromancer. The others didn't last long, once she figured out they didn't have the right skill set. They could work the death magics, to some extent, but no matter how hard they tried, they couldn't open a door to the moors. There aren't

too many who have the skill for that. And even if there were . . .'
He trailed away.

Alice racked her brains, trying desperately to remember what
she'd read in Proctor's Fellowship files, but it felt like a lifetime
ago now. Images of the dead floated across her memory, alongside
flashes of the glinting lancet.

'She's killing people, isn't she?' she said. 'Her own Fellowship
members. She's forcing them to sacrifice themselves to Death.'

One corner of August's mouth lifted in a slanted grin, and he
glanced away from her.

'Yeah. When they're standing at an open window, she sweet-
ens the deal by telling them they'll be compensated with a blissful afterlife in the moors. Then she gives them a mental nudge
and, next thing, they're lying on the street with a broken neck.
Once her blood is in their system, they're powerless to stop
themselves.'

'But . . . I don't understand why she's doing it. Her membership numbers will go down until there's no one left.'

He coughed out a puff of smoke and side-eyed her. 'Two
reasons,' he said. 'The first, she genuinely believes that every sacrifice she makes raises her profile with the Lintuvahti – they're
gifts to him. Secondly – and this is the clincher . . .' He paused.
'She wants to walk into the moors herself – but *alive*, not dead.
Unfortunately for her, the moors . . . Only the dead can find
them. The living don't even know where the door is.'

She nodded. Proctor had said as much.

'Her sacrifices are supposed to open that door for her; that's
how you get inside without having to kill yourself first. You get
a necromancer to summon a dead soul in the moors to open the
door *for* you – *from the other side.*'

Alice's mind scattered. All she had to do was get him to

summon some dead person to open a door for her, and she could walk right inside.

'But it hasn't worked,' she said. 'She's still looking for a way in. If she can use the sacrifices to open the door . . . why hasn't it worked?'

He shrugged. Suspicion worried at her.

'It's you, isn't it? You're her necromancer, but you don't want to open the door for her,' she said slowly as understanding dawned. 'She's killing people to open the door, but you're . . . keeping it closed. You're not summoning them back to open it at all, are you? You're failing on purpose.'

'No.'

August's nightjar ducked, and Alice held her breath. He was lying. She leaned into him, peering more intently at his nightjar. Certainty resonated through her head. He *could* open the door – he just wouldn't.

'Why won't you do it?' she breathed. 'If not for Marianne, do it for me. I'm not trying to start the bloody apocalypse!'

He stood up abruptly and crushed his cigarette under his heel.

'Because it's twisted,' he said roughly. 'People can only be summoned to the door if they haven't died willingly. If they can't be at peace, because unfinished business or revenge is stopping them from letting go and passing on – through the moors to whatever comes next.' He was shaking. 'She's a sick bitch. You know she killed her own family years ago? It's a wonder her dead sister hasn't clawed the door open to get to her anyway.'

His eyes locked on Alice's. He looked wild, and she swallowed thickly. 'Do you see what the price is? Who are you going to wrong so badly that they'll fling open the door to the moors to get to you?' he demanded. 'Who's going to die to get *your* door open?'

Her mouth snapped shut. It couldn't be true. There had to be another way. She had to get to Jen's nightjar.

'So there you go,' August said quietly, sliding down the forge's stone wall and angrily yanking another cigarette from the packet. 'That's my useful legacy. I get to be complicit in murder for it to work. I get to tell Marianne the door's still closed, so she makes more and more sacrifices. I get to watch them die, knowing I could stop it – but that if I did, she'd be one step closer to her twisted plans to slaughter the whole city. I believe her about the purge, you know – she's evil enough to be capable of anything.'

24

Vin Kelligan's office had been destroyed. He sat in the ruins he'd created, jaw clenched and seething with rage at the news he'd just been delivered. The silly bitch – the silly bitch was working with the Fellowship, and she'd managed to end up on the run. How long would he have to wait to get hold of her *now*? And what if she'd signed herself up as an official member? If Marianne got her claws into her, his plans were dust. He would have to send a warning . . .

He dragged himself to his feet, kicked aside the chair, which lay splintered across his carpet, and leaned against his desk, panting with exertion. It was a handsome desk – solid walnut with polished bureau drawers.

'Vin . . . please . . .'

Lattimer had brought the message about the girl. Lattimer *knew* he didn't like to hear bad news on a full stomach.

'I told you,' said Vin. 'No more cock-ups.'

He folded his arms across his chest, and the man cringing in the corner flinched.

'Next time, Lattimer . . .' he said, eyeing the busted chair malevolently. 'Next time it will be you, not the chair.' There was a heavy pause. 'Now bring me some better news,' he snapped.

It was dark and Crowley still hadn't returned. Alice and the necromancer had spent the last several hours waiting, sometimes making desultory small talk. Alice had tried to engage August in various schemes to open the door to the moors. He had ruthlessly dismissed every proposal.

'You know what?' he mused some time later, his head resting on a sack of iron filings. 'Chaining myself to that sociopath was the worst mistake of my life. If I could go back in time . . .' He sighed. 'I knew I should've opted for that sex cult in Soho instead.' He suddenly lifted his head to look over at her. 'Are you listening?'

'No.' Her finger idly traced the outline of a nightjar in the dirt.

He grinned. 'That's the spirit. You can tell a lot about a person by how they deal with setbacks. Throw another madcap scheme at me. I'll do my best not to mercilessly unpick it straight away.'

She ignored him. She was rapidly becoming light-headed with hunger and despair.

'What's your legacy?' he asked, changing tack.

Her gaze drifted over to his face. 'I don't know. I thought maybe Mielikki's, but I probably imagined it . . .' She shrugged.

'Right, this is no good,' he said, sitting up with exasperation. 'We can't just sit here for hours. What are we waiting for?'

'Nothing,' she said. 'I'm on the run from the police, and it was all for nothing. You're impotent and I'm a failure.'

'Hey, steady on!'

Frustration and anger ballooned in her throat.

'It's true,' she said bitterly. 'I'm no closer to saving Jen's night-jar than I was the night she got hit by that car.'

She turned away from him.

'What happened to your neck?' he asked, coming closer.

She'd forgotten all about it. It was no longer even tender. Soon, the scab would fall off and there'd be no sign at all of what she'd tried to do to save Jen.

'Marianne did it,' she murmured. 'It doesn't hurt.'

There was a heavy pause. Then he said, ominously, 'Did she give you the lancet? Is her blood in there, controlling you?'

'No.'

There was a rustle of clothing behind her, then a banging creak. Alice turned to find August opening the forge's wooden door.

'Don't go out there,' she hissed. 'I'm on the run now, and they'll be after you too!'

'I'm taking you to see something interesting,' he said. 'You think you might have Mielikki's legacy? Where better to research than in a library?'

She frowned. 'I don't—'

He headed out of the forge, into the crisp evening air. Feeling she'd lost all control of the situation, Alice scrambled upright and raced after him.

They exited a door in a part of the Rookery – or London – that she didn't recognize.

'It's dark. We won't get caught,' August said. 'The Runners don't know where we've been hiding anyway. And I doubt they've got patrols out, looking for the legendary outlaw, Alice Wyndham.'

'This isn't Kings Cross . . .' she said.

'Well spotted.'

'But you said . . . I assumed we were headed for the British Library.'

He glanced away, and Alice reached out and squeezed his arm tentatively. He hissed in pain and snatched his arm away. She stared at him in confusion.

'Are you okay?'

'Fine,' he murmured, pulling down his sleeve and massaging the wrist. He stalked off, leaving her hurrying to catch him up.

'Marianne said there was a failsafe,' she said, deciding to approach her impossible problem from a different angle. 'There's some sort of security measure to stop people just wandering into the moors. Do you know what it is?'

August shook his head, and she stiffened. His nightjar practically radiated deceit. She bit down on her lip to stop herself calling him out for the lie and smiled at him. *Softly, softly.*

The streets narrowed, and their footsteps echoed on the cobbles. Alice felt very exposed. She imagined the Runners dogging her footsteps, lurking in the shadows, and increased her speed. They trudged onwards, until they finally came to a cobbled square.

She recognized this. When they'd first moved to London, Jen had insisted on dragging her to every market in the city, no matter what they sold – fresh vegetables, second-hand clothes, jewellery, fish. She hadn't cared what she bought; she'd just wanted to try her hand at bartering.

She looked about her, trying to picture the place cluttered with stalls. *Bermondsey Antiques Market.* Jen had bought a brass candlestick holder but couldn't afford to buy its matching twin. She suppressed a smile. Jen really was terrible at bartering.

There was no market here now. Instead, the square was dominated by an ancient stone abbey gradually being strangled by thick, leafy vines. At the back of the crumbing building was a bell tower, while out in front, a huge spire rose up above the door, spearing the night sky.

'What is this place?' asked Alice, awestruck.

'Bermondsey Abbey,' said August. 'It used to be, anyway. It's the Abbey Library now. Come on.'

'Bermondsey doesn't have an abbey,' she said as she followed him across the square.

'It did. Once. Anyway, what we want to see is down in the atrium.'

Aside from the stone walls and stained-glass windows, the building didn't look much like an abbey inside. It was one vast rectangular room, almost empty, carpeted with dust and grit. A well-worn path through the dust led from the door to a hole in the floor.

Alice followed August to the hole and peered inside, expecting to find an equally grimy basement. Instead, she found a gloomy staircase. The steps were smooth and worn and seemed to stretch far below the ground.

'Call me sceptical, but that looks like an oubliette with its own hundred-metre staircase.'

'Scout's honour,' he said. 'It's not a French dungeon.'

'You were in the Scouts?' she asked, momentarily distracted.

'For a whole week.'

'You grew up in the mainland, then? Or do they have Scouts in the Rookery?'

He'd already galloped off into the narrow gap without responding. After a brief hesitation, she followed him on a meandering descent down the subterranean staircase. The quality of the air changed as they wound their way down. Alice had expected warm, stale air and a damp smell, but it grew fresher as the staircase, lit with oil lamps, broadened, and the roughly hewn walls became smooth and polished.

They dropped lower and lower, sinking below a maze of sloping corridors that branched off from the stairs like spokes from a wheel. She couldn't see where they led – they faded into impenetrable darkness – so she quickened her pace to lessen the distance from August. She felt much relief when they finally emerged, footsore and panting, into the upper floor of a huge atrium.

'What's—' Alice froze, looking up in wide-eyed astonishment. 'But that's . . . How?' she managed.

There was a tree. Indoors. It had to be two hundred feet tall. Its thick, twisted trunk was growing right out of the atrium floor, some four or five storeys below, and reached up, past her, to a huge glass ceiling that was level with the ground outside. It looked like the tree was holding up the now-thunderous sky.

'You like?' August asked with a grin.

Alice nodded dumbly.

The crooked grey boughs snaked up over her head. The crown was crushed against the glass, but the canopy of leaves was so voluminous they ruffled Alice's hair when she moved. Dull green on one side and brighter on the other, the unfamiliar leaves were elegant and tapered.

It was both breathtaking and fearsome. Far too immense for the vast atrium, the tree's branches plundered every inch of space, chasing along corridors and twining around arches and pillars like an infestation. The stooped lower boughs pressed against the walls as though fighting to burst from the seams of the building. She couldn't help but be reminded of a magnificent, kraken-like sea creature, its tentacles straining against a net.

The atrium was dimly lit, illuminated by pinpricks of yellow light dancing up and down the more spindly offshoots of the tree.

'Fairy lights,' she murmured, reaching out to touch them.

'Fireflies,' August corrected.

There was a bustle of movement behind her, then a sharp voice said, '*Don't.*'

Alice turned.

A tall woman with steely-grey hair and a book in her gloved hand nodded at a placard erected on the floor. 'Young lady – read the warning signs,' she said. 'The Lampyridae – the fireflies – bite.' With a smooth flourish, she slid off her glove and angled her hand. It was missing a little finger. 'See?'

Alice withdrew her hand from the tree, and the woman gave her a stern nod before moving away.

'Probably a librarian,' said August, watching her go. 'One of Mielikki's – they tend to the books. Made of paper – wood pulp, see? And she's right. If you touch a firefly, there's every chance the little fuckers will chew all the skin and muscle off your hand. They protect the tree – and are only supposed to attack if you actually pierce the bark, but they've made one or two "mistakes" over the years.'

Alice paled and turned away.

A granite staircase wrapped around the trunk of the glowing tree in a spiral. Landings ran off it, leading to the other storeys – to doors and passageways and more narrow alcoves filled with shelves and shelves of books. The Abbey Library, it seemed, was like a vast honeycomb burrowed out of the earth.

When she finally staggered from the bottom step, she found herself in something like an indoor courtyard. The base of the trunk was buried in the ground only feet away, surrounded by grasping roots that bulged from the courtyard's tiles and vanished into the earth below.

There were people milling around in silence. They sat on the floor or leaned against shelves in the alcoves, their noses buried in books. Stacks of handwritten manuscripts and journals dotted the library in haphazard piles. There was an air of scholarly disorganization about the place. So much for the librarians.

'How is there a tree growing inside a building?' she asked. 'Or . . . under it?'

'Mielikki put it here,' August said.

Alice closed her eyes, breathing in the earthy scent of the ridged bark and the abundant leaves, her senses filling with the low, lilting violin music she'd heard in House Mielikki long ago. The image of Ronan Bishop's face when the roof collapsed at the dogfighting ring and his confused 'What have you done?' resurfaced in her mind. She badly wanted to know if she'd pulled down that roof – if she'd caused the barrels to explode, cracked the begonia vase and if she'd grown a branch from her floorboards. If she had Mielikki's legacy, might that, somehow, help her help Jen – despite what Crowley seemed to think?

'I thought you'd like it,' said August, grinning at her. 'This is a special tree.'

'Of course.'

'No. *Really* special. It has a ton of names, in every language, but in the Rookery it's known by an older name. Its first name. This is the Arbor Suvi. The Summer Tree – better known as the Tree of Life.'

'*The* Tree of Life?'

'Yes.'

Alice expelled a deep breath.

'Can you feel it?' he asked. 'I've heard that people with Mielikki's legacy can hear the tree's heartbeat.'

She stepped closer to the magnificent roots tangled around the courtyard, a flutter of hope in her chest . . . but there was no heartbeat.

Disappointment punctured her, and she shrank away from the tree. Had she imagined some connection to Mielikki, because she'd found her aviarist skills so intangible?

'Hey, don't be put off,' said August, turning towards one of the small passageways twisted around the tree. 'I'm not saying *every* member of House Mielikki can hear it. I'll show you something else.'

She hesitated. 'August, I think we should leave. This is too public. If the Runners—'

'Stop worrying and follow me,' he said with a fixed grin. 'You never know, this might trigger something for you, even if the Arbor Suvi hasn't.'

She hesitated, then sighed. 'Isn't *arbor* the *Latin* word for *tree*?' she asked. 'I thought this place was obsessed with all things Finnish.'

'It is, but England – the mainland *and* here – is a mosaic. A patchwork quilt of cultures and historical influences. Everyone who landed on our shores stamped themselves on the shape of the language: the Saxons, the Normans, the *Romans* . . .' He smiled and thumbed at his chest. 'History buff,' he explained.

She forced herself to return his smile. 'History graduate.'

'Are you serious?' He laughed delightedly. 'This is fate.'

The passageway was filled, floor to ceiling, with bookshelves. They were crammed with books in an assortment of covers: some hand-bound in decorative cloths, cards and leather; others simply wads of handwritten unbound sheets, gathered together with thick string. Many of the cover illustrations were embossed or pressed in ornamental gold leaf, and some were hand-painted. The books, however, didn't appear to be borrowed often enough to shake the dust loose from the yellowed pages.

'You're allowed to read anything you want, as long as you're respectful,' said August. 'The librarians' penalties for damage to a text, or late return, are . . . let's just say *steep*. Be careful.'

Alice greedily scanned the titles as she passed, one finger trailing along the delicate spines. *Doorways of the Western Isles*; *Chancellor Westergard: A Life in Service*; *Jagatsingh-Carroll's Encyclopaedia of Tree Genera . . .*

'How am I doing so far?' asked August, startling her.

'With what?' she asked, dropping her inspection of the shelves.

'First proper date,' he said. 'Marks out of ten?'

'This isn't a date!'

'It's a ten, right? I can see it in your face.'

'This *really* isn't a date.'

He clutched his chest and gave her a wounded look.

The passageway widened, and Alice found herself in an empty circular room. There was a warning placard fixed to the pale stone floor: *Warning: Lampyridae*. Fireflies drifted overhead, each glimmer illuminating a series of thick tapestries draped around the curved walls.

'What are those?' she asked. The tapestries were bleached by age, though they had clearly once been rich blocks of colour. They were embroidered with geometrically patterned hems, and near the top, there were rudimentary symbols woven into the coarse material.

'Our family trees,' August said with a self-satisfied grin. 'They're linked to the four Masterbuilders of the Rookery. See the names of the House members?' He gestured at the indecipherable letters stitched into the material. 'I think those were sewn in when the tapestry was made. But it wasn't sustainable to keep making permanent additions, so they gave up.'

He was right. The stitched names quickly gave way to small, faded pieces of card pinned to the tapestries instead.

'No one adds their names any more. Not now they're guarded by the fireflies.' He sighed. 'The books are the only things you can touch in this place.'

'Which tapestry is which?' asked Alice.

He quirked a smile and turned back to the wall hangings. 'That one there is for Ahti, the water Masterbuilder. They reckon he copied the Thames or rerouted some of it through here.' He pointed at the nearest tapestry, which was a dull navy blue with a faded red hem. There was a crest at the top displaying a line drawing of a boat, similar in style to the Stone Age petroglyphs chipped into cave walls.

'Then there's Pellervoinen's – he mapped out the city and built the doors . . . and apparently, he had a real thing for Mielikki. Over there is Ilmarinen's banner. Rumour has it he had a very famous great-great-grandson called Thomas Farriner, who tried living in London and accidentally burned it to the ground. That last one is Mielikki's. Among her many talents, she was responsible, as you know, for growing the most famous tree in . . . I suppose the world? The tree breathes life to the Rookery. And there are *tons* of superstitions about the tree that reach way beyond these walls, but this is their origin.' He paused, waving a hand at Mielikki's green tapestry.

Family trees. It was the first time it had really hit her, really and truly sunk in. She was *not entirely human*.

'It's my biological family . . .' she breathed.

'What about them?'

'They're the ones who've done this to me. It's their crazy blood running through my veins. And I knew nothing about them at all, not for years, until the exact moment their DNA ruined my life.'

'That's family for you,' said August, with a wry shrug.

It was hard to stifle her sudden rush of bitterness. She glared at the tapestries.

'There are five,' she said, nodding at the final swathe of white fabric, hemmed in black, which loomed over her shoulder. 'Five tapestries, not four.'

'Aha! Well spotted.' He glanced at her. 'The fifth one is for Tuoni: the Lintuvahti. But the Lintuvahti wasn't a Masterbuilder. He was—'

'Death.'

'Yes. And still is.'

She stepped back to examine them better. 'Death has a family tree? So Marianne was right? Death really does have a child?'

'Tuoni's is blank,' August said pointedly.

'Tuoni . . .' she repeated.

'Yeah. *Death*. The Lintuvahti.'

'How many names does one person need?'

He laughed. 'Are you kidding me? The personification of Death has hundreds of names, in hundreds of different cultures. The Grim Reaper, Mot, Thanatos, Meager Hein, Azrail, La Santa Muerte, or Tuoni for the Finnish . . . To put it another way, Lintuvahti is his job title. But Tuoni is his actual name. But most often, people call him by his title and his name has been forgotten.'

'Right,' Alice said. 'And what about his family tree?'

'There are songs and stories about Tuoni. Folktales that the Väki brought to the Rookery from Finland. They claim Tuoni has a wife, named Tuonetar, and a family – the whole works. The Fellowship are obsessed with the stories. Their thinking is that the original Finnish myths about him having a family have to come from somewhere . . . but if he did have children, surely they'd be right up there on that tapestry – and they're not. Believe me, the Fellowship spent years looking and couldn't find any trace of his offspring.'

She knew this story.

'Marianne forced Proctor to help, but he's practically blind. Couldn't find his own arse with a mirror, and no sign at all of Death's children. But the Fellowship are still convinced that Tuoni, when he's ready, will choose a mistress to bear his children. Children who will then—'

'Purge the world?' she said.

August nodded. 'But outside of the Fellowship, most think it's impossible for the Lord of Death to procreate. Their argument is that it's impossible for death to create life. So, no kids, no names on the family tree.'

'Then why bother putting up a tapestry for him at all?' she asked. 'If it's just going to stay blank?'

He grinned and nodded at the worn fabric. A glyph-like symbol of a tree was threaded in black near the top of the tapestry. 'That's the Fellowship's other obsession, and this is the capper for them – *no one knows who put it here*. Marianne is fixated on this tapestry. Fixated. She thinks the fact that it exists at all means that the Lintuvahti either does have a bloodline or has the capacity to beget one. It's as good as proof to her.'

Alice peered at it. It was nothing special. If it were for sale in a shop, they'd have had to pay her to take it home. It was frayed and unravelling, with several suspiciously dark stains on the hem.

She stepped past August, drawing closer to the other family

trees. She was dwarfed by the swathes of fabric dangling from the stone. She scanned the names pinned to them. Henry Morgan. Joshua Myles. James Keenan. Martin Donnellan . . . Her eyes drifted over to Mielikki's faded green tapestry.

'Did you pin your name on one of these – before the fireflies started guarding them?'

He shook his head. 'I'm not a member of a House. Not yet, anyway.' He nodded at the furthest tapestry. 'Maybe I'm distantly related to Ahti, though. He had a knack for water, and I'm a Rhone – August *Rhone* – like the French river. Water's not my dominant legacy, obviously, but – funny thing – I never need an umbrella. Rain just . . . bounces off me.'

She nodded absentmindedly. Was Crowley's name up there?

'Marianne has studied *every* story about Death to bolster her beliefs,' he said. 'Finnish, Hellenic, Christian—'

'I saw her paintings,' Alice said.

He nodded. 'Then you must have seen the lamb's blood on the front door too. Can we talk history buff to history buff here?' he said. 'You've heard of the Exodus story?'

She nodded. 'Well, yes.'

'Wasn't there a Disney film about it?' he said snidely.

'Yeah – that's not how I know it, August.'

He laughed. 'The ancient Egyptians wouldn't let the Israelites leave the country, so ten plagues were sent to free them, culminating with Death. And the Israelites put lamb's blood on their front doors, so the Angel of Death would know to spare them and pass over their houses.'

'I remember. But the Lintuvahti isn't the *angel* of Death, is he?'

'No.' He ran a hand through his hair anxiously. 'I could really do with a smoke.'

'Let's go back upstairs then,' she said. 'If we get discovered by Runners—'

'Not yet,' he said quickly. 'Just . . . There's still more to show you.'

When he saw that she was watching him, eyes narrowed with suspicion, he attempted to renew his smile. His nightjar seemed unsettled too. Her skin prickled with unease.

'The Exodus story is about plagues,' he said abruptly, distracting her. 'And in some of the Finnish myths, Death's daughter, Loviatar—'

'Wait. She's his daughter?' Alice asked, thinking back to Marianne's hideous painting of the skull woman giving birth on the rocks. 'So is this Loviatar going to . . . purge the world at some point?'

'No,' August said. 'She's just a story. There's been no sign of her whatsoever in real life.' He shook his head. 'My point is, there are these old Finnish stories about Loviatar, and her diseased children were basically *plagues*.' He raised an eyebrow, waiting for a reaction.

Plagues . . . she mouthed silently.

He nodded. 'In Exodus, there are ten plagues, which end with the plague of death. In the Finnish stories, Death's *child* gives birth to nine different plagues.' He paused. 'Two different belief systems, and they both end up with a connected idea about Death. Funny coincidence, right? So when Marianne says she wants to bring on a purge, what she's actually talking about is a *plague* – and she thinks the connection between the different stories of Death, like the tapestry, are proof it's possible.' He was becoming more animated, circling the room while he talked. 'Have you figured out why she puts lamb's blood on the front door of the Fellowship yet?'

Alice's brow wrinkled. 'Because . . . that's what happens in Exodus? And in Judaism, it's the paschal lamb – the sacrifice of Passover – that saved them from death.'

He stopped suddenly. 'Yeah. Lamb's blood symbolizes innocence *and* represents protection. That's why the Fellowship paint it on the door to keep them safe when the purge – the plague – comes.'

'But . . . Marianne said it would be an honour to die.'

'Yeah,' he said. 'But *she* wants to go *last*. She imagines herself walking off into the sunset with Death – the last of all; the most special. That's why we always have lamb's blood on the door. To keep her alive long enough to go last.'

'That's . . .' Alice shook her head.

'Yep.'

She was watching his nightjar carefully, and it seemed restless, its wings fluttering and its head darting around. He couldn't keep still either, she realized. He kept tapping the tops of his thighs. Why was he so agitated?

'August,' she said. His anxiety was infectious. Coming here had been a bad idea; the Runners might be circling upstairs right at this moment. 'I really think we need to go—'

He smiled at her. 'It's a lot to take in all at once, isn't it?'

'I . . . Yes,' she said. 'Well . . . I suppose it's a good job that the Lintuvahti's tapestry is blank. If Marianne could get her hands on Death's bloodline, who knows where it would lead.'

There was a long pause before either of them spoke, as Alice's suspicions about Marianne's motives formed into a terrible new shape.

'I know what she wants. Oh my God. I know why Marianne wants to open the door – but it's madness.'

She turned to August, a shocked laugh escaping her, but he was staring at the floor and she knew, instantly, that something was wrong. Any warmth and camaraderie had been sucked from the atmosphere, and there was a sudden gulf between them.

'*August?*'

She felt a sudden surge of rage. Had he tricked her into coming here – to get caught by the Runners?

His eyes darted up, but not to look at Alice. They were focused on a blur of movement over her shoulder. She turned sharply.

Marianne stood in the passageway, a smile playing around her thin lips and a lancet rolling between her fingers.

25

'A pleasure to see you again,' said Marianne, her voice brittle.

She moved into the circular room. She wore a blood-red slash of lipstick, and her dark, greying hair was tangled down her back. She gave the impression of something withered and cruel. Alice almost backed up against the tapestries, but stopped and held her ground. She wasn't going to be intimidated by this repulsive crow of a woman.

'You wanted *her* to find us?' Alice hissed to August. 'So you lied about staying in jail to avoid her? But . . . your nightjar . . .'

It didn't make sense. August's nightjar *had* suggested he was frightened of Marianne. And yet . . .

'Alice,' he whispered. '*Help me.*'

She frowned, confused. Whose side was he on?

'Have you come for August?' she said. 'Or me?'

Marianne circled Alice, studying her with interest. Alice gritted her teeth and stared straight ahead.

'I've come for my necromancer,' said Marianne.

August was pale and stiff as a cadaver. He was staring directly at Alice, his eyes pleading. It was unnerving. He was clearly terrified. Why, then, had he urged her not to leave earlier? Staying in one place had only made them easier to track.

Marianne turned to the tapestries, addressing Alice as she examined them from afar. 'Imagine my surprise when you backtracked on our arrangement.'

'Look at him,' said Alice. 'He doesn't want to go with you. You can't make him.'

Marianne laughed. 'Of course I can.' Smiling, she strode to August and took his hand. He didn't react as she peeled back his sleeve to reveal his arm, littered with old scars. There was a scabbed gash on his wrist; Alice remembered him wincing when she'd squeezed it on their way here.

'See?' said Marianne. 'He's as docile as a sleepy kitten.'

She was right. But he'd been fully conscious and talkative until Marianne had shown up.

'You've used the lancet on him,' Alice murmured. Was that how much control she had as a hemomancer? She could click her fingers and her victims would slip in and out of her spell, like someone under hypnosis?

'August,' said Marianne, her voice clear as a bell, 'tear off that filthy scab and dig your fingers into the wound on your arm. Nice and deep.'

He was clammy now, his skin ghostly. Alice saw the flare of alarm spark in his eyes before quickly dying out. She inhaled in horror as his fingers twitched and rose above the scabbed skin, curling in upon themselves – and as though he were an automaton, the movements strange and robotic, he plunged his fingernails into the gash, burrowing in deeply. The blood pooled in the wound and dribbled around his wrist, rich droplets splattering to the floor.

'Stop it!' Alice shouted.

Marianne turned to August and put a hand on his arm. 'You may stop.'

He pulled his fingers free and let his arms fall by his sides. His wrist was a mess of oozing flesh.

'What's wrong with you?' snapped Alice.

Marianne was staring reverently at one of the tapestries on the wall, her chest heaving and her hand tightening around the knife-sharp lancet. August moaned in panic; something must have broken through the barrier of Marianne's control – maybe her grip on him was loosening. And Alice wondered desperately if there was something she could do to distract her.

'I know why you want him to open a door to the moors,' she blurted out. 'And why you didn't want me to search for the Lintuvahti's offspring, to kickstart your so-called purge.' She paused. '*You* want to appear on his tapestry – on Death's family tree. *You* want to be the mistress that has his children!'

Silence fell, then Marianne reluctantly tore her eyes away from the wall.

'And why not?' she said, her voice low.

Alice exhaled heavily. 'But even if you get inside, aren't the moors protected? You said so yourself. You can't just wander in, or everyone would do it.'

'He will keep *me* safe,' said Marianne. 'I've proven my devotion to him, over and over, and I'll do it again when I give him a child. It will be *our* son who purges the Rookery, gifting his father with all the sacrifices he could ever wish for.'

She was insane.

'You killed your family,' said Alice, suddenly remembering August's words. Marianne flinched. 'You killed your own family. Sacrificed them to your *Lord*. And now you want to spawn another one with—'

'I didn't kill my sister – I liberated her,' spat Marianne. 'Helena's mind was so riddled with disease that she married a monster who despised us. Imagine! She enslaved herself to a man whose family had hunted us for generations. He didn't love her. How could he?'

Alice frowned. 'Did . . . your sister marry one of the Beaks?'

'She married Sir John Boleyn – now *leader* of the Beaks,' said Marianne. 'She polluted our bloodline with his filth, and my father disowned her for it. My father was a great man, the vice-leader of the Fellowship in its prime. But Helena dishonoured him, and he lost his position.'

'So you . . . killed her?'

'She left me with no choice. She didn't even raise a hand to defend herself from me. Nor did her in-laws either. We caught them by surprise, and they tried to run instead of fighting. *Weak*. But John wasn't even there. He left them to die alone . . . so I spared the baby, to torment him,' she said quietly.

'She'd just had a *baby*? You're disgusting.'

'I wanted John to see Helena's face every time he looked at it.' She broke off and took a deep, steadying breath. 'But it was a small, sickly-looking thing. It had been born too early. I doubt it survived long anyway.'

Alice's face was taut as she pored over what she'd learned. No wonder the Beaks thought the Rookery was a city of evil. And Marianne was a monster. She almost didn't dare breathe.

'Helena was naive and easily tricked,' said Marianne. 'But it wasn't a punishment I brought down on her; it was salvation.' She spun the lancet through her fingers, the metal glinting warmly in the firefly lights. 'But for you, this *will* be a punishment. Now that you've returned my necromancer, I have no need of you – or any other aviarist at all.' She turned to August, who was standing rigid, his jaw set. 'Hold her down,' she ordered, moving to block off the exit.

Alice's pulse quickened. *Surely, he wouldn't.* But his eyes were hollow as he lurched in her direction. *Shit. He would.* She cast around for something she could use as a weapon, but finding nothing, she scrambled backwards towards a tapestry. The rough fabric billowed as she darted behind it, the threat of the Lampyridae ringing alarm bells in her mind. *Mustn't touch . . . Mustn't . . .*

A hand grabbed at the tapestry, and she shrank sideways to avoid it. *The tapestry. The Lampyridae.* The fabric was clenched tight between August's fingers, and Alice stared at them in horror as a sound like a buzz saw tore through the room. It was the drone of small wings rapidly beating the air. The hum grew louder, reverberating off the walls as a swarm of tiny glowing fireflies shot into the room like a hail of bullets.

They descended on August with malevolent speed. Razor-sharp barbs lining their heads sliced into his skin. He barely flinched. They crawled all over his arm, a mass of shiny black abdomens reflecting the yellow glow, hacking at his flesh. Blood poured down his wrist and pooled on the floor. Panicked thoughts crashed around Alice's head – they'd go right to the bone; she couldn't watch him get hurt on her account. And anyway, she still needed him!

She gritted her teeth, sick with fear, and dashed them from his arm. A few fell away but the bulk clung on, heads burrowed into the bloody wounds in his skin.

'Get off him!' she roared.

She wrenched the tapestry from his pale fingers. Her stomach clenched in anticipation – they would come for her now, instead . . . Except, they didn't. *Go,* she urged them. *Fuck off.*

And as one, the fireflies rose into the air, hovering as though dazed – then hurtled away, down the passageway. Alice exhaled heavily and released the tapestry. Why hadn't they attacked her?

'Interesting,' said Marianne, watching her with narrowed eyes.

Alice dropped back behind the tapestry, her mind racing. She had to get out – past Marianne. A familiar sense of calm settled over her, and her jaw tensed; she knew what to do, and she only had seconds to act. Creeping sideways, she peered out from behind the ancient fabric.

August stood nearby, his face expressionless despite his ravaged arm bleeding out. His nightjar was suspended in the air above his head. She fixed her gaze on it, then targeted Marianne's bird too.

She exhaled. 'Look away.'

At Marianne's urging, August swept the tapestry aside. This time, there was no sign of the Lampyridae. And no sign of Alice.

'Where's she gone?' demanded Marianne, moving away from the passageway, leaving the way clear for Alice to escape . . . but she just couldn't. She couldn't leave August behind.

Marianne was so close she could smell her musky perfume. She wavered for a fraction of a second, but Marianne was a mass murderer. If ever violence was justified, it was now.

Unseen, Alice twisted her body and snatched at Marianne's glowing cord. She yanked it closer, and it pulsed and shuddered in her hands. She flushed with the heady buzz of joy she'd come to expect – but she knew pain and dread would follow.

Marianne stumbled, the back of her skull slamming into the wall. Her eyes widened with horror, but her mouth was slack. Alice's calm deserted her and the cloak vanished. Marianne's bony hands clawed at her, trying to shove her away, and Alice dropped the cord – just as August kicked Alice's feet out from under her.

She threw out an arm, and her palm caught the tip of the lancet as she fell. Alice's coccyx slammed onto the stones, and she gasped. Shooting pains tore through her spine.

Her slashed palm bled onto the stones, and she rolled sideways to avoid August's boot as he swung a foot back . . .

'Stop!' she breathed.

Marianne groped drunkenly at the wall and pulled herself upright, her expression filled with menace.

Alice's eyes darted to the empty passageway as August's boot headed for her face, and she threw herself sideways to avoid him. A trickle of her blood ran into the earth and mortar between the stones, turning it a rich red . . . and beneath her, the solid floor rippled like a rug pulled loose. A cacophonous rumble filled the space as the paving flags juddered, and a cluster of dried roots burst out from under them. They thrust upwards like grasping hands. Tree roots? Vines? Had she done this? The stones shifted and Marianne and August were thrown off balance. Marianne's head ricocheted off the wall, and she crumpled, out cold. August smashed down next to her, and Alice leapt to her feet.

August released an explosion of air and sagged back against a patch of bare stone wall. Marianne's control over him had slipped, now she was unconscious – and he was blinking furiously, trying to regain his senses.

'Oh God,' he moaned. 'That mad bitch. What did she—'

No time. Alice grabbed August's jumper and yanked him to the passageway and out of the atrium, to safety.

Lungs burning, Alice stumbled along the pavement, dragging August behind her, her mind reeling. She had to get back to Jude's forge. She quickly surveyed the main thoroughfare, waiting for a gap in the traffic. After several frustrated moments, she darted into the road – but her strength seemed to have abandoned her and she was clipped by a passing dustcart. She landed on the cobbles with a winded gasp, pulling August down beside her like a broken doll.

'My arm,' he gasped.

Tears beckoned. Fuck it all – she was still no nearer to rescuing Jen's nightjar.

'August,' she hissed. 'I can't drag you across the entire city.'

'I can still feel her,' he croaked. 'She's in my veins.'

Shit. She hadn't thought of that. She'd just escaped with Marianne's puppet; he could turn on her at any minute.

'How long until her blood wears off?' she asked. 'It must, at some point.'

'I don't know,' he panted, his face pale with agony.

They looked at each other, and she knew they were thinking the same thing. Marianne could have him shove her straight into traffic any minute, and there wasn't a thing he could do about it.

'When did she give you her blood?' asked Alice. 'It replaces itself every few weeks . . .'

'The day I was arrested,' August groaned. 'My arm is – *fuck*.'

Damn – her blood was still in there. 'We need to get you somewhere you can't hurt yourself, or anyone else, until it's left your body. Coram House,' she said. 'It's more secure than the forge.'

'You don't understand,' he wheezed.

'Did you *want* Marianne to find you?' she asked suspiciously. 'It was *your* idea to go to the library . . .'

'No. At least . . . I don't think so.' He'd pulled off his jumper and wrapped it around the wound to stem the blood. 'Maybe. I think she might have planted it in my head. The Abbey Library is usually patrolled by Runners because of the tree – it's precious – and in my head, I thought it was perfect. But now I think she might have—'

'Perfect for what?' asked Alice. 'Why would you think it was a good idea to go somewhere there might be Runners?'

He looked at her, and cold understanding settled over her. 'You *did* want me – us – to get caught!' she said. 'I knew it!'

'I wanted . . . to be safe from Marianne's influence,' he gasped, his jaw clenched against the sensation in his arm. The shock was clearly wearing off – the pain would kick in, full throttle, any minute. 'She's been forcing her blood into me for years. But she can't use it to *force* me to open a door for her. She tried that with her other necromancers, and her blood was too powerful; it over-whelmed them and weakened their own legacies. But she's still been injecting me with it every couple of months, to make sure I don't stray too far. She withholds it and makes me go cold turkey when she wants the door open. And then when it fails, she puts that poison inside me again to control me while she thinks of another ploy.'

'You sound like a drug addict,' she said.

His face twisted with hatred. 'It's a fucking toxin. I don't want her polluting me any more. That's why I needed to stay in Bow Street as long as possible, but you pulled me *out*!'

Alice looked away from him, her heart pounding. Angular taxicabs rolled past, and a black Beardmore slowed to a stop by the kerb. She flinched instinctively as swift footsteps drew closer.

'Alice Wyndham—'

Her mouth fell open and she stared in horror as two Runners rushed towards her. They descended and her arms were wrenched backwards and twisted behind her. She could hardly breathe . . .

'Take me!' she heard August yell. 'Take me as well, you bastards!'

26

Risdon met them at the main doors of Bow Street Station.

'Come to my office,' he said. 'Please.'

Alice blinked away her fury and confusion. Why weren't the Runners taking her straight to the cells?

'Where's August?'

He frowned. 'August Rhone has been refusing to leave our custody for weeks. That he's no longer blocking a cell is a cause for celebration.'

Please. Please let August have travelled to Coram House. She'd have lost any chance of him opening the door to the moors if Marianne had got to him.

Risdon closed the main door and reopened it to darkness. They spent a moment in the void before he opened the door again and they stepped directly into his office.

'I didn't think it was possible to travel in the station,' she said numbly.

'I make the rules – I don't abide by them,' he said. 'Rather like yourself and Crowley, I am uncommonly skilled with the doorways. Sit. Please.'

She took the seat opposite his desk, and he sat in the far comfier chair on the other side. 'Can I get you anything? Tea?'

She shook her head. What sort of ploy was this? Drug her so she'd go peacefully?

'You'll be glad to know that I've rescinded the warrant for your arrest and lifted your suspension.'

'Are you serious?'

He folded his hands. 'Very much so.'

'But . . . *why*? I broke into your cells. I . . . I helped someone escape.'

He sat back and poured himself a cup of black tea. 'You removed a nuisance who was refusing to leave.'

She watched him in silence. There had to be more to this. There was no way she could have trespassed twice without punishment.

'You want something from me,' she said slowly.

Risdon took a sip from his drink and set it down on the desk. 'I wish to offer you a new role within the organization. Something more suited to your talents.'

Alice swallowed, her eyes tracking away from his face and across the shelves of books lining the wall behind his desk. She scanned a few of the titles – *The Kalevala, The Codex Sinaiticus, The King James Bible, Magellan's Metaphysical Treatise: Sielun, Magellan's Nightjar Compendium* . . .

Her breathing stilled and her gaze sharpened. Why did he have that rare book? She opened her mouth to speak. He was watching her with an expression of patience. He didn't know she was an aviarist – or did he? Was he trying to flush her out?

'What are my talents?' she demanded.

'I believe you have an uncanny knack for rooting out lies,' he said. His face was the very image of bland patience. So he did know she was an aviarist? Who had told him?

'Imagine the good you could do,' he went on. 'You could be

involved in the cut and thrust of investigation – sitting in on interviews with suspects, reading their nightjars, revealing to us their truths and motives. It would be so much *more* than a dead-end post in the archives.'

She paused. Did she really want to work for the Runners again? Hadn't one day been enough? Marianne had infiltrated the Runners too. She was as good as a serial killer, and yet she seemed to be free to do as she liked; the whole thing smacked of corruption.

'August *told* you what Marianne wants to do,' Alice retorted. 'He said he told you she wanted to open a door to the Sulka Moors, so that she could start a city-wide massacre. Why hasn't anyone investigated her? She's the reason he wanted to stay in your cells – to stay safe. You *know* this.'

'Miss Wyndham,' Risdon said calmly, 'Marianne Northam's beliefs are fanciful.'

'Fanciful,' she repeated. 'Right. But not too fanciful, because she's managed to get her hooks into some of your own Runners. Maybe *that's* why she doesn't get investigated.'

He paused. 'Is that an accusation?'

She swallowed hard and stood up on shaky legs. 'No,' she said. 'No, it's not. It's one of those truths you wanted me to root out.' She turned to him and plastered a smile on her face. 'Thank you for your help with the arrest warrant and the suspension. Does that mean I'm free to go?'

'Of course. And my offer?'

'I'm sorry,' she said, 'but I think I'll have to pass.'

Risdon sighed gently, but she feared he hadn't given up on her. 'Very well. You may, if you wish, return to your previous post in the archives at your convenience.'

Alice nodded, but she had no intention of returning.

'Thanks again,' she said as she slipped out of his office and hurried off through the darkly lit station.

When she reached the exit barrier, Chalmers was on duty, red-faced and corpulent as ever, and her footsteps slowed to a stop. He'd had the opportunity to stop her the night she'd broken August out of the cells – but he hadn't. She'd been grateful at the time, but now she felt sickened; here was another Runner mired in corruption.

'You again,' he said.

'The one and only,' she said tightly.

He suddenly leaned over his desk and grabbed her hand.

'I've been waiting to see you again,' he said in a low voice.

She frowned and tried to pull back. 'This is a public place,' she murmured. 'If Marianne thinks she can—'

'The moors,' he hissed.

Alice stiffened. 'What are you talking about?'

'They want to help you. You'd be a fool to turn them down.'

'Who is "they"?'

'The Beaks,' he murmured. 'They'll get you inside and help you cheat the protections in place – they have a way – if you're willing to meet them.'

'But . . . don't you work for Marianne, not—'

'And if you *don't* go . . .' Chalmers glanced nervously out over the entrance hall. 'You'll put your loved ones in jeopardy.'

She froze. They were threatening her family? And *Jen*?

'Here,' he said. His free hand reached down behind the counter. He lifted up a suspension file and shoved it at her chest. 'Take this as an incentive. You've no chance without them.'

He released her, and she staggered backwards in surprise.

'Go to the London Eye – back through the Arch. When you want to meet them, buy a ticket for the Eye and they'll find you.

Any night. Give your name at the booking desk and they'll find you there.'

He swung the barrier at last, and it clanked shut behind her, leaving her on the other side. Her stomach lurched, and she shook her head, biting back her anger.

'You tell those bastards,' she hissed. 'You tell those bastards I'll kill them if they go near Jen or my parents.'

She hurried out of the station and down the steps. Outside, she flung herself back against the wall, breathing great lungfuls of cold air. She was free. Chalmers was in league with the Beaks. Her loved ones were in danger. And August . . . ?

Her legs trembled. She was torn between rushing back inside and smashing that bastard Chalmers in the face and racing up to Risdon and revealing what he'd said. She swallowed thickly. But the Beaks wanted to help her. A few hours ago, things had seemed hopeless, but now . . .

No. It was a trap. They wanted to lure her out. Vin had already tried to drag her away, and this was their second attempt. They needed her to examine nightjars, to unmask people with Väki genes for them to murder.

She looked up at the many windows of the eerily quiet station, but some thread of unquestioning trust had snapped. The Runners didn't always catch the bad guys. And sometimes the Runners *were* the bad guys.

27

'Finally,' said Crowley, his face slack with relief as he opened the door. 'After a day spent pulling strings with Risdon, I went to deliver the news of your exoneration. Only to discover you'd vanished from the forge with that halfwit.'

She trudged past him, into the hallway, then stopped and frowned.

'What halfwit?' Her eyes widened. 'Is August here?'

She poked her head into the kitchen, where Sasha and Jude made a welcomingly domestic scene. Sasha was at the cooker, her shirt sleeves rolled up, and Jude was chopping carrots at the table. It seemed there'd been another leak, too; the ceiling was dripping water into a saucepan on the counter.

'Is he here?' she repeated.

'We've locked him in the attic,' said Crowley grimly. 'For his own safety. And ours.'

'It's not as inhumane as it sounds,' said Jude. 'He has blankets and cushions. We've fixed up his arm and given him something for the pain. He's out cold.'

Crowley frowned. 'He'll remain in the attic until he's free of Marianne's influence. I've asked Josef Skala to visit tomorrow, in case he can speed up the process of red blood cell replacement.'

'You're going to donate to—'

'Absolutely not,' he said. 'Josef's going to detoxify him, not fit him with a skeleton key.'

She glanced up the stairs.

'Don't even *think* of visiting him before Josef has cleansed his system.'

She nodded. 'I'm going to head up to my room.'

She wanted to be alone with her thoughts – and the file Chalmers had given her. She didn't dare tell Crowley about the offer; he'd brought her to the Rookery to get her away from Vin and the Beaks. But if she didn't meet them, what was the risk to her family? Were they bluffing? And at the back of her mind, the niggling worry: what if they really were the only ones who could get her into the moors, to find Jen's nightjar and escape with it?

She sank onto the bed. And despite the encroaching darkness stealing the light from the room, she flipped open the file's front cover.

> *The Black Menagerie lies in the heart of the Sulka Moors and is home to an almost infinite number of nightjars. Each nightjar is secured within the menagerie upon the death of its former owner. This is when the cord binding them together is severed and the soul-bird free to fly to the moors. Death, known to many as the Lintuvahti, tends to the nightjars in his care.*
>
> *Source: Louisa Williams, survivor of a trip to the moors*

Alice squinted at the page, trying to comprehend the words fully. This Louisa Williams had actually survived a trip to the moors.

So it *could* be done; it was possible not only to go to the moors but also to return safely. But how? She continued skimming through the file, her eyes dancing across the aged pages, searching for answers.

She finally came to a small blue ledger tucked into a plastic wallet, the handwriting elegant but clear. Only the first few pages had been filled in, but she fell upon them eagerly.

The Sulka Moors are difficult to access. This makes visiting Death's 'Black Menagerie' – which houses nightjars after our souls pass over – doubly so. Eamon Pickford, latterly of Paignton, Devon, reported several interesting findings on the matter of travel there, before his death in 1873. An aviarist and a necromancer by trade, Pickford was paid a handsome sum to enter the moors with a view to passing on a message to a Mrs Agnes Naysmith, former wife of Arthur Naysmith, a local publican. Pickford made several short trips to the moors, collating all he learned there upon his immediate return.

Pickford discovered that when he set foot inside the Sulka Moors, the door to an empty cage in the menagerie opened. He reported chest pains and the sensation of drowning after approximately two minutes journeying across the moors. He noted, also, that the cord binding him to his nightjar seemed to be fading – though their connection fully re-established itself when he left the moors. Finally, he concluded that this was the Lintuvahti's safeguard to protect his lands from an invasion by the living. Namely that every living person who entered the moors would lose their nightjar, after only a short

*time – resulting in severe chest pains as separation
occurred and eventual bodily death.*

*He reports in his diaries that his conclusions were
correct, having – on his last visit – allowed Arthur
Naysmith to accompany him to the moors to seek out the
publican's deceased wife. The trip was not successful: they
found no sign of Agnes Naysmith, nor any other soul.
Moreover, Arthur collapsed and died within moments of
arrival. Pickford reports the horror of watching as the cord
binding Arthur's nightjar to his body was rent in two. The
cord dissolved and the nightjar abandoned the publican's
corpse, flying directly to one of two empty, opened cages –
one for each of them. Somehow, Pickford's nightjar's
connection lasted longer – presumably due to his aviarist
legacy. This allowed him just enough time to leave. Pickford
reports seeing other nightjars flying over the moors, and he
watched as the cages opened for them and then closed once
they were ensconced inside. 'Each nightjar is the key to a
cage,' he wrote. 'The cages open and close for them alone.'*

*Pickford never returned to the moors. His diaries
detailing the event were only found several years after his
death. But from other writings, we have concluded that
he was correct. Upon a living person entering the moors,
a cage in the menagerie will open. This will attract the
nightjar to it, via some form of magnetic pull. This, as
Pickford noted, acts as a safeguard, ensuring that the
living are not tempted to venture into Death's lands. For
those willing to take the risk, the price of dallying there
will be the loss of their nightjar and near-instant death.
We cannot, therefore, ratify the practice suggested by Sir
Thomas Liddle, assistant to the commanding officer – who*

*advocated sending Bow Street Runners to the Sulka Moors
in an attempt to commune with, and glean information
from, the souls of murder victims.*

Signed:
  The Right Honourable William Garrick,
  Lord Chief Justice

The pages fell away from Alice's fingers, and she tipped her head back to stare at the ceiling. So this was Death's safeguard. This was what stopped the grief-stricken from travelling to the moors to be reunited with their dead.

Even if she managed to get into the moors and steal Jen's nightjar back from the menagerie, she would probably lose her own. And then die before she had a chance to save Jen's anyway. How long had Pickford lasted? Minutes? Could she rescue Jen's nightjar and escape from the moors in only minutes? She exhaled heavily. *Unlikely.*

'Did you know?' she accused.

Crowley flinched. He was in the hallway, blowing dust off the Bakelite phone.

'Know what?' he asked, eyes sliding away from hers.

'If I go to the Sulka Moors,' she said, descending the last few stairs, 'then a cage in The Black Menagerie will open and . . . I'll lose my nightjar to it and die there myself.'

His face relaxed and he nodded. This clearly wasn't new information. 'It's true that you would be required to sacrifice a nightjar to the open cage. But it's also true that once the cage receives a nightjar, it will close. The nightjar you sacrifice acts as a key: the cage door opens when you arrive and closes once a nightjar enters.'

'So I'm just going to lose my nightjar then?'

'No,' he said wearily. 'You have to sacrifice a nightjar to one of the menagerie's cages, but no one said it had to be your own. You're an aviarist; you can do what others can't. Bring a spare nightjar with you.'

Silence fell while Alice digested his words. 'Where would I find a spare nightjar?'

'You don't *find* a spare nightjar, Alice,' he said. 'You *take* one.'

She stared at him, but his expression was unyielding. What was he suggesting? That she tear a nightjar from its owner? If she wanted to save Jen, she had to sacrifice someone else's nightjar? Someone else's soul? How? How could she sever a cord? And this was on top of the apparent murder she'd have to commit for August, so he could call a vengeful soul to open the door. No. It was too much. All of it.

'Why didn't you tell me this before?' she asked, aghast.

'Because I've not yet found a palatable solution – but I had hoped to do so,' he said. 'One obvious solution is to be present when Marianne is sacrificing one of her members to her *Lord*.'

She recoiled, but his face had taken on a musing expression.

'Consider it carefully,' he said. 'It would be a death you couldn't stop anyway. An inevitability. There would be no blood on your hands. Though it might be unpleasant to watch, the act of snatching the nightjar – within moments of their demise – would be harmless.'

'That is . . . disgusting,' she managed, her throat tight. That he would even suggest it . . .

'Yes,' he said darkly. 'Well, sometimes the only options are bad ones.'

Alice watched in helpless silence as Crowley strode from the hallway. She hesitated for a moment, then hurried towards the kitchen, where she could hear him loading the sink with plates. She raised her fist to the closed door, took a deep breath to steel herself and—

The door was whipped open before she could complete the movement. Crowley towered over her.

'What?'

She let her hand drop and blew out a breath.

'I . . . I just . . .'

She fell silent, unable to find the words.

'Well, as enthralling as this little tête-à-tête has been, if you will excuse me,' he said, swinging the door shut.

On impulse, she shoved her hand into the gap, and the door crushed her fingers before bouncing back open. She gasped and stumbled against the doorframe as tears instantly sprang to her eyes. *Bugger!* She gritted her teeth.

Crowley took one look at her, cursed, grabbed her elbow and pulled her into the kitchen. He spun the tap, shoved a tea towel under the cold, rushing water and turned back to her. She allowed him to carefully wrap her throbbing fingers in the towel. The icy water made her wince with pain.

'That wasn't one of your better ideas,' he said.

'I know,' she murmured.

'If you expect me to feel guilty, because you recklessly shoved your hand into a doorway, then you can think again.'

She stared at him incredulously. 'You just don't know how to be a normal human being, do you? Your social skills are as—'

'Calm down,' he said, his voice unexpectedly soft. 'Stop getting your knickers in a twist.'

Her cheeks flamed. 'Leave my knickers out of this.'

He raised an eyebrow.

There was a moment of silence so thick you could have tarred a road with it. Then his eyes flicked down to the towel and he seemed to remember he was still holding her hand, his thumb brushing gentle circles over her knuckles. A thrill spiralled through her, and she couldn't tell if she was tingling because of the pain or her hopeless despair or something else. Then he released her hand and glanced quickly away. There were two bright spots of colour on Crowley's cheeks. Was he *shy*?

'You should . . . get some rest,' he said, nodding awkwardly at her and slipping out into the corridor. 'We should *all* get some rest.'

'There was a letter on the rug for you,' said Jude, wheeling into the kitchen the following evening.

Alice put down the potato peeler and frowned as she took the proffered envelope. Sasha peered over her shoulder while she opened it. It contained an old photograph of a laughing bride and groom with their arms slung around each other. Along the bottom, *We asked nicely* had been scrawled into it. Every muscle in her body tensed, and she thrust it under Jude's nose.

'My parents,' she croaked.

'I'll phone the Runners,' said Sasha, storming into the hallway.

Alice spun abruptly on her heel. She sprinted down the basement stairs, her heart jackhammering against her ribs, and pummelled Crowley's door so hard that it rattled against its frame.

'Has my door insulted you in some way?' he asked when it creaked open. 'Why must you insist—'

She shoved the envelope under his nose. He glanced down at it.

'What? Is it my birthday?'

'You *said* they would be safe if I stayed away from them!' She pulled out the photo. 'My parents . . . This was delivered to the house. They only had one copy of this, and that was kept in their *living room*.'

Crowley's eyes widened.

'Which means that those lunatics have been in my parents' house!' Alice shook the photo in a pale, clenched fist.

She'd wasted time today when she should have *been* there. She should have gone straight back to London, but she'd thought there would be time to negotiate, to plan what to do. What if her parents were already—

'I've had enough of this,' she raged. 'All of it. I'm going home to check on them.'

'That's not a good idea,' said Sasha. She was standing at the top of the stairs with a grim look on her face. 'It could be dangerous if you travel in this state. You won't be able to concentrate properly—'

'I don't *care*,' Alice shouted. 'What choice do I have? What if they're—What if those bastards have—' She screwed her eyes shut. Now was not the time for hysterics. She needed to keep it together. 'Close the door, Crowley,' she rasped.

His eyes glittered in a way she'd come to expect. 'You will not use this door to travel there.'

'Fine,' she said. 'Fine.' She'd use another fucking door then. She whirled back to the stairs.

'You will *stay here*.'

'I'm going.'

'No!' he said, a desperate edge to his voice. 'I'll make sure they're safe, but you must stay. I'll – let me fix *this* for you, at least.'

He flung his door wide and snatched up his coat before closing the door.

'Sasha. Make sure she stays here. Where it is *safe*.'

'Stop talking about me as though I'm not here,' Alice said. 'They're *my* parents.'

Crowley turned back to her, his face awash with sympathy. He placed a soothing hand on her shoulder, as though calming a wild animal.

'Alice,' he murmured. 'You're in no fit state. Your emotions are running so high you're going to get yourself killed, and your parents too.'

'Fine. We'll go together then. Me and you.'

He grimaced, impatience sweeping away his gentleness. 'Someone needs to stay with August. Josef will be here soon; if he can't help, it may be weeks before August is capable of opening a door to the moors. Speak to Josef when he comes. Impress upon him the importance of detoxing our guest as soon as possible.'

'Sasha and Jude can stay with August,' she protested.

'Finding a necromancer with the skills to open a door to the moors has taken forever,' he retorted. 'And now you're happy to take your eye off the bigger picture? We – you – need him. Desperately. Would you really trust anyone else to take care of him?'

She hesitated. 'You could stay to look after August and I could—'

'No. You can't travel right now, and I will not babysit that fool. He's your responsibility.' He paused. 'August . . . is the key to helping Jen. Trust me to do this for you. I'll return when I'm certain your parents are safe.'

Trust. The magic word. Again.

She nodded shakily. 'And what if you don't return?'

'I will.'

Alice held up the photograph in both hands. 'The Beaks know where I am now, and they have people working for them here in the Rookery. I found out Chalmers is one of theirs yesterday, and

God knows who else. They can get to me, Crowley.' She paused for a sharp breath. 'So what if you don't come back?'

His eyes met hers, and his face relaxed. 'Then assume I've failed,' he said softly. 'And you must *run and hide*.'

She frowned. Run and hide? Something twisted in her chest. When he turned away, panic overwhelmed her, and she darted closer and grabbed at his sleeve. She wanted to say . . .

He paused, waiting for her to free the words straining at her lips. The moment lengthened, and they remained frozen in silent tableau.

Crowley swallowed hard. With a nod, he gently shrugged her off and wrapped his hand around the doorknob. He pulled open the door that usually led to his room but which now opened only into darkness. He made to step forward—

'Crowley,' she said. 'Thank you.'

He paused. A brief expression of pain flashed across his face, and then he slammed the door shut.

She raced forward and pulled it open as though to follow him, but the darkness had gone. Instead, she found herself standing in Crowley's bedroom, trembling and alone.

The house was filled with a powerful silence. The kind of silence that made its own demands. You *must* not speak. You *must* slip from room to room like a ghost, muffling your footfalls on the creaky floorboards. The kitchen, usually a hub of warmth, was drab and cold.

Jude, Sasha and Alice sat waiting there, unspoken questions hovering in the air above them.

Where was Crowley? Why hadn't he returned? Was he still safe? Was he alive?

Jude placed a bowl of steaming lingonberry porridge in front of Alice, and she stared at it. She couldn't eat.

Her fingers drummed against the tabletop. She was wired. Restless. She'd had a pathetic amount of sleep, having spent most of the night on the basement steps. She had waited for Crowley. But Crowley hadn't come back.

Then assume I've failed . . . And you must run and hide.

She shivered at the memory and stood up abruptly. It had been almost twenty-four hours. She couldn't wait any longer.

'Alice,' said Sasha, puncturing the silence at last. 'You can't. It's not safe.'

Alice forced a smile. 'I'm just going to bring this up to August, that's all,' she said, lifting the bowl of porridge.

Josef Skala had worked his magic on August's kidneys, plasma and platelets, and his blood was now clean and free of Marianne's insidious influence. Whatever Josef had done to him had wiped him out, however. He was expected to sleep through the night, recuperating.

Sasha frowned, scepticism plastered all over her face, but she returned the attempt at a smile. 'Yeah. He must be starving.'

Alice nodded, but didn't move. The bowl was scalding her hands, but she barely noticed.

'Crowley will be back soon,' Jude said gently. 'He always is. He just likes a dramatic exit, that's all.'

Alice excused herself and walked calmly up the first set of stairs. However, once she was sure she was far enough away, she raced up the next flight.

She closed the door behind her, dumped the bowl on the floor and hurried to the spindly writing desk in the corner. Inside was a Bowie knife she'd borrowed from Jude's weaponry collection.

He'd insisted on kitting them all out, now that whoever worked for the Beaks knew where to find her.

Her knife was perfect. The handle was made of polished deer antler, and it fitted snugly in the palm of her hand. Not too small and not too big: the Goldilocks of knives. She shoved the sheath into her jeans pocket and pulled on a fleece-lined coat. What else would she need? The feather. She snatched it up from her chair.

Maybe Crowley and her parents were fine. Maybe her mum had delayed him by forcing him to stay overnight and giving him the full-on Wyndham hospitality treatment. Yes. She nodded jerkily to herself. That certainly sounded like Patricia Wyndham.

She took a deep breath, visualized and ran her fingers along the crack of her bedroom door. Then she pulled it open and was met by darkness. Perfect. Her adrenaline spiked, and she could almost feel the blood racing full throttle through her veins. She stepped forward into the void, the image of her parents' red front door fixed firmly in her mind.

Her fingers brushed against a door handle. *Yes!* She pushed open the door and—

Shit! She was in Coram House's bathroom. She growled with frustration and kicked at the forlorn-looking toilet against the wall. Fear squeezed her chest tight. Her parents and Crowley might be getting tortured and murdered in London, and she was standing here taking it out on a toilet.

It was *her* the Beaks wanted. She had to fix this. Jen, her parents, everything . . .

She paused, her hand flat against the door, as something dawned on her. Marble Arch. Sasha had said it was one of the only ways in and out of the city, so she couldn't go directly to her parents' house anyway. She'd have to go back the way she came.

She blew out a breath, opened the door and thought furiously,

The janitor's outhouse at Goring University . . . She pictured the stone shed and the glossy black door with the ring handle.

The door now opened onto the perfectly manicured gardens, bathed in shadow and moonlight. The row of fir trees hiding the outhouse threw monstrous shapes across Alice's path. But she paid them no mind as she jogged around the wing of the building, her focus utterly bent on reaching the Arch.

It wasn't yet midnight, and a few Rookery students still meandered around the university's central building, with its impressive domed roof. But the lights began to wink out as it closed for the night.

When she reached Marble Arch itself, her stomach swooped at the sight of it. She sprinted across the road, darting sideways to avoid a horse and trap. Then, without pausing, she steeled herself and hurtled through.

There was a group on the other side of the Arch, and she gasped. Had anyone seen her materialize out of thin air? But they were consulting a tube map and not paying her any attention at all.

She slumped against the nearest column of the Arch, trying to get her bearings as the lights blinded her and the noise disoriented her. London was a far brighter, louder, busier version of the Rookery. A city with the volume turned up. Had it always been like this?

Flashy cars were beeping their way through the streets, stopping at traffic lights as groups of men and women, dressed to impress, staggered across the road, thumping bonnets in high spirits. Ornate fountains lit with rainbow lights spewed a cascade of coloured water nearby. Tourists roved the streets in gangs, admiring perfectly ordinary things, like phone boxes and buses.

It was all so familiar, and yet . . . not. London was the same, but she was different.

Alice took a deep breath. *Focus.* She scanned Edgware Road. Where could she go? Which doorway could she use?

Finally, her gaze alighted on a tiny upmarket wine bar over the road, called Franc's. She hurried towards it, ploughing through a flock of pigeons then braving more traffic.

Once inside, she located a large gold arrow hanging from the ceiling, pointing at the bathroom. Alice checked there was nobody behind her and shoved the door aside.

My old bedroom in my parents' house . . . My old bedroom in my parents' house . . .

Alice staggered through the blustery space of the void once more and stumbled right out of her old bedroom wardrobe. She collapsed onto the bed. She'd done it! She'd made it home! But the joy was short-lived.

Alice sat up, careful not to make a sound, and slipped the Bowie knife out of her pocket. Then she tiptoed over to the door to the landing. She had the benefit of surprise and didn't want to waste it. She gently pushed the door aside and crept out.

As she searched the house, the obvious grew impossible to ignore. There was no one there. No Crowley. No Mum. No Dad. No little white dogs, even. *No Beaks.* And yet, something had happened here. Something very bad. The living room had been trashed. The coffee table had been upended, and the TV was lying face-down on the floor. Plant pots had been smashed, and there was mud scattered over the carpet, mingling with the shards of glass from a shattered mirror. There were scorch marks on the carpet and the wallpaper, as though someone had tried, and failed, to set the place on fire. Crowley?

Dread settled in her stomach. What should she do? Given the

circumstances, the police were out. They'd never believe her. She felt strung out, her nerves tight as guitar strings as she made herself sit and think in the dining room. A pile of old newspapers caught her eye, stacked on the table.

LOCAL WOMAN STILL MISSING! screamed the headline. She scanned it distractedly until she hit upon a name she recognized and sat bolt upright. Alice Wyndham. There was a quote from the Met police, pleading for information. She read the article greedily, but the more she read, the more sickened she felt. *Mr and Mrs Wyndham . . . Their daughter Alice has been missing since . . .*

The room seemed to shrink, the walls crowding her, suffocating her. Crowley had lied. He'd said he'd delivered her letter to her parents, that he'd 'taken care of it'. And all this time they'd thought she was *missing*. Her eyes flew to the article again. The words *bogus police officer* leapt out at her.

That man. That bloodyfucking man! She'd thought he was helping her. She'd finally begun to accept his skeleton key donation as a sign of trustworthiness – he'd given her his *blood*. But – of course! What an idiot she was. Couldn't she follow his blood through the doors?

Wasting no time, Alice rose and headed for the nearest door. She took a deep breath, put her hand against the dining room doorframe – her fingers tingling – and pulled it open to the void.

Crowley's blood . . . Follow Crowley's blood . . .

Another door appeared in the darkness, and she opened it quickly, entering an unfamiliar room. She stared around wildly, the knife thrust out in front of her in a fighting stance.

'Mike! Oh my goodness! Mike, she's here! She's here!'

And then a short woman with bobbed white hair and oval glasses barrelled forward and swept her into a bone-crushing hug. It was her mum.

28

She woke suddenly, going from a deep sleep to total alertness. Her neck ached from the angle she'd been lying at on the sofa and her arm was prickling with pins and needles. She jerked up, and her two dogs launched themselves at her, an explosion of fur and wagging tails.

Alice buried her face in their coats and exhaled a shuddering breath before squinting around the room.

'Crowley?'

There was no sign of him. Her dad was flicking through the TV channels with a remote control. Her mum was sitting rigidly in the chair opposite, a magazine on her lap, which she was ignoring completely. When she realized Alice was awake, she pushed her glasses further up her nose and swallowed convulsively.

'We thought he'd killed you,' her mum said quietly.

'I thought *you'd* been killed,' said Alice.

Her mum scrunched the magazine in her hands, her fingers bone white. 'I let him into the house,' she said, 'and then – he took you.'

Her dad was staring straight ahead, unmoving, as though he didn't dare breathe. As though breathing would ignite the tension in the room and consume them all.

'*I let him in*,' her mum repeated.

Alice stared at her, shocked. 'It wasn't your fault. He could have got in anyway. And besides . . . I was okay. Really. I'm so, *so* sorry—'

'No,' said her mum, holding up a trembling hand. '*I'm* sorry. I'm the one who—'

She struggled off the sofa. 'Mum—'

There was a muffled sob, and then Alice was snatched into her mum's arms, their cheeks pressed together so tightly that when they finally parted, her face was wet with tears that weren't her own.

'He said he'd delivered a letter to explain,' said Alice, 'so that you wouldn't worry.'

'Oh,' said her mum, wiping her face with the hem of her cardigan, 'he's explained everything *now*. But that doesn't make up for the weeks of torture we went through before we found out.'

'We thought he was a lunatic,' her dad croaked. He'd turned the TV off and was looking at her as though he'd never seen her before. He didn't seem to have shaved in a long time, and his usual stoic West Countryman persona seemed off-kilter. 'Turning up on the doorstep after all that time, telling us all sorts of crazy stories about birds and places no one could see. I swung for him, but the bugger ducked. Good job, really, because then I thought he might be our only chance of finding out what he'd done with your—with you.'

His face flushed.

'And then . . .' her dad said, 'and then he said we were in danger, and he pulled me through the kitchen door. And it – it didn't lead to the kitchen. It led to, well, to here.'

'Where are we?' asked Alice, getting to her feet and peering out of the living room window. Outside, iron-grey waves smashed against a harbour wall, splattering foam across the stones before sweeping back into the pushing-pulling tide. Across the sea there were rolling green hills, dotted with small bungalows still visible in the darkness.

'We're in Ireland – somehow,' said her mum.

Alice turned from the window. 'I followed him here, but . . .' She swung around, ears strained for sounds of movement. 'Where is he?'

'There was some trouble when we were leaving,' her mum admitted. 'He sent your dad and the dogs through all right. But then, when it was my turn . . .' She frowned. 'Another man burst into the house and there was a bit of a . . . scuffle.'

'A scuffle?' Alice said blankly.

'A fight. They nearly destroyed the house. The man, the one who smashed through the front door, he punched that – that Crowley and came running at me, so I had to grab the first thing to hand, that awful ceramic flower pot, and smashed it over his head. Well, I tried to, anyway, but I missed and got his shoulder instead. I slowed him down though. I don't think he was expecting it. Then Crowley and him, they charged at each other, and there was fire – I don't know where that came from – but there was fire and blood and, oh God, it was awful. Just awful.'

'And then what happened?'

'Crowley grabbed me and shoved me out of the kitchen door. It opened right into here. He got blood all over my jumper, and he said to me . . . he said, "When you get there, rub that blood on the door and don't wipe it off. Don't wipe it off the door and she'll be able to find you." And he was right, because you did. Is it true?'

Alice's mind was reeling. 'Is what true?' she whispered.

Her mum glanced over at her dad. His face was pale and strained. 'What he said you are?'

Their eyes met, and she found tears pricking painfully at her. She nodded, and her mum laughed. A tearful, panicked laugh.

'Oh!' she said. 'Oh! Well! That's . . . We always knew you were special. Always said you were. Remember when you won the swimming certificate for the ten metres?'

'Everyone got one, Mum.'

'We still have it,' she said proudly. 'It's in a frame in the dining room.'

Her dad stood up on his creaky legs and lumbered over to envelop her in a tight hug. Something snapped inside her then, and she collapsed against him, snuffling into his shirt.

'It's okay,' he said in his gruff voice, doing his best to comfort her.

'It's not,' she said. 'Everything's going wrong. Jen's accident was all my fault—'

He pushed her away, holding her at arm's length so he could see her face properly.

'It wasn't your fault,' he said firmly. 'Life is hard enough without blaming yourself for things you can't control. Don't do that. Jen loves you.'

He crushed her to him again, and then gently pushed her away and cleared his throat. 'I need to go and chop firewood or dig a trench. There's too much oestrogen in this bloody room.'

Alice laughed weakly.

'Will you have a cup of tea?' he said.

She nodded. Tea. That great bastion of comfort.

'Mum,' said Alice. 'The man that attacked you and Crowley? Did you know who it was?'

She shook her head. 'I'd never seen him before in my life.

I only saw him properly after I hit him on the shoulder. You know, I think I might have broken it. Can you break a shoulder?'

'What did he look like?'

She paused, her face screwed up as she searched her memory. 'Tall,' she said. 'Taller than me. Well, everyone's taller than me, of course . . . Stocky. And strong. He had a shaved head – sort of stubbly – and a scar on his face. No, two scars. One right down his cheek.'

Alice nodded. Vin. Vin and the Beaks. Thank God Crowley had arrived in time. What would have happened to her parents if he hadn't been there? The memory of Jen splayed out on the road, surrounded by a pool of blood, jumped into her mind and left her stricken.

'Are you okay, love?'

Alice plastered on a fake smile. 'I'm fine.'

She turned around to hide the horror on her face and found herself inches from the blood smeared across the kitchen door. Crowley's blood, dried and flaking. What if he was—

She inhaled as though she'd been winded, swaying on her feet. He had done this for her. He didn't have to, but he had – and now where was he? *Something* constricted her chest. *Crowley* . . . If he was hurt . . .

'Why don't you go for a proper lie-down, in the bedroom?' said her mum. 'You only slept for an hour or two.'

Her mum's hand came up to rest on her shoulder, and she patted it shakily.

Alice squeezed her eyes even tighter to hold herself in check. 'Okay,' she whispered. 'Okay.'

'Good. I'll go and put the heating on; it's like the Arctic Circle in that room.'

She listened to her mum's footsteps receding and paused for

just a second – and then rubbed at the blood on the door, spitting on her sleeve to clean the waxy wood.

Crowley had been in a fight, but he hadn't come back to Coram House – and he'd been bleeding. She had to find him. Maybe if there was no blood on this door, she could track him to wherever he was. What if he was bleeding out?

She wrapped her hand around the door handle and tried to focus. She opened it to darkness and prepared to hurry through, but a voice called out, full of alarm.

'Alice?'

Alice turned to her mum, her face strained.

'I'm sorry, Mum,' she whispered. 'I have to find Crowley. He saved you – I have to help him. I love you.'

And then she stepped backwards, into the void, the dogs' barking ringing in her ears.

29

The first thing she registered was the dripping. A steady stream was falling from the cracked ceiling, splashing onto the exposed pipes and dribbling off to pool on the kitchen floor. The room smelled damp and stale. There was one tiny window above the kitchen cupboards. But it had been painted shut and was covered by a dirty grey net curtain. Where was this place?

Alice fumbled for her knife and edged her way into the next room, eyes alert for any signs of movement. An ancient velvet sofa stood sentry in the corner of the living room. Dozens of paintings of birds cluttered the walls: doves, hummingbirds and robins.

She tiptoed into the hallway and surveyed her options. The front door was right in front of her. She could leave, find out exactly where she was and maybe learn whose house this was. Or she could go up the stairs. She took the stairs.

The landing ran off to three closed doors. The first, predictably, led to the bathroom. The second led to a bedroom that had been used as a dumping ground. Old ladies' clothes were spilling out of the wardrobe. A walking frame was balanced, upside down, on the dressing table, next to a wooden jewellery box engraved with feathers.

Impatient now, she pushed open the last door. The furniture here was equally old-fashioned, the carpet was the same pea green, and the bed was in the same place – covered with another patchwork throw. But this room had Crowley in it.

He was slumped on the floor, his back to the wall. The carpet near Crowley was not pea green. Even in the dim light, it was red.

Alice dropped the knife and flew to his side, reaching for his neck to find a pulse. A faint tick drummed against her fingers.

'Crowley? Crowley, can you hear me?'

She peeled his eyelids back and patted his face urgently. Sweat plastered his hair to his forehead, and he was so pale she could almost see the colour of the veins throbbing at his temple.

'Crowley!' she yelled. 'Wake up!'

A low, guttural groan escaped from the back of his throat, and he sucked in a breath. His body went rigid and his eyes flew open. He rolled sideways and coughed into the carpet – a hacking, violent cough that left him trembling and pale.

He flopped onto his back again, his breath coming in short, hitched bursts.

'Tell me where you're bleeding,' Alice begged.

He shook his head and closed his eyes, sinking back into oblivion. She shuffled forward on her knees and brushed the hair back from his face. His body had gone utterly limp.

'Crowley? Crowley! Wake up. Please wake up or I—'

She bit her lip and reached for his coat, pushing it back over his shoulders and pulling it as far down his arms as she could, hampered by the fact that his full weight was lying on it. She inhaled sharply at the sight of his shirt, once white but now damp with oozing blood. It had spread across the right-hand side and soaked into his sleeve. Her hands jumped to his shirt collar and she tore at the column of buttons, tugging the fabric up out of the waistband of his trousers and carefully peeling it away from his damp skin.

There was a deep, ragged gash in his shoulder, about three inches long, and his chest was a canvas of purple bruises blossoming under the skin. Scrapes and cuts spiderwebbed across his ribs and down his stomach. And beneath these were older scars, slashed here and there across his skin.

She immediately reached for the shoulder wound but hesitated. It was very inflamed, a swollen stretch of skin that continued to drip blood in long rivulets down his arms and chest.

She needed to clean the wound. She'd watched enough *Holby City* to know that much. But with what? *Think, Alice. Think.* She clambered to her feet and hurried into the bathroom. Above the sink there was a small mirrored cabinet. She opened it so violently she nearly pulled the damn thing right off the wall.

'Shit!' she hissed as the contents spilled out. She dropped to her knees to gather them into a pile and quickly inspected her hoard. One small glass bottle with a faded label was TCP. She hunted some more and found an old pack of yellowed bandages, some paracetamol (out of date) and some white(ish) fabric tape.

She sprinted back to Crowley's side and uncapped the TCP. This was going to hurt. Steeling herself, she took a deep breath and poured the liquid directly into the open gash.

His eyes snapped open and he convulsed as though electrocuted. His eyes rolled back, and he moaned through clenched teeth.

'I'm sorry!' she wailed. 'I'm sorry. I'm so sorry!'

Shaking all over, Alice used her knife to tear six thin strips off the fabric tape. She had to take several breaths before gathering her nerve, then reached out and pinched the edges of the wound together.

He spasmed under her, perilously close to throwing her off, but she didn't let go.

'Shh, shh,' she soothed frantically, even as her fear for him grew. 'It's okay. It's going to be okay.'

She hurriedly stuck the strips of fabric tape across his sliced skin, closing the wound, albeit temporarily. Then she bandaged his arm.

When she was all finished, she sat back on her heels and sobbed into her hands – just once, before focusing on the task at hand.

'Crowley, I need to get you onto the bed,' she told him.

His eyes flickered open again, and a confused frown tugged his eyebrows down.

'I'm going to hook my arm under your shoulder – the other shoulder,' she explained. 'Now I need you to lean forward,' she said as she straightened up and tried to pull him with her into a standing position. They stayed upright for a split second, him leaning heavily against her. But then his legs failed, and she had to push him towards the bed so that he didn't crash back to the floor.

She swung his legs up and collapsed down beside him, breathing heavily with exertion. She'd done it. And all she wanted to do now was to curl up in a ball beside him and sleep. Instead, she placed a hand on his forehead and instantly snatched it back. He was feverish and sweating. In the bathroom, Alice wearily soaked a worn towel in cool water and headed back to wipe his face and chest.

And that was how she passed the next four hours.

***

She woke slowly. First, aware of breath against her cheek, then the searing warmth of a body down her side. Gradually, she sensed she was being watched. By Crowley. Whose half-naked body was pressed close to hers. It was, after all, a single bed.

Her eyes flew wide open and she scrambled off the mattress, clunking her knee on the bedside drawers.

'Did you get me drunk and take advantage of me?' he croaked from the bed.

'What?' Alice rubbed her knee. 'No, I did not!'

He glanced down at his ripped-open shirt and slowly fastened the few buttons still attached. She looked away, embarrassed. It wasn't like she hadn't seen a half-naked man before; what was wrong with her?

'How are you feeling?' she asked, her gaze fixed on the bedside lamp just six inches to the left of his face.

'Like I've been trodden on by a herd of wildebeest.'

She winced. 'We need to get you to a hospital. I put some tape on your wound, but it needs stitches. It's still bleeding, even with the bandages.'

Crowley pulled aside his shirt to check. He grunted. 'There's a sewing box under the kitchen sink. Bring it up to me. Please,' he added, as an afterthought.

Her mouth opened and closed. 'You can't be serious! You're never going to sew the stitches yourself?'

'Certainly not. What do you think I am – an idiot?' He rolled his eyes. '*You're* going to do it.'

She sat on the mattress with the sewing kit.

'I'm going to have to undo these again,' she said, touching one of the few buttons on his shirt.

His eyes slid down to watch her fingers, and after a moment he nodded.

She swallowed thickly and slipped the first button from its hole. Her fingertips accidentally brushed his skin, and he closed his eyes with a sharp intake of breath. She freed the other buttons, her heart hammering at the intimacy of it. She was *undressing* him. Here, in the charged silence of a bedroom. On a bed they had shared only the night before. She lingered over the last button until his eyes snapped open, and they stared at each other. His breathing quickened, his chest rising and falling under her hands. She pushed the shirt fully open and cleared her throat, trying not to let her gaze wander across his chest, at the dusting of dark hairs that ran down to the waistband of his trousers.

'Which colour thread?' she murmured, reaching across to rifle through the cotton spools in the sewing box.

'Does it matter?' he managed.

'The green thread would match your eyes.'

He laughed, but then hissed with pain. 'You are ridiculously impractical. Choose the strongest.'

She inspected the light grey cotton and measured it against a length of neon pink. The pink was slightly thicker. She began to unspool it, but he gave her such a withering look that it stopped her in her tracks.

'What? You said you didn't care about the colour.'

He stared at her.

'Fine,' she sighed, tossing it aside. She picked up the grey and threaded the needle.

Then she took a deep breath and put the point of her needle against Crowley's skin. 'I failed my textiles GCSE,' she said suddenly. 'The teacher said my sewing was more crooked than Al Capone. You're sure you want me to do this?'

'Of course I don't. I'm not a masochist. However, I *need* you to do it.'

'But you don't have anything for the pain.'

'Then talk to me. That should be as good as any anaesthetic.' He smiled slightly, to remove the sting.

'Okay,' Alice breathed. 'What shall we talk about?'

He gestured for her to start.

She swallowed and located the edge of the wound with the needle. He jerked and she panicked and violently stabbed at the wound.

'Oh my God! I'm so sorry!'

'Just. Get. On with it,' he said through gritted teeth.

She pulled the thread through, trying not to let her hands shake. She'd never liked the sight of blood. Crowley had turned so pale he was practically camouflaged against the white bedsheets.

'Tell me—Tell me whose house this is!' she said.

'It's Sylvie's,' he moaned.

'Oh,' she said. Her eyebrows flew up. 'I'd thought it might be Sasha's house.'

'Why on earth would you think that?' he bit out. He was clammy with fever.

She hesitated. 'The kitchen is leaking. And at Coram House, the problem with the pipes . . . It's Sasha, isn't it? She's non-practising, and instead of her legacy vanishing, it's trying to burst out. Did something happen to—'

'That's not my story to tell,' he said firmly.

Her mouth snapped shut, and she bent over her sewing. She pushed the needle through again and he groaned.

'I'm sorry,' she whispered. 'I wish . . .' She shuddered and searched for something else to focus on. 'Tell me about the infamous Sylvie then. How exactly *did* you know her?'

'She was my wife,' he said. His breathing changed as he focused on it, becoming slower and deeper. Calmer.

'*What?*' said Alice, momentarily forgetting that her needle was half buried in Crowley's skin.

'For God's sake, I was *joking*,' he said tightly, his lips thinned with pain. 'Keep sewing. Talk *and* sew!'

'Sorry,' she mumbled. 'So how did you know her really?'

'None of your business.'

She glowered at him, but he had closed his eyes. 'Fine.' She sighed. 'Tell me more about why she gave her feather to me then.'

He swallowed. 'Aviarists like Sylvie see other nightjars but never see their own. Not until they're about to die. So . . . she finally saw hers and knew her time was up.' There was a pause. 'She had cancer. Terminal. Her nightjar gave a feather after her diagnosis, and she knew—' He hissed as the needle pierced his skin again. 'She sensed you were the one meant to inherit it.'

'How *did* you know her, Crowley?'

'Be careful with that needle!' He opened his eyes and fixed his gaze on her until she grew uncomfortable. 'I've been waiting years to find out who Sylvie's successor was going to be,' he said finally. 'She lost much of her aviarist sight when old age set in. But a long time ago, she—' He shook his head. 'It doesn't matter. We were . . . old friends. Once. I used to stay here. She trusted me.'

'You used to stay *here*? But it's . . .' *a dump*, she thought. 'Were you a lodger?'

'No. I was a boy who needed somewhere else to go, and a peaceful terraced house in Battersea seemed as good a place as anywhere. In many ways she . . . saved me.'

Oh. That made sense. Alice remembered Josef, the skeleton key locksmith, saying Crowley used the doorways to escape when he was a child.

'What were you running from?' she asked.

His eyes darkened, and she knew she'd gone too far.

'I think I'm half finished,' she said. He closed his eyes and gave a tiny nod, and she concentrated on her macabre sewing project.

'So, Coram House,' she said at last. 'Do you own it or—'

'Yes.'

She nodded. 'It's a big house. Was it your family home when you were small?'

He stiffened. 'I have no family.'

She smiled. 'Everyone has a family. Biological or not.'

He said nothing, so she turned back to her stitching. Okay, so family was obviously a touchy subject too.

'They were all very worried about you at the house,' she said. 'I didn't tell them I was coming to find you, you know. I just disappeared.'

'I expect your beloved August will be tearing his hair out over your safety,' he said.

'August?' she said, confused.

She paused the movement of her needle and glanced over at him. His eyes were still closed. And despite the cold set of his face, a rush of heat pooled in her stomach and caused her skin to prickle. Even with the snarl, he looked . . . defenceless, for a change. Lying there, eyes closed, giving himself up to her inept ministrations.

'You just don't get it, do you?' she whispered. 'For someone who seems so clever . . .'

His eyes opened, and she bent over her needlework.

'I seriously doubt August cares about anyone but himself,' she said. 'Besides, he's probably got a thing for Sasha.'

Crowley snorted. 'Pointless. Sasha has been pining for *Jude* for the better part of a year.'

Alice's mouth dropped open. 'Sasha has feelings for Jude?'

His lips quirked. 'Obviously. You're supposed to be the one who can read nightjars.'

'But – she never . . . What else don't I know then?' she demanded.

'Now there's a question that could take years to answer,' he said, a glint of repressed laughter in his eyes.

She resisted the urge to punch him in the shoulder. 'Come on, tell me some more gossip.'

'I never gossip,' he said. 'Gossip is for the inane.'

'What about you then?' she asked offhandedly. 'Do you have a mystery woman tucked away somewhere?'

Something changed in the very air of the room. The atmosphere was charged with tension.

'No,' he said. 'I don't care for . . . relationships.'

'Ever?' she asked. 'You've never been . . .' Her throat nearly closed with embarrassment, but she ploughed on regardless. 'There's never been anyone you've ever cared about, or . . . ?'

'I've loved two women in my lifetime,' he said, his voice a silky whisper. 'One was my mother . . . and the other . . .'

He shook his head, his face pained; she didn't know if it was because of the question or his wound.

Alice swallowed and pulled the last stitch tight. She screwed up her courage and forced herself to exude nonchalance. 'So . . . what was she like?'

He hesitated. When he spoke his eyes were unfocused, caught in anguished remembrance.

'Estelle was . . . *incomparable*.'

And though he was looking at Alice, she knew he was staring right through her. She had never felt more insignificant in her life.

The moment finally passed, and he asked, 'Are we done here?'

She nodded and knotted the cotton thread, trying to ignore the churning in her gut.

'Good.' He pulled his shirt back over his shoulder and tugged up the quilt. 'Then I think I ought to get some more sleep.'

He closed his eyes, and she knew she'd been dismissed.

30

That night, Alice slept next door. She spent half the night scratching and coughing dust out of her lungs. So she was beyond relieved when the sunshine blazed through the window the next morning.

She hurried next door and froze on the threshold. Crowley's bed was empty. She stared at it in shock. Had he left? She wandered through the empty rooms in a daze. After all the worry and stress he'd put her through, he'd just upped and left without—

The back door slammed and Crowley limped into the kitchen clutching a box of cornflakes.

'Have you been outside?'

'Shop,' he said. 'Breakfast.' He rattled the box and, with a hiss of pain, bent to retrieve some bowls from a cupboard. She watched him in silence as he looked for one that wasn't too cracked or filthy. He filled it with cornflakes and pushed past her, bowl in hand.

'But where's the milk?' she said. 'You can't have cornflakes without milk.'

He glanced over his shoulder. 'It slipped my mind, all right?' he said testily.

She sighed and turned to the grubby bowls. Every single one looked like it might be harbouring deadly bacteria. She grabbed the cornflakes box instead and traipsed after him.

'How's your shoulder?' she asked as they settled in the living room.

'Fine,' he said. 'It was only dumb luck that he managed to hit me. Still, I managed to burn him before I got away.'

'It was definitely Vin Kelligan?' Alice asked, crunching on a handful of cornflakes.

He nodded, and they lapsed into silence. Finally, she broached one of the many questions that had occurred to her lately.

'If the Beaks want to annihilate the Väki, why don't they just storm into the Rookery and – I don't know – shoot everyone?'

He didn't answer immediately. He chewed his cornflakes for so long that she wanted to tip the box over his head.

'The Rookery is difficult terrain,' he said at last. 'It's not a place the Beaks can travel to unscathed, which is why, as a rule, they don't attempt it.'

'But . . . why is that?'

'The Rookery was built for the Väki, and only them. Those humans who have no Väki DNA, who somehow manage to enter the Rookery, slowly lose their minds. Travelling to a different plane of existence causes a loss of nerve cells in their brain, similar to dementia. You've heard of the madness of King George? You must have, considering your history degree.'

She nodded.

'Well, contrary to popular belief, his madness was actually caused by a prolonged stay in the Rookery. Since George the Third's reign, the government has known all about the Rookery's existence. The fact that the place sent the monarch insane became an issue of national security, so fell under the Official Secrets Act. *That* was when the Beaks were given funding and enfolded into the Ministry of Defence.' He sighed.

'Anyway,' he said. 'What's important about this is that we're safe in the Rookery. However, not every Väki makes it there. Some of them have such diluted blood that they can happily live their lives here in the mainland, without ever even knowing their heritage. Nevertheless, no matter how diluted their blood, the Beaks believe them to be an abomination. An abomination that must be wiped out.'

'Because of the crusades? Something that happened a thousand years ago?'

'Yes.'

Alice hesitated. 'Or maybe the Beaks hate us because Marianne and the Fellowship murdered their leader's family?'

'Who told you that?' he asked.

'Marianne did. Her sister was married to Sir John Boleyn. He can't have hated the Väki much if he married one. So it must've been his hatred of Marianne, for what she did – what they were capable of – that tipped him over the edge.'

'The Boleyn family has been the driving force of the Beaks for decades, and he's been personally responsible for the deaths of many, many Väki,' said Crowley. 'His marriage was a blip in an otherwise unblemished record of extermination. He killed before the wedding ring was put on his finger and he killed after it. I wouldn't care to dwell on his excuses. The only fact that matters is that their aim is to slaughter us all. And they want you to help them do it.' He paused. 'They can't tell the difference between ordinary humans and the Väki. But a Väki nightjar is different to a human's. Didn't you look at your parents'?'

'I . . . There wasn't time. I didn't think.' She sighed, suddenly bone-tired. 'The Beaks . . . want to use me to identify Väki – those hiding in the mainland – for them to kill. I *know* that. But I can't stay in the Rookery forever, Crowley. No. After I've retrieved Jen's nightjar, I'll disappear,' she said. 'I'll go somewhere with my parents, once I've helped Jen. Somewhere far away, off the Beaks' radar, and I'll just . . . never come back.'

He blanched at this, and she gave him a long, hard stare. Did the idea of her leaving really bother him?

'If the Beaks can't find me, they can't use me, right?' she said carefully.

He nodded absently; he couldn't seem to meet her eye. She looked down at her hands and took a deep breath. Now was not the time to lose her nerve. He'd once told her she had to prioritize, and that was what she was doing. She had no choice.

'I know how to get inside the moors,' she said. 'And I know exactly how to work around the safeguard now too.'

'How?' he asked.

She shook her head. She wasn't about to tell him – or anyone else – what she had planned. Ever.

'Crowley, I'm ready to take my chances in the menagerie.'

He stood up so abruptly that the empty cornflakes bowl crashed from his lap to the floor. It cracked cleanly in two.

'You're too inexperienced,' he said. 'You know nothing about the Sulka Moors yet. We haven't even planned how you could cross the river—'

'What river?'

'My point exactly. The river *Lethe*, which runs right through the moors.'

'I'll swim.'

'The river Lethe, or river Huonomuistinen, is also known as the River of Forgotten Things,' he bit out. 'You'd know this if you were prepared. You'd know your memories wouldn't survive a swim.'

'Then prepare me,' she urged. 'That's why you took me to the Rookery, isn't it?'

He shook his head irritably and bent to pick up the broken bowl.

'I took you there to keep you safe – *for Sylvie*. And to keep the Beaks from using you against us.'

'No,' she burst out, 'you said you'd help me with Jen. That was why *I* agreed to go.'

'Well maybe I've changed my mind,' he snapped. 'Maybe— Maybe it contradicts my promise to Sylvie. What you're planning isn't safe. None of it. If I let you go, and you—you leave, what am I supposed to—Sylvie would never forgive me,' he finished bitterly, his chest heaving.

Where had this come from? He *had* said he wanted to help her with Jen; he'd arranged for Josef to cleanse August, so that August could open the door to the moors . . . And yet, he'd mentioned nothing about her needing a spare nightjar or she'd die, and nothing about this so-called river. He'd been keen enough to get her into the moors, but now it seemed like he was trying to block her. Sabotage her. Was it really because he'd suddenly decided it was too dangerous?

Alice searched for his nightjar, but his back was to her and it must have been hiding – as usual – against his chest. The incandescent cord around his wrist glowed brightly, beads of light pulsing along the radiant twines. Her hand moved to clasp the feather in her pocket, but her gaze was fixed on the luminous cord. It was a two-way street, Proctor had said. A path that led from the nightjar to the soul itself.

The shimmering light was entrancing; she couldn't look away. She held out her hand, the feather clutched tightly in her fist. She was across the room from him, but she felt as though she were sitting by his shoulder. The cord palpitated and began to . . . *unravel*. She inhaled sharply. A single thread of light twisted loose . . . then another, his cord fraying like a rope . . . and Crowley's hidden nightjar began to sing. A looping, churring noise washed over Alice, rising to a crescendo. It was in *pain*.

Her eyes widened and she staggered backwards. The birdsong vanished. She hadn't even touched his cord . . . She'd never heard . . . She blinked rapidly and tried to regain her composure. Her hands were trembling. She glanced up at him. He was still crouched down, absolutely still. Had she damaged him – again?

He groaned quietly and rose. He'd cut himself on the cracked pottery; he was still gripping the sharpened edges fiercely.

'Are you . . . okay?' she asked.

He nodded and looked down at the blood on his palm. 'Funny turn,' he murmured.

His hair was stuck to his clammy forehead. Where before he'd been pale, now he was red-faced and feverish again.

'We need to get you back to Coram House,' she said, concerned. Her eyes traced his cord, careful not to focus her attention on it for too long – she didn't know what had happened – but thankfully, it looked perfectly intact.

'I'm fine,' he said gently. 'Stop fussing.'

She nodded.

'The river . . . in the moors. You're not ready. If you swallow enough of the water, it will wash away your memories, your mission. I don't imagine it will be easy to rescue Jen's nightjar when you've forgotten who she is.'

'I'll keep my mouth closed,' Alice said calmly.

'You're being reckless,' he retorted. 'You haven't even mastered sighting nightjars on command, without that damn feather.' He whirled from the room, and she had to rush after him into the grotty kitchen.

'Then I'll take the feather with me.'

He dropped the broken bowl into the sink, his voice rising. 'And if you lose it—'

'I won't lose it. I'll Sellotape the bloody thing to my forehead. I'm going to do this, Crowley, and I'm not going to wait any longer. The sooner I get Jen's nightjar, the sooner I can—'

'*Disappear,*' he said coldly. 'Yes. So you said.'

Her heart pounded. *Was* he upset because he wanted her to stay? Was that why he'd been blowing so hot and cold about helping her enter the moors? She swallowed hard. It didn't matter what he wanted – or what *she* wanted. She couldn't stay; Jen needed her.

Crowley looked at her, but the clear concern in his eyes was at odds with his aloof tone. 'Very well,' he said. 'I'll speak to a contact of mine who can supply directions to Jen's nightjar's cage. The Black Menagerie is practically labyrinthine. Without the location of her nightjar, you'll never find it.'

'How soon can you speak to your contact?'

He turned back as he headed for the door. 'Tonight.'

On the other side of the city, deep in the heart of Westminster, Major-General Sir John Boleyn was furious. However, he surveyed the man he considered his colonel with an almost preternatural calm.

Sir John's blue eyes were sharp with the experience of age. But his bearing and sinewy build were those of a man much younger than his sixty-something years. And his impeccable dress, side-parted dark grey hair and wire-framed glasses were coupled with an air of natural authority.

His face showed no outward signs of displeasure, but a practised observer might have spotted a tell-tale sign: the corded tendons of his right hand, which had blanched as his fingers clenched an engraved fountain pen. Of course, the biggest sign of all was the fact that he was smiling. He was not a man who smiled often. And those who knew him best had learned to fear it, because this was a man whose amusements came only from cruelty.

'The girl,' he said, gesturing with his hand. 'She did this to you?'

Vin Kelligan glanced at the bandages mummifying his burned arms and hesitated. 'Not exactly. She had . . . help.'

'Help. I see.'

Kelligan sucked at his teeth and stared hard at the major's desk.

'I gave you one command. One. I want the girl, Vincent. But so far you have failed. Is that correct?'

'Yes,' he said roughly.

'Yes?' said Sir John, feigning confusion.

'Yes,' he bit out. 'I failed, *sir*.'

Sir John sat back in his seat. Kelligan shifted uncomfortably, but his feet remained rooted to the spot. The bandages itched something chronic, but he dared not scratch them in here. Finally, Sir John leaned over his desk with a sigh and began writing furiously on a sheet of thick, creamy paper.

Kelligan waited. He waited an indecently long time. Long enough for the tingle in his bladder to become insistent. Long enough for his legs to shake and the tingle in his bladder to morph into painful, stabbing cramps. Sir John ignored him. When he had finished writing on one sheet, he moved swiftly onto another.

The room echoed with the ticking clock on the wall, counting out a metronomic beat to match the wave of each cramp in Kelligan's abdomen. Soon, his legs burned with the effort of holding his weight. He shifted from one foot to the other, but a sharp glance from Sir John stilled his movements. He looked down at the floor, the tips of his ears turning red. How much longer would he be forced to wait?

When his eyes next drifted to the clock, his vision was blurred with exhaustion. How many full rotations had the minute hand spun? Three? Four? His tongue was stuck to the roof of his mouth, and he swallowed painfully. He squinted at Sir John, who was still writing at his desk. An empty plate was beside him, and he had slung his jacket on the back of his chair. He had been busy. Pages and pages had been filled with his scrawling handwriting, and a towering stack had been built, teetering dangerously close to the edge of the desk.

The room swam dizzyingly before Vin. He forced his breaths to come gentler, since every inhalation brought fresh agony in his bladder. Still, he waited. He waited until he could wait no more.

His muscles tensed at the last moment, but it was a futile effort, and when it failed, the hot, spreading stain across his groin was unstoppable. He grunted with relief and shame. When the urine pooled in a trickling pitter-patter at his feet, Sir John finally looked up from his paperwork and tutted.

'How disappointing,' he said softly. 'At moments like these, you remind me of the reprobate you were when I plucked you from the gutter. You are *dismissed*.'

Kelligan's face was stony as he turned to leave, his boot squelching on the tiled floor.

'You will . . . persuade the girl, Vincent. And if she cannot be persuaded, you will use your imagination.'

'Yes, sir,' he croaked, balling his hands into fists. Alice Wyndham would pay for his humiliation. She would pay – and so would Crowley.

31

Alice's Coram House homecoming was bittersweet. Sweet in a very literal sense, as Nella – the ever-mysterious next-door neighbour – had dropped off a batch of sugared Finnish pastries. Sasha was trying to shove these down their throats to 'get their strength back'.

The bitterness came from Crowley, who had not spoken a single word to her since he'd vanished through a doorway in Sylvie's kitchen. She hadn't even known for certain that he was going straight home. She'd thought he might go to his contact for information. But no, he was sitting stiffly at the kitchen table when she scrambled back home herself.

'Crowley, you're burning up,' said Sasha, peering down at him in alarm. 'Look at the state of you.'

'I'm fine,' he said.

She raised an eyebrow and whipped the cups and plates from the table. 'Your collar's soaked with sweat. You're *not* fine.'

Alice had to agree with her. He was looking worse by the minute.

'A glass of water, perhaps,' he murmured.

'What about Josef? You need a proper doctor,' said Alice.

He ignored her suggestion and turned to Sasha, who shoved a

glass into his hands. 'Might I ask a favour, Sasha? Would you take a look at my shoulder?'

'What's the matter with it?' she asked.

'I was . . . stabbed,' he said calmly, 'and I suspect it's become infected.'

Sasha cursed in horror.

Crowley glanced at Alice as he went on. 'The wound has already been cleaned and stitched, but I fear this may have done more harm than good because of my "nurse". Would you fix the damage?'

Alice shot to her feet. She locked eyes with him for a split second – hers all fire and righteous indignation, his indifferent. She shook her head. Being around Crowley was like strapping yourself to an emotional pendulum. He was better than this, but she didn't have time for these games. There were bigger things at stake than Crowley.

'You should get some rest,' she said flatly. 'Take care of yourself.'

She thought she saw him flinch at the finality in her tone, but she turned away. She had an appointment to keep.

Alice had chosen a cafe only a short distance from the London Eye. From her seat by the window she could see the slow progress of the illuminated capsules as they spun on their Ferris wheel through the dark sky. She had not, so far, spotted anyone acting suspiciously near the attraction. Well, besides herself. She'd been nursing a mug of now-cold hot chocolate between her hands for almost an hour, and she'd had more than a few looks from the staff.

Her ticket for the Eye said 7 p.m., and it was drawing ever

closer. But she couldn't afford to let nerves get the better of her. She was about to be locked in an inescapable glass pod with someone who wanted to massacre people with her DNA. No big deal.

She exhaled shakily. What could Vin do to her in public? Nothing. He couldn't attack her in such an exposed place. Which meant that she would be safe.

Despite her attempts to soothe her anxiety, Alice couldn't shake the creeping sense of dread or slow her rapid heart rate. At this rate, Vin wouldn't have to kill her. She'd go into cardiac arrest before she even set eyes on him.

It was time. She took a deep breath and strode out of the cafe, into the chilled evening air. She had no intention of helping them in any way, of course – but they didn't know that yet. They wouldn't – not until she'd got what she needed. Not until Jen was finally safe and she was far away with her parents.

She trekked along the South Bank, the Thames rippling beside her. It was mostly inky black in the dark, but warm reflections from riverside cafes and restaurants illuminated its shoreline.

The ramp that led to the Eye was only half filled with tourists when she finally reached it. But her ticket was for priority boarding, so she soon found herself at the front of the queue.

A man in a grey fleece waved her towards a descending glass capsule, but she just stared at him mutely.

'Fear of heights?' he asked.

Fear of death, more like.

She backed away, scanning the capsules. The next glass pod came to a gentle stop, and a dozen or so people tramped out. Vin Kelligan was sitting on the oval bench in the centre. Then the doors snapped shut – and as the pod began to rise again, Alice saw a brief flare of anger cross his face. He thought she'd stood him up. Good. She wanted to be the one in control. Once the capsule was moving, he'd be stuck in there until it completed a full rotation . . . but she wouldn't, given her newfound skills with doors.

She hurried down the ramp and sprinted back to the cafe, heading straight for the bathroom. She flung the door wide, took a deep breath and stepped into the void, the image of Vin's capsule doors fixed firmly in her mind.

She stumbled into the capsule with less finesse than she'd been hoping for, and the door snapped shut behind her. Vin grinned up at her, the light catching the scars on his face.

'And there was me thinking you weren't going to show,' he said. 'Well now. Maybe you're braver than you look.'

Alice glanced around the pod and now saw that there *were* others with Vin. Two men and two women stood against the far wall by the rail, backs to her, staring out through the glass. She was outnumbered, five against one. A pulse of nerves shot through her: it was too late to change her mind.

A hand clamped on her shoulder.

'Why don't you take a seat?' said Vin, shoving her down onto the bench.

Vin had been staring at Alice, and it was starting to irritate her. Finally, her nerves shredded by the silent inspection, she snapped at him, 'Well? Don't tell me you wanted me here just to admire me. What happens now?'

He smirked at her in a frustratingly patronizing way. 'Some women look pretty when they get angry. Fire in their eyes, you know,' he said. 'You don't.'

'I was told you could help me,' she said, ignoring the taunt. 'Can you, or not?'

He slid closer on the bench and put a sweaty hand on her knee. She flinched and glared at it as he inched it up her thigh.

'There's a lot I can do for you,' he said, his voice throaty.

He squeezed her leg with his claw-like fingers. She snatched at his hand and flung it away, trembling all over with suppressed rage.

'You don't touch me. Ever,' she hissed.

His lips curled in a snarl, and his fingers twitched as though he wanted to strike her, but he gripped the bench and visibly composed himself.

'Can we just get on with this,' she snapped. 'You know why I'm here.'

He gave her a slow nod of acknowledgement. 'Yeah. Seems to me you must be pretty *desperate*, to come to us.'

She refused to rise to the bait.

'Still. Better us than the Fellowship. You can't imagine how angry I was when a little birdie told me you'd got involved with Marianne.' He sighed. 'We just want you kept nice and safe. Sacrifice isn't going to be an option. Not for you. We always look after our interests.'

Who was their 'little birdie'? Chalmers?

'By the way,' said Vin, 'such a pleasure to meet your parents.'

'Spare me the pantomime,' she said through clenched teeth. 'What the hell is it you want from me?'

He smiled. 'Did you know extracts from the birch tree can be used to fight cancer? Amazing things, trees. And there's a whole forest of trees in the moors . . .' He shrugged. 'In exchange for our help, we want a piece of tree bark.'

Alice nearly choked. Had she misheard? She thought he'd said—

'Cut off the bark from a trunk, a root or a branch, and bring it to me. And maybe, just maybe, I won't go looking for your parents.'

She tamped down the urge to laugh. She'd never heard anything more ridiculous in her life. 'A piece of tree bark? What are you planning? Setting up your own herbalist business?'

'Yeah,' he said, raising a hand to his scarred cheek. 'I've heard there's a big market for tree extracts – oils, balms and tinctures – in the Rookery. We're after its medicinal properties. It's going to fix my skin and make me baby-faced again.'

Alice didn't need to search for his nightjar to know it was a lie. Her flippancy drained quickly away.

'What do you really want it for?' she asked. 'Tell me the truth.'

Vin laughed. 'All right. I'm going to build a tree house with it. Or, better yet, I'll use it for firewood.' He stared at her. 'It's none of your fucking business. But that's not all,' he said. 'When you bring it back, you stay here, with us. You're going to be our special little pet.'

She noted the badly burned skin on his hands from his fight with Crowley, and felt a savage pleasure.

'All right. I'll bring it back to you, and if you think you can keep me here, I'll let you go ahead and try.'

She couldn't just agree outright to become his personal lapdog, now, could she? The lie had to be believable.

Vin stared at her, his face pensive. 'Good,' he said. 'I think my night is about to get a hell of a lot more entertaining.' He stood up abruptly. 'I want you back from the moors by midnight. And if you don't have something for me by then, well, maybe I'll go and reintroduce myself to your parents.'

He grinned at her, and she wanted to knock the teeth out of his ugly mouth. But his threats didn't matter. Her parents were far away, and he'd never find them.

'How have you found a way to get around the safeguard?' she asked.

He shrugged. 'A little birdie told us . . .'

'So?' she said. 'How do I get into the moors, then, and what do I need to do when I get there? How do I get out without the moors claiming my own nightjar?'

He smirked at her. 'You take a spare.'

She shook her head. 'But that's exactly what I'm *not* –'

'Show her.'

Alice's heart leapt into her throat. She'd been so focused on Vin she'd forgotten there were four people behind her. Two men and two women. When she turned, she saw only two of them were Beaks – the two others were captives. One was her old boss, Colin. The other was Sandra, his PA.

Sandra was standing like a statue against the glass wall; she seemed to have frozen solid with shock. Colin, however, swayed drunkenly between the two Beaks as they turned him around. His shirt was half unbuttoned and there were damp patches spreading under his arms. His eyes were glazed and his face was blank.

'What—Why is—'

Vin's face split into an unpleasant grin. He now had something white in his hands – a pair of latex gloves. 'You needed some spare nightjars,' he said, pulling them on. 'So we've brought you a pair. We thought these ones might . . . amuse you.'

Oh my God. No. What had they done to Colin? He looked as though he'd been drugged. Had they poisoned him? Sandra just stood there, her eyes wide and her skin like porcelain.

Vin nodded to one of the other Beaks – the woman – and she keyed something into her mobile phone. The London Eye juddered to a stop. The dim blue lights inside the capsule winked out, pitching them into gloomy darkness, the capsule lit only by the moon.

'Get ready,' said Vin, and he whipped a blade out of his coat pocket.

'Wait!' Alice shrieked. 'Wait! No! You *can't*!'

Colin's head lolled sideways, but his mouth puckered, working itself into shapes, and he managed to slur, 'Al-isss.'

The knife! She fumbled in her own pocket and pulled out the Bowie knife she'd brought for extra security. But her quivering fingers mishandled it, and it sliced her palm as it clattered to the floor, spinning towards Vin.

'Kind of you to offer to do it yourself,' he said, bending to retrieve it. 'But don't worry, I don't mind getting my hands dirty.' He twitched his gloved fingers. 'Figuratively speaking. Mind you – I think your knife might be sharper than mine, so I'll use yours.'

She gasped and clamped her bleeding hand around her sleeve cuff, to press the feather harder against her skin. She could go for his cord! But she was too late. She watched in horror as Vin lunged forward and plunged the knife deep into Colin's chest. Blood spurted and collected in Colin's matted chest hair, staining his shirt red. He thumped to his knees, and Alice snapped out of her horrified stupor, rushing to him. She pushed her hand against the hole in his chest, trying and failing to hold back the tide of gushing blood.

'Colin . . . Colin, no, come on,' she managed. 'Not like this. Please.'

His weight pressed against her. She couldn't hold him upright, and he slumped to the floor, her fingers slippery with his blood. He tried to draw breath, his lungs spasming and failing, and then, in a matter of minutes, he lay dead.

'No,' she murmured. '*No.*'

'And for my next trick . . .' said Vin.

Alice screamed as he hurtled towards Sandra, who was still standing like a catatonic mannequin against the wall. Sandra made no move to run; she did nothing to save herself at all. Vin grabbed her by the arm and used his free hand to drive the knife right into her abdomen, thrusting upwards. He wrenched the bloodied knife out and Sandra instantly collapsed at his feet with a soft sigh, her eyes fluttering closed.

Alice was blind with tears, her body racked with sobs as she surveyed the devastation around her. A pair of hands hauled her to her feet. She shoved them away and staggered backwards. Bile rose in her throat and the capsule spun around her, but Vin grabbed the back of her coat and thrust her forward. She slipped on the blood and fell towards the glass wall.

'Don't be shy,' growled Vin. 'Take the fucking nightjars.'

She shook her head wildly. Was he out of his mind?

'If you don't take them, they just died for nothing. Make their deaths worth something.'

She stared out the window, grasping the rail for support, her panting breath clouding the glass. Their pod had stopped at the peak of its ascent into the skies, and all of London was spread out below her, the city lights twinkling like a blanket of stars. Below Big Ben and the parliamentary buildings, Westminster Bridge was busy with traffic. Two boats were carving through the Thames, their headlights cutting into the icy water. The other side of the river was illuminated by restaurants and bars. London was so . . . alive. And here, in this capsule, was only death.

Colin and Sandra . . . How could he have done this? This wasn't . . . She'd thought . . . Alice shoved her clenched fist into her mouth and bit down on it, hard. Colin. Sandra. Innocent people had died because of her. How many more? Would Jen be next? Could she let Jen wait even longer without helping her? Could she refuse this opportunity to help Jen now?

Her eyes flew open just in time to see Colin's nightjar's wings unfold as it broke loose. Its silvery cord, no longer connecting it to Colin, hung down as it wafted its wings and took flight. She lurched forward and dived for the end as it started to fade. Once she had it, its light seemed to strengthen in her hands, growing brighter – more solid.

The cord was lighter than air, like a whispering breath somehow moulded and wrapped around her hand. She shoved away the revulsion shuddering through her and tugged gently at it. The nightjar dipped its head and soared directly into her blood-soaked hands. She had to force herself not to shake it off her traitorous skin as it sat there, perfectly calm, seemingly unaware that she'd just snatched it from its murdered owner. She tentatively reached out with a shaking finger and stroked its feathered back. She tried to be soothing, to put her feeble apologies and regrets into every stroke.

'Do you have it?' asked Vin.

She nodded, not quite trusting herself to speak.

'Good. Get the other.'

Sandra's nightjar was perched on her body, pecking at its slowly dimming cord. Hands shaking, she reached for it.

'Why . . . Why did you kill her? Why kill both of them when I only needed one?'

'Our little birdie said you'd need two. One for you and one for your friend. You can't remove her nightjar without leaving one behind,' Vin said, clapping her heartily on the back. 'Now then, you just make sure you're back here before midnight and I won't have to set any more nightjars loose, will I? Oh, and Alice, if that's not enough to tempt you back here – well, there's always this,' he said, jerking his head at Colin's body.

She dragged her eyes away from the nightjars to look at him. She was dazed and swaying slightly on her feet.

'He's got your DNA all over him,' said Vin. 'If you don't come back we'll make sure someone finds him. The knife too. Got your fingerprints all over it, hasn't it? Disgruntled former employee seeks vengeance on bullying ex-colleagues,' he said. 'That could work.'

'You sick bastard,' she whispered.

'Midnight,' he said, amusement dancing in his eyes.

'It makes no difference,' Alice said. 'I still can't get into the moors, even with these. I've got no one on the other side who can open the door for me.'

Vin laughed out loud and jerked his head over his shoulder, at the corpses on the floor. 'You do now – they're good for that too. We've employed a necromancer for you as well,' he said. 'He's very well qualified. He'll summon one of them back to open it for you.'

Her breath caught. *August?*

'His name's Berthold Lehmann. Took all of our resources to find him. Picked him up on the border with Poland, trying to do a runner – must've known we'd put the word out we needed someone with his particular talents. You're going to meet him in the Rookery,' said Vin. 'Here. He's waiting for you at this address.'

He shoved a piece of paper at her, and she stuffed it into her pocket with barely a glance. She didn't need their crooked necromancer; she had her own.

'Oh – and don't leave it too long. Get what you need for your little trip and then get me that fucking tree bark. Okay? Go on then – the doors are that way.'

Their capsule was over a hundred metres in the air, and the exit was tightly closed. What if it failed to open to the void? What if it just opened into clean air and she stepped out into empty space and plummeted to her death? Maybe that wouldn't be so bad. A quick, clean end to the horror show her life had become.

'The electronics are off, so they'll open manually,' said Vin. 'Do it *now*, before the technicians on the ground get too antsy about their broken Ferris wheel.'

Alice swallowed, and her fingers rhythmically stroked the two birds sitting on her wrist. She was very careful not to glance down at Colin's or Sandra's fallen bodies or the pools of blood seeping out from under them.

She fixed an image of Franc's wine bar in her mind and pushed the doors apart. With a judder and a metallic creak, they wrenched open and she fell forward into the gap. A hand snatched her backwards to safety, and she gasped in shock as a blast of freezing wind rushed into the capsule.

It was horribly black beyond the doors, and she couldn't be certain whether they had opened to the void or simply to the sky.

She didn't turn, but Vin whispered into her ear, 'Midnight. I'll meet you down there, at the queue for the Eye.'

32

By the time Alice made it back to Coram House, she found that she was shaking uncontrollably. She was reluctant to go back inside in case her housemates recognized her guilt and guessed at the repulsive thing she'd done. Except that she had to, because Crowley would be there with the directions she so badly needed and August was holed up in the attic.

She closed her eyes and tried to push aside the visions of blood and knives, the finality of Colin's last gurgled breath and Sandra's defeated sigh. Because she'd wanted to save Jen, two innocent people had had their lives ripped away from them, and she could never – ever – make this right.

She peered at the forcibly stolen nightjars. She'd expected them to thrash at her with their sharp claws in revenge, but in fact they were ridiculously placid. Once she'd tied their cords around her wrist, they were content to sit on her shoulder, in the crook between her neck and jaw. There was something so intimate about this that, stricken with guilt, she'd had to fight the urge to dash them from her shoulder. The least she owed them was some kindness, some comfort.

She wondered what her own nightjar was doing, whether it had accepted the intrusion. She reached up and stroked them, and they nuzzled against her skin. Humans' nightjars *were* different. Their beaks were slightly bigger, but their bodies were smaller and darker, their feathers much plainer than Väki nightjars'.

'You shouldn't have done it.'

Alice shuddered and snatched her hand back from the birds.

A tall, skeletal figure was watching her from the shadows of Nella and Gideon's house next door. For a second she thought it was Death, come to claim the birds from her. But then the figure moved into the light thrown by the nearby street lamp, and she relaxed. It was just Proctor.

'Shouldn't have done what?' she said, her heart slamming against her ribs. How good was his eyesight? Could he see that she was standing there with two extra nightjars?

'You shouldn't have gone to them for help. You should've just let your friend go peacefully. Not like this. Not stealing nightjars like a graverobber.'

She wanted to throw up. He *could* see them. He could see the birds, and he knew what she'd done to attain them.

'You know this is wrong,' he said quietly, lumbering up near to her, so close she could smell his stale clothes and see the rasp of hair on his unshaven jaw. He looked tired. 'You can still choose to let them go. They should be where they're supposed to be.' He reached out his hand to her and – for one insane moment – she thought he was going to stroke her cheek. Instead, he grabbed at her wrist, dragging her right up to his chest and his burned-out eyes. She tried to shove him away, but in one swift movement, he'd wrenched one of the cords off her wrist, tearing Sandra's nightjar away from her. With one mad flutter of wings, it soared off into the moonlit sky, free at last, and slowly faded away.

'Why did you do that?' Alice cried angrily. 'I needed it! Now she died for nothing!'

'Because what you're doing is wrong,' Proctor said. 'It's my fault too, and I have to make it right again.'

She sobered up then, clutching Colin's nightjar to her protectively. 'How is it *your* fault?'

'They've been paying me.'

'Who?' she asked, her voice shaking. 'Who's been paying you, Proctor?'

'Vin Kelligan,' he growled. 'He wanted to find you, so I went to London to help him. I saw you that night. Before your friend was . . . And I told him you were the one he needed.'

'*You're* the reason Vin tried to get me into his car that night? *You're* the reason Jen was there, trying to help me! I – I saw you in the bushes, didn't I?'

'I didn't know,' he protested. 'I couldn't be sure what they'd do, and I didn't trust you anyway. I'm not stupid. Crowley – and probably Risdon, too – they were going to groom you to take over from me, weren't they? Because my eyes don't work but yours do. But Vin still thought I was useful. Could still do a job. So I—I told them things.'

Alice sucked in a breath that flayed her throat.

'Like what?' she whispered. 'What did you tell them?'

He inhaled sharply. 'I told them you needed to get to the moors to rescue your friend's nightjar.'

She flinched and stumbled away from him. '*You're* Vin's "little birdie"? Not Chalmers?' she said, aghast. 'But that's why they *killed* Colin and Sandra. God, Proctor, you—' She sputtered uselessly. 'You're worse than me!'

'You can't go to the moors,' he said calmly. 'Not now. I had to stop all this. You'll kill yourself if you go now, with only one nightjar.'

'Well maybe I'll kill *you* if I stay,' she yelled as she raced up the worn stone stairs to Coram House. She slammed the front door shut behind her, leaving Proctor the Judas behind.

August was sitting on the wooden chair in her room, his arms crossed and a mulish expression on his face.

'I wouldn't do it for Marianne, and she was constantly threatening to kill me if I failed. So why should I do it for you, especially after what you've done?'

'Please, August,' she begged, as Colin's nightjar tilted its head to look up at her. 'Marianne wanted to spawn a devil-child that could kill the entire population. I only want to save someone's life. Help me do that. Please.'

'You don't understand,' he said quietly. 'No one does. My legacy is like this . . . diseased part of me.'

'You're right,' she said after a moment. 'I *don't* understand. If I thought I could save a life I'd help without question . . .'

His nightjar fluttered anxiously and ruffled its feathers against his neck. 'Look, my stepdad died when I was ten,' he said. 'I didn't even know what I was back then, but the Beaks did. They didn't need to look at my nightjar; I'd already given the game away about what I was.' He looked up at her, his eyes flat. 'It was so stupid. Just coincidence. I was waiting for the tube, and there was this fucking cockroach . . . One of them *saw* me do it.'

Alice nodded, her mouth pinched.

'It was like . . . magic. I didn't know how I was doing it, but I could make it dance, do whatever I wanted.' He shuddered. 'They must have followed me home, because they knew how to find me. They set up a car crash to get rid of me – the abomination – but they hit the driver's side by mistake,' he said bitterly. 'So my stepdad died, and I didn't.'

'So . . .' She hesitated. 'That's why you hate your necromancy? Because you think it's your fault he died?'

'No,' he said hoarsely. 'I was ten years old – how could it be my fault? It was theirs.' He wiped his mouth with the back of his hand. 'Most necromancers can't summon the dead from the moors, but I can. I'm not the rarity that you are, but I'd put myself in the most unusual top five or ten per cent of the Väki population. Remember I said it was possible to summon someone if they think you've wronged them? Well, I was eleven when I accidentally discovered that. Guess how?'

Her face creased in sympathy. *His stepfather.* 'God, August. I'm sorry.'

He shrugged. 'Why? Wasn't your fault, or mine – again, it was the Beaks'.' He paused. 'The thing was, we'd always got along pretty well, I thought . . .' He laughed humourlessly. 'But he blamed *me* for his death. A kid.' He shook his head. 'I don't like what I can do. Other people, they can make heat or light, or help things grow. Productive things. What can I do?'

Alice looked him in the eye. 'You can help save my friend.'

The basement door opened an inch, and Crowley glared down at her through the crack. Without a word, he swung the door open. He'd obviously had some rest, because his bed covers were mussed and his awful, sickly pallor had gone.

'Has Josef been to look at your injury?'

He nodded and shut the door, but the motion jarred his wound. He winced and pressed a hand against his shoulder.

'Crowley—'

'*I'm fine.*'

'Good. That's good.' Alice paused, but decided to plunge on

before the awkward atmosphere smothered them both. 'I'm here for the instructions that will lead me to Jen's nightjar cage.'

'I'm not—You're not ready,' he said hoarsely. 'You can't go; it's too soon.' She frowned up at him, and he looked away, clearing his throat. 'We need to spend some time strategizing.'

'We don't,' she said. 'There *is* no time. Vin went after my parents. Everything is coming to a head. It has to be now.'

'Travelling to the Sulka Moors is tantamount to suicide unless—'

'I've already sorted it out,' she said, without glancing at the sedate bird perched on her shoulder. 'The safeguard won't be a problem.'

'How?'

'Marianne. Sorry, but I went to meet her again, and she told me how to trick my way in,' she lied easily. She just couldn't tell him about the stolen birds. 'Anyway . . . August has agreed to open the door to the moors. Did you get those instructions from your contact?'

He pursed his lips and gave a sharp nod.

The clock on the wall seemed incredibly loud, ticking through the silence. Finally, Crowley moved to his desk and retrieved something from the top drawer. It was a wooden jewellery box engraved with feathers. He laid it on the desktop and she sidled closer. There was something familiar about it, but she couldn't quite figure out what.

Crowley plucked a piece of folded, yellowed paper from inside. He didn't immediately hand it over; he simply held it to his chest, as though it was something precious.

'Those are the instructions?'

He nodded. 'In a manner of speaking.'

'But who could possibly have known where her cage is?'

'That's unimportant,' he said, his voice clipped.

'Can I see them?'

Seeming strangely reluctant, he passed the paper to her. She unfolded it, frowned at the page and glanced up at him.

'I don't understand.'

'It's a piece of her nightjar's cage. I obtained it from my contact.'

Alice examined the small, blackened piece of . . . something . . . resting on the paper. What was it? A shard of wood? The edges were ragged and splintered. But she'd never seen wood this black before, and it wasn't simply charred. Stone, then? Or metal? There was something staining the edges, something that had dried and darkened. Blood, maybe, or sap.

'What is it?'

'I *told* you. A piece of her nightjar's cage.'

She rewrapped it in the paper and stowed it in her pocket. 'How is that going to help me find her nightjar?'

'It ought to act as a compass – or a divining rod. The nightjar cages are . . . self-healing. If they're broken, they fix themselves; they regrow.'

'The cage . . . grows?'

'The broken piece will seek out its cage. It will want to affix itself to the cage again, to help it to mend. I'm told it will vibrate the nearer you get to the correct cage; it will experience something of a magnetic pull.'

Alice nodded, processing the information. What wasn't he telling her? Who could possibly have acquired this? If someone had been that close to Jen's cage, and was involved, why hadn't they rescued Jen's nightjar for her? She shook her head – it didn't matter; the time for talking was done. Her eyes strayed across the room, finally settling on Crowley's desk.

'That box,' she said slowly. 'That jewellery box. I knew I'd seen it somewhere before. It was in Sylvie's house.'

'Don't be absurd.'

'It was. You said you were getting the instructions from a contact.' She frowned. 'But . . . you must have already had it at Sylvie's that whole time. Why didn't you just give it to me when we were there?'

'I didn't have it then,' he snapped.

'Did Sylvie give you this broken piece of Jen's cage? Did *she* give you the location of Jen's nightjar?'

'Of course not,' he hissed. 'She *died* and left you that cursed feather *before* your friend nearly got herself killed.'

Alice stared at him without blinking, the harsh tone barely registering, searching for his nightjar. Yet it was, as always, hiding out of sight. Refusing to betray his secrets.

'Listen,' he said with a weary sigh. 'The cages – you must be careful. *Don't* break them, whatever you do. If you touch the sap—'

'I'll be cautious,' she said. 'I'll treat everything in the moors as a threat to be avoided. Satisfied?'

He fell silent, his eyes searching hers. 'No. How has Marianne found a way around the safeguard?'

Alice hesitated just a fraction too long. 'She's given me some of her blood,' she lied. She could see the suspicion forming in his eyes, so she rushed on. 'It's complicated, but it's done now. I'll be fine. You're going to have to trust me.'

His eyes widened at the mention of trust, so often used by him to prevent her getting the answers she'd wanted. She couldn't afford for him to get cold feet now; she needed to do this. *Jen* needed her to do this. No more waiting.

'I need you to be safe,' he murmured. 'I need you to . . . succeed. Are you certain you—'

Something fluttered in her chest at his words. She quashed it. 'I'm okay, I promise.'

He nodded, and then they simply stared at each other. She didn't know what to say. Maybe there *was* nothing else to say. Except, perhaps, goodbye. After this they would have little reason to see each other again. But she hated goodbyes. And there *were* things she wanted to say to him but didn't dare to: words that threatened to choke her; confessions she forced herself to swallow for the sake of her pride. He should be glad to be rid of her; she'd brought him nothing but trouble since they'd met.

'Well,' she said, turning towards his door. 'I guess that's it. I finally have everything I need.' She gave a rueful smile to hide the nerves and patted the shard of broken cage in her pocket. 'Now . . . for the easy part.'

When she opened the door to the corridor, August was standing stoically by a small built-in storage cupboard.

Crowley inhaled sharply when he spied the interloper.

'Are you ready?' asked August.

'Yes.'

August nodded and moved to the cupboard door. He placed his forehead against the wood and closed his eyes. He said nothing, but his breathing became erratic. His left hand slid sideways and his fingers burrowed into the crack between the door and the frame. The air in the corridor chilled, and the tiny hairs rose on Alice's forearms.

She turned back to Crowley for a last reassurance, but he didn't smile. Would he see Colin and Sandra on the other side? Would he hate her if he saw them and realized what she'd done?

There was a click, and she shot round. The door was ever so

slightly ajar. There was a flicker of movement through the gap, and Alice held her breath, her stomach churning. Was that . . . a shadow? Colin? Or—?

'Good luck,' August murmured, making her jump. He held her eye for a moment, then quickly left the basement.

She wrapped her hand around the door handle, steeling herself with a deep breath . . . and pulled it open an inch. It didn't open to the void. It opened directly to—

'The moors,' whispered Crowley.

Alice tensed, anticipating her old colleagues vengefully hauling her inside – but there was nothing. Had they vanished, their forms too insubstantial once they'd opened the portal? Relief warmed her chest. No Colin and no Sandra. How could she have faced seeing Colin most of all, when she was standing here holding on to his nightjar?

Forever a master of stealth, Crowley had crept up behind her, so close that she could have leaned back and rested her head against his chest. His scent – his Crowley scent – engulfed her, and she felt almost light-headed.

'Alice,' he breathed into her ear. '*Don't go.*'

She turned and looked up at him. They were mere inches apart. The air between them warmed as they traded breaths. She could feel his heart beating through his shirt, pounding a quick tempo against her own.

His hand inched up towards her face, and she anticipated the brush of his fingers along her cheek. Instead, they wrapped around a length of her loose hair, and he carefully tucked it behind her ear.

'I have to go,' she murmured. 'It's the whole reason I'm here.'

She saw the exact moment the indifferent mask slid across his face, and she felt something inside her plummet. She hadn't meant it to come out like that. However, she *did* have to go, he knew that – but he'd already stepped back from her, leaving a gulf between them.

'Of course it is,' he said stiffly. 'Then I suggest you leave immediately. The sooner you've completed your goal, the sooner you can *disappear*.'

His words were laced with such ice that they seemed to freeze the air in the corridor.

'Take this,' he said, digging into his pocket and pulling out a crumpled glossy photograph. It was her parents' wedding photo. 'I spoke with a necromancer—'

'Who?' she asked, taking it from him and clutching it tightly. 'August?'

'No. It doesn't matter who. You will need the photograph to cross the Lethe. You *need* a memory in order to *keep* your memories. The photograph should ground you and prevent your entire sense of self from being washed away.'

'Thank you,' she said quietly. He offered no response; he merely stared at her, stony-faced. She shivered and turned back to the doorway, still open just a crack. She could hear something beyond. A rushing, swirling roar. What was she going to find when she stepped through?

She took a deep breath, poised to cross the threshold.

'I wanted to thank you,' Crowley said quickly, as though the words had been wrenched from him.

She turned.

'For coming to find me when I was injured. For my shoulder. For – helping me. I just . . . needed you to know.'

She opened her mouth to speak, but it was too late. She was through the door, and it slammed shut, leaving her on the other side. Alone. And in the Sulka Moors at last.

33

Her breath puffed a cloud in front of her that was swept away by the raging winds. The air was different here; it tasted metallic, and so cold that every inhalation knifed her throat. The frigid wind chafed at her eyes, making them stream, and she wiped them with her sleeve as she turned on the spot.

She was standing on a steep riverbank, under rays of murky sunlight that split the grey sky. Jagged stony outcrops stretched downhill, to be met by icy running water. It rushed downstream, splattering a frothy spray halfway up the bank and pummelling the dark and glistening rocks that jutted from below its surface.

Rolling fields stretched out beyond the far bank of the river, dusted with a glittering frost. The moors lay in the distance, and a thin, scrappy mist partially obscured a forest of bare trees spread across them. Their branches reached into the gloomy skies, dark and angular and exuding quiet menace.

Something fluttered against Alice's skin, and she jerked her head. Colin's nightjar was still on her shoulder. Of course. She'd almost forgotten. She stroked its head and it closed its eyes, relaxing into her ministrations. She turned slowly on the spot, galvanized by the warm little body pressed against hers. Where was the doorway she'd come through? Where—

She froze. There were two tracks of footsteps along the bank. Her breath hitched, and then she frowned. Sandra and Colin? But the footsteps led *away*. So they had . . . opened the door and gone?

She shuddered and looked out across the moors, searching. There was no sign of them. There were also, she realized, *no* doors here. No buildings. Nothing. It was a barren landscape. Had she opened a door into thin air? More importantly – with no physical doors, how on earth was she going to get home? She exhaled loudly. Maybe it was best not to think about that just yet. She was here now, and that was that; she'd have to worry about how to leave later.

Alice took a shaky step forward, and frozen tendrils of grass crunched underfoot. She winced, expecting the noise to broadcast her presence as she walked. Yet after a while, the ball of tension in her stomach began to unwind. The feeling that Colin or Sandra was going to lunge out at her faded. There was no one around, but shouldn't there be . . . *something* here? Other dead people? Ghosts? Souls? All that was here – inescapably here, right in front of her – was the river. She could walk the length of the bank for miles, but it would lead her nowhere. The only way forward was across.

She gritted her teeth and started down the riverbank. The rocks grew wet and slippery as she neared the water's edge, and she almost lost her balance as she clambered lower and lower still. She finally lost her footing on a slippery outcrop. The nightjar on her shoulder was flung into the air, where it fluttered in panic, tugging at the silvery cord lashed to her wrist. She threw out both hands to break her fall, but her body slammed onto the slick rock face. She cried out as something sharp tore at her skin and she plunged into the icy water.

Alice just had time to gasp in shock as the water swallowed

her whole and punched the air from her lungs. Her arms and legs thrashed as she broke through the surface, spluttering and coughing. She kicked, trying to propel herself closer to the far side, but the weight of her sopping clothing held her back as she flailed. Her parents' photograph floated free, and she cursed and lunged for it. Too late. It was stolen away by the current, and she knew a brief moment of terror as the icy water filled her lungs and dragged her back under.

She was thirteen, and it was winter. She was standing outside the head teacher's office in her grey school uniform – and a pair of neon green socks. Forbidden socks. Only black ones were allowed. It wasn't a protest against the strict regime; she'd just shoved on the first pair she'd sleepily picked up that morning.

'What are you out here for?'

That was her form tutor, striding past clutching an armful of exercise books.

'I've got green socks on,' she said. 'So I was sent to see Mrs Duffy.'

He raised a disapproving eyebrow as he disappeared around a corner. 'You'll be late to your next class,' he shouted over his shoulder.

She shrugged and leaned against the wall. Waiting, waiting, waiting. She certainly would be late if the head didn't get a move on. She'd knocked five minutes ago and still hadn't been called in yet.

'You'll get detention tomorrow lunchtime,' said Jen, her red hair in a ponytail and wearing round glasses too big for her face. She was sprawled on the comfy seats lining the hallway outside the office. The special seats reserved for visitors.

'I know,' she said glumly.

'Here,' said Jen, grinning. 'We might as well give her two for the price of one.' She wriggled out of her left shoe and peeled off her black sock.

Alice stared at it dumbly.

'Swap!' said Jen, waving the sock in the air like a flag. 'Give me one of yours. We can have a green and a black one each. Then she'll give us both detention. At least we'll be together!'

Alice grinned and pulled off one of her shoes.

She was cowering under a table, and the Year Two teacher was annoyed with her.

'There are no birds in my classroom, Alice. It was just a puppet. An owl. I brought it from home for our habitats project.'

Her pacing feet paused. 'You gave everyone such a fright, screaming like that.'

Mrs Mosley hunkered down, and blue eyes peered in at her.

'If you don't come out from there, I'm going to have to phone your parents.'

'You can't!' she squeaked. 'You can't phone them – they'll send me away.'

She was trembling all over. It was her worst fear. The birds had only come after she'd found out about her adoption – and if her parents knew about the birds, they might not want her any more.

Mrs Mosley's eyes filled with concern. 'Alice –'

'There's nothing wrong with me,' she babbled, clambering out from her hiding place. 'There's nothing wrong. I was being silly, but I'm sorry, and I'll be good now.'

'He's an idiot.'

They were stretched out on Jen's bed, flipping through magazines.

'No, he's not,' said Alice. 'He got an A-star in his biology exam last week.'

'Biology. That figures.'

'He really likes you. You should say yes.'

'I don't want to go out with him,' said Jen, readjusting her new, rectangular-framed glasses. 'He's a complete idiot! And besides—'

'Go out with him.' Alice swallowed and flicked her fringe out of her eyes. 'Put him out of his misery – all those puppy-dog eyes he keeps giving you in French . . . I don't like him any more. Honestly. And it's not as if he ever liked *me*, anyway.'

'Well, that just proves my point,' said Jen. 'He's got bad taste. Which makes him an idiot.'

Alice sighed. 'You know I wouldn't mind, right? What chance do I have with boys, anyway? They all think I'm mad.'

Jen smiled and stabbed her finger at a picture in the magazine, expertly changing the subject. 'We need to double-date one of these,' she said, nodding at the rock star brothers clutching guitars on page twelve. 'I wouldn't mind studying a bit of biology with one of them.' She paused. 'Or French, for that matter.'

'We said we'd tell her. We said we'd explain it to her when she was old enough.'

'I've changed my mind.'

'But, Patricia—'

'No, Mike. She's only seven.'

'She asked me yesterday why she didn't have any brothers or sisters.'

Patricia gave a huff of frustration. 'What does she want with sisters? She has Jen.'

'She might *have* sisters, darling. That's the point. We don't know anything about her real family. We don't know whether her biological parents had twenty other children or none.'

There was a long pause, broken only by the sound of muffled sobbing.

'We need to make a decision and stick by it. Do we tell her sooner rather than later? Or do we wait until she's a grown woman with a family of her own? We could see the adoption counsellor. They could give us some advice. Maybe we should never tell her at all.'

'I'm her mother. Me, Mike. *I'm* her mother, and no one is taking that away from me – not social workers or counsellors, not anyone.'

'Sshhh. I know. I know, darling . . .'

And out in the hallway, sitting rigidly on the stairs with her knees tucked up to her chest, was Alice. She stared through the gap in the banisters, tears streaming down her face, dripping onto her thin cotton nightdress. She wouldn't let anyone take her away. She wouldn't. If a social worker came to take her, she'd scream and scream and scream—

She was screaming. Perhaps. Or perhaps it was someone else. She couldn't be sure. She couldn't be sure of anything very much. She was so very tired. And warm. Funny, when the little voice in her head kept insisting she was freezing.

A hand came towards her, striking her cheek, but the pain was nothing. Nothing. She just wanted to sleep. Why wouldn't they let her sleep?

'Give it up,' said a croaky voice in her ear. 'Give it up before it takes your own nightjar!'

She let the voice wash over her and sank back into sleep, her limbs heavy as—

Crack!

A sharp slap made her ears ring, and her eyes flew open. She tried to focus on the face looming over her, but her eyes had already begun to roll back into her head. Bony hands gripped her shoulders and shook her fiercely.

'Wake up! This place is not for you! Not yet, do you hear?'

Alice's eyelids were weighted down, and she felt herself sink back into the icy grass.

'Where is it? I know he must have given it to you,' mumbled the voice beside her.

The jagged shard of broken cage was thrumming in her pocket, insistent and niggling – and then, suddenly, it wasn't. The voice hissed and tutted and then – *crack!* – another slap rocked her sideways. She sat upright. She suddenly felt very present, very real . . . and very weak.

Her head jerked to the side and a wave of nausea rose in her throat. She doubled over and retched into the frosted grass. The unfamiliar hands whacked her on the back as she spluttered and expelled a spray of putrid, watery bile. When her stomach was mercifully empty, she rocked back onto her knees and wiped her mouth. The world was spinning.

She fought to steady her breathing as white spots began to dance in front of her eyes. *Breathe. Breathe.* Then gradually, very gradually, the world slowed and sharpened into focus.

She was on the other side. The other side of the river Lethe. The forest was ahead of her, dark and foreboding. It dominated the moors, a vast tangle of blackened branches stretching to infinity, eclipsing the landscape so that there seemed to be nothing beyond.

She pushed the wet hair off her face, trembling. She was shivering so violently she thought she was going to dislodge a vital organ.

'Hypothermia,' said a voice behind her.

She whirled around.

A little old lady with beady eyes and cotton wool hair was studying her with no small amount of concern. She seemed . . . familiar, somehow.

'What – who – where did you –' Alice stammered.

'I pulled you out of the water,' she said. 'Before the hypothermia got a grip on you, I hope, but you'd better get home to a doctor soon.'

'Are you here alone? You're the first person I've seen.' *Person.* Was she a person?

'The others are beyond the forest.'

'Others?'

'Other souls, other spirits, other shades. Whatever you want to call us.'

'You're dead?'

'I certainly hope so. Otherwise my cremation must've hurt like hell.' The old lady tottered closer and smiled. 'Alice Wyndham. I've been waiting for you. Can I have my feather back now?'

Alice stared at her stupidly, mouthing the word *feather* in silence. Realization was slow in coming. It fought through the treacled fug of her brain.

'Who are you?'

'Sylvie,' said the old woman.

'Sylvie,' Alice repeated. She knew that name, didn't she? She searched her mind but found only . . . gaps. 'I can't quite . . .'

'It's the water. You spat some out, but you drank some too. Not much, I don't think, but enough to make your memory foggy. Sit,' Sylvie said, pushing Alice back onto the crunchy grass. 'Rest your brain a minute before you go gallivanting.'

Alice nodded and allowed her eyes to lose focus as she retreated to the depths of her mind. She remembered all of her times tables and her ex-boyfriend's phone number. She remembered that her dad supported Swindon Town football club and that her mum's eyes were blue. She remembered lots of things. Tons. But there were things missing. She didn't know what they were, but she felt their absence just the same. What if she'd forgotten something vital to her plan? She stood up abruptly on unsteady legs.

'You're Sylvie,' she said to the old woman. 'I remember you. And you're . . . here?'

Sylvie nodded patiently.

'Your feather – I need it,' Alice said.

'No, you don't. You can see just fine without it.'

'I can't.'

'The feather is making you blind. You rely on it because you've got no confidence in yourself. Give me the feather, little birdie.'

Alice reached into her pocket and tugged it out. She clutched it to her chest, but Sylvie gently prised open her fingers and took it from her.

'Now,' she said, 'open your eyes. And look around.'

Alice frowned. 'Look at what? I can't even see Colin's nightjar without your feather.'

'That's because it's gone,' said Sylvie. 'I couldn't untie the cord around your wrist, so I cut through it with that broken bit of Arbor Talvi in your pocket.'

Alice's mouth fell open.

'Don't look at me like that; I had to, and you know it. The Black Menagerie demands its price.'

'You gave Colin's nightjar to the menagerie?'

'Of course I did. Never mind that now. *Look. Over there.*'

She pointed at something over Alice's shoulder, and she turned.

The breath whooshed out of her. The forest – with its dark and shadowy trees clawing at the sky like skeletal hands – wasn't just a forest. The knuckled branches had grown into contorted, intertwining shapes. They twisted and criss-crossed, jagged wooden fingers wrapped around each other, and in the narrow spaces between the branches . . . there were nightjars. Fluttering, sleeping, preening birds. The forest was *teeming* with nightjars. Because it was both a forest and not a forest. It was an *aviary*. It was—

'The Black Menagerie,' said Sylvie. She pressed something into Alice's hand. 'See?'

It was the broken piece of cage, and it felt warm in her grasp, vibrating against her skin.

'That bit of Arbor Talvi can sense its home,' said Sylvie.

'You used this to cut the cord around my wrist, to free the other nightjar,' Alice said. 'But how did you know it was in my pocket?'

Sylvie laughed. 'Well, I'm the one who gave it to Crowley in the first place, aren't I?'

Alice looked at her in confusion. But Crowley had said she hadn't. Because Sylvie had died *before* Jen's nightjar vanished. Unless she had managed to find the cage, break a bit off and somehow send it to Crowley *after* her death.

'But Crowley said you didn't. He said—'

Sylvie patted her arm. 'He says a lot of things. And a lot of them sting. You don't want to pay much attention to his words. It's his actions you want to mind.'

Alice nodded. 'What does Arbor Talvi mean? It sounds like . . . the Arbor Suvi? The tree in the Abbey Library.'

'Oh, I know. It's because they're opposites. The forest in the Sulka Moors is made up of Arbor Talvi trees. The trees of death – or winter – to the Arbor Suvi's Tree of Life. *Suvi* means *summer*, you know. That's a piece of Arbor Talvi bark, from the young lady's cage.'

Alice clenched her fist, and the bark's vibrations tingled through her arm like pins and needles. 'Will you come with me? Into The Black Menagerie?'

Sylvie shook her head. 'I'm afraid not. But I can give you some words of wisdom. You mind yourself with that bit of Arbor Talvi. Don't go swinging it around, or else you might sever your own nightjar's cord clean in two. That's what it does, and that's why you won't ever see an Arbor Talvi growing anywhere but here. The Arbor Talvi trees respond to nightjars like nothing else. You'll need to hold on to your own nightjar for long enough, so it can open the cage that matches that shard.'

'*My* nightjar will open the cage?'

Sylvie's eyes widened. 'Any nightjar will do it – didn't Crowley say? The nightjar is a universal key. They open and close the cages: any of the cages. But I thought you had something clever planned? I thought you and him had concocted some way of . . .' She trailed away as a dawning sense of horror filled her eyes. 'You mean to say, with those great big brains of his, he's sent you in here with only one spare nightjar? And no plan for retrieving your own from the cage?'

'What do you mean? I open the cage with my nightjar and then . . . What? Why would there be a problem? I call out the other bird, and then I go home.'

Sylvie's face creased with sympathy. 'After you've opened the cage and retrieved the nightjar you're seeking, your own nightjar will fly inside. It's a straight swap. A sacrifice. The other girl's will come out, but yours will be *stuck* in the cage. And the only way to reopen the cage, to free your own little birdie, is with another nightjar. You were supposed to bring two: one to get into the moors safely, and one to get into a cage.'

Alice's mouth opened and closed. She'd *had* two nightjars, but . . . Fucking Proctor. She put her hands over her eyes. The Arbor Talvi pressed into her cheekbone. She took several deep breaths. Proctor had tried to tell her she couldn't do it with one nightjar. Crowley must have known, but she'd shut him down, insisting she'd chosen a different solution altogether . . . Why on earth hadn't she considered the fact that the cages might be *locked*? That she couldn't just waltz in and open them by hand?

'I'll think of something,' she murmured, rubbing her eyes and turning to face the menagerie head-on. 'Will you walk with me? Not into the forest, just a little of the way?' Alice felt very alone now that the small nightjar had been torn away from her.

Sylvie nodded. 'Of course. I'll come as close as I dare, but . . . My own darling nightjar is in there somewhere. I don't want to see it caged, pining for me as I do for it.'

They set off in silence across the icy moors. The wind pulled at Alice's hair, flicking the wet tendrils into her face and chilling her skin. The walk was arduous, every step sluggish and exhausting. Frost had begun to crystallize on her woollen coat, freezing the soaking fibres. She still trembled, her feet and hands so numb that the pulsing Arbor Talvi in her palm was the only thing she could feel.

'Y-you've known Cr-Crowley for a long t-time?' she chattered. Every word was punctuated by a burst of steaming air. She was getting colder. Worse, not better.

'Since he was a scared little thing.'

'What w-was he s-scared of?'

'His blood.'

Alice frowned. 'Blood?'

'From his dad, mostly,' said Sylvie. 'His dad was a bad lot. There are some things you can't run from, though. You know that, of course.'

Alice nodded distractedly.

'Crowley's a good man, though,' said Sylvie. 'Oh, I know he doesn't always give that impression. He's just damaged. There are plenty of folk like him around, but maybe none so affected. He's been scarred. By death, mostly. And sharp tongues.'

They tramped onwards, the forest looming out of the white landscape like a monstrous thing. Every step that drew her closer felt like a wrench, a slow and painful hardship she wasn't certain she could endure. Jen, she reminded herself. She was here for Jen. Jen, who would've sprinted into death for her, if things had been reversed.

'Have you ever seen his n-nightjar?' she asked. 'He's always h-hidden it from me, and I always wondered wh-what he didn't want me to see.'

'Crowley's bird? Oh yes, I've seen it all right. It's the sort of bird that sticks in your memory. Powerful-looking thing, it is.'

Alice nodded. 'What about me? Can you s-see *my* nightjar?' she asked suddenly. What if this was *it*? What if she died here and never saw her nightjar—

Sylvie smiled. 'I can see better now than I have in years. And yours – it's a real beauty. I caught a glimpse of it when I first saw you on the bus.'

'How do I g-get it to open the cage if I can't even s-see it?'

'It will fly right in by itself. You won't need to do anything but find the right cage.'

Alice nodded and bit her lip, her gaze raking the many night-jars nestled in the branches of the Arbor Talvi.

'Can I always see them now? Other people's nightjars. Without the feather?'

'Aviarist sight is like blinking, my love. You can see and not see them whenever you want. Like a switch, turn it on and off. Assuming you . . .'

Live. The word went unspoken, but Alice heard it just the same.

They had stopped on the outskirts of the menagerie. Two rows of trees stood sentry before her, like a guard of honour, calling her to step beneath the canopy of their twisted arms. The meagre light from the dark skies dappled the frosted ground and illumin-ated a winding path through the forest.

In her fist, the broken Arbor Talvi shard jumped wildly, and she opened her palm. It spun like the needle of a compass, as Crowley had promised, then suddenly arrested its movement and sat straight and still as a fallen arrow.

'It will point the way,' said Sylvie, stepping back from her.

Alice took a shaky breath and poked it with a finger. It was immovable. It had set its course.

'Good luck,' said the old woman.

Alice wanted to say thank you, or goodbye, but she found she couldn't say anything at all. So she only nodded and stepped into The Black Menagerie.

34

Whereas before they'd been silent, now the birds cawed and twittered above. They clamoured at the branches, hundreds of beady black eyes watching her pass, announcing her arrival with shrill screams.

Every nerve in her body was alive with electricity. *I'm in the Land of Death. Please don't let the Lord of Death find me here. Please don't let the Lintuvahti find me stealing from him.*

The Arbor Talvi in her hand jerked to the left, and she reluctantly abandoned the path to clamber over huge tree roots and duck below low-hanging branches. The quality of the light seemed to change as she trekked deeper into the heart of the menagerie. Beams of light from overhead sliced through the branches in glowing columns and cast long, distorted shadows between the trees.

The tree trunks themselves grew twisted, stretching diagonally across her path so she had to crouch to avoid the coarse bark and knobbled branches. Vin Kelligan's request for a piece of the bark resurfaced, but she dashed it from her mind. She would do the Beaks no favours. Their threats and bribes were nothing to her now.

The Arbor Talvi led her on a meandering journey, a winding,

fumbling trail through the wild forest, turning left and right and back on herself. The chunk of wood nudged her this way and that – directing her, at last, to one dark tree.

Alice held her breath, her gaze sweeping up and down and around the trunk. She could see no missing piece, but the Arbor Talvi thrummed in her hand like something alive. Maybe it wasn't missing from the trunk – maybe it had been taken from a branch?

Her eyes hunted the black, claw-like branches, where thirty or more birds stared down from their perches with bright interest. Each one was trapped within a tangle of interlocking twigs and boughs. Her breath hitched in surprise – these were the cages. But which one was it? Which bird had she come for? She thought she might be able to sense Jen's spirit or personality, somehow – the way she'd noted August's extravagant nightjar and Sasha's coolly defiant one – but . . . she just didn't know. They all looked alike from here.

Fear gripped her. Had she come all this way for nothing? What was she supposed to do? She couldn't take the whole tree back with her. Her pulse quickened, and it seemed to her that the nightjars sensed her distress, because they suddenly exploded into a burst of activity, slashing the branches of their cages with their claws and pecking frantically at the bark.

'Shhhh,' she whispered urgently. 'Please be quiet. Please.' If the Lintuvahti found her trespassing, then all was lost.

Despite their frantic activity, the birds left no permanent scars on their cages. Red sap bled from the slashes and pecks and quickly repaired the marks. Crowley had told her not to try and break the cages. Was it because they simply couldn't be broken? Because they repaired themselves instantly? Maybe Vin had been telling the truth when he'd said he wanted the bark for its healing properties.

Alice held out her Arbor Talvi compass and drew closer to the tree. She clambered up onto a knot of roots, searching desperately for the gouged hole. The Arbor Talvi vibrated rapidly, and she tightened her fist to keep it from leaping out of her hand. It sensed she was getting closer . . . *There!* A thin, tapering branch with spiny barbs – it had a narrow cut of bark missing, showing the smooth, light sapwood beneath its crust.

This was the cage! Jen's nightjar was trapped in these branches. But she couldn't quite reach . . . She clung to a lower offshoot for balance as she pushed upward . . . and shoved the missing piece into the hollow.

The tree seemed to pulse under her hands, and she watched in mounting awe as gloopy red sap, like clotted blood, spilled out around the edges of the broken piece. It hardened before melting away and vanishing entirely. She shuffled closer – but there was nothing to see now. No ragged edges, no splinters; the bark looked perfect and whole.

Her stomach fluttered. She'd done it. So . . . where was Jen's nightjar? She arched backwards, to better peer into the cage. But her foot slipped, and she threw her hand out, grabbing a spindly twig to steady herself. She was too heavy. The twig snapped in a splatter of wet sap and she was flung backwards.

She landed with a thump, but scrambled up, still clutching the broken twig. The red sap had sprayed over her hands, so her palms seemed drenched in blood. She tossed the twig away, and watched as a thin film began to settle on her skin. Before it had the chance to harden, she wiped it off on her jumper, scraping sap down her chest. Her head darted up to re-examine Jen's cage. She wanted that cage open. *Now.*

And yet – all thoughts were pushed from her mind because there, looped around her wrist, was a pulsing, diffuse glow. Her cord. Adrenaline and surprise surged through her. She laughed and spun around, searching for her nightjar.

Her excitement lasted only seconds. As she turned, the ground tilted beneath her feet and she staggered backwards, white stars bursting in front of her eyes and a terrible shooting pain doubling her over.

What was wrong? What was happening?

A screech from above punctured her confusion. Dazed, she squinted into the air as an indistinct shape hurled itself straight at the branches of Jen's cage, tugging her wrist skywards with it.

Through her pained stupor, she tried to focus as the branches shuddered and unravelled themselves, straightening and unwinding like the unclenching of a fist. They scooped her blurred nightjar out of the air just as another bird, this one with rumpled feathers, exploded out from the tree. With her nightjar now in their embrace, the branches tightened and twisted around it, meshing together to form an impenetrable cage once more.

Alice was left, open-mouthed and with an intense pain in her heart, to stare helplessly up at it. The silvery tether that bound her to her nightjar was still intact, but growing thinner and fainter with every second. The dishevelled brown bird that had taken the opportunity to escape the same cage flew straight towards her and thrashed at the air. She swallowed and attempted to concentrate on the bird – Jen's nightjar – but the ache in her chest was tearing her body in half. She staggered upright, pressing her fist against her heart to ease the pain.

Jen's frantic nightjar followed her, trilling with agitation. She swiped at it and plucked it from the air. Its cold, needle-like claws perched on her hand, pinching the skin painfully, and she hissed out loud. She wrenched her other hand from her chest and fumbled behind the nightjar, searching for some sign of a silvery cord.

She found it, but it was very short and very faint. She managed to loop it around her wrist, tie it, and then lurch back to the tree.

She couldn't leave her nightjar here. The pain was knifing through her like a hacksaw, slicing and slashing away at her arteries and tendons. It felt like sharp fingers were prising open her ribcage and trying to dig out her heart. She needed to get it back.

This was something beyond physical pain; this was a vital part of her being ripped away. She moaned, and her blundering foot came down heavily, crunching the vibrating twig she'd discarded on the ground earlier. The pulse it sent up her leg acted as a catalyst.

Cage – she'd break the cage – didn't matter – she'd break every bone in her hands before she gave up trying. She flung a hand up to the lowest branch and planted one foot against the trunk as she strained to haul herself to the next one.

She caught it with a gasp, but the momentum had caused her foot to slip from the trunk, unmooring her. She was too weak. Her fingers loosened and her head lolled drunkenly.

No. She'd come too far to fail. She tried to push the pain in her chest away, but it was spreading. The palms of her hands were on fire. Spikes of agony raced down her thighs and into every limb. She fought the blackness threatening to engulf her and tightened her fingers. She swung all of her weight sideways and lashed out with her feet. Her shoes found the trunk again and she scrambled to wrap her ankles around it, using the temporary stability of her position to hoist herself up to the next branch. Her silvery cord was needle-thin now. It couldn't snap. She couldn't let the cord snap, or she'd lose her nightjar forever.

She tried to breathe deeply, but it sent a shot of searing agony through her lungs, so with quick and shallow breaths she angled her arms higher, bending them at the elbows so they hung over the branch. Then, with one final burst of strength – her last – she swung one leg up onto the branch and grabbed at the wood imprisoning her nightjar.

With a yell of rage and anguish, she tore the branches aside, cracking and splitting the wooden bars of the cage. Red sap gushed out over her, splattering her chest and dripping down her neck and under her jumper. She heard the sound of frantic wings beating at the air before her balance slipped and she fell. She crashed onto the frozen ground in a broken heap and watched as red liquid pooled out around her. Blood or tree sap, she didn't know. She couldn't move. She couldn't feel her limbs.

Her sight dimmed until it was a pinhole surrounded by darkness. She had the vague sensation of something hovering above her. A blur of flapping and feathers. Her nightjar? The breath rasped out of her, and a trickle of blood coursed from the corner of her mouth. She could feel its soft feathers as it nuzzled at her hand. It had come to comfort her.

She fought to stay conscious, to force her eyelids just that bit wider. It wasn't supposed to be here. Everyone knew that. Aviarists didn't see their own nightjars. Not until ... *Oh* ... the moment of their death.

Her eyelids flickered shut, and then there was only blackness.

35

Crowley had had dealings with most of the Rookery's necromancers over the years, and this one – Eris Mawkin – was no exception. The only difference was that Mawkin was allowed to practise her illegal art, while the others tended to get themselves thrown into Newgate Prison. She was given special dispensation on the grounds that she practised it in the Council's name. She was affiliated with the Runners, in much the same way he was, although her job title was much more official than his own. They had bonded over this common ground – both despised by Risdon, but tolerated for their useful abilities.

'So what's the problem?' asked Mawkin. She leaned back, her battered brown leather boots propped up on a stool. One hand hung over the back of her chair, a glass dangling precariously from her fingers.

Crowley looked about him with a guarded air. Even in his own House, he didn't take his privacy for granted. House Ilmarinen was a hub of constant activity. Aside from the offices and workshops in the other parts of the building, the bar's twenty-four-hour licence meant that company – and unwanted listeners – was never far away.

They were sitting in the rotunda, a circular hall crowned by a domed glass roof. There were three storeys, and each one had its own ornate cast-iron balcony running around it. It always reminded Crowley of the tiers of an extravagant cake.

The top-floor bar was his preferred Rookery drinking establishment. Small braziers of hot coal stood on the round tables, lending warmth and light. Portraits of long-dead House Ilmarinen members smiled approvingly from gilt-edged frames on the walls. And display cases of fossilized plants – coal's foremost ingredient – were built into the bar's countertop. The building used to be the old London Coal Exchange.

He glanced down at the collection of empty glasses in front of him, then up again at Mawkin. She'd dumped her fedora on the table, and the chin-length brown hair beneath was mussed and tangled. She was here as his guest, and yet she had the audacity to treat the place like her own living room. She never changed, a fact he found somewhat comforting.

Despite her rare misinformation over Ronan Bishop's suitability, it had been Mawkin whom he'd consulted about crossing the Lethe river. She already knew some of the truth – she was one of the very few he trusted – and he needed her professional advice again. So it was that he proceeded to explain as much as he felt necessary about Alice's trip to the moors.

'How long has she been in there?' Mawkin said at last, looking at him keenly.

'Nearly twenty-four hours.' He snatched a shot glass from the scattered pile on their round table and threw the amber liquid down his throat. It eased the painful twinge in his shoulder. 'She lied to me. I thought she'd found safe passage, but I found Proctor gibbering on my doorstep. The bastard took one of her spare nightjars.'

Across the bar, a group of men burst into raucous laughter, and Crowley sat back with a sigh.

'I think she'll have broken a cage. She hasn't returned, and it was the only option open to her.'

'Then why are we having this conversation?' asked Mawkin. 'She's already dead.'

Crowley went very still. 'I have to work under the assumption that she's not. What can you tell me about the Arbor Talvi?'

'The sap is deadly.'

He nodded. 'But there's an antidote.'

Mawkin dipped one finger delicately into her glass and licked the bead of whisky she collected. It was, to his mind, deliberately provocative, and his mouth tightened with mild disgust.

She hooted with laughter at his reaction. 'Believe me,' she said, 'you're about as far from my type as it's possible to be. You and at least fifty per cent of the population.'

In frustration, Crowley stood up and made to leave, but she waved at him to sit. 'The only antidote is the sap's polar opposite,' she said. 'You need sap from the Arbor Suvi. The Tree of Life will counteract the poison produced by the trees of death.'

'But the Arbor Suvi is heavily guarded, night and day. It's impossible to get past those carnivorous bloody *fireflies*.'

'It's guarded *now*,' Mawkin said. 'But it wasn't always.' She tilted her head and gulped the whisky. 'The stuff is like gold dust in the medicinal field. It's not just an antidote to poisons; it heals virtually everything. You might be able to pick some up on the black market, but . . .' She shook her head. 'I doubt you have anything valuable enough to trade.'

'Who's the seller? Christ, don't tell me it's as obvious as Forrester's herbalist's?'

'Josef Skala,' she replied. 'Though my understanding is he only had a very small amount. He may not have any left.'

'Josef?' He shook his head. 'Impossible.'

She shrugged. 'That's what I heard. Take it or leave it.'

Crowley stood again, shaking his coat free of the chair. 'I need to go. She might be back by now. I need to be there when she returns.'

'If she's broken a cage, the poison will get her. And you won't even have the *opportunity* to save her with Arbor Suvi sap if her body's stuck in the moors.'

'Then I'll drag her back myself.'

Mawkin lounged back in her seat and gave him a quizzical look. 'How? You're many things, Crowley, but you're no necromancer.'

'I don't need anyone to open a door to the other side for me – not when *she's* there. Her blood will open it for me.'

Mawkin gave him a look of amusement mingled with pity. 'You might be able to open a door to the moors, Crowley, but you can't go through it without a spare nightjar. If you try, you'll lose your own within the first two minutes.'

'Two minutes, is it? *Watch me,*' he said, spinning on his heel and walking away.

Sure enough, she wasn't at Coram House when he got back. He paced the rug by his desk, his eyes drawn obsessively to the clock ticking out the hours of her absence. He couldn't wait any longer. He had to get her out, whether she'd rescued the missing nightjar or not.

He turned sharply and strode to his door. He hesitated, his fingers clasping the handle. Was his Pellervoinen traveller blood strong enough for this? It wasn't infallible. He couldn't access

Marianne's home; he couldn't access parts of Bow Street Station – and on very rare occasions he'd even had issues with doors in the mainland. He couldn't afford for it to fail him now.

He closed his eyes and concentrated. The moors were frigid, but her blood was warm, a beacon in a frozen sea. Throbbing. Calling him. She was just there, beyond the door . . .

He snatched it open and gasped as the harsh wind of the Sulka Moors blasted through the doorway. The cold bit into his cheeks, but he stood unmoving. He'd done it. Satisfaction blazed in his chest, but he quickly pushed it aside. He had to find Alice.

All he could see beyond the door were tangled black branches and a carpet of frost; the icy crystals glistened under the glow of moonlight striping through the trees.

He angled his neck, hunting left and right for any sign of her presence, for footprints or broken branches or—His breathing stilled. *There*. A crumpled blot in the shadows, lying still in a pool of something dark.

Two minutes? That was how long Mawkin had said he would have before his nightjar was torn away from him. He rushed back to his bed and yanked the blanket off it, bundling it into one hand and hurrying back to the door.

Without a second's hesitation, he stepped through the doorway, his strides eating up the ground and his hair flying about his face.

The black trees and frosted ground cast the landscape in harsh monochrome. The wind that pierced the gaps between the branches was chilled enough to shave the skin from his face. His cheeks stung and his limbs felt leaden, but there was no respite from the bleak environment.

He reached Alice and flung the blanket over her before scooping her into his arms, careful to avoid touching the deadly sap. The pain in his shoulder burned with the extra strain. He stormed back towards the doorway, chased by the bitter wind, his boots kicking frost into the air as he moved swiftly through the menagerie.

He was less than a dozen paces away when he felt something tear open in his chest. He staggered, and his hold on her slipped momentarily. This was nothing to do with his shoulder wound; this was a wholly incorporeal torment. Gasping at the crippling pain searing through his ribs, he bowed his head into the wind, gritted his teeth and pushed forward. He stumbled at the threshold and clattered to his knees, shoving Alice through the doorway and doubling over, clutching at his chest.

Crowley squeezed his eyes shut as a shot of agony lanced through him. Maybe he was having a heart attack. A harsh burst of laughter escaped his mouth. A heart attack. Didn't you require a heart for one of those?

He slammed his hand onto the wooden floor on the other side of the doorway and allowed it to take his weight. He clawed forward until he was balanced precariously on his hands and knees. The wind blew a spray of frost onto his back, but he ignored the chill as he crawled into his room on all fours. Once inside, he kicked the door closed with his trailing foot and collapsed onto his back, his chest heaving. His head thudded onto the floor and his hands went to his coat; he tore it open and rested his palm on his heart. It was still there. It was still pumping. He breathed deeply, gulping at the warm air. He was alive. He had walked through the moors and lived.

36

She was dreaming. Strange dreams in which birds flew at her, tearing her skin from her bones with their razor-sharp beaks. She threw up her hands to protect herself, but they sliced oozing scratches into her face and arms. She moaned in her sleep and the dream switched abruptly. Now she was running through the menagerie, with Tuoni – Death – following close behind. He shouted something, and the tree roots suddenly tugged free of the earth and shot out in front of her, sweeping her clean off her feet at his command. She hit the ground and scrambled backwards as the Lintuvahti loomed over her, but her fear was extinguished the moment her eyes found his face. He was so very, very beautiful –

'Crowley hasn't visited her at all.'

'What did you expect? You know what he's like.'

The voices punctured the hazy world of her dreams, and her eyelids flickered.

'Because I'm pretty sure she's *dying*, Jude. That's why. The least he could do is say goodbye.'

She could see them. Almost. She was looking at them through frosted glass. Their shapes were indistinct, faces blurred, but she knew they were there. Sitting beside her. Tucking a warm blanket tightly around her shoulders.

'Why do you keep doing that?' asked August.

'What?' said Sasha.

'Why do you keep leaning over her like that? She can't see you.'

'Because . . . if she does wake up, I want the first thing she sees to be someone smiling at her. Okay?'

'You're not smiling. Are you crying?'

'Look,' she said, 'why don't you both just go and get some sleep? It's after midnight.'

'We're not leaving,' said Jude.

There was a pause, then, 'Where's Nella? Has she gone home yet?'

'She's trying to concoct something with herbs in the kitchen. Something Finnish. She's convinced that if she finds the right combination, she can heal her.'

'Do you think Crowley will come to see Alice?'

'No.'

'He's a cruel bastard,' said August.

'He's not. He's just . . .' Jude sighed. 'He's just Crowley.'

⁂

Many miles away, on the other side of Marble Arch, Vin Kelligan was sitting in Jubilee Gardens on the South Bank, staring into the depths of the Thames.

The bitch had not come back.

He'd waited almost twelve hours, first at the foot of the London Eye. Later, as midnight and then one o'clock and two o'clock passed with no sign of her, he had tramped down to the gardens and perched on a bench to wait some more. Dawn broke, and he'd merely swallowed, his gaze fixed on the choppy waters.

He clenched his fists in a burst of anger, but the cold had so numbed him that he could no longer feel his limbs. His muscles were locked in place, and he wasn't sure he could get up off the bench even if he tried. Why hadn't she come? She'd understood the cost of failure.

He unfurled one hand and glanced down at the address scrunched in his palm.

Mike and Patricia Wyndham, Harbour View Cottage, Dublin. Of course he would have sent them there.

'Crowley, what a surprise!'

Crowley gave a tight smile as the old man, wrapped in a chequered dressing gown, ushered him inside the shop. 'Josef. My apologies for calling on you so early.'

'Not at all, not at all. Is the shoulder troubling you?'

'No, it's fine.'

'Wonderful. No need for me to doubt my talents then,' he said, smiling. 'Tea?'

Crowley nodded. 'Thank you.'

Josef bustled out to the small kitchen. Crowley heard the clinking of china and the whistling of the kettle on the hob.

He paced around the shop, picking up syringes and knives and replacing them, his restless fingers fiddling with a box of tourniquets. He startled when Josef shuffled back in, bearing hot drinks and biscuits on a round tray. Crowley ignored the biscuits but drank the scalding black tea in silence.

'So,' said Josef at last. 'Out with it. I know you're fond of brooding, but I'm an old man. Your silences make me wonder whether I've actually gone deaf.'

Crowley drained the cup and swirled it in his hands, shifting the tea leaves at the bottom into a brown clump. 'I'd like to purchase something from you.'

Josef looked taken aback. He smiled through his obvious confusion. 'But you know you have only to ask and I'll give it to you.'

'You might want to hear what it is first,' Crowley said carefully. His head darted up to meet Josef's bright gaze. 'I hear you have a store of Arbor Suvi sap.'

Josef's mouth fell open and his eyes lost their sparkle. He swallowed and cleared his throat. '*Crowley—*'

Crowley closed his eyes. 'It's for Alice. I can pay you enough that you'd still make a profit.'

'Good God, I would never deny you out of greed. But, Crowley, my debts are . . . quite serious. And Evelyn . . .' He put his cup aside and trailed away, his eyes glistening with tears.

'What is it? What's happened?'

'Her arm,' whispered Josef. 'It's gone. From the elbow down, there's . . . there's . . .' He clamped a hand on his mouth and stifled a moan.

'Tell me,' said Crowley in alarm. 'Josef, speak to me. What's happened?'

Josef flapped his hand and swallowed, regaining self-control. He shook his head and took his glasses off. 'My debts were bad, and she thought she was helping,' he said hoarsely. He began to clean the lenses with the cord of his gown.

'What did she do?' Crowley asked.

'She crept out to the Arbor Suvi one night and attempted to retrieve some *more* of its sap.'

Horrified understanding settled on Crowley's face.

'She knew that it would help to pay off my creditors, since we could either sell it on or use it in my work. She thought that her House Mielikki membership would give her some protection from . . .'

The fireflies. The carnivorous fireflies.

375

'. . . the Lampyridae,' said Josef. 'But it didn't, and she's . . . Half of her arm is . . . gone,' he finished. 'And the creditors are still threatening us. They shoved burning newspapers through the letterbox last night and—'

Crowley unbuttoned his coat and flung it onto the medical bed. He lowered himself to the mattress and met Josef's stare with a steely glint in his eye.

'A skeleton key,' he said. 'Use my blood and the both of you can get far away from here. No one will be able to track you but me, and you'll be able to lock the doors so tightly no one will ever be able to enter.' He rolled up his sleeve. 'You'll both be safe. And if you make enough to pay them off in the future, you can come back.'

Josef's eyes widened and he ran an agitated hand through what remained of his hair. There was a pregnant pause, and the old man's hand groped for Crowley's and squeezed it.

'Then . . . let me give you something in return.'

Crowley frowned. 'Josef—'

'You said it was for Alice? The girl you brought here?'

He gave a cautious nod.

'Very well,' Josef murmured. He looked up into Crowley's face, peering at him thoughtfully. 'I had never dared hope that you would love—'

'I don't *love* her,' said Crowley. 'I need her. That's all.'

Josef pursed his lips and hurried to prepare the tourniquet.

37

She was drowning in pillows. Virtually every pillow in Coram House was piled under and around her, like sandbags in a barricade. Jen's nightjar kept darting over them and back again. There was something very odd about its movements; they were erratic and ill-balanced. She hoped it didn't signify anything about Jen's state of mind – if the coma hadn't already *robbed* her of her mind.

'She's unwell . . .' Jude's voice floated up the stairs. The doorbell had gone two minutes ago, and she was trying to listen, to learn who it was.

Unwell. That was one way to put it.

'She's too weak for visitors.'

Not strictly true – thanks to Crowley and his trusty bottle of healing miracles. Apparently she'd been at death's door and he'd appeared to give her some medicine. At least, that's what Sasha had told her. She hadn't seen him once in the four or five days she'd been confined to her bed since. She'd wanted to thank him, when she'd first woken up. But as the days passed with no appearance from him, she began to feel less grateful and more frustrated.

He'd literally *walked through death* to save her. And then the minute she was safe, following his brave and noble deed, he'd decided to completely ignore her. Why bother saving her in the first place? Was it out of some warped sense of duty to Sylvie? *Still?*

Frustration was safer than the throat-closing fear that had gripped her when she'd first woken up. She'd been so close. So close to death . . . and to failure.

'She's bearing up well, but she's not up to seeing visitors,' she heard Jude say.

A voice mumbled in response, and she stilled while she tried to identify it.

'We'll pass on your regards, Commander Risdon, of course we will,' said Jude.

The door creaked closed and she tensed. Risdon. What the hell did he want? She held her breath. She didn't know how or what to feel about him any more.

Her bedroom door cracked open.

'We come bearing gifts,' said August.

He crept into the room, followed by Sasha, who was carrying a plastic shopping bag only slightly less orange than her garishly patterned blouse.

'What's that?' Alice asked suspiciously. 'It's not grapes, is it?'

Sasha grinned and plonked the bag on the bed. She shoved her hand inside and dramatically pulled out an enormous bar of Dairy Milk chocolate, three packets of crisps and a rattling box of fruit pastilles.

'Where did you get all this?' Alice asked in awe.

Sasha grinned. 'We went to a supermarket. A proper one, in Manchester. What do you want first – savoury or sweet?'

'Do you really need to ask?' said Alice, reverently unwrapping the chocolate bar. She handed them equal shares, and for a few minutes the only sound in the room was chomping.

From the corner of her eye, she sensed Sasha's nightjar watching her. She turned towards it, but it vanished. August's too. It had been like this since she'd woken up . . . since she'd returned Sylvie's feather. She hadn't completely lost her aviarist sight, but it had dimmed to nothing more than tunnel vision. Blurred, indistinct and always just out of reach. The only nightjar she could see clearly was Jen's. She wasn't sure why – possibly because she'd been concentrating on retrieving it for so long. There was no way she was letting it out of her sight.

When the last of the chocolate was gone, Alice clambered gingerly off the bed and paused to check herself over; her legs were still a little weak, but her balance was good. She moved to inspect the clothes on her coat rack.

'You're feeling back to normal, then?' asked Sasha, tidying away the discarded wrappers. 'Because you know how I feel about sick people.'

'Yes,' said Alice. 'You hover over their deathbed so they can see you smiling lovingly if they wake up.'

Sasha gaped at her. 'You heard that?'

'It was very touching.'

'I . . .' She shook her head, speechless for probably the first time in her life.

'This is like that scene where Dorothy finally sees behind the curtain,' said August, 'and discovers that the Wizard of Oz is just this old guy in a suit.'

'No,' said Alice, smiling at Sasha. 'It's the scene where the Tin Man finally gets a heart.'

'Next time you're sick,' Sasha muttered, 'you're just getting grapes and water.'

Alice grinned. 'Anyway, I feel fine,' she said, shoving aside half a dozen hangers and rifling through a collection of jumpers and T-shirts.

The only things that had survived her trip to the moors were Jen's nightjar, herself and a tiny shard of the cage, which she'd apparently still been clutching in her hand when Crowley rescued her. Sasha had found it when she'd undressed her. She'd cleaned it thoroughly with a tiny dab of Arbor Suvi sap, to nullify any trace of the poison, then fashioned it into a keyring – telling Alice that it was a talisman. It was proof that she'd passed through death and lived to tell the tale. It wasn't as beautiful as Sasha's own spectrolite talisman, but Alice had grown strangely fond of it – and she needed all the good luck she could get.

Alice took a blue jumper and a pair of jeans off a hanger and spun around. The sudden movement made her dizzy, and she put a hand to her head.

Sasha gave her a worried look.

'I don't suppose *you*'ve seen Crowley lately?' Alice asked before Sasha insisted she get back into bed.

'I think he's been busy,' she said.

'Busy,' Alice repeated in a flat voice.

'I bumped into Eris Mawkin the other day,' said August, ripping open a packet of crisps. 'Crowley went for a drink with her in House Ilmarinen a couple of nights ago.'

Alice's cheeks flamed instantly. Of course he had. She grabbed up the clothes and stared meaningfully at August.

'I'm getting dressed now,' she said.

Sasha opened her mouth. 'But—'

'If I lie around in bed any more I'm going to forget how to use my legs. I have Jen's nightjar. I'm going to give it to her.'

'You're not well enough,' said Sasha.

'I'm fine.'

Sasha and August exchanged a sceptical look.

'We'll come with you,' said Sasha.

Alice shook her head. 'I appreciate your offer, but really – I don't need babysitters.'

'Stop acting the martyr and just get dressed,' said August, gesturing at her clothes. 'We'll wait outside. Call us back in when you're ready.'

'Hang on,' said Sasha. 'Let's plan this out properly. We should talk to Jude too.'

'We don't need a plan,' said Alice. 'She's in hospital, not Fort Knox.'

'Which hospital?'

'I . . .' She faltered. 'I'm not sure. She was at St Pancras to begin with, but Crowley arranged for her to be moved so that Vin Kelligan wouldn't know where she was.'

'See,' said Sasha. 'I hate to break it to you, but you're crap at this stuff. Look at where bad planning got you last time.'

Alice frowned. 'This is different. I'm not risking death now. Anyway, Crowley knows which hospital she's in.'

'But Crowley isn't here,' said Sasha. 'So we'll have to wait.'

Wait for the Invisible Man to put in an appearance?

'No need,' said Alice. 'I'll just ask Jen's parents where she is.'

'Well, in that case I'm definitely going to get Jude,' Sasha muttered. 'He stayed to babysit you while we went to the supermarket, but I bet he's up for his first trip to the mainland.'

Jude had not been as quick to agree to the trip as Sasha had expected. He'd argued that they hadn't spent enough time discussing potential pitfalls. It was only when Alice pointed out that Oxfordshire, where Jen's and her parents lived, was quieter and less dangerous than London that he'd been convinced. He'd agreed to come, she suspected, purely to keep her and Sasha out of trouble.

Once in the mainland, they used Franc's wine bar, home of unpronounceable French coffees, to make their final doorway jump. And though Alice had named her destination as the more general 'my parents' house', she'd fully expected to stagger out of her old bedroom wardrobe again. It was a shock, therefore, to meet a blast of icy rain.

They'd exited through her parents' front door, right out onto the doorstep, which was cluttered with her dad's now-shrivelled pot plants.

'Jen's parents live next door,' she shouted over the battering rain.

They nodded frantically and hurried away from the shelter of the house. The rain had churned the garden into a slippery mudbath, and the front path was no better. Jude's wheels looked like an off-road biker's, spraying wet mud out behind him as he picked up speed.

Alice burst through the gate that led to the pavement. But she was so blinded by the sheets of water thundering from the skies that she didn't see four men leaping out of a red Ford Escort parked opposite.

They were splashing towards her at a run, and Alice crashed headfirst into a tall, stocky man with a leering grin. *Vin.*

'Hello, sweetheart,' he murmured, grabbing her by the elbows. She was so startled she hardly resisted as he yanked her closer and wrapped a sopping-wet arm around her neck, pressing her face into the crook of his elbow.

'*Alice!*' Jude's voice sounded far away. He was still on the path, his hands striking at the empty air as though tearing at something invisible. There was a brittle, deafening crack. The tips of the metal railings surrounding the garden were snapping off and falling to the ground. Jude slashed his hand, sweeping his arm in front of him, and one of the short metal spikes shot through the air like a bullet. It buried itself in Vin's thigh.

'*Fuck!*' He screamed right in her ear, but instead of dropping her, he gripped her more tightly, ignoring the blood soaking through his trouser leg. 'Get the others!' he growled.

Jen's nightjar fluttered back and forth in frantic distress, and Alice had to bat it out of her way as she tried to jam her elbow between their bodies, but Vin twisted and smashed his fist into the side of her face. She thought she felt her skull crumple as a ringing filled her ears, and she rocked backwards, hissing in pain.

All around her, she could hear the sounds of a scuffle that she couldn't see. She didn't feel quite . . . present. The throbbing pain had carried her away from the wet streets and the brawl. She heard Sasha yelp and then fall worryingly silent, but August . . . Was that him shouting and swearing? She could hear thumps, like someone kicking a sack of flour, and a shouted 'Leave him!'

Then there was nothing but blackness.

38

The first thing she did when she woke was check her head to make sure it hadn't caved in where that bastard had punched her. The second thing she did was gasp and flinch when her fingertips brushed the bruised flesh.

Oh God – the others. Panic skittered through her, and she sat bolt upright. The pain in her head intensified, and she sank back to the floor, white-faced and trembling. She was soaked through too, her hair slicked to her face and her body chilled to the bone.

'It's okay,' said Sasha, from somewhere in the corner of the room. 'We're all still alive. My ankle's sprained, and August's . . . eye socket doesn't look right. And his shoulder is –' she swallowed – 'floppy. I think it's come out of his socket, only I don't want to touch it in case . . .' She trailed off. 'They left Jude in the garden. I think he's okay.' She took a deep, shuddering breath. 'His first trip . . . I'm going to fucking kill them.'

Alice pushed herself into a sitting position and tried to ignore the throbbing in her head. The stone floor underneath her was black with dirt, and the bare brick walls were no cleaner. A thin slice of light speared through the only window in the room. It was high up on one wall, right near the ceiling, and was so narrow a mouse wouldn't have fitted through it.

The only thing in the room was a staircase with smooth, worn stone steps. And, set into its side, right in the corner where it was most shadowed, was a small door. At only around a metre high, it was too small to be a door to another room, but might be the hatch to a storage cupboard.

Alice staggered over and thumped down onto her knees before it. A cloud of dust blossomed up, and she coughed it out of her lungs before tugging at the handle.

The hatch suddenly gave way, sending her sprawling to the floor, but she scrambled back to it on all fours. It was just a cob-webbed cupboard. There was a shelf with an old sweet wrapper on it and a name scratched into the paint – Louie or Louise? – but nothing more.

'I tried it too,' said Sasha, 'but it wouldn't open to anywhere else. And the only other door is *that* one. I tried that too.'

She jabbed a finger at the door at the top of the stairs. It was a solid rectangle of metal, the type Alice imagined you'd find in bank vaults.

'Why isn't he wet?' Alice asked, coming to sit down beside Sasha, whose wet hair was soaking into the front of her blouse. August was shivering violently, but, strangely, he was bone dry.

'He reckons he's somewhere on Ahti's family tree,' said Sasha. 'Didn't you know?'

She nodded, now recalling their conversation at the tapestry. Ahti – the Masterbuilder who built the rivers in the Rookery. But Sasha was a water Väki too, and yet she was drenched.

August moaned and cracked open one puffy eye.

'Am I dead?'

'Not yet,' said Sasha.

'Those . . . bastards,' he managed. 'They'd better not have ruined my good looks.'

His eyelids flickered and he blacked out again.

Sasha gave him a shake, but the arm attached to his popped shoulder rolled into an unnatural angle. Alice leaned over him and smoothed his hair away from his swollen face.

'Do you think—'

Alice never heard what Sasha had intended to say, because the metal door at the top of the stairs clanged open. A stocky figure stood backlit in the doorway. His face was cast in shadow, but she could still see his scars.

'Well, well, well,' Vin said to Sasha as he descended the stairs. 'What's a nice girl like you doing in a place like this?'

Sasha swore, and Alice lurched to her feet, to stand protectively in front of August's battered body. Vin made to grab for Alice's arm, but she ducked and took the opportunity to boot him in the shin. Despite her weakness, he grunted and clutched at his leg. The elation of hitting her target emboldened her. So that was his bad leg. The one Jude had stabbed with the railing. With a shot of adrenaline urging her on, she pulled her arm back and slammed it at his face. He shifted his weight and jerked upright so that she missed. The momentum sent her staggering.

Vin took the chance to dive for her in a scrambling lurch. He grabbed for her arms and pinned them behind her back, nearly yanking them from their sockets with such terrible force that she cried out.

'Get the fuck off her!' shouted Sasha, trying – and failing – to scramble to her feet on her useless ankle.

'I'm starting to lose my patience with you, sweetheart,' he rasped into Alice's ear, ignoring Sasha's flailing. 'You try that again and I'll tear you limb from fucking limb.'

As if to underscore his point, he leaned right over her and clamped his warm mouth on the soft flesh of her neck. She gasped in revulsion, and his lips drew back from his gums, his snarl widened and he bit her.

She stumbled, but refused to give him the satisfaction of a scream. His teeth broke the skin and he licked the wound with the tip of his foul tongue, then kissed her on the cheek before dragging her up the stairs.

'Wait,' she breathed. She shook her head, desperately trying to pinpoint his nightjar; she could sense it somewhere, on the periphery of her vision. If she could just see it, she could snatch at his cord and incapacitate him . . . but she couldn't see a fucking thing. She knew she should never have let Sylvie take back the feather; she was useless without it. Even any stress-induced Mielikki talents seemed to have abandoned her.

'I did try to come back when I left the moors. But I had an accident. I was bed-bound for days.'

'Lies,' he sneered. 'But you're *ours* now; so you're going to make yourself useful.'

Alice winced at the bright light as he steered her roughly out of the basement and along a corridor. She tried to take in some clues about where she was – but she couldn't figure out anything other than that this seemed to be a big, grand old house. The chandeliers and oil paintings suggested a stately home. She couldn't see any phones, but plenty of windows and doors. All she needed was one proper door. If she could just slow him down so she could hunt for one . . .

Limping badly, Vin jerked her to the right and smashed her, face-first, into a closed door. Her lip burst open when it hit the wood, and she tasted blood.

'Ladies first,' he said in a mocking voice, pulling the door wide and shoving her through it.

He released his hold on her and she spun around to face him, only to find herself staring at the slammed door. She heard the scrape of the key in the lock and then his retreating footsteps. She turned to see where he'd imprisoned her now and found herself surveying a ground-floor bedroom. An iron bedstead took up much of the space, but there was a grand mahogany desk in the corner, a window – locked, unfortunately – and . . . another door.

She stared at it. Could it be a trick? Why had he left her in here? She tiptoed cautiously over to the door, her adrenaline fizzing with the awful possibility that there might be someone else on the other side. She held her breath and nudged it open with her foot. It led to an en-suite bathroom.

Alice raised her head to the ceiling in silent prayer, closed the door properly, wrapped her fingers around the handle and gently clicked it open. Her knees nearly gave out as the relief washed over her. It had opened to the void.

She dived inside and closed the door behind her. The wind drove into her bones, fully waking her from her exhausted stupor, making her more alert. Where should she go? Back to the Rookery for reinforcements? She tried to concentrate while the void's sharp breeze blustered around her suspended body. *Reinforcements.* If she could just get to Crowley, or Risdon . . .

Franc's wine bar . . . Franc's wine bar . . . Franc's wine bar . . .

She felt a door handle materialize at waist height and grasped it with a burst of joy. She twisted it and shoved it open, stumbling out of the darkness into . . . the room she'd just left.

'What?' she breathed. 'No!'

She tried again. Maybe if she was more specific . . . *The bathroom in Franc's wine bar . . .*

She opened the door . . . to the same room again. But she was no longer alone. There was an older man, with salt-and-pepper hair swept to one side, wire-framed glasses and eyes like chips of ice. He was leaning on the desk, and straightened at her arrival.

She guessed he was in his early sixties. He was dressed in a fine waistcoat and shirt with mitred cuffs, and he was tall but not heavy-set. He moved with a gracefulness that she found unnerving. *Snakes move elegantly*, she thought, *before they strike*.

'Alice,' he said quietly. 'I'm glad to finally meet you. You may call me Sir John.'

Her breathing stilled. Major-General Sir John Boleyn. Leader of the Beaks.

'What do you want?' she said, raising her chin.

He raised a corresponding eyebrow but didn't immediately respond.

'I trust you have found that Cranleigh Grange meets your satisfaction? Vincent put you with the rats in the cellar, I hear. But he didn't quite appreciate the delicate balance of our burgeoning relationship.'

'What are you talking about?'

'We are going to be friends. One does not put friends in the cellar.' He gestured at the room. 'These will be your rooms while you stay with us.'

'Where's Jude?' she asked. 'What have you done with August and Sasha?'

The door crashed open, and Vin appeared with a sullen expression on his red face. 'He's here.'

Sir John frowned. 'It is customary to knock, Vincent. Your manners are deplorable.' He waved him away, and Vin scowled and stormed out.

'I must apologize. Even as a child he lacked civility.' He moved closer to examine her, smiling at whatever it was that he had found.

'I've waited a long time for this, for my very own aviarist,' he murmured. 'And now you're here, you do not disappoint.'

Footsteps approached along the corridor, and Alice darted a look at the window, weighing up her options. Could she survive a jump through a panelled Georgian window?

'Ah, at last,' Sir John said, looking towards the door. 'Louis? We're in here. Come and see what I've found.'

She was going to be tortured. She knew it with a deep, unwavering certainty. This Louis was coming to pull out her teeth with pliers, or break all her fingers to force her to work for them.

She held her breath—

'Alice,' said Sir John. 'I'd like you to meet my son, Louis Boleyn.'

Louis strode into the room and stared at her distastefully. 'You found her then?' he said coldly.

Alice's throat closed up until she couldn't breathe, and she stiffened in shock.

Louis Boleyn was no stranger to her. They'd met several times before. In fact, she lived in his house.

It was Crowley.

39

'*You?*' she whispered. 'You're a . . . Beak?' She stared at him in stunned silence as the world and everything she thought she knew tilted on its axis. Crowley was a Beak. The son of the Beak's leader. He had lied to her *all this time*. Even his name was false. Louis Boleyn.

As the shock wore off, rage erupted, almost blinding her.

'You treacherous *bastard*,' she shouted, lunging at him with fists raised.

She smashed one fist hard into his ribs and the smile fell from his lips. He grabbed her wrists, the fierce look in his eyes almost scalding her, and flung her from him.

'You *liar*!' she gasped, spinning back around, her face on fire with anger and her breath coming in sharp bursts.

Crowley jerked his head at his father, who was watching the exchange with curiosity, and narrowed his eyes.

'Pity there were no other aviarists available,' he said to Sir John. 'This one's clearly deranged.'

'You fucking bastard!' Alice spat. 'Why are you doing this?'

'Because you're an abomination,' Crowley said simply. 'And your kind make my skin crawl.'

She recoiled. The truth. At last. That was why he'd refused to visit her. Why he never reciprocated the way she felt – the way she'd mistakenly *thought* she felt.

'My kind?' she said. '*My* kind?'

She hurled herself at him and landed a blow on his cheek, leaving a satisfying red weal. She drew back her arm for another assault, but it was snatched out of the air by Sir John.

'I think that's quite enough,' he said.

He twisted her wrist at a strange angle, and something inside it pinged and cracked. She shrieked, her chest heaving.

'Vincent?' Sir John called softly. 'Our guest is ready. Please escort Alice to the drawing room, where our other guests are now waiting.'

This time, she didn't bother fighting.

'Observe,' said Sir John. He nodded at Vin, who sauntered towards Sasha and grabbed at her hands, which were now tied together. He wrenched her sideways and dragged her, cursing, across the wooden floor. He dumped her in the middle of the room, next to a bucket of water, a jug and a towel.

Then he knelt beside her and dipped the towel into the water. For one bizarre moment, Alice thought he was going to wash Sasha's face. But then he laid the wet towel over her face, covering her air holes, scooped water into the jug and poured it in a gushing waterfall over the towel. Her shouts were muffled, but she kicked her legs in panic until the jug was empty. Waterboarding? They were going to *drown* her?

August, similarly restrained, lunged towards them – but a handful of other Beaks stomped into the room. One threw him to the ground and smashed his boot heel down onto August's busted shoulder, and he blacked out again. Two others restrained

Alice from behind as she tried to get to Sasha. She bit and kicked for all she was worth, but their strong hands held her tightly.

'Sasha!' she yelled. 'Fight!'

She was a water Väki! Why didn't she fight? Water was her legacy – it *couldn't* drown her, could it?

Vin smirked at her as he pulled the towel from Sasha's face. She gasped, great heaving breaths, as water trickled out of her nose and spewed from her mouth. Her eyes were hollow with fear, and it was as though she were somewhere far away.

'Z-Zara—' Sasha sputtered incoherently.

Alice remembered the name. The young girl she'd seen die in Sasha's memories – the reason she was non-practising. Sasha . . . was just going to let herself drown.

'Stop!' Alice cried. 'Please!'

Sir John smiled and gestured to Vin. The towel was thrust back onto Sasha's face and blasted with water. She didn't shout this time; she lay immobile as the water cascaded over her.

'Stop!' Alice begged. 'Why are you doing this? Stop!'

Vin tore the towel from Sasha's face. Her eyes rolled back and her limbs jerked into a seizure. Tears spilled down Alice's face as Sasha rolled onto her side and vomited a white, frothy bile onto the floor.

'This is what happens when people disappoint me,' said Sir John, looking at Alice.

Alice's face paled and she began to shake. What else could she do? Wait until they'd killed Sasha right in front of her? She searched the room wildly for – something – anything.

This room must be full of nightjars and cords she couldn't see. But how could she ever expect to hear the rustle of feathers over the sound of her own thundering heartbeat? She closed her eyes, trying desperately to calm herself enough to concentrate. There were two men holding her. If she could just . . . There! A flutter to her left! Her eyes flew open and she lashed out to grab handfuls of feathers . . . but the nightjar had already vanished from sight. The man holding her wrenched her arm, and she cried out.

Crowley was standing in front of the door, watching them with his teeth gritted and his hands bunched into fists. Her eyes flicked over to August, who had tried to push himself into a sitting position. A burst of hope exploded in Alice's chest, and she shivered.

'All I asked for was a simple favour from you,' said Sir John.

Alice swallowed and glanced at Sasha.

'I'm not going to work for you,' she said, her voice shaking. 'I'm not going to identify Väki for you.'

Sir John's eyes darkened. He spun on his heel and nodded at Vin.

This time, as Sasha drowned under the water, Alice waited until August started growling and fighting to get to her. Her heart was pounding as she threw herself towards him, yelling, 'Let him go! Get your hands off him! You're hurting him . . .'

Vin paused his assault, and Sir John laughed, looking from Alice to August and back again.

'She clearly favours him over the girl,' Crowley drawled, leaving his hiding place and glancing down at August, his mouth a hard line.

He glared at Alice before crunching down on August's fingers – making him howl in pain – and coming to stand by his father. Sir John smiled and nodded at Vin, who swiped up the wet towel and flopped it over August's face. The Beak who had stamped on his arm earlier thumped down on top of him and straddled his legs to stop him from lashing out with his feet.

The water was duly poured over August's face, and Alice screamed until her throat was raw. She was still screaming when they pulled the towel away. She was the only one who noticed that although his hair was sopping and his skin was glistening with a watery sheen, no water spilled from his lips or his nostrils. August thought he was one of Ahti's descendants – the Masterbuilder of the river Thames. He'd been impervious to the rain that had drenched Sasha and Alice before their capture. And though he was playing along – magnificently – in response, he was impervious to their waterboarding torture now.

'One favour,' Sir John said placidly as he walked towards her. 'Just one. To bring me something – something so very innocuous – and yet you refused me. You bargained and bartered, and then you went back on your word.' He shook his head as though gravely disappointed.

Alice stared at him in shock. 'Are you serious? This is about the piece of tree bark?'

'Of course,' he said. 'We upheld our side of the bargain, and now you'll see the consequences of not upholding yours.'

Her stomach turned. There was a piece of it in her pocket. The talisman keyring Sasha had made for her. But she couldn't let them have it. Not if they wanted it this badly. Her mind raced as she tried to work out what to do. What *were* they going to do with it? It was the sap that had nearly poisoned her to death, but there was none of it left on the wood in her pocket. If it was the sap they wanted, would it be safe to hand it over in exchange for their release?

She glanced up at Sir John through her eyelashes. He wanted it, would do anything to get it – and so she couldn't let him have it.

'Kill the girl, Vincent,' said Sir John, without taking his eyes off Alice's face. 'If she's irrelevant to the aviarist, then she's of no relevance to us either. When you're done, you may have the aviarist's parents as well, if you wish. You know where to find them.'

Vin stood up with a leering smile, and Alice's stomach lurched.

'No,' she breathed. Crowley had moved her parents to Ireland, to a safehouse – but Crowley was a traitor. Her parents . . . She had to . . .

And then, a chink of light appeared. A luminescent rope, glowing brighter every second as it stretched from Vin's wrist to the small, dark blur in her peripheral vision. She stared at it, hard, willing it to become clearer. The feathers grew more distinct, the beak sharpened . . . and Alice's legs almost gave way with relief, but she held her ground. If she could just get a little closer . . .

Vin, still grinning, withdrew a small knife from a sheath wrapped around his ankle and stalked towards Sasha.

'Stop it!' cried Alice.

Her concentration broke and his nightjar disappeared. Her frustration and fear spiralled, but Vin didn't even pause.

'Stop! *I have it!*'

Alice yanked the shard of wood out of her pocket.

'Take it,' she breathed. 'Just . . . take it.'

Sir John bore down on her, smiling in animated disbelief before plucking it gently from her fingers. He studied it in wonder.

'Take them all downstairs,' he murmured. 'Put them in the cellar while I check this is genuine.' He nodded to two of his men. 'Arrange transport for midnight. The witching hour seems appropriate, I think. It will be quieter then.'

They were back in the basement. Sasha was shivering against the wall, and August was trying to warm her up by squeezing the water out of her clothes.

Over the next few hours, Alice found herself alternately pacing in extreme agitation and staring into space, caught between frantically poring over escape options and the horror of Crowley's betrayal. Her parents . . . She had to reach her parents . . .

She was filled with anger and the most awful, gut-wrenching hurt. She hated that she felt so wounded. The fact that Crowley was capable of bruising her so badly gave him a power over her that she resented. She didn't want to be made to feel anything, not by him. Why had he bothered taking her to Coram House at all? Why hadn't he just brought her here as soon as they'd met?

She shivered and slid down the wall next to August.

'What time do you think it is?' she asked.

'Late,' said August. 'They'll be coming back for us soon.'

She nodded and tipped her head back, resting it on the rough brick.

'I'm sorry,' she said.

He shifted in the gloom. 'For what?'

'Everything. I couldn't even—'

'This is *not* your fault.'

She gestured helplessly at her wrist. 'I can't see nightjars properly any more. Only Jen's, and right now, that seems to have vanished too.' She took a shaky breath. 'If I'd practised without the feather . . . If I'd been able to—'

'You can't torture yourself like this,' August said gently. He reached out and squeezed her arm. 'Be patient. The nightjars will come back.'

She touched his hand, and they fell into a thick and hopeless silence. No one knew where they were. No one was coming to their rescue. Even if Jude was safe, he'd never be able to find them to bring help. The only person who could have tracked them down, using the blood connection, was Crowley. She closed her eyes. If she could just *stop thinking* about him for a few moments –

Her eyes snapped open in the darkness. 'What was that?'

August shifted beside her. 'It came from the side of the stairs.'

She pushed herself to her feet. There was a scrape of wood against stone and then the sounds of scrabbling against something hollow. She tensed. Could it be rats? She was practically blind in the cloaking darkness, but the noise sounded too deliberate for rats.

A deep voice called, 'Alice?' and all the breath exploded from her lungs. It was Crowley.

She stared in stunned silence.

'Alice?' he repeated, closer than before. 'Are you there?'

He emerged from the dark corner and strode across the room towards her. His hand reached out for her arm and, on instinct, she lashed out and shoved him away.

'Stop. I'm here to help you.'

'Help?' she said, her voice breaking. 'Like you helped Sasha when she was being drowned to death in front of you? And August?'

'You don't understand. If you would just *listen*—'

'How the hell did you get in here?' asked August, his arm around Sasha, who was staring at Crowley wide-eyed. 'The door didn't even open.'

'I didn't use the basement door,' said Crowley. 'I used the cupboard.'

'But I tried the cupboard when we were first dragged in here,' said Alice. 'It didn't open to the void at all.'

'It has a lock,' he said. 'An . . . unusual lock.'

'But how did—'

'I grew up here,' he snapped. 'What? You think you're the first ones to get locked in this basement? I spent half my childhood in here.'

Alice couldn't see his face in the darkness, but she could hear him beside her. 'I can get you out of here,' he said. 'The cupboard will open for me.'

'Why should we believe you?' she asked, her voice dripping poison. 'You're a liar and a traitor.'

'I'm no traitor,' he said. 'Look. We don't have time for this. If you want to shout and rage, then fine – but not here. Wait until you're somewhere safer. August, I'll take you and Sasha first. I can get you as far as Marble Arch, and you can get home from there yourselves.'

'Why the hell would we go anywhere with you?' hissed Alice.

'What's your alternative?' he said angrily.

What *was* the alternative? Go wherever Crowley wanted to take them – possibly to be tortured and killed – or stay here – and be tortured and killed when Vin came back for her anyway.

'What about Alice?' asked August, struggling to his feet.

'This doorway is locked,' said Crowley. 'It only opens for me – so you can't help with the navigation, and I can't transport three of you by myself. Two is already going to be pushing it. I'll come back for her. At least they won't kill her.'

'I'm not leaving her here on her own,' August replied. 'Take Alice and Sasha first, and come back for me instead.'

Alice's heart swelled with a rush of affection for him.

'No,' she said. 'You go. Sasha's in a bad way, and she needs you. You know the Rookery better than me; you'll know what to do if something goes wrong.'

She turned to Crowley while August helped Sasha to her feet. 'How can we trust you now?'

'Because I'm here, aren't I?'

'Maybe it's a trick. How can I be sure of anything when everything about you is a lie, *Louis*?'

'You know me, Alice.'

'No I—'

'Yes, you do. You *know* me,' he said, almost pleading. 'You *can* trust me. And anyway, you don't have any other choice.'

Alice wished she could see his expression properly in the dim light. But August had already managed to get Sasha onto her feet, though she was swaying back and forth.

'Crowley – Louis – is taking you somewhere safe,' Alice whispered to her. 'He's going to get you home, okay? And when you get back, Jude is going to look after you. He'll be there, waiting. I'm sure of it.'

She couldn't see Sasha's face clearly, but she jumped when her hand came out and patted her on the arm. Suddenly, she found it difficult to breathe, and she gave Sasha a quick, tight hug before releasing her and squeezing August's hand.

'Take care of her, won't you?' she said.

'Of course I will. But you're following us. You're coming back to Coram House too.'

Alice hesitated. No, she wasn't going back to Coram House. She was returning Jen's nightjar, and then she was going to make sure her parents were safe. The three of them would go and start a new life somewhere else. Somewhere the Beaks wouldn't be able to find her. Sasha could barely stand because of her. August looked like he'd lost a fight with a steamroller. And Jude – God knows what had happened to Jude. Everyone would be safer if she just left them alone.

'I'll see you later,' she said, her voice strained.

She watched in silence as they squeezed through the cupboard door. It scraped closed, and then she was alone in the cellar.

40

She was drifting in the quiet space between sleep and wakefulness, head bowed over her knees for comfort, when she heard the grinding rasp of wood against stone. The cupboard door. She peered into the darkness with bleary eyes.

'Can you stand?' asked Crowley.

Alice nodded, but remembered he probably couldn't see her. 'Yes,' she croaked.

He reached out to grab her arm, but she slapped his hand away and used the wall to manoeuvre herself upright.

Crowley opened the small door and the wind from the void blasted through it, kick-starting her brain. Where would he take her? Could she *really* trust him? He crouched down and shouldered his way through first. She took a deep breath and followed him in.

She emerged into the gloom of Sylvie's grubby kitchen. There were still a handful of cracked bowls on the countertop from their last visit.

Crowley busied himself with a cupboard, pulling out glasses and a small cardboard box while she peered out of the window.

It was dark outside. It must have been several hours since she'd left the Rookery.

'Painkillers,' he said, holding the box out and filling the glass at the sink.

She stared at the box. What if they weren't painkillers at all? What if they were rat poison or something to drug her?

'*Please*, Alice. They'll help.'

She snatched them from him, popped out two tablets and swallowed.

'Why have you brought me here?' she asked.

'I needed you to listen.'

Anger knotted her stomach. 'I'm not interested in anything you have to say.' Her eyes narrowed. 'No, actually I am. There's only one thing I want you to tell me. Which hospital was Jen moved to?'

He swallowed, and his eyes flicked to her shoulder as though trying to picture the invisible nightjar nesting there. 'I will tell you after—'

'No!' she shouted. 'No deals. No bargains. Just tell me which hospital, *Louis*.'

He winced. 'My name is Crowley.'

'You are *not* Crowley. I don't know who you are. Give me Jen's hospital and ward details. Now.'

His grip tightened on the counter, and his face paled as his eyes searched hers.

'Very well,' he said at last.

He pulled open a kitchen drawer, producing a pencil and an old envelope. Wordlessly, he scribbled something on the back.

'Do me a favour,' she said. 'Tell Sasha and Jude – and August – I said thank you. For everything they did. Tell them . . . goodbye.'

He looked up at her, seemed about to say something, but

appeared to think better of it. She glanced at the envelope and frowned.

'But this is the same hospital. St Pancras.'

He nodded grimly.

'So she wasn't moved at all? Another lie?'

'It wasn't meant to be a lie,' he said. 'I . . . had no choice.'

'Why? Because – what? You don't want me to find her and fix her? You selfish *bastard*.'

'Of course I want you to fix her,' he said roughly. 'But as soon as you take that nightjar to the hospital, this is over! You'll leave, and you'll never come back.'

She shook her head, incredulous. 'This will be over? *This* isn't anything. You made that perfectly clear when you called me an abomination.'

'That was an act,' he snapped.

'But how would I know?' she said, almost shouting now. 'Maybe *everything* has been an act. Those times I thought that maybe you felt . . . Maybe everything about you is a lie.'

He looked as if he was struggling to respond, his face torn by warring emotions.

'Not everything,' he rasped. 'Not the things that mattered.' He pushed past her and up the stairs. She followed in confusion, her anger rising once more.

'It's late. You can sleep there,' he said, indicating the cleaner of the two bedrooms. 'I'll be next door.'

'I don't want to sleep,' she said. 'I need to go to the hospital.'

'They won't let you in,' he said wearily. 'Visiting hours are after nine o'clock in the morning; if you open a door to get there at this hour, it will only draw suspicion.'

She hesitated, her jaw set, and he looked down at the carpet.

'Fine,' she said coldly. 'I'll wait. But I deserve some answers.'

She moved past him and sat on the bed. 'You wanted me to listen to you. Well, I'm listening now. Tell me why you're not a traitor. The Beaks hate us. Why don't they hate you?'

He expelled a breath. 'What makes you think they don't?'

She didn't respond, merely waited in hostile silence.

He raked a hand through his hair and leaned against the dressing table.

'My mother was Väki. Pellervoinen . . . though she was always convinced she had a drop of Mielikki in there too.'

'Your mother was Marianne's sister,' said Alice.

'Don't mention *her* name to me,' he said. He continued more softly, but his voice was a brittle thing. 'My mother was kind and gentle. Marianne is poison. She led her gang of brainwashed fools to the house and butchered everyone. My mother, almost the whole Boleyn family . . . I only survived because I hid in the cellar, but—'

'You said the Boleyns had been the driving force of the Beaks for decades,' she interrupted. 'So why did they allow your mum – a Väki – to marry into it?'

'They . . . didn't know what she was,' he said. 'Only an aviarist can tell the difference outright. She didn't broadcast what she was; she repressed it. She set her legacy aside so that her husband's family would never learn the truth.'

She crossed her arms. 'So your dad didn't even know?'

He held her eye. 'He knew. He loved her just the same.'

Alice didn't understand. 'But . . . if he loved her, why would he dishonour her memory by turning against her people? By hunting them down and killing them?'

Crowley frowned, his face strained. 'Because he arrived home to find his entire family slaughtered by Marianne and her followers – by *Väki* hands. *Her people* did that. He was angry and needed an outlet. And over time, when her memory began to fade, he questioned the reality of their relationship. He'd been taught contempt for the Väki from birth, so why *had* he fallen for her? She was charming and beautiful, certainly, but plenty of women are. He convinced himself that she had him under a spell. He's paranoid, and that paranoia has sparked a terrible hatred in him.' His voice had risen, and he paused before continuing in a more dispassionate tone. 'I've never been able to figure out if he hates her because he thinks she tricked him into loving her, or if he hates her because she was "weak" enough to die, and leave him behind. Both, I think.'

They fell into silence while Alice tried to comprehend all he'd said.

'But the Beaks' origins go back to early Christianity, not Marianne's massacre; they were formed in the crusades,' she said. 'And their hatred of the Väki . . . It stemmed from their religion. I just don't get it. Murder doesn't seem very religious. How can—'

'They believe it's justified. The Väki are devils whose existence is blasphemous.' He shrugged. 'Matthew Hopkins, the seventeenth-century witchfinder general, was a puritan with deeply religious convictions. There will always be people like my father. The Beaks have existed for hundreds of years; he didn't create them – *they* created *him*.'

Alice glanced over at him. She was tired and angry, and could no longer work out if he'd betrayed her or not. But she had to wonder how bad it had really been for him, growing up.

'But what about you?' she said cautiously. 'What am I supposed to think? He seemed to treat you all right back at the house.'

Crowley hesitated before speaking again. 'He finds me useful, that's all. I learned to survive his violent episodes as a child, and I suppose I've become used to them as an adult. But does he treat me well, or like a son? I'd *never* say that.'

His vehemence startled her, but she also felt strangely re-assured. Perhaps he really was more than the spy he'd seemed.

'The basement,' she said, suddenly remembering. 'You said he locked you in the basement when you were little?'

'Yes. It was probably the safest place in the house.'

'But . . . you have Pellervoinen blood. Couldn't you just escape from a locked—'

'I did. The first time I fled to the Rookery, he brought me back.'

'How?'

He shrugged. 'The Beaks had captured several Väki. My father forced one to take him through the Arch, so that he could drag me home.'

'How long was he there?'

Crowley gave her a humourless smile. 'I know what you're thinking, and yes, sometimes I've wondered the same. Did an extended trip to the Rookery induce his madness? But I don't believe so. My mother's death was the catalyst for that, and he never returned to the Rookery for a repeat visit. In fact, he had the doors in the house locked – by the same fool who'd given him his first taste of the Rookery – so that I couldn't escape through them again.'

He sighed. 'Luckily, my mother's Pellervoinen blood was stronger. Sasha and you – despite your skeleton key – may have been unable to open the basement door. But it has never been a barrier for me, despite his attempts. The second time I used it, I found myself in Josef Skala's living room. I was six – a scrawny, bruised little runt, covered in muck from the basement.'

'You went straight there?' she asked. 'You didn't have to go through the Arch?'

'It's not uncommon for legacies to be heightened during moments of stress or danger.'

Alice nodded. Wasn't that what had happened whenever she'd shown traces of Mielikki's legacy? When she was angry or in danger . . .

'What happened then?'

'Josef didn't want to let me leave.' Crowley's face creased with misery. 'But I was frightened. I knew my father would come for me, so I returned home. I visited Josef and his wife after that, many times over the years, but never stayed long enough to arouse my father's suspicions.'

'You must have felt very alone.'

'I was never alone,' he said sharply.

She glanced at him quizzically, but he looked away.

'Have you been living with your father all this time? Splitting your time between there and Coram House?'

'Of course not.' He laughed, but there was no humour in it. 'When I'm not in the Rookery I've been staying here, at Sylvie's. I haven't lived in my father's house since I was twenty.'

Her lip curled. 'How can you even stand to be in the same room as him?'

'My relationship with my father is one of necessity,' he said, holding her gaze this time. 'I've convinced him that I despise what I am. He allows me to live in the Rookery because he *thinks* I'm the perfect double agent. I spend my days dancing a tightrope you can't imagine –' He broke off, taking a breath. 'I've been feeding him so many lies that I can barely keep track myself. But never once has he questioned my commitment. In his own, peculiar way, he's come to trust me. To rely on me, even. Perhaps that's part of his madness.

'And if he insists on my working by his side, who am I to argue when it gives me the opportunity to help others like me – like my mother? Tonight I helped you, didn't I?' He looked at her, imploring her to understand. 'I've helped Sasha, and Jude, and others before them . . . When they've found themselves in difficulty, I've given them a safety net – jobs, a home . . . just as I did for you. I've spent *years* trying to balance out my father's evil with good deeds.'

'Out of – what? Some clinical sense of restorative justice?' Alice said, looking at him, assessing.

'No. Because it's the right thing to do. Because I care about those I've helped.'

'Is that the reason you agreed to help me find Jen's nightjar? To balance the Beaks' actions?' She remembered the shame she'd sensed when she'd touched his cord. 'Or are you trying to make up for your own terrible actions too?'

His face paled, and he swallowed thickly, unable to look at her.

'I've only ever wanted to . . . fix things. But I'm only one person. I can't take down the Beaks alone.'

Her chest felt tight; how could anyone live such a miserable existence? So weighed down with deception and a twisted sense of duty?

'Doesn't Vin know the truth, though?' she asked quietly, the anger all but dissipated now. 'He saw you when you helped get my parents to safety. He stabbed you. He must know you're not on their side, so why hasn't he told your father?'

'Tell my father he stabbed his only son?' he scoffed. 'To my father, the Väki might be devils, but Vin is a *cockroach*. Vin would *never* risk his position by unmasking me to my father – unless he had absolutely cast-iron evidence.' He hesitated, frowning. 'Besides, my history with Vin is . . . complicated.'

She searched his eyes, trying to find some connection there, but he had closed down again. For some reason, Vin seemed to be a revelation too far.

'Complicated?' she said, stiffening. She knew an excuse when she heard one.

He pushed off from the dressing table and shook his head. 'It doesn't matter. It's late.'

'Yes, it is late,' she said, standing up. 'But I'm listening now. I'm sick of lies.'

'I've given you the truth. I'm *not* a traitor, and now you know why.'

'But your nightjar is *still* hiding. Why is it always hiding from me?'

He had moved closer, anger and hurt written on his face.

'Do you want to bleed me dry of *all* my secrets?' he said, raw emotion in his voice. 'Don't you think I've shared enough?'

Something hardened in Alice's chest, and her gaze sharpened. Had he really told her the truth? About the Beaks – about everything?

'No,' she said. 'Not after everything that's happened today. How else am I supposed to know, for sure, that you're *not* like your father?'

He stepped away from her without a word, turning to leave. And despite everything, she automatically caught at his sleeve to draw him back.

He spun around, his eyes flashing. 'I'm not my father.'

She tilted her chin defiantly. 'I want to see your nightjar.'

'*Why?*'

'I want to know what it's hiding.'

'You're asking to see into my soul,' he said, his voice low. 'Are you really prepared for what you might find?'

Tension coiled in her body, and she lifted her eyes to meet his penetrating gaze. His chest was heaving as he struggled with his emotions, and there was no sign of distance in his expression now. His lips had parted, and a fluttering sensation in Alice's stomach was making her dizzy.

'I want to see,' she breathed.

His eyes were still pinned on hers. But the anger had vanished, and now she could see the pain afflicting him in every line on his face.

'*Show me.*'

'Alice,' he murmured brokenly. '*This* is what my nightjar is hiding.'

He bowed his head, crushing his mouth to hers. She was overwhelmed by the familiar pinewood scent that clung to his woollen coat and hair, and she closed her eyes as she breathed him in. Her skin was electrified by his touch, and when she opened her lips to his she tasted the faint tang of whisky in the warm depths of his mouth. His tongue slid against her own, and she gasped as a surge of adrenaline thundered through her veins. Her heart beat wildly in her chest, and she arched herself against him with a muffled groan.

The noise seemed to bring them to their senses, and they broke apart and stood staring at each other breathlessly, their faces flushed. A line had been crossed. But she had wanted the truth, and now she had it at last. She watched him carefully for any sign of hesitancy, and then, finding none, placed her palms against his ribs, feeling his racing heart beneath them. She slid her hands up his neck and into the hair at his nape, pulling him back down towards her.

'Are you certain this is what you want?' he asked, his voice ragged.

'Yes,' she said, reaching up to trace a gentle finger along his cheekbones, his brow, and down the bridge of his nose. She definitely wanted this. To touch him in ways she had never dared before. The vulnerability she'd witnessed earlier – she wanted to see it again: Crowley as he really was, behind the carefully constructed facade and the sharp words. She wanted something real. Something raw and wild and untameable.

She brushed her lips over his, urging his mouth open, and he closed his eyes as he leaned in to her. His tongue slipped from his parted lips and into her mouth as he wrapped his arms around her. She rocked her hips against him, and he inhaled sharply, hardening against her stomach.

He abruptly tore himself away from her and she thought, for a moment, that he'd changed his mind, but then his fingers swept across her stomach, leaving tingles of electricity in their wake as he searched for the hem of her jumper. He found it and tugged it up over her head, quickly followed by her bra. He took a moment to gaze at her, his eyes alight with appreciation, before he reclaimed her mouth, overbalancing her so that she fell back onto the mattress.

He bent over her, and her fingers darted up to yank open the buttons of his shirt. She shucked it down his shoulders, and he tossed it onto the bedroom floor as she ran her hands over his chest, following the trail of fine dark hair that disappeared into the waistband of his trousers. She couldn't help but glance at the scar on his shoulder, and she hesitated, stilling her movements, until he pressed a desperate kiss against her lips, distracting her, and her eyes fluttered closed with a soft sigh.

He trailed his lips down her throat, his teeth nipping gently at the delicate skin. His tongue darted out, and he ran it along the sweep of her collarbone and down her ribcage. She gasped and dug her fingernails into his shoulders, and he stifled a moan against her.

'*Alice.*'

She shifted her body, opening her legs to cradle his hips and urging him higher, pulling at his shoulders. She strained to find his mouth, groaning as he pressed his weight against her, pushing her down into the soft mattress.

His hips bucked and she fumbled for his zip, her nimble fingers snagging the waistband of his trousers and tugging them down. Her fingers reached between them and he gasped in shock as she brushed his sensitive skin. His eyes flew open, and he suddenly scrambled off the bed, away from her.

'What?' she breathed. 'What is it?'

She sat up, watching in mounting horror as he snatched up his shirt and dragged it back on. His fingers shook as he closed the buttons, and dread crept through her.

'This . . . was a mistake,' he said, his voice shaky.

Nausea bubbled in the pit of her stomach.

'I don't understand,' she said.

'I think you would . . . regret this . . . in the morning.'

'What?' She shook her head in confusion. 'What are you talking about? I know my own mind, Crowley, and I've wanted this for a long time.'

He froze and stared down at her, his lips parted and his eyes burning with something she couldn't understand. 'I can't . . . I can't do this,' he said hoarsely. 'Please . . .'

Blood rushed to her face and flushed her cheeks. She was shaking all over now.

He gave her one last unfathomable look before striding from the room. She heard him curse next door – something incomprehensible – but she didn't care. She didn't care. She pulled up the blanket and rolled onto her side, hot tears sliding down her face.

She would never set eyes on him again. Never. Confusion fought with the ache in her chest, and she screwed her eyes shut. Tomorrow, she would get up early and she would leave, and she would not speak to him or look at him or feel anything for him ever again.

41

Alice hadn't bothered with the woman behind the hospital information desk. She'd simply smiled at her as she hurried past, clutching Crowley's envelope and its scrawled written directions. Jen's ward was in an annexe off the main hospital.

There was almost no activity on the ward when she finally reached it. No hustle and bustle, no one crowded around the nurses' station. But, if she listened very closely, she could hear a musical churring noise, rising and falling in distant corridors. Nightjars, all around her. Her stomach fluttering, she bit back a hopeful smile and pushed on.

The blinds were down on room 201, and she hesitated for a moment. She crept closer and pressed her ear to the door, but all was silent within: no surprise; there were no nightjars in this room. All Alice could hear was machinery beeping and the whirring of the air conditioner.

She pushed the door open. How long had she waited for this moment? Too long.

'Jen,' she whispered, moving urgently towards the bed. The figure beneath the sheets made no sign that she'd heard. Alice frowned. She was painfully thin. Her eyes were sunken and her cheeks hollow, and her hair . . . was not red. The woman in the bed wasn't Jen.

She stepped back in surprise. She was in the wrong room. She turned to leave quickly, before she was found by a nurse. But almost as though a switch had been flicked, Jen's nightjar materialized on Alice's shoulder.

It fluttered madly in the air, shrieking and straining against the cord that bound it to her wrist. She stared at it in confusion. Why was it doing that? Why had this stranger so excited it? She tugged it away and it whirled on her, slashing its claws at her face. She threw up her arm to protect herself, and it soared around her and pulled her back towards the bed.

Alice began to tremble as she watched it. Slowly, with a terrible fear descending on her, she moved towards the pale figure. She unclipped the chart from the end of the bed and swallowed, searching frantically for dates, for . . .

No.

She dropped the chart and it clattered under the bed. She couldn't breathe. Then the door flew open and Crowley stood before her, a grim look on his face.

'So,' he said. 'Now you *know.*'

Alice clawed at her chest; there wasn't enough air in the room.

'Please,' she breathed. 'Please tell me this isn't – that this . . .' She couldn't finish. She put her head in her hands and squeezed it tight. She stayed like that for several moments, gathering herself, but when she dropped her hands, she was furious.

'Why is *Estelle Boleyn* lying in Jen's hospital bed?'

Crowley swallowed and came towards her, but she flung out an arm to stop him.

'*No!* You stay over there, away from me.'

His jaw tensed, and he nodded. 'Estelle, as you see, is in a coma.'

'Estelle,' she repeated. 'Your Estelle? The one you said was *incomparable*.'

'Yes.'

'But . . . But she has your name, Crowley. Your real name!' Her voice had risen, and she fought to keep herself under control. 'So she's your wife.'

'Don't be ridiculous. She's my *sister*.'

Alice's mouth fell open. Sister?

'She's . . . But you've never . . .'

She couldn't deal with all this. It was too much. Too much.

'You gave me that piece of Arbor Talvi to guide me to *Jen's* nightjar cage,' she said. 'But this *isn't* Jen's nightjar at all, is it? It's Estelle's. I knew I didn't recognize it. I knew it didn't feel like hers.'

He stared at her blankly, offering no response – no denials or apologies.

'Sylvie found that bit of cage for you. She told me. She brought it back for you years ago, didn't she? Why didn't she get Estelle's nightjar for you while she was there?'

'She . . . wasn't strong enough. She was already losing her sight. But she promised me that, when the time came, she would give me her successor's name – your name – so you could retrieve it instead.'

'Where's Jen?' Alice spat.

He shook his head.

'I travelled all the way to the Sulka Moors for *this*.' She jerked her wrist, and Estelle's nightjar angrily batted its wings. 'Now I have to go back there for Jen's, after I nearly *died* the first time around.'

Crowley strode past her and thumped down into the seat by Estelle's bed.

416

'You don't understand,' he said, pleading with her now.

'What don't I understand?' she said with force. 'You'd better start talking, Crowley, or I swear to God I'll go to the moors right this second and let her precious nightjar fly back in!'

His eyes darted up to meet hers. He looked bone weary. 'I know that you hate me, Alice. Feel free. You're not the only one – and I deserve it. But honestly, it's not too late for Jen . . . and Estelle is innocent. She's lying in that bed because of me, and she deserves to be given her nightjar back. She's done nothing wrong.'

Alice laughed incredulously. 'Nothing wrong? *Everything's* wrong with this. My God, you've been lying since the start! Where's Jen? I don't give a shit about your sister or her nightjar, Crowley!'

'Enough!' he almost shouted. 'Estelle is the reason I was never alone as a child. You have *no idea* what it was like. She's been *everything* to me.'

'Don't you dare try to—'

'I *had* to save her. Like you had to save Jen – but she's my *family*,' he said, his face contorted.

'You should know all about family,' she breathed, the pain of his betrayal stabbing deep. '*Louis.*'

'Alice, please. Please just listen. Let me explain.'

She glared at him, bright spots of rage nearly blinding her.

'Estelle asked for none of this. She's—'

'*Incomparable?*'

He winced. 'Yes. Estelle and I . . . We protected each other from him. She's . . . Everyone who ever met her adored her. Even *he* loved her, despite himself, and even Marianne spared her the night she murdered our mother.'

'How did she end up in a coma?' Alice asked in a brittle voice.

He turned to her, a broken expression on his face.

'It was Vin's fault – as well as mine. He grew up with us too, in a way; his father was the gardener, and when he died, Vin took over. He was . . . almost family. But when Estelle was sixteen and I turned twenty, I inherited some money from my mother. We could finally escape. We were going to go to Ireland and disappear in the countryside. Rent a cottage.'

'Your dad found out?'

He shook his head. 'No – it was Vin. He begged me not to do it. He didn't want to be the one left behind. I told him to come, but he was terrified of my father – terrified of being caught helping us, but also desperate to impress him. When we crept out at night, he refused to let us leave. We argued on the landing, and – somehow – he grabbed at Estelle and . . . she fell down the stairs. He was glad. Glad because it meant we would have to stay. But she fell into a coma and never recovered.'

His eyes darkened and he clenched his fists. 'And after, I joined the Beaks and I hunted people – people like me – for my father. You can imagine how proud he was.'

'Why?' she whispered. 'If you hated him so much, why would you do that?'

'I was mad with grief. And because from the moment Vin pushed Estelle down the stairs, I hated him even more than my father. And it *burned him up* to see me finally gain the affection from my father he so craved. And you know what?' He glared at her fiercely. 'I was *good* at it . . .' He faltered. His shoulders sagged, and he shook his head. 'But Estelle . . .'

He shrugged helplessly. 'She's only here because of me and my plans. And she needs that nightjar. I have to fix her. I have to.'

Alice fixed her gaze on the bed.

His face was pained. 'Alice, I didn't know you. I was already set on this course before I knew you at all. Over a decade I've been waiting for Sylvie's successor. And never, in my wildest imaginings, did I expect that you would—that I would ever care for . . .'

'What about Jen?' she demanded. '*Where is she?*'

Crowley drew a breath, and it seemed everything had been leading up to this moment. 'At home.'

Alice looked at him in stunned silence. 'What?'

'I didn't know,' he said quickly. 'Not until I started making the arrangements to move her from St Pancras and discovered she wasn't even there. I thought . . .' His voice cracked. 'I made an assumption about her coma, but I was wrong.'

'What . . . What do you mean?' she said.

'This is all I've ever known about the damage done by a coma,' he said, gesturing desperately at Estelle. 'I thought Jen would suffer the same fate, losing her nightjar while her body slept, but . . . she didn't. It wasn't a true coma. I misunderstood. The doctors only induced her coma to prepare her for an operation, after the car accident, but she came out of it a few days later. She left hospital . . . She went home.'

'She was . . . never in a real coma?' Alice gasped. 'She's okay?' She rubbed at her face as the full horror of his schemes crashed down on her.

Jen was okay. Crowley was a bastard, but . . . *Jen was safe*. Relief mingled with rage, and her words were laced with pain. 'You had this planned – right from the start?'

'No,' he insisted, his eyes wild with alarm. 'I had *no idea* Jen was going to get hit by a car. I came to you because Sylvie *did* beg me to keep you safe, but she didn't even need to ask – of course I wanted you to be safe. But I also needed you to help Estelle. I thought the two goals could fit well together, that I could convince you to help me, since she was an innocent. But when it came to it, I couldn't find the words. And you just didn't understand . . .'

Her mouth thinned.

'I'm not blaming you,' he hurriedly added. 'I was a stranger, and I fumbled my explanation so we got off on the wrong foot. And then the car crash, and Jen . . . and *Vin* . . . Alice, he knew your name and how to find you. You were in danger. I had to get you away, and the Rookery was the only place that was safe. But Jen's nightjar – when I said you could bring it back, I really believed it was the truth. And I thought . . . I thought if you came to the Rookery, you could just rescue two nightjars – Estelle's and Jen's – instead of one.' His face was a picture of terrible anguish. 'It was a stupid, split-second decision that led me down this path. A terrible one, I know. But once I'd started – once I realized Jen was okay – how could I tell you? I owed it to Estelle to keep quiet, but then it became so *difficult*; I didn't want you to be put into danger on my account, not when I'd started to—'

'You've been lying to me from the second we met.' Alice's voice came out in a harsh rasp. 'You terrified me about Jen. I thought it was my fault. I thought she was going to die. You sent me through death too – and it wasn't even for her!'

'And I walked through death to rescue you,' he whispered.

She stabbed a shaky hand at him. 'No. No, you didn't. You walked through death because I had *her* nightjar!'

Alice whirled around. 'Here,' she yelled, yanking at the silvery cord still around her wrist. 'Take her precious nightjar. I don't care – just take it, and never, ever come near me again. All that talk, when we first met, about staying at Coram House and earning my keep – it was for this, wasn't it? Well you can fucking have it!'

She untangled the cord and flung it at the bed. The glowing thread twisted as the bird flew through the air towards Estelle.

But the nightjar stopped short before it reached her – as room 201's door glided open and a tall, slender man swept inside in a bluster of wind. It was as if he had brought winter with him. The air chilled and frost crept across the windows, spreading icy spikes and swirls across the glass. His cloak was glazed with hoarfrost, and the wind whipped it carelessly about his ankles, scattering frozen crystals across the floor.

He stepped forward, the ice crunching beneath his boots, and a pale hand reached out and snatched the nightjar's cord from the air. Then he turned to Alice, revealing the finely sculpted face of a young man: pale except for berry-red lips, and framed by ice-white hair. His eyes were the lightest green she had ever seen, lined by lashes so delicate and colourless they seemed hardly to exist at all. There was nothing out of place: no blemishes, no freckles . . . nothing. His features were so perfectly symmetrical it was unsettling. He smiled at Alice, and her stomach tightened in fear.

'You have stolen something of mine,' he said in a clear, neutral voice. His breath billowed a white cloud in the air, and she shivered.

Her eyes flew to Crowley's and back to the stranger. She'd *dreamed* about this man. Back when she was delirious, after she'd returned from the moors. She backed away.

'Who are you?' she whispered.

He stepped closer, his movements quick and darting like a bird's, and peered down at her.

'I believe you know me best as Death.'

42

'*Tuoni*,' Crowley murmured.

The figure turned to him. 'I am not Tuoni,' he said, to their surprise. 'Tuoni was the first Lord of Death. I am the last.'

Alice frowned as adrenaline pulsed through her, making her brave. 'How is that possible?'

Crowley gathered himself too. 'You're the *second* Lord of Death? The second Lintuvahti?'

'Of course,' said the pale figure standing between them. 'Death is a responsibility – a role, not a person.'

August's words came back to Alice as her mind raced. Lintuvahti, he had said, was a job title, not a name. Just as different people sat on the throne, but the job – the role – was always the same.

'Tuoni abandoned his duty, and so I stepped into the breach to take his place.' His lips quirked into a smile, but it seemed unpractised, as though his muscles had not quite mastered human expression.

'Why did he do that?' Alice asked.

But he didn't answer. 'You stole this nightjar,' he said simply. 'Now I am entitled to one in return.'

'I . . .' She paled.

'You broke one of my cages. And though it has been mended, it must be refilled.'

Crowley stepped forward, his face stony. 'I can get you a spare. If you could just give me some time.'

'I do not wish for a spare.' Death cocked his head on one side, examining Alice carefully. 'I think I would like yours.'

He raised his arm, like a falconer calling its bird. A terrible tearing sensation ripped through her, and she staggered against the frosted window, clutching at her heart.

'No,' growled Crowley, lunging to stand in front of her, to hide her from Death.

But he was too late. A puff of frigid air caressed her face as her nightjar appeared at last. She watched it through slitted eyes as it circled.

Death's eyes brightened with triumph as her nightjar flew to him and perched on his forearm.

'You have a very beautiful nightjar.'

'I bet you say that to all the girls,' she managed.

He laughed and strode closer. '*Look.*'

He held out his hand, and another bird materialized on it. It was taller, more regal-looking than her plump little nightjar. Its eyes were white where her bird's were black. But its feathers were the exact same colour: snow white.

She smiled dazedly through the pain in her chest. Her nightjar . . . So pretty. And she could see it so perfectly – no blindness, no peripheral vision. The ruffled tips of the vanes were soft as silk, and its tiny beak no more than a dainty nub. The pale wing feathers seemed to shine in the sunlight pouring into the room, making the contrast between its huge, glossy black eyes more remarkable.

'I have never seen another so pale,' he said. 'I would like to keep it. But you will have to accompany me. You cannot stay here without it.'

'No. Please,' Crowley entreated. 'It was because of me that she stole from you . . . Take mine.'

'Ah,' said Death. 'But you cannot see it. You cannot appreciate why I would like to keep hers.'

'Why are they the same colour?' Alice gasped, through the burning in her chest.

'Do you really not know, Alice?' He flashed his unpractised smile again. 'Do you really not know why your nightjar might share similarities with mine?'

The Fellowship of the Pale Feather, she thought – all looking for Death's descendants. No. She shook her head. Her parents were Patricia and Mike . . . Not her biological parents, no, but still . . .

'It's not true,' she whispered. '*You're lying.*'

'I never lie,' he said. 'I sensed you in my menagerie. You left a trace, *Alice Wyndham*. The living and the dead have their own auras, but you . . . You are neither living nor dead. You should not exist at all.' He smiled. 'Now. Do you really not know who you are?'

She was growing weaker. She gripped the cold window sill, her legs threatening to give way.

'Tuoni,' she managed. 'Why did he abandon his duty?'

'Tuoni's soul was severed from his nightjar,' he explained calmly, 'so it was unleashed on the world, devouring all it touched. The severance turned him into a killer, a role that troubled him over time.'

Alice's face screwed up as she remembered Marianne's tenth plague painting – the white nightjar watching a shadow sweep across Egypt. The nightjar *watching* as the soul murdered everything in its path?

'My role is different. Nightjars and the souls they guard come to me – when it is their time,' he said, stroking his nightjar. 'I am a custodian, tending to those in my care.'

'Marianne,' she breathed. 'She said the Lintuvahti used to kill people – but had stopped because it was beneath him. But . . . it wasn't because he *stopped* killing, was it? It was because it was a *different* Lintuvahti altogether. He was a murderer, but . . . you're not?'

He nodded. 'My nightjar and I are as one. Tuoni became a killer only when his was severed.'

'But you're killing *her*,' Crowley shouted.

Alice shook her head, clutching at her chest. The silvery cord tethering her to the bird was stretching and losing its vibrant glow. Soon it would break.

'As long as I'm not in the moors, surely I won't . . . die without my nightjar – or even without my soul, if it leaves with no nightjar to guard it,' she groaned. 'I'll be . . . like her.' She gestured at the bed.

Comatose, hooked up to machines to survive.

'No,' said Death. 'Your body *will* die, because you *must* accompany me to the moors. It is where you ought to be anyway; it is your homeland.'

She flinched. 'No, it's . . . How could it be?' She took a deep, steadying breath. 'Tell me more about Tuoni. *Please.*'

He blinked slowly, and then began to recite, 'The Lord sent a pestilence on Israel from the morning until the appointed time, and there died seventy thousand men . . . And when the angel stretched out his hand towards Jerusalem to destroy it, the Lord relented from the calamity and said to the angel, "It is enough."'

'I don't understand,' Alice breathed.

He tipped his head to one side and continued. 'Words. From your human books. The Old Testament. There's more: "All the firstborn in the land of Egypt shall die, from the firstborn of Pharaoh that sitteth upon his throne, even unto the firstborn of the maidservant behind the mill . . . But for those who take the lamb's blood, the blood of innocence, and paint it upon their door, there shall be mercy. For when the Lord goes through the land to strike down the Egyptians, He will see the blood on the top and sides of the doorframe and will pass over that doorway, and He will not permit His destroyer to enter your houses and strike you down."'

'Those are from the Bible. But that's got nothing to do with—'

'This is just an example you might know, to show the weight we bear, as Lintuvahti. But Death has always existed in every culture, and Death does not discriminate between different beliefs. He comes for you all.' He paused. 'Tuoni grew weary of these many duties. So I took his place.'

'You took his place? How? Were you . . .'

He smiled. 'We all, eventually, find the places where we belong. Tuoni found that his place was elsewhere, but my place is with my nightjars.' He looked at her calmly. 'As is yours. I do not think it wise for you to stay here once your nightjar has been taken. I will take you to the moors immediately.'

'*No!*' hissed Crowley.

And then the most extraordinary thing happened. Crowley's nightjar, so long hidden from her, stretched out its wings and soared over his head, its wings arched behind it. It flew straight at her nightjar, still perched on Death's hand, and slammed into it. Her bird tumbled from Death's arm, and its wings burst open to slow its fall. Crowley's nightjar – so dark where hers was pale – strutted arrogantly onto Death's arm and stared him right in the eye.

Her heart stuttered and she exhaled sharply. Death was examining Crowley's nightjar with something like amusement.

'I cannot take yours,' he said. 'Courageous little bird though it is. I will have either the thief's or the stolen bird returned to me. There must be a balance.'

A gust of breath exploded from Crowley, and he buried his head in his hands for a moment before nodding.

'Take it, then,' he rasped brokenly.

Crowley stepped aside, and the sense of betrayal roared in Alice's ears like white noise. He walked away from her without a backwards glance, his attention fixed on Estelle. He smoothed her hair and reached down to lay a kiss on her forehead. Alice looked away; she couldn't watch.

'Fine,' she croaked. 'Let's not drag this out. Just get on with it then.'

Death nodded and gestured, causing Crowley's nightjar to fly back to its owner.

Death sliced at the air by Estelle's bed, and a dark rectangular hole appeared. Frost blasted into the room, swirling about Death's cloak, and he nodded at her before stepping through the hole – the doorway – into the Sulka Moors.

Alice made to follow him, but he held out his hand. Her cord began to shine so brightly it blinded her, and a sudden warmth filled her chest. The pain evaporated. What was he doing to her?

'My home is your home, always,' he said quietly.

The doorway vanished without a sound. The wind dropped, and the warmth in her chest eased. She stared at the empty spot in stunned silence. She was still here. Still breathing. But – she searched out Crowley, who was watching her with utter misery on his face.

'The nightjar . . .' she said.

'He took it.'

'But . . . not mine?'

He shook his head, a shattered look in his eye. They stared at one another. The beeping of the heart monitor echoing through the room was the only sound.

The silence coiled around them like a twisting, dangerous, suffocating thing. Tears pricked at Alice's eyes, and she glanced at the bed. It was too late. *He* was too late. She couldn't forgive him. Not now.

She took a deep, trembling breath, and then nodded at him and left the room. She closed the door behind her and leaned against it for a moment. And then she walked away.

43

'Tea?'

Alice nodded, and smiled up at Jen as she handed her a steaming cup then settled down in the patio chair next to her. They sat in silence on the balcony, looking out to sea. Alice had to force herself to stop glancing over at Jen to check she was really there – really safe. Jen's legs were covered in fading scars, but the most visible sign of the car accident was a new pair of round glasses. Her old ones had been smashed.

The weather was wilder here on the Irish coast, more extreme, and the wind whipped up Jen's red hair. Alice was bundled up in jumpers and had a coat over the top of her pyjamas. She sighed with contentment – she was far away from London, the Rookery and the Beaks; her parents were here; Jen was here. Everyone she loved most was safe.

They watched the waves smash on the rocks near the harbour wall, hypnotized by the rhythmic swell of water. She loved sitting here with her sketchbooks. Every morning when she woke, she felt more rested and at peace than she had for months. She had closed her mind and her eyes to nightjars, and doors were now merely objects that closed off one room from its neighbour.

She thought, sometimes, of Sasha and Jude, August – and even Proctor and Marianne – but she never thought of *Tuoni*. And she certainly never thought of Crowley. She didn't wonder whether he'd returned to Coram House or to his father's side, and she certainly didn't dwell on the look in his eyes when she'd left him and his strange world behind.

'So what are you going to show me tonight?' asked Jen, jolting her from her thoughts.

Alice glanced sideways at her and grinned. Only Jen Parker could venture out to drink tea in sub-zero temperatures wearing only a thin cardigan and a pair of shorts.

'What do you mean?' she asked.

Jen rolled her eyes. 'You abandoned me for months to come to this middle-of-nowhere place. You're telling me there are no touristy things we can do?'

Alice frowned into her cup. They hadn't told Jen the truth. How could they? Instead, they'd cobbled together a story about Alice going AWOL after Jen's accident, running away to Ireland to cope with the anxiety and guilt. The reports about her being kidnapped by a bogus police officer had been brushed off as a laughable misunderstanding.

'Is there a cinema?' pressed Jen. 'There's *got* to be a cinema at least. This is Dublin.'

'*County* Dublin.'

'Let's have a movie night in then,' she said, checking the time. 'Or a movie afternoon.'

'Sounds good,' said Alice.

They fell silent for a while, before Jen said plaintively, 'You are coming home, aren't you?'

Alice wasn't sure how to respond. Leaving here would be

leaving a carefully built cocoon. And the Beaks were still out there, after all – somewhere.

'You never know,' said Alice, 'by the end of your holiday, you might want to stay. You could get a job here.'

'Maybe we should go out to a pub instead,' said Jen. 'Once we've both checked the local talent, I'll let you know.'

Alice exhaled shakily. 'I don't want to meet anyone. I'm done with men.'

'You can't let one two-timer put you off.'

Alice blushed. Her mum had mentioned Crowley's name on the third night of Jen's holiday. Crowley had been quickly remodelled as a brief fling, someone she'd had a drink with just before Jen's accident and who'd been calling her since – until she'd discovered his other woman, waiting in the wings. Which was pretty accurate, actually. God, she hated lying to Jen.

'That . . . Crowley of yours, he's—'

'He's not "my" Crowley, Jen. He never was.'

Jen nodded, but her glance was just a little too probing. Luckily, she left soon after for the supermarket, to get snacks for the film. Alone on the balcony, Alice stared at the crashing waves, her mind determinedly blank.

Alice's parents had also gone out, window-shopping for a short-let retirement cottage, so the house was quiet. They'd fallen in love with Ireland, after a few months away from their usual routines. But they didn't want to be beholden to Crowley and his rented place any longer.

It was starting to get dark when she heard her phone buzz and saw Jen's number come up. Why was she texting? Wasn't she back from the supermarket yet?

Hello, Alice. We've got your little friend. Do you want her back in one piece?

She frowned as her fingers tapped out a response.

Very funny. If you're still there, will you get chocolate?

Several minutes passed. And when a reply finally came through, Alice felt sick and light-headed. It was a picture taken with a camera-phone. Jen. In a dark, narrow space, a strip of silver masking tape over her eyes and mouth.

Alice's fingers shook as she peered closely at the picture. There were red marks on Jen's cheeks where the masking tape had been applied too tightly. She was bound with frayed rope to a rickety chair, and there was a piece of corrugated iron in the dingy background. Was it a freight container?

The phone beeped again, and she started. Heart in her throat, she swiped the message open.

Tonight. Marble Arch. 2am. If you're late, she dies.

44

She hadn't had time to say goodbye. She hadn't even left her parents a note. She'd simply fled, crippled with guilt. After everything she'd done to try to save Jen – and now she was in the hands of the Beaks, because of her.

She felt inexplicably nervous as she waited on the steps of Coram House. What if they turned her away? She was poised to knock again, but the door was pulled open and she almost fell over the threshold, right into August's shocked arms.

'Fucking hell!' he shouted. 'She's back! It's Alice!'

Thundering feet pounded through the house, and she stood there, embarrassed, as they poured into the entrance hall – Jude wheeling out from the kitchen and Sasha emerging from upstairs, her hair scraped back.

Sasha flung her arms around Alice and then shoved her away angrily.

'Where have you been?' she cried. 'We thought he'd done something horrendous to you!'

'Who?' she asked. 'Crowley?'

'Of course!'

But . . . She'd asked him to pass on her goodbyes.

'He was supposed to be bringing you back,' said August. 'From the cellar. And when he didn't, we thought he must have done something to you. Handed you over to the Beaks or something. So we reported him to the Runners.'

'We locked him out of the house and haven't seen him since,' said Sasha. 'Jude did it.'

Jude nodded solemnly. It was clear it had given him no pleasure.

'Where have you *been*?' asked Sasha, grabbing Alice's hand and pulling her into the kitchen. She sat down and they crowded in after her, watching expectantly.

'I went to stay with my parents,' she mumbled. 'In Ireland. Crowley . . . moved them there a while ago.'

'So he didn't hurt you?' asked Jude, frowning.

She shook her head. He'd certainly hurt her, but not physically, she supposed. 'No. He didn't. Actually, he's been paying my parents' rent since they moved to County Dublin, so . . . I don't know. I suppose he's been trying to help.'

'You've come back for good now?' asked Sasha. 'We've kept your room exactly as you left it.'

'Yes,' said August. 'A dump. Clothes everywhere. I wanted to rent your room but I've settled for the attic – it was tidier.'

Sasha whacked him on the back of the head.

'I'm not back permanently,' Alice said. 'Although I'd like to stay until tonight, if that's okay with you.'

'If that's okay with us?' said Sasha. 'This is your home.'

No. It wasn't, actually. But she couldn't think of a polite way to say that right now. 'I had to come because the Beaks have taken my friend, Jen. After everything I've done to save her. Vin Kelligan has her.'

'Not that bastard again,' said August.

'I've got to meet him tonight and, somehow, get her back. But

434

I need to speak to the Runners . . .' She hesitated. Could she really trust the Runners? 'I need to phone Risdon.'

Trust was a luxury. The Runners were all she had.

She'd been awake since 8 a.m. and her body was running on empty. It had been almost nine in the evening when Risdon left. He'd listened to her rambling recollection of events, from Vin's attack on her house to the picture of Jen he'd sent to her mobile earlier that evening.

They now had a plan, of sorts. But there were almost five hours before it would be put into action, and she couldn't stop fidgeting. What if there weren't *enough* Runners for this? What if Jen was already dead?

She sat on the edge of her old bed in Coram House, frantically going over everything that could, and probably would, go wrong.

She started when the door swung open and Jude appeared.

'We're going to come with you,' he said. 'Sasha, August and I. We'll be there, with the Runners.'

Alice shuddered a breath. 'You don't have to do that.'

He gave her a lazy, lopsided grin and reached into one of his chair's hidden compartments.

'I made you something,' he said, holding it out to her.

She blinked and edged forward on the bed.

His gift was a piece of origami. The white paper had been folded intricately to produce a sharp-angled bird with outstretched wings.

'I made a nightjar for you,' he murmured. 'This was supposed to be the template – I was going to make it out of metal at the workshop. But Sasha was convinced you were, that you'd . . .'

He shook himself, and his tone became more businesslike. 'The Finnish pagans made their own sielulintu out of wood and arranged them around beds and graves. They were supposed to stand guard over the soul when it was vulnerable.'

They'd thought she was dead? She found she couldn't speak.

'Now that you're back,' he continued, 'I thought you could keep this one by your bed. And since you can't see your own nightjar, you could decorate it with the things that matter to you. The things your soul . . . can't keep hidden from its nightjar.'

She stared at him in silence, and he blushed.

'It's a terrible idea, isn't it?' he said. 'Sentimental rubbish.'

He wheeled backwards sharply, but she called after him.

'I love it, Jude. It's really beautiful. Thank you.'

He grinned sheepishly and made to leave.

'Jude?'

He paused and looked back.

She stared at him. 'Can I ask how you . . .'

'Spina bifida,' he said. 'It's okay. Everyone asks eventually.'

She shook her head, her cheeks burning. 'Sorry, no, that's not what I was going to ask.' She pointed to what he'd written on one wing. 'How did you *know*?'

He smiled. 'I don't need to be an aviarist to see it. It's all over your faces. Both of you.'

She bowed her head as he left the room. She couldn't tear her eyes away from the origami bird where, on the wing, Jude had penned *Crowley*.

She sat bolt upright, the sensation that she was being watched prickling all over her skin. The room was dark and gloomy.

'Go back to sleep,' rumbled a voice from the wooden chair.

A figure was sitting in it, leaning forward with his elbows on his knees and his face in shadow.

'Crowley?'

There was a pause. 'Yes.'

'Why are you here?'

'Jude sent me a message. I was sorry to hear about—'

'Don't,' she burst out. 'Don't you dare.'

He dropped his head and nodded.

'I'm surprised you didn't know about Jen anyway. You must have gone down in the hierarchy if they didn't tell you what they were planning. Or maybe they did tell you and you just *let* them kidnap her.'

'They didn't tell me *anything*. Vin clearly wants to keep this one all to himself. More chance of personal glory that way.'

She took a shaky breath, and when she spoke again her voice was softer, more entreating. 'Can't you find her, Crowley? Can't you help her like you helped us?'

'I don't know where he's keeping her. If I did . . .'

'Well it's not much use you being a Beak then, is it? If you can't do a simple thing like that.'

'Simple?' he said. 'Do you know how paranoid my father has become since your escape? He doesn't trust his own shadow, never mind me – or anyone else.'

'Yes, well . . .' Alice shook her head and stood up suddenly. 'What time is it?'

'Midnight. You have two hours. Get some more rest.'

'Rest?' she said. 'I need to get *out there*. I should . . . I could take them by surprise.'

'And do what, exactly?'

She drew a dagger from her pocket. 'Jude gave it to me. It's one of his best. I could—'

'Vin, alone, is four stone heavier than you. Stronger, taller, with a greater arm reach. You'd be dead in seconds. What else can you do?'

She shook her head. 'I don't know. When I've been in danger before . . . maybe Mielikki's legacy helped . . . but even that seems to have vanished with the feather.'

'You did something to me, once,' he said. 'I collapsed on the floor by your feet.'

She'd grabbed his cord.

'I can't do it any more. Since Sylvie took the feather back, the only nightjars I've seen clearly were . . . the ones I saw in the hospital room,' she said carefully. 'Whatever it was I could do, I've lost it.'

'It merely requires practice and patience to see without the feather,' he said. 'What you can do . . . You can't lose it. It's inside you.'

'Well, not any more,' she said sharply. 'And despite having lost my abilities, I have to let them take me anyway.'

'I know. Jude told me.'

'Risdon's going to station Runners in the buildings around Marble Arch – some in London and some in the Rookery, where Vin can't see them. As soon as Jen is safe, they'll rescue me. But . . . what if they don't let me go when the Runners appear? What if the Beaks outnumber them? I mean –' She swiped at her eyes. 'I'm not saying it's a bad plan. It's just that there hasn't been time to think of a better one.' She took a deep breath and turned to look at him.

'I'll get you out, Alice,' he said softly. 'If it goes wrong, I'll come for you. I'll always come for you.' There was something tender in his eyes for a moment. 'I've done it before, haven't I? What's a hostage situation or two between friends?'

'I was sorry,' she said after a moment. 'About what happened at the hospital . . .'

'You were in danger because of me,' he said, 'so I had to end it. It's fine.'

'It's not. Nothing's fine any more. But for what it's worth, I'm so sorry about Estelle.'

There was a pause so drawn out she thought he'd fallen asleep.

'I can't remember the sound of her laughter any more. I think . . . that maybe it's better that way. Maybe she and I are both free now,' he murmured, before they were swallowed once more by silence.

Alice was leaning casually against the Arch, but she was trembling. She was trembling so badly that she worried the knife in her pocket might accidentally stab her in the leg. She rubbed her hands together and breathed on them, a steamy, billowing cloud that quickly dissipated in the wind. She checked her watch: 2.01 a.m. Vin was late.

The night was unusually quiet. Was it always this quiet at 2 a.m. on a Monday? She couldn't see anyone on the streets. In fact, there was hardly any traffic either. It felt *wrong*.

She tried not to glance at the buildings across the street, where she knew the Runners and her friends were waiting and watching. Then her phone shrieked, and she nearly jumped out of her skin. It was Jen's number.

'Hello?'

'Get in the taxi.'

'What?' She spun around, searching for some sign of Vin or Jen.

'There's a black hackney cab on its way to you. Get inside it when it stops.'

'But—'

The phone went dead, and she looked up, her eyes wild. How would the Runners follow her now?

The black cab roared up beside her, and she stared at it dumbly. Then she stepped in.

The tyres squealed as they tore up the pavement. The car hurtled down Oxford Street and took a sharp left turn, slamming her against the window. Then the driver pulled to an abrupt stop and Sir John climbed in.

He nodded to the driver, and the locks clicked down in the back doors, securing her inside as the car tore off again.

'Where's Jen?' she demanded.

'Let's not jump ahead,' he chastised. 'First let's check we're not followed by your Runners.'

'What Runners?' she said.

He gave her a cool look. 'Let's go for a little drive until they lose us, shall we? Buckle up. I'd hate for you to go through the window if we crash.'

'You got your piece of fucking wood,' Alice said through clenched teeth. 'So why all this? Why kidnap Jen? Why bring me here?'

He smiled. 'I wanted to bring you here the night you escaped from my cellars. I was . . . displeased when you denied me the opportunity.'

'Well, I'm here now,' she said. 'Now what?'

'Now I want you to do a little sightseeing with me. London is very beautiful at night.'

She stared at him blankly.

'And if you make this difficult,' he added, 'I'll annihilate

Jennifer. I'll spill her ashes over every unconsecrated inch of this city, so that her parents will have nothing left to bury.' He smiled pleasantly. 'And then I'll tell them you could have saved her.'

'If you hurt Jen –' she fumbled in her pocket – 'then I will come at you a thousandfold, you twisted bastard.'

She pulled out Jude's dagger and shoved it right up under his chin.

He laughed. 'Go ahead. But then you'll never find out where she is. You have nothing to gain by killing me.'

'Take me to Jen.'

'Give your knife to my driver.'

'*No.*'

'You can't kill me. If I die, she dies.'

Alice clenched the handle so hard her fingers went numb.

'Give your knife to my driver – or she dies right now.'

Alice swore and shoved it through the driver's hatch. She searched desperately for Sir John's nightjar, but the cab remained empty, so she sought to calm herself down, to focus. *Patience and practice.*

'Where's Jen?' she said. 'If you don't show her to me, I'll fight your plans every step of the way.'

'You should never have given up your pretty knife so easily,' he replied. 'Your friend is right *there.*'

He gestured, and the driver pulled a U-turn. The city streets flew by as the car raced back the way it had come and jerked to a stop about fifty metres from Marble Arch. Too far away from the Runners.

'See,' he said.

A van sat opposite the Arch, and when its back doors opened Alice could see Vin sitting there in the shadows – with a figure heaped under a blanket.

'Is that her? Under the blanket?'

'Of course.'

'But how do I know it's her? Bring her out.'

'No.'

She searched the empty street by the van, willing the Runners stationed nearby to notice. *Come on. She's right there.*

'I've told Vincent that when my driver flashes his headlights, it means you've been uncooperative. When the lights are flashed, your friend will die. Understood?'

She wiped her sweating palms on her jeans, her pulse hammering hard. The plan had failed.

'I can help you,' she said quickly, a hazy, desperate plan forming in her mind. 'Your daughter, Estelle . . . I can help her.'

Sir John flinched. His gaze slid sideways towards her.

'I know she's in a coma. But if you let Jen go, I'll go to the Sulka Moors. I'll bring back Estelle's nightjar. If she has her nightjar, she can wake up. Let me help you, please,' she begged.

He gave her a pitying smile. 'What makes you think I want her to wake?'

Alice inhaled in surprise.

'My daughter is sleeping. Asleep, she is so perfect . . . everything I ever wished for in a daughter. I can think of nothing worse than interrupting her slumber, awakening the poisonous legacy in her veins. Now then,' Sir John said softly, leaning close to Alice, 'shall I tell you a little secret?'

He withdrew a small ring box from his breast pocket and stroked the lid lovingly.

'We know who you are, Alice Wyndham. We've known for quite some time. And we know that you are special.'

She tried to shake off her panic, to focus on what he was saying.

'Proctor Sinclair told us the colour of your nightjar weeks ago, and, I don't mind telling you, we were astounded. We'd been hoping merely for an aviarist. But then who walks into our lives but you, of all people. Someone who most of us didn't believe existed. *You*, Alice, with your pale-feathered nightjar. Daughter of Tuoni. *Child of the Lord of Death.*'

45

'Drive to the Arch,' Sir John shouted to the driver.

He started the engine and the major leaned closer to Alice, his eyes glinting. Finally, he opened the ring box to reveal a small shard of wood – the wood he had taken from her.

'Arbor Talvi,' she said, frowning.

'From the famed Black Menagerie.'

'How do you even know anything about that place?'

'Every good soldier discovers all he can about his enemy,' he said. 'Imagine! You, of all people, handed me the very thing I most required. I *had* thought that I could use it on individuals. But then I discovered who you were, and I knew I could achieve so much more.'

'Like what?' she asked. He was giving her the strangest look.

'The Rookery is a nest of evil, with the Fellowship at its rotten core,' he said. 'They'll always pose a danger, to every man, woman and child in London, unless they're eradicated.'

The car revved and thumped right up the traffic island's kerb, raced over the pavement and skidded to a stop only feet away from Marble Arch. The locks on the doors flew up and Sir John dived across the seats. He threw open Alice's door and she fell out of it backwards, her body hitting the pavement and the back of her head smacking onto the stone. Sir John scrambled out too and stood over her.

Her vision doubled for a moment as she fought to control her anxiety. She needed a weapon. *Patience and practice . . .*

Her mind stilled, and Sir John's nightjar erupted into view. She felt a rush of adrenaline as the bird swooped around his head. The glowing cord trailed from its foot, and Alice surged upwards, her teeth gritted and her hand outstretched. His cord!

Too late.

Sir John slashed the Arbor Talvi through the air above her. And in that single, solitary instant, the world slowed down and Sylvie's words came back to her: *You mind yourself with that bit of Arbor Talvi. Don't go swinging it around, or else you might sever your own nightjar's cord clean in two. That's what it does.*

Snap!

The world jerked into sharp focus and time sped up, bringing Alice back to the moment, back to the swinging arc of the Arbor Talvi slicing through the air above her and then . . . and then her body fell away, discarded on the pavement like a costume that no longer fitted.

Crowley had started running the second the cab had mounted the pavement. He hurtled towards the Arch and his father. But his father was quick. The second Alice's body began to seize, he had thrown himself back into the taxi and it had roared off the traffic island and vanished into the streets of London.

Crowley threw himself down beside Alice as she jerked and twisted on the stone. He grabbed her arms and clamped them down by her sides.

'Alice?' he shouted. 'Alice!'

Slowly, the tremors left her body, and she lay on the ground, drained and still.

'Open your eyes!'

He dragged her into his arms, resting her body across his knees, and cradled her to his chest. He bowed his head over her, trying to control the helplessness, the burning rage. *Not again.*

He was dimly aware of the noise and activity around him. The Runners had poured out of the other buildings and Risdon was barking orders at them. Someone called his name – his real name – but he ignored it. He knew who it was. Vin was on his knees with his arms pinned behind his back, surrounded by Runners on all sides.

'Louis, you fucking traitor!'

He had no energy left to care. His father had abandoned Vin, left him to take the blame. And while this might have given him pleasure once, now he was numb.

'We've secured the other girl,' said Risdon, trudging over. 'She was under a blanket in the back of the van. God knows what Kelligan's done to her. She's very confused; it's possible he's drugged her. My Runners are seeing to her now.'

Crowley nodded. He didn't care.

'I had medical assistance on standby on the other side of the Arch, just in case there were any casualties. I'll have them come through and take a look at Alice.'

'There's no point,' said Crowley, his voice monotone.

'Of course there is. Look at her. She needs someone to see to her. We could take her to one of the London hospitals if our people can't fix her.'

'She's in a coma.'

'She's what? Don't be—Crowley, are you all right? You don't

446

look yourself. Here, pass her to me and I'll carry her through the Arch.'

Crowley's grip tightened on Alice's body. 'No one is taking her.'

Risdon frowned and hunkered down. He cast an eye over Alice's limp body, over the pale face and the still-breathing chest.

'She needs to be taken to someone who can help.'

'There is no *point*. I'll bring her back. We'll—' He swallowed, growing more agitated. 'Coram House – I'll look after her there. No more bloody hospitals. No more sterile white rooms.'

'She needs medical attention, Crowley, and she needs it now. Let go of her.'

'*No.*' He turned to Risdon and his face crumpled. An anguished laugh burst out from him. 'You don't even know!'

Risdon was fighting to keep calm.

'How do you know she's in a coma, Crowley? What do you think he did to her?'

'He had the fucking Arbor Talvi! He took it off her and I couldn't get it back. I tried, but he'd put it somewhere.'

'What are you talking about?'

Crowley stared up at him, a savage look in his eyes. 'He must have known what she was, or he never would have done this. But *I* didn't tell him who she really was, so it must have been her. Playing the fucking martyr. *Why* did she tell him?'

'Tell him what, Crowley? What has he done to her?'

'He's cut her cord. I saw him swing the Arbor Talvi at her. She's lost her nightjar, Risdon. All that, and she's lost it anyway.' He buried his head in his hands and took several shuddering breaths.

'Why would he do that? I don't understand.'

'Because of what she is. She must have told him.'

'And what is she, exactly?'

447

Crowley stared at him. 'She's an aviarist – but more than that, she's Tuoni's child.'

Risdon glanced down at Alice and shook his head. 'No, she's—'

'*She is*,' Crowley said bitterly, his tone leaving little room for doubt.

'Tuoni . . .' Risdon shook his head as though unable to accept the truth. 'No. You're mistaken. Marianne has turned your mind . . . You're unwell.'

'I'm telling you,' Crowley snarled, 'her father is Tuoni.'

Risdon stared at him in shocked disbelief. His eyes searched Crowley's face, and, seemingly unable to root out the lie, he cursed loudly.

'She's *Tuoni's daughter?*'

Crowley nodded.

'My God, Crowley . . .' Risdon's face paled. 'Tuoni's child has had her nightjar severed? Do you know what this means? The nine plagues of Loviatar, and the tenth plague of Exodus – the old scholars, the stories, even the paintings agree . . .'

'What are you talking about?' Crowley snapped.

'Magellan wrote about the very nature of nightjars, in *Sielun*, his book on the metaphysics of the soul—' He broke off and shook himself. '*Your* nightjar guards your soul and keeps it safe. And when you die, it flies away, so that your soul is released to Death.'

'So? This is common knowledge.'

'Magellan theorized that Tuoni's nightjar was different. That it had a different purpose.'

'What are you—'

Risdon rushed on, his voice growing louder in his determination to be heard. 'Magellan believed that Tuoni's nightjar was not *protecting* his soul, but imprisoning it. Acting as its jailer,' he said. 'Tuoni is *Death*, Crowley – without his nightjar, his soul wouldn't need to head for the moors, to find death; his soul *is* death. Magellan theorized that Tuoni's nightjar guarded his soul to keep *us* safe – to keep the *whole world* safe from it.'

'But . . . why would he theorize any such thing?' asked Crowley.

'He wasn't the only scholar to believe it,' snapped Risdon. 'Death is a lethal destructive force in most cultures. I *know* you've seen Marianne Northam's Exodus painting too.' He was almost shouting, urging Crowley to understand. 'It shows Death's severed nightjar, watching as his soul is unleashed on the world, sweeping across Egypt like a shadow, harvesting the firstborn.'

'But it's just a story,' Crowley murmured, suddenly numb as he pieced everything together. Death – in the hospital – had spoken of this; Tuoni had become a killer once his nightjar was separated from his soul.

'In every story there's a grain of truth,' said Risdon, his voice hoarse. 'Magellan's theory – can you not see how like the Exodus story that is? How much Tuoni resembles the Angel of Death?'

Crowley stared down at Alice in alarm, still held tight against his chest.

'If Tuoni's child is the same as her father, her nightjar was *incarcerating* her soul, not safeguarding it. Keeping the world safe from it. And if her nightjar has been cut loose . . . Crowley,' Risdon murmured, grey-faced, '*she's a plague*. Her soul is going to sweep through the whole city – the Rookery – and murder everyone in its path.'

No, Crowley thought. It couldn't be true. Not Alice. And yet . . . The look of euphoria he'd seen on his father's face – this was their dream: to kill all the Väki in the Rookery at once. *A purge.*

Risdon turned, looking for something. He moved towards the

group of Runners standing smoking and chatting nearby, Vin at their feet. Jude, Sasha and August – the convict – were hovering by Jennifer. The rescued girl. The redhead was sitting on the kerb, a blanket around her shoulders, huddled against the biting wind.

'I can stop this,' Risdon murmured.

Her body was long gone, and she was soaring. But she was not a bird; she was a soul. Her nightjar had flown away, pale wings mere streaks against the moonlit sky. Her nightjar – Death's twin – had abandoned her, but there was no pain this time, because she was free.

'*You can't*,' rasped Crowley.

'I have no choice,' Risdon said blankly.

'Then – use Vin.'

'He's too damaged. It must be an innocent.'

'Use me. I volunteer.'

'No,' snapped Risdon. 'You're no innocent either. And you're Väki – I must use a *mainlander* for this to work on this side of the Arch. And there's no one else; we cleared everyone from the area this evening, under pretence of a gas leak.'

'I won't allow this.' Crowley stood, gently placing Alice onto the cold pavement. 'She'll never forgive me.'

'How will she feel when she has the deaths of every Väki in the Rookery on her conscience?' growled Risdon. 'Will she get past that?'

Out of options, Crowley ran at Risdon, his face contorted

with pain. But a handful of Runners grabbed him. He could only watch in horror as Risdon knelt down in front of Jen.

'She needs an ambulance,' said Jen shakily, pointing at Alice. 'Please tell me you've called for one.' She paused. 'And what *happened*? She was in Ireland. *I* was in Ireland . . .'

'She followed you,' Risdon said kindly. 'To save you.'

She bit her lip to keep from crying. She smiled. 'Well, of course she did. We're best friends.'

'I know,' he said. 'And I'm so very sorry.'

Jen looked up at him, confused. But she didn't have the chance to ask what he meant, because he had already pulled the glinting blade from his pocket. With one graceful movement he slashed it across her throat, the cut clean and precise. Her eyes widened, but then, almost instantly, they dulled with the glaze of death.

Risdon put his hands on her drooping neck and began to lather himself in her arterial blood . . .

Alice was rushing through the air. *Like* the bird but *not* the bird. The bird was white, and she was a dark and shadowy thing. A grasping, hungry thing as she hurtled through the air, towards the Arch.

Crowley stared at Risdon in shock, gasping for breath.

'You—She's—'

'She was pure. An innocent. A lamb,' Risdon said roughly. 'Half the religions in the world believe in the power of sacrificial lambs, Crowley. This is our only hope. Better to sacrifice one in order to save many more.'

And then, as in ancient Egypt, he anointed the doorway with

blood. He swiped his hands across the marble white stone of the Arch, painting great streaks of Jen's blood across the gateway to the Rookery so that the daughter of the Lord of Death would show mercy and *pass over*.

On the floor by Crowley's feet, Alice began to stir. And then her eyes flew open and she screamed. The pain seared her chest, burning through her in agony. She was back in her body. But where was her nightjar? Alongside the agony of separation from her nightjar, there was another pain. It was a dark and shadowy, all-consuming pain, gnawing at her belly. A hunger. Oh God. She'd been about to kill, to feed, to destroy. Her *soul* had hungered for it.

'The blood has repelled her from the Rookery and sent her soul back to her body,' said Risdon. 'But it will leave again soon. Without her nightjar to stop it, it will target the rest of London next. We need to—'

'You will *not* kill her!'

'The moors, Crowley. We must get her to the moors.'

'No! Without her nightjar to offer to the menagerie, her soul will leave *there*. And her body will die in the moors without its nightjar and soul. At least *here* there are hospitals to keep her body alive while—'

'The girl is a child of Death. That's her homeland. She belongs there.'

'She belongs *here*!' Crowley's voice rang out in the cold night air.

'We don't have time for this.' Risdon gestured frantically at the nearby Runners. 'Get the necromancer. I need Eris Mawkin here, *now*,' he roared, and they scattered to do his bidding.

Crowley glanced up, half stupefied. 'Mawkin can't open the door to the moors.'

Then a figure shifted nearby. It was August, kneeling by Jen, his face horror-struck.

'No,' he said. 'But *I* can.'

Crowley stared at him in shock. 'Please. Don't do this.'

'I . . . believe him,' August said.

'It's the only way she stands a chance – the only way *we* stand a chance,' growled Risdon. 'Death is her companion, not her enemy!'

Crowley gasped. 'No. You'll have *murdered* her even more surely than you murdered her friend.'

46

She lay on her back, staring up at the sky. It seemed on the verge of thunder, clouds blackened and swollen and the wind steering them across the horizon like giant ships. A stab of pain knifed through her chest again, and she gripped the frosted grass, crunching it in her fingers. She screwed her eyes shut as the pain built, waves of crippling agony crashing through her and then ebbing away like the tide. She breathed slowly and opened her eyes.

A face was hovering over her, peering at her with interest.

'You came,' said Death.

Alice closed her eyes. 'Please. Make it quick.'

He shook his head.

'I'm dying anyway,' she rasped. 'I have no nightjar to guard my soul. How long do I have before my soul abandons me too and I die here?'

'You have a little time,' he said evenly.

'I don't want more time.' The pain spiked, and she squeezed her eyes shut. 'I was so . . . *hungry*. I nearly . . . Oh God, I nearly . . .'

The pain ebbed once more.

'*Please*,' she begged. 'You know what I am. You know what I'm capable of now. I'm a plague. Loviatar. The . . . Angel of Death.'

'Will you stay with me?' he asked. 'As my companion. Your nightjar alongside mine.'

She shook her head. 'I don't want to stay anywhere. I don't want to . . . exist at all. I never saw Jen's nightjar. Her real nightjar. I bet her soul was beautiful. But mine . . . Oh God, mine . . .'

'Anguish is beautiful too,' he said gently. 'Your anguish will hold you fast to your moral compass, Alice. I see in you the same turmoil your father felt.' He frowned, a thoughtful expression on his face. 'I can repair your nightjar's cord. If that is your wish.'

He lifted his hand into the air and smiled at her.

It was quiet, at first, but it was growing louder. Alice tried to concentrate, to listen, as the distant flapping of wings fluttered ever closer. A bird circled, then threw itself into a headlong dive. It swooped onto Death's hand and tucked its white wings away. She could see herself reflected in its shining black eyes.

Death flicked his wrist and Alice's nightjar was thrown into the air, then disappeared. The pain in her chest vanished, and she took a deep, gasping breath.

'I thought . . . I thought if a living person entered the moors, its nightjar's cage in the menagerie opened and called to it. Shouldn't mine be going now anyway?'

'No,' he said. 'I reached inside you and brought your true self to the surface.'

'Wh . . . What?'

'At the hospital,' he said.

Alice clutched at her chest. She remembered the feeling of warmth and the brightness of her cord, blinding her.

'A cage will no longer open when you come, and you need make no payment. You are welcome in the Land of Death, because you are made of death.'

'I—' She shivered, but not from the cold. *Made of death*. She felt made of life, not death. Life was thrumming through her bones now, exploding along every nerve.

'Your nightjar is returned to you, for now,' he said. 'If you insist on living, you must not lose it again.'

She nodded bleakly.

'Jen . . . is dead. I saw it,' she said, her voice catching in her throat.

Jen was dead – and Sandra and Colin had died for nothing. The futility of it all caused the pain in her chest to return. But this time it was the pain of loss. *Jen was dead.*

Death smiled.

'You know, I am not so dour as you might believe,' he said, though she didn't immediately understand why. 'It is very grey here, and I enjoy the colour, very much . . . The girl with the blood-red hair.'

He moved away from her, on feet so light that he might as well have been floating. He paused a short distance away and nodded at something – someone – further down the riverbank. Someone stepping carefully along the stones that lined the water. Her red hair was swept out behind her by the wind, rippling like a living thing.

Alice's heart leapt into her mouth as Death approached the wild-haired girl. He said something to her – Alice was too far away to hear – and Jen smiled at him. Death took off his cloak by the water's edge, where the stones were more polished and less abrasive. He laid it down for them both, and Jen laughed. She sat down beside him, skimming stones across the Lethe.

Alice turned away, blinded by tears. They turned to ice as they fell to the ground.

EPILOGUE

The thing she liked most about Glenhest, a tiny village in the West of Ireland, was the darkness at night. In London, and in the Rookery, artificial lights eradicated the shadows. Here, no one saw her when she left the house and walked the crooked lanes under cover of darkness. She walked because she couldn't sleep. And she enjoyed the darkness because it hid her shame.

She ambled past one of the countryside's many derelict houses, skimming her fingers through the long wild grasses that grew by the side of the lane. She knew he was there. Watching. He often visited, using the doors of abandoned houses and barns.

She risked a glance at him. He reclined in the shadows, his hip resting against the doorframe. He searched her face, a question in his eyes. The same question as always. She nodded, and the tension in his shoulders relaxed. He gave a brief smile and bowed his head as she trudged onwards, her eyes straight ahead. Yes, she was okay. Yes, she was safe, out here in the wilderness.

But she didn't need – or want – Crowley to keep her safe. *She* was the monster in the shadows, the nightmare under the bed. She wasn't scared of the Beaks any more. She was scared of herself – of where she'd come from and of what she'd nearly done. The purge – she had come so close to being an architect of death.

She had longed to see her nightjar, once. But since she'd almost lost it – and herself – she'd found it was no longer hidden from her. She wished it was. The pale feathers fluttered in the corner of her eye, an unwelcome reminder of what lived within her soul.

A door closed, and she felt Crowley's absence the second he vanished. She turned back to look. To make sure. The door he'd used was green, with cracked and peeling paint, at the end of an overgrown path. When she reached it, she laid her hand flat against the wood and closed her eyes. She might have been laying her palm against his chest. She felt the call of his blood through the door, warming her, persuading her.

She tore her hand away, her face flushed. Maybe if she ever managed to forgive herself . . . maybe then she might forgive him too. She sighed and shoved her hands deep into her pockets, her fingers tingling with inexplicable pleasure. She made it almost as far as her parents' cottage before she stopped dead in the middle of the lane. The urge to fling open a door and seek him out was overpowering.

The tingling travelled up her arms, wrapping its warmth around her chest and squeezing her tight, robbing her of breath. Crowley . . . Crowley made her feel like that, when he kissed her. Alive and dying, all in the same moment. Crowley made her *feel*. Those feelings – they grounded her; they reminded her what it was to be human.

She took a deep, shuddering breath and reached into her jeans pocket. She pulled out the paper she'd folded and unfolded a thousand times this past week. It was confirmation of her new employment: research assistant to a Professor Reid. It was her security blanket, proof of the second chance she wasn't sure she deserved.

The porch light outside the cottage lit up the gravelled drive-way, and she glanced down at the letterhead. *Goring University. Department of Natural Sciences.* It was time to make her choices count. She had to live a life big enough for two now. She owed Jen that much.

She was going to work hard and master her craft. She was going to learn who and what she was – and she was going to make sure her parents were fully protected. The Beaks weren't finished with her yet – she knew that much – and next time she'd be ready.

As she walked to the back door, moonlight fell across the ivy crawling over the cottage's rear wall. It was interlaced with twigs of willow, horse chestnut and heather. The willow had tested her the most. As she gently nudged them, the horse chestnut leaves began to shift colour, becoming a deeper, richer green. She stroked the thick vines, and small clusters of yellowish-green flowers burst from the ivy beneath her fingertips. She would miss this place. But the real House Mielikki was waiting for her, and she hoped to achieve a kind of peace there too.

She was going home.

She was going home to the Rookery. And maybe she and Crowley would find each other again there.

ACKNOWLEDGEMENTS

Thanks everlasting to:

Jemima Forrester, a literal angel who changed my life because she wasn't afraid to take on a (then) 145,000-word monster. An eternal optimist to my eternal pessimist, you are simply the best. Bella Pagan, who is as much a blacksmith as an editor, for hammering this story into shape. Thank you for making the dream real and for making me better at this! All of the fantastic team at Pan Macmillan, who believed in this story and made all of this possible. Thanks to Georgia Summers for fielding my inane questions; Natalie Young and Toby Selwyn for their superb desk-editing and copy-editing skills; and to Matthew Garrett for designing such a brilliant cover. To the Tor US team – Diana Gill, Kristin Temple, and those I haven't yet met – thank you for your support. To all of my foreign publishers – it's truly an honour. Thanks go to the Pan Macmillan foreign rights team for sending this story across the world!

David Hewitt, for the unwavering belief I'd get this far – thanks for never suggesting I give up and settle on a more achievable dream! Pippa Davies – all the library trips were worth it in the end (this isn't the Catherine Cookson-style book you wanted me to write, but I hope it'll do for now!). Christopher

Davies – introducing me to Terry Pratchett, my first fantasy author, changed everything, so this is basically all your fault. Brona Morgan and Sean Keenan, who got all the good genes – I'm hoping that printing your names in the acknowledgements buys me some good credit for any future birthday cards I forget to send. Robert Hood – I literally wouldn't be here without you. Liz Keenan, Darryl Morgan, Henry Morgan, James Keenan, Joshua Keenan, Myles Keenan, Lisa Wild, Sammy Wild, Natasha Hewitt and Peter Hewitt – brilliant, all (and two of you are very much missed). Thanks to my immediate and extended family (Irish, Scottish and English) for being the best people.

My Doris, Emma Saphier, who has kept me sane these past twenty-five years, knows me better than I know myself, and who is the Jen to my Alice. (Special mention also to Cooper Cawley-Saphier, Nathan Cawley and Harry Cawley, who make up the Cawley-Saphier dream team). The super talented Junior Rhone, who took my writing pipe-dream seriously and made me think it was possible – thanks for being a brilliant creative sounding-board for fifteen years and counting (I know – shocker!). Lynn Jagatsingh (née Carroll) who was kind enough to read all my earliest stories even though they were absolute dross, but encouraged me anyway. Mike Kilroy and Pat Kilroy, the kindest people I know, who make the best Sunday lunches and whose names I stole for this story.

The GFA ladies, who have travelled the writing road alongside me, supporting all the way – Gemma Cooper, Corinne Duyvis, Lacey Edwards, Michelle Krys, Lori M. Lee, Amy Christine Parker, Natalie Parker, Ruth Lauren Stevens, Amy Tintera, Kim Welchons and Stephanie Winkelhake.

To the FPPS family – an assortment of misters and misses who work hard and laugh harder – thank you for the steady supply of tea, cake and chatter. Writing is a lonely endeavour, so a day job with the best teaching staff in town keeps all my marbles in the right place.

To the children in my classes – past, present and future: this is the only page you're allowed to read! You should know that this book is about the millionth draft of this story. That means I made 999,999 mistakes before this version – and each one made me a little bit better. Mistakes are brilliant – be brave and make lots of them! I plan to make many, many more!

Finally, to Seb Hewitt and Archie Hewitt (top boys!) I'm so proud of you both – always and unconditionally. This one's for you . . . *everything's* for you!